The War Wolf

The Sorrow-Song Trilogy

Part One

By

Peter C. Whitaker

D1707202

ISBN-13: 9781492969570

ISBN-10: 1492969575

The War Wolf

Acknowledgements:

For my wife Donna for believing in me,

my parents, Eddie and Beryl for having me,

and Paul Burnett, Patrick Gladstone, and David Moody for being friends for life.

And for Roy.

Grateful thanks to Mike Christou, Tanya Rucosky Noakes, and Cassie Wren for all their help and support in the writing of this book.

Sincere thanks to Rick McDonald for allowing me to use his translation from Old English of the Anglo-Saxon poem 'The Wanderer'.

Table of Contents

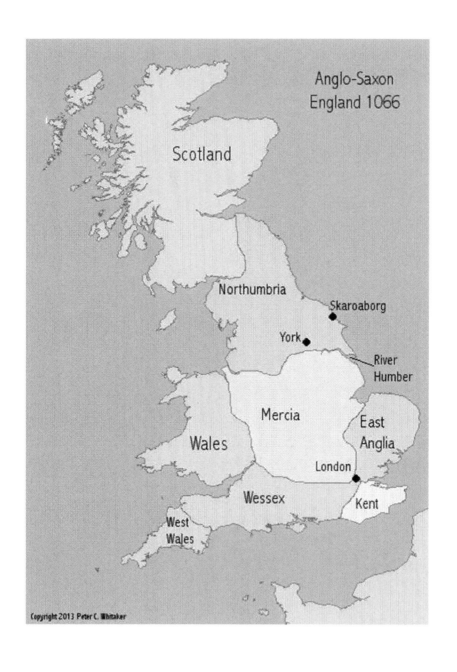

Anglo-Saxon
England 1066

Scotland

Northumbria

Skaroaborg

York

River
Humber

Mercia

East
Anglia

Wales

London

Wessex

Kent

West
Wales

The War Wolf

Monday 15th May 1066

The Village of Grim's By, Mercia

"War-wolf horrid, at Heorot found a warrior watching and waiting the fray" – Beowulf

Tostig Godwinson cleaned the blood stained steel of his fine sword on the poor cloth tunic of the dead ceorl who lay at his feet. He returned the weapon to an equally fine leather scabbard decorated with gold fastenings that glinted in the sunlight. The body of the man lay on its left side, he was still holding onto the hoe with which he had attempted to defend himself and his family. The sword stroke administered by Tostig had not granted instant death, however. The unfortunate peasant had had time to pull himself into a foetal position as his life's blood ebbed through the wound in his stomach and stained the hard packed earth beneath him. His eyes might have seen the last death throes of his people as he lay helpless at the feet of his killer but now those eyes would see nothing more.

They did not see the black smoke rising lazily into the beautiful and cloudless early morning sky. Undisturbed by so much as a breath of wind it formed into a slowly twisting and expanding miasma, hanging heavily over the land like a shroud that was about to fall. The scent of burnt flesh tainted the air. Many of the bodies were animals such as oxen, hogs, horses, hounds even, many more were human. Their hair had been singed and blisters licked by naked flames formed on heads, torsos, and limbs, the skin cracking and spitting out fluid to reveal a raw redness beneath. All had been trapped with no hope of escape.

It had been a village, so typical of the many small settlements dotted along the eastern coast of Mercia, in the region known as Lindsey. A habitation made up of simple timber framed buildings with daub and wattle walls enclosing single rooms in which entire families lived together. Thatched roofs, dried by the long hot summer, were quickly consumed by the fire that fed the dark smear on the endless blue of the sky above them. A palisade and a ditch surrounding the village had offered some degree of protection to the occupants, but it had proven to be no kind of barrier to the determined band of raiders who had broken through the defences as the occupants rose to greet their last day.

Indeed it was no obstacle at all to the men who had come out of the early morning mist in many ships, which even now could be seen moored just off shore. Ships crewed by warriors who did not even know the name of the village that they had attacked obediently at their lord's command. If they had taken the time to ask any of the inhabitants before putting them to the sword they would have discovered that the place was known as Grim's By, a Danish name that meant 'Village of Odin' in the old Norse. It would have made no difference to them, however, whether the village had belonged to the Danish Odin or the Saxon Woden or to any other god for that matter; its fate would have been the same.

Death by fire and its place in the landscape signalled by the winding grave-marker of black smoke that rose from the charred remains. Death brought by Saxon swords and Saxon spears. The people of Grim's By had been largely Saxon as well.

Tostig looked around, taking in the destruction that his men had wrought, but gave it no further thought because he was looking for something in particular; or rather someone.

"Osberht!" he exclaimed in a tone that indicated that he was both used to exercising authority and to being obeyed.

"He is here! He is here!" the man named Osberht appeared from behind Tostig with an exaggerated bow from which he did not fully rise. His entire manner was one of supplication; there was fear in his eyes too. "I saw his banner as we approached, My Lord; I saw his banner."

Tostig hoped that the peasant was telling the truth because there was precious else here to make this adventure worthwhile. The men might find supplies for the fleet, mayhap some weapons too, but little else. The village had possessed no buildings of note, nothing that they could put a torch too that would hurt his brother Harold and his allies in the north. The fight was already over, which was not surprising as there had been barely a hundred people in the village, including women and children, when the struggle had commenced. Tostig's force was significantly greater than that which these peasants of Lindsey had been able to muster in their own defence. Some might have escaped in the confusion of battle but most had been caught within the palisade.

"I will exact some form of revenge in this midden, be it against Gunnvor or yourself!" he told the cowering man.

"He is here just as I told you, My Lord!" Osberht insisted with a weak smile. "He is here."

"The peasant does not lie," Oswyn, once a high-theign of Northumbria and still a loyal supporter of his exiled lord, announced as he approached Tostig from the centre of the village. He had barely broken into a sweat during the fight despite his heavy armour and numerous weapons that a Saxon warrior habitually carried into combat. Behind him came a group of fighters dragging a man with them. "We have captured the rat in the trap."

Two of the weapons-men stepped forward and pushed their charge before them, keeping a tight hold of his arms. The captive wore good quality armour, stained with a little blood mayhap, but the stain could not hide the quality of the harness. His face was damp with sweat and besmirched with ash and dirt. A ring of gold the thickness of a man's finger still kept his hair in place however, so there was no mistaking the face. If they had expected to see fear written there it was absent from his eyes; instead he expressed nothing but contempt for his captors.

"High-Theign Gunnvor." Tostig recognised him with satisfaction. He noticed that blood ran freely down the side of the man's face from a wound to the scalp. It did not surprise him that the theign had been in the thick of the fighting. If nothing else he was known to be a brave man.

"Tostig Godwinson!" Gunnvor replied with a sneer.

Suddenly he spat catching both his captors and Tostig off guard. His spittle hit the Saxon lord in the face. Oswyn responded by driving the pommel of his sword into the other man's stomach. Even with his steel byrnie to protect him, a coat of chain mail that only the rich could afford, the force of the blow drove the wind from his lungs. His guards let Gunnvor fall to his knees at their lord's feet, expressing their contempt for his enemy with laughter.

"What is a man of your towering station doing in a hole like this?" Tostig asked in a reasonable tone as he wiped his face with the edge of his expensive cloak. "Moreover, what do you in Lindsey, your lands are in Northumbria as I recall?"

"I came to be the cause of thy doom," Gunnvor replied once he had recovered his breath. With a little difficulty he climbed back to his feet so as to be able to look his enemy in the eye.

"It is as I said, My Lord," Osberht had retreated at the sight of Gunnvor but now he sidled back to Tostig's side. "Eorl Morcar sent High-Theign Gunnvor to be of assistance to his brother Eorl Edwin. He makes a tour of Lindsey to see how things lie within the elder brother's lands."

"You will be paid for this act ceorl!" Gunnvor promised in a cold tone.

"He will, but not by you," Tostig retorted. He pulled a linen bag from his purse and shook it gently so that they could hear the coins it held. "This is the price of your head, Gunnvor, a treasure to this peasant, a trifle to me, and much less than what you probably value your own hide at."

He gave the coins to Osberht who bowed repeatedly in his annoying fashion as he received them in his cupped hands. The peasant glanced at the captured theign and gave another bow towards him. Oswyn noticed this unnecessary display of etiquette and wondered at it, but Osberht withdrew quickly from their presence and once more the captured theign attracted all of their attention. For his part Tostig noticed that Gunnvor's hair had greyed since they had last met and that there were many more creases in his face now. He looked as if he had lost weight too. If he could see beneath the grime of battle, if he had seen the theign when he arrived at Grim's By yester-even, then he might have noted that he did not look hale and hearty at all. Gunnvor was getting to be old but that would be a condition that would not haunt him for much longer.

"I will have revenge all the same," Gunnvor declared defiantly.

"You seem to be somewhat lacking in spears for such a grand ambition," Tostig observed. "Were these ceorls to be your power, these farmers of swine with their pitchforks and langseaxs for swords, tools that are poor enough for the butchering of their animals never mind for matching the steel of my wariors?"

"It sorrows me to use such people to the end I designed," Gunnvor admitted, "but you left me no other means to bring you in off the whale-road and make you tarry."

"Why would I stay?" Tostig enquired with a frown. There was something in the manner of the theign that vexed him. He had expected Gunnvor to be at least angered by falling into the hands of his enemy but he seemed calm, almost resigned to his fate. "There's nothing for me here. The best that I can say is that my men got some exercise and I rubbed a little salt into Edwin and Morcar's envy; although laying hands upon you, one of my accusers before the king, was the sole purpose of this endeavour."

"Aye, I swore against you in York and cast my lot for Morcar to take thy place as Eorl of Northumbria, and I'm proud to admit it," Gunnvor pulled himself up straight and glared at Tostig. "You were never fit to be our eorl! You were ever a cruel and spiteful lord over men, a man without honour; a nithing true."

"Cruel am I? Mayhap we can put that to the test." Tostig spoke in a calm voice but a sudden wave of hatred for his former vassal washed over him. Gunnvor's words had opened a wound that had had barely anytime to heal. Indeed, it was the chance to ease that very sore that had brought Tostig to such a place as this in his quest for vengeance. "Oswyn, he raised his hand against me."

It was all the prompting that Oswyn needed.

"Bind him to that cart!" he ordered.

The warriors knew what was to come. They roughly stripped the theign of his mail byrnie, then the thick woollen jacket that he wore beneath it, and finally the fine linen shirt. Next they stretched out his arms and tied a hand to either end of a large cart that someone had been loading with vegetables before the surprise attack had interrupted their plans. The ox that was to have drawn the vehicle lay dead between the spars in a pool of its own blood, several arrows protruding from its body. One of the warriors thought to remove for himself the theign's circlet of gold, his badge of rank, letting the captive's shoulder length hair fall free about his head.

Oswyn hefted his fighting spear and looked at the theign speculatively. He lunged forward suddenly and thrust the point into the man's right palm. With a quick twist he withdrew the gleaming steel as Gunnvor, a man of Danish descent, bit his lip in cold determination to fight his pain. Fresh blood began to course down the side of the cart.

"Your hand offended me," Tostig repeated with a cold smile. "Though this may cause my enemies little pain even a prick from a small thorn causes festering, as they say."

"I would that my hand were about thy throat," Gunnvor retorted between clenched teeth.

"You would do better to beg me for mercy, before the pain robs you of your manhood."

"This is nothing!" Gunnvor asserted.

Oswyn stabbed again, this time aiming for the bicep on the theign's left arm. The sharp steel of the spearhead cut through skin and muscle with ease, nicking the bone but not proceeding through to the wood where it might have become stuck. The spear was quickly withdrawn again.

"You will have no place in the shield-wall again." Tostig observed. A warrior who could not heft a shield into position was of little use to his fellows in battle and of what value was any man who could not acquit himself on the field of combat?

"I will have my revenge," Gunnvor hurled back defiantly.

"How?"

"You will wonder at it," the theign promised him through gritted teeth. "My son has inherited my title, my lands, and my fortune, my line will continue, but this day I bring about your ruin and he will not ever be at thy mercy for it."

"Intriguing." Tostig now affected a bored tone.

Oswyn pressed the point of his spear against the theign's right thigh and began to lean against the shaft of the weapon. Gunnvor clamped his teeth together and fought against the pain. Oswyn looked into his face and smiled. With a slight movement he twisted the spearhead as it penetrated the muscle. He pushed and twisted, working at breaking down the other man's will to resist the hurting. Blood ran freely down the theign's linen trousers and began to pool at his feet, staining the leather of his shoes. Eventually it proved too much for Gunnvor and his scream rang out at last. Again Oswyn withdrew the spear, making sure that it would not become stuck in the thick and heavy thigh muscles.

"Your position is hopeless," Tostig told him. "Pain is your only future until such time as I allow death to claim you. You see, I am your master once again. You have no power over me."

Gunnvor's head had fallen forward and his loose hair masked his face. Tostig thought that he heard something uttered from between the man's lips but he could not make out what might have been said. He glanced at Oswyn who stepped forward, grasped a hand full of hair and pulled the man's head up again; with every intent of causing further pain.

"You do not agree?" Tostig asked.

"I have power over you now!" Gunnvor summoned up enough strength to answer clearly.

"I fail to see your power," Tostig looked bemused. "Clearly you have taken all that you can, which is much less than some men I have known. You do not deserve an honourable death. You give us no sport."

"It is my power that kept you here." Gunnvor tried to shake Oswyn's hand away with a defiant twist of his head but the other kept his painful hold.

"Kept me here for what?" Tostig demanded with some irritation.

"FOR DEATH!"

It did not rest well with Coenred that they had to sit and wait beyond the bounds of the village and offer a brave man like High-Theign Gunnvor up to Tostig Godwinson's reavers. He recalled to mind the passage from the poem where Beowulf had lain and watched the monster Grendel consume his brave Geat warriors before he stopped the carnage by challenging the creature.

"...he seized a sleeping warrior for the first, and tore him fiercely asunder."

The oft remembered lines ran through the warriors mind and gave rise to the question once again;

Why had Beowulf not acted sooner?

To his own thinking the warrior was the shield of his people. Coenred would no more stand by and see one of his own men come to harm if he could prevent it than he would command ill prepared men into the fight.

He glanced at the eorls who lay some feet behind him. They were both dressed in fine armour, their helmets scarcely hiding the excitement that filled their young faces. Their duty was to protect the people but they had offered the ceorls of Grim's By up to Tostig as bait, seasoned with the presence of High-Theign Gunnvor like a rich dish, for there was nothing but bitterness between the eoldermen of the house of Aelfgar and the exiled Tostig Godwinson. It was true that Gunnvor had come willingly to the eorls and counselled such a scheme as this, but Eorl Morcar's offer to reward the theign's son if Tostig could be brought to battle had been the honey to seal the compact. It may also be true, as some of the men honestly stated, that Theign Gunnvor felt his last days were upon him and that he looked willingly to go from this middle-earth at the point of a spear rather than in a sickbed, but it seemed a needless waste of life to the huscarl all the same.

The eorls had about them a power sufficient to oppose Tostig; there had been no real reason to suffer this unnecessary bloodshed. The eorls feared only one thing; that Tostig Godwinson would simply take to ship again and sail out into the northern sea where they could not reach him. Unlike King Harold they did not have a sizeable navy on which to call.

The land around the village was flat. To the north stretched the great River Humber, the powerful estuary that led out into the wide northern whale-road. The flat land stretched many miles to the south, offering no cover whatsoever. For this reason the warriors had approached the village like skulking brigands in the night. They had lain wrapped in their fine cloaks as dawn had broken over them and patiently had each and every one of them waited for the king's exiled brother to take the bait.

For his part Tostig Godwinson had ravaged the eastern coast of Mercia since being forced from Sandwic in Kent when his elder brother Harold arrived with a considerable power of ships and weapons-men. The settlements of Lindsey were easy prey, as the Vikings had discovered many generations ago, but they offered little in the way of a tactical gain. Nevertheless Tostig had pushed ever northwards towards Northumbria and although not certain Grim's By had seemed a likely victim to fall before the king's outlawled brother. Getting word to Tostig that one of his chief accusers was present in the village had been the lure that they had set; the capture of a seeming traitor was the encouragement to take the bait.

Eorl Edwin and Eorl Morcar both admired and envied the Godwins and believed that defeating even a disgraced son of the famous Eorl Godwin would attract to them some of the glory and power that had raised Harold Godwinson up to be the King of England. Despite their motive it was an expected duty for the eoldermen to defend their people. In that respect no one could condemn them for being here no matter how they had come to be laying in the grass watching the smoke rise slowly into the clear blue sky. Tostig represented a real threat to the peoples of Mercia and Northumbria and a successful repulsion of his raids would at least protect the majority of them from further harm.

The warriors watched as a figure came around the wooden palisade and hurried towards the gathering although he could probably see nothing of the weapons-men in hiding. A Saxon huscarl positioned in advance of the main body rose and intercepted the man, telling him to crouch and accompany him back. When he came close Coenred recognised High-Theign Gunnvor's servant Osberht. The peasant and the warrior fell to the soft grass beside him.

"Is Tostig present?" Coenred demanded.

"Aye and my lord doomed," Osberht answered in a voice wracked with emotion. "They kill him slowly."

"You know that this was Theign Gunnvor's intent," Coenred told him, not unaware of the loyal servant's pain but more concerned about the violent encounter that was about erupt.

"He will die bravely and not in his sickbed," Osberht said to no one in particular. "But I will not keep this! It is cursed." He held out the bag of coins given to him by Tostig as if it contained something loathsome.

"Give them to the poor for that is an act that would anger Tostig greatly," Coenred told him. He turned to the young warrior who waited on his command. "Aethelmaer, pass the word, we go."

Aethelmaer smiled, such a grim expression on so young a face, and crawled back to where the eoldermen lay with their favourites around them. The word spread quickly and the army began to muster, rising from their hiding place in the long grass. Normally they would advance in close order, shield overlapping shield and bodies pressed together for mutual protection but such a formation did not allow for speed of movement. Instead they were more loosely placed, far enough apart to be able to move unencumbered, but close enough that they could form the shield-wall if threatened with danger.

Coenred glanced left and then right as they strode on legs that ached with muscles kept too long in one position and inactive. He was rewarded with the sight of the front line keeping its integrity. The left was commanded by Hereric, the right by Thrydwulf; both fellow huscarls. They were professional warriors in the pay of the eorls. Their armour of mail byrnies and steel helmets were the best that money could buy. The rank of a huscarl was not held by a poor man, as attested by the gold, silver and rare stones that decorated their weapons, their armour, and their rich clothes of many bright hues. Their swords were the badge of that rank, embellished with gold and silver. Their large round wooden shields were highlighted in many colours and styles, some abstract, others with stylised animals. The gold dragon of Mercia on a black background was a favourite with many of these men for that was the land of their birth or, in the case of the professional fighting men, their allegiance.

The brightly mailed warriors demonstrated their discipline, the product of countless hours spent training as only professional men at arms could afford to do. They all moved at the same pace with their shields held ready before them. In their right hand they gripped their fighting spears or large Dane-axes at the ready. There were about a thousand Saxon warriors descending upon Grim's By. Almost to a man they were huscarls; the elite of the Saxon army. Their numbers were added to by several high-theigns and sons of eoldermen who were companions of Edwin and Morcar. Like the huscarls they wore mail byrnies and steel helmets for they were all rich men who owned large estates or the sons of such. It was also the way of many to wear their wealth for all to see. Saxons did not hide their station in this life; least of all upon a field of battle.

The warriors kept the walled settlement immediately to the front of them to mask their approach and made no noise whatsoever. Normally battle-horns would be blowing, standards waving, and the men tapping out a marching rhythm with spear or axe shafts or sword pommels against their large wooden shields. Today they were as silent as the early morning mist that had hidden Tostig's coming from the villagers.

It was as they had hoped it would be.

No alarm was shouted from the enemy's ranks, they were clearly distracted by something else, something that the Saxons could only guess at. When they came within a few paces of the village's ditch the warband swung south in a smooth, controlled motion, heading for the gate that they had spied out earlier in the evening. The front ranks began to increase their pace despite the weight of the arms and armour that they carried. The second, third and fourth lines followed suit. They were men practiced at war, their muscles hard and strong. Their breath came deep and slow. Their minds were dark with thoughts of violence. At last a battle-horn ripped the smoke stained sky.

The sound of the horn grabbed everyone's attention within the village. Heads snapped round, looking for the source of the challenge, and then the warriors who stood in and around the gateway to the village saw it. A dark mass punctuated with many gleams of sharp steel coming around the wooden palisade, moving in one direction, with one intent and with one mind.

"Morcar?!" Tostig snarled disbelievingly. He had wandered towards the gate at the sound of the horn and saw the excited reaction of his men. His quick mind deduced the true nature of his position; the trap had been sprung. He looked back at High-Theign Gunnvor. "You knew this?!"

"It was my purpose all along," the other laughed back despite his pain and weakness from the blood that flowed too freely from the wound in his thigh. "You listened too greedily to my spy, he did not lead you here for your gold; he brought you here for my revenge! You have no time to take to the sea and escape this time Tostig, cur of Godwin. Morcar sends his huscarls to take you, the best swords he commands; your dogs don't stand a chance."

"My Lord, you must to the ships," Oswyn urged with some alarm.

"They are too close," Tostig answered, his experience of previous military command coming to the fore. "Form the men up. Form a shield-wall. FORM A SHIELD-WALL!"

Oswyn knew that his lord was correct in his assessment, but he knew also that Gunnvor was right too. They had some 800 warriors, many of whom were former theigns like himself who had followed Tostig into exile, but mostly they were mercenaries, hired swords, adventurers looking for plunder. The weapons-men coming on at a quick pace did indeed look to be huscarls, their armour was of undoubted quality, their carriage purposeful, their weapons held in trained hands. They were experienced warriors who had sworn death-oaths of loyalty to the brother eorls of Mercia and Northumbria, not adventurers in search of loot.

The reavers began to form up but with many a longing glance back at the ships that lay behind them, rocking gently on the waters. The safety offered by those stout timbers called to the men. Fighting peasants caught unawares was one thing, fighting huscarls was another. Their hearts were more for flight than fight.

Coenred gave a moment's assessment whilst they were still some paces from encountering the enemy. If it had been Vikings that they were about to face then he would have halted the men and had them form a proper shield-wall, close packed and presenting a hedge of spears. He saw, however, the lack of will evident in the faces of the cowards that awaited the inevitable clash of arms. They were not concentrating upon their defence; they were hesitating. He decided to move to a full charge and announced his decision with a war cry that his brother warriors picked up and yelled with disdain at their enemy.

Tostig's men had tried to form up with the remains of the palisade on their right and the still bound High-Theign Gunnvor just beyond the open gateway. There was insufficient room to form up within the village itself so the reavers had to exit Grim's By and draw their lines in the open where they could better encounter their enemy. The captive could not see the Saxons rounding the settlement from the west but he could see the hated Tostig trying to prepare his men to receive them. He hurled his vocal abuse upon them with a passion and longed to be free from the cart to wield his sword once more despite the wounds that he had suffered.

The huscarls came within a few paces of the roughly formed mercenary shield-wall and hurled their throwing spears in a coordinated volley. It was a manoeuvre that broke their stride but it was a drill that they were much practised in. The throwing spears were not aimed at individual men but rather at the large round shields that they held up for their own defence. The weapons struck home and added a considerable weight to the shields, dragging the wooden implements down. Inevitably some of the spears did find flesh to bite into as well. The blood began to flow again.

With another cry the huscarls charged the mercenaries with stabbing spears, chopping Danish axes and gold decorated swords that sliced through muscle and tendon. Tostig urged his men to stand firm, to maintain the shield-wall, to resist the onslaught. He was not new to war, his family were well steeped in the art, but it was that very experience that told him that his cause was already lost. He realised too late that

Gunnvor had indeed been the bait to entice him to wait until the Saxon spears had closed upon him in this trap. Knowing that there was now little else that he could do Tostig chose to obey his own courage and stood in the foremost rank with his sword in his hand.

The two forces came together and for a moment it seemed that they would resist each other, but that notion was deceptive. The shock of the impact went only one way. Tostig's adventurers lacked not only the quality of armour and weapons of the huscarls; they also lacked their unity. The reavers' brotherhood was disparate in origin and bound only through the same desire for wealth gotten through the sword. They lacked the Saxon's cohesion, spirit and single minded determination. A huscarl swore to obey his lord, to defend him with his life, and if that lord should die on the field of battle to remain upon it until either death took him too or all of his enemies were slain. In the face of this grim resolve it was not long before the first of the mercenaries broke away to escape their formidable enemies. As soon as one left the fight others quickly followed.

Coenred pushed hard from the centre of the front line, keen to cross swords with the king's brother. He fancied that he could see him, a little to his right. There stood a Saxon lord some forty years old, his head protected by a fine gold decorated helmet and swinging an equally fine sword. His face was clean shaven and fierce, his carriage tall and powerful. He gave the impression of being the son of a fabled eorl, a man born to command; one who had trodden over fields of battle previously. He was what Coenred expected a Godwin to look like.

Determined to reach him by breaking through the enemy ranks immediately in front Coenred dropped his fighting spear and drew from his belt the large Dane-axe that all huscarls carried. Powerful muscles propelled him forward until he collided shield to shield with the enemy. The huscarl's axe head rained down on the man who held the opposing shield, the bright steel biting into the wooden rim. By the strength in his trained arm Coenred beat down that shield, hewing large pieces of wood out of it in the process. When the opportunity offered itself he cut into the man's body, smashing through his collar-bone, rendering his left arm useless. A fighting spear flashed over the huscarl's left shoulder and pierced the mercenary's now unprotected chest. The warrior wielding it was adept in his art; he twisted the shaft of the spear to stop the blade being held by the muscles and bone of the now inert body, and then drew the weapon back ready to thrust forward again.

The breach having been made Coenred surged into it with his axe going to work once more. Brother huscarls followed him, their shields pushing the enemy away to the left, their weapons hewing and stabbing to the right, irresistibly opening the gap. The enemy front line began to buckle under such merciless pressure. Coenred pressed to his right, coming behind the front two ranks of the enemy. He used his large shield to deflect spear thrusts and half hearted sword swings on his left, trusting to his comrades to follow him and kill anyone who dared now stand against them.

Oswyn glanced to his right and saw the Saxons open up the shield-wall with their ferocious attack. He marked the tall huscarl who was busy with a blood stained Dane-axe. Their eyes met in the madness of the violence and Oswyn read a cold intent there. Ever loyal to his lord Oswyn decided to press him to retire now before that huscarl could carve a path to them through the thinning ranks of their hired adventurers.

"My Lord!" Oswyn beseeched Tostig.

He had no need to say anymore. Tostig, although unaware of the huscarls pushing through the ranks to his right, understood the danger only too well. He had stood as long as he could to face his enemies, now was the time to sacrifice the men who followed him for pay and loot in order to save his own life. He turned and ran for the beach.

Many thought to follow their leader but those at the front of the shield-wall were pressed too hard and too closely to disengage from the fight without presenting their unprotected backs to the huscarls' weapons. They had to stay to preserve their own lives and in doing so they helped to save the former Eorl of Northumbria as well.

"Quarter!" Voices called out from among the dismayed ranks. Men stepped a pace or two backwards and shields and weapons were dropped quickly, empty hands raised to show that they no longer offered any resistance. Better a life as a slave than a harsh death before these grim warriors thought many a sorry individual.

"Give quarter," Coenred commanded when he saw that the mercenaries were giving up the fight. The discipline of the huscarls saved many a mercenary's life as they responded to their captain's order, sheathed their weapons and took to binding their captives' wrists instead. Try as he might Coenred could no longer see the man he had presumed to be Tostig Godwinson and that disappointed him greatly.

The fight itself had been short but bloody. A large number of the adventurers lay either dead or wounded. An equally large number could be seen running north towards the mud flats of the Humber, or south along the beach. They would find little comfort out there in the wilderness no matter in which direction they ran.

"The eel escapes the net," Sigbert, a brother huscarl, commented and pointed out to the breakers with his long fighting spear. They could see a small boat being rowed furiously towards a larger sailing ship. On board that vessel men were already preparing it for getting under way, the dark rectangular sail unfurling. "The wind, such as it is, is a south-westerly; it will blow them to Scotland if not into the mouth of some whale."

"His power is broken," Coenred masked his own disappointment. "Tostig Godwinson will not be ravaging these lands again."

"Coenred! Coenred!" a young voice called out from behind them. Turning the warriors beheld Edwin, Eorl of Mercia, approaching.

"My Lord," Coenred closed the ground between them and gave him the bow that etiquette required of a servant to a lord.

"Do we have him? Do we have Tostig?" Edwin asked with youthful excitement. He removed his heavy helmet and his shield-bearer took it without waiting to be asked.

"He escaped us, My Lord," Coenred confessed. "His power is broken, however. Many of his men have deserted him and he leaves behind a number of ships that you can press into Mercia's service."

The last was added to dull the edge of disappointment that he knew the young eorl would feel at the news. It did not seem to work. Edwin had only one thought on his mind, the humiliation of his brother-in-law's younger kinsman.

"All gods damn him!" Edwin railed. "How could this fail? How could he escape us?"

"He turned and ran before our spears," Coenred replied. He removed his own heavy steel helmet to let the cool breeze kiss his sweating head, revealing a beard that was uncommon amongst his kind. His shield-bearer, a man by the name of Eanfrid who was some ten years his senior and dressed in good quality armour, took the helmet and also relieved his master of his shield and throwing spears. Eanfrid had already recovered the tall fighting spear that Coenred had dropped earlier in the fight.

"Your men did well," Coenred commented.

Edwin only scowled. His younger brother Morcar joined them, still touched by the excitement of the fight. In his wake came several of their followers, all of a similar age to the eoldermen.

"We have taken many prisoners," Morcar told his brother elatedly, "there will be many slaves to work the land."

"Tostig Godwinson has escaped us but cost us not a single man," Coenred added. "You have defeated him, taken prisoners in war, captured arms and armour and several ships that once belonged to him. Today has been a good day."

Edwin considered the words of his captain of huscarls and it changed his mood. He looked around at the scene that surrounded them. He did not acknowledge the burnt buildings, the dead animals or the peasants who had already died this day. He looked at the several hundred defeated men who now sat on the ground with their hands bound, the bodies of the fallen, broken spears and abandoned swords. He saw his own men, splendid in their armour and exuding a martial strength that reflected his own authority as an eorl, a nobleman of Saxon England, and this moved him.

"It was worth the effort wasn't it?" The question was entirely rhetorical; Eorl Edwin was merely justifying the fading of his initial anger at the escape of Tostig Godwinson. The thought of the new possessions that had fallen into his hands did not overly concern him, that place was taken by his ambition to rival the greatest of the aethelings; the House of Godwin. Today he felt that he had taken a step in that direction.

"The village can be rebuilt," Morcar assured him.

"The village will be rebuilt," Edwin agreed. "It will ever remind Tostig of how we bested him here. We will send riders to London to tell Harold of how we put his brother to flight. If only we had killed him too."

"My lords, High-Theign Gunnvor," Hereric approached the group respectfully but a note of concern coloured his voice. Like all of them he had removed his helmet to allow the fresh air to cool his forehead, and in doing so revealed a handsome face that did not indicate the years of experience that he had earned as a huscarl.

Without another word they followed the warrior back to the laden cart where a group of the Saxons had gathered around the theign who now lay free of his bonds, stretched out upon a cloak taken from one his former tormentors. The men made way for their young noblemen.

"High-Theign Gunnvor," Morcar called out to his vassal.

In truth he barely knew the man but he was astute enough to realise that Gunnvor had had a hand in his promotion to the earldom of Northumbria and valued his support accordingly. His expression of concern would not be lost on the warriors gathered at that spot either.

"Is he dead, My Lord?" Gunnvor asked in a rasping voice. His face had paled from the loss of blood that he had suffered and he seemed much older than he had looked only yesterday. It appeared that Oswyn's spear had cut the femoral artery in his thigh. Hereric had tied a leather belt tightly above the wound but a lot of blood had already escaped.

"Sadly, My Theign, Tostig Godwinson escaped us. He had the luck of the Godwins again," Morcar told him. The young eorl glanced over his shoulder at Coenred who read the meaning of the look. He shook his head to indicate that the brave man would not survive his wounding.

"But you broke his power?" This was said with some urgency.

"Aye, we broke his power," Coenred answered. "We have captured many of his men, his ships, his weapons. The rest have deserted him."

"Then that is good," Gunnvor asserted. For some reason his vitality decreased rapidly following this statement.

"We will take you back to Northumbria," Morcar told him, "your people will know of your bravery on this day. Your son will be proud of you."

"My son will rule in my place as your loyal theign?"

"On my honour, as we agreed so will it be," Morcar reiterated their bargain. At another time he might have been irked being so pressed by a servant in respect of an oath already made but the thrill of the battle still coursed through him and he was acutely aware that he was in the presence of many brave warriors; he wanted to appear to be a deserving lord of such men.

"Give me my sword?" Gunnvor requested. From somewhere a weapon was produced and pressed into the dying man's hand. He did not look to see if it were indeed his own but just gripped the hilt with both hands, the tip of the sword pointing to his feet. He sighed and closed his eyes as if allowing the last of his strength to escape him only now that all things seemed settled as he had desired.

"He fulfilled his wish to die with his sword in his hand," Hereric said with approval.

"A fair death honours a man's life," Morcar added, somewhat moved.

"May he be the last Saxon to die in battle this year," Coenred said.

Wednesday 8th September 1066

The Town and Port of Dives Sur Mer, Normandy

Duke Guillaume of Normandy sat disconsolately astride his horse, one hand loosely holding the reins and resting on the saddle before him, the other holding his cloak fast. The wind tore through the sky like a demon, whipping flags and the canvas of the tents with a ferocity to make them crack loudly into the air. Men walked with an effort or were pushed by an invisible hand depending on the direction they were taking. The sky was as dark as his mood and the threat of yet more rain only added to the misery of everyone in the camp.

"The Devil finds work for idle hands," Odo, the Bishop of Bayeux, observed dryly. He looked around the city of temporary accommodation and noted how battered and beaten everything appeared. "We have spent too long in this place."

The duke glanced north. Windblown sand stung his face as he squinted into the hard blown gale. Odo was right; the weather had held them trapped here for far too long. The men had grown restless with little else to do other than training and foraging for fuel. It was inevitable that their minds, fired by the prospect of plunder abroad, should seek diversion here at home when there was not much else to do other than sit around and wait.

He looked down at the two soldiers who awaited his attention. Their faces were dirty and fearful, as they had every right to be. It was unfortunate that they were Normans too. However, he could not show leniency in this matter and expect the army to retain its discipline regardless of who committed the crime. Around them were gathered a large portion of that army, enough to communicate to the others what they saw today and what it meant for anyone else who did not respect the duke's commands.

"What is the charge?" Guillaume asked loudly in his most authoritative tone.

"Theft and rape Your Grace!" A young officer responded promptly, his hand on the pommel of his sword, his back straight and true. The soldier's hair was cut short on top and shaved both at the back and on the sides in the current popular fashion. He looked like the epitome of young Norman martial stock. Against him the two accused hardly compared with their wild eyes and cowering postures.

"And how do they plead?" Guillaume pressed.

"Not guilty, Your Grace." The officer spoke promptly again. No one was surprised by his answer, however.

"The complainant."

A middle-aged townsman was bustled forward at the duke's command. He looked almost as terrified as the prisoners, wringing his velvet hat in his hands, but unlike them his manner had also about it a degree of determination, he was here for a reason and would not balk now no matter what authority he appeared before.

"Speak your charge," The duke instructed him.

"Sir, I left my daughter to mind my shop whilst I did business in the market. When I returned I found that she had been vilely assaulted and robbed of many things of value from our house. Neighbours told me of a disturbance and when they came to see what it was they were pushed aside by two soldiers who were then seen running back towards the camp. I followed and made my complaint to the officer, this one here, who found through his questioning that these two were seen entering the camp in haste and carrying goods that did not belong to them." He rushed his words as if he still pursued the offenders but he also spoke with conviction. At the end of his speech the man glowered at the two soldiers and then turned a more respectful face to the duke.

"Officer?" The duke looked to the young man.

"It occurred as the townsman says, Your Grace. Upon hearing the complaint I questioned the sentries and these two were named as entering the camp hastily. Upon apprehension we found goods for which they could not account and not in keeping with a soldier's equipage." He answered smartly and again with confidence.

"The woman?"

"Too distressed sir," the father insisted with a touch of anger. "She is but a child, stained by these beasts!"

The Duke glanced at the accused again. They looked like time served men, a sad loss that would be to an army about to invade a foreign land. Nevertheless, he had issued a general order to govern the behaviour of the troops whilst they camped within the vicinity of Dives Sur Mer; the local population were not the enemy.

"Admit your guilt and seek clemency," Bishop Odo suggested to them.

"My Lord, we did nothing." They looked at their commander with fearful eyes and then around at the soldiers and officers gathered for the impromptu court. They believed that there was little hope for leniency and ignored the words of the clergyman. Odo also knew the military worth of the two men and had hoped to offer both them and the duke an alternative to summary execution by the intervention of some Christian compassion, but they had just ignorantly spurned his help.

"You broke the curfew and went into the town?" The young officer demanded, fully understanding the path down which the court must now be seen to go.

"Yes sir," one replied meekly.

"You ran back to the camp with this man in pursuit?"

"To avoid wrongful accusation sir."

"You were seen carrying goods for which you cannot account."

"We bought them," they insisted together.

"You maintain your innocence?" The duke demanded having grown weary with the proceedings already.

"Yes sir." They both spoke and raised their hands to him in supplication.

"Have them whipped and then hung," Guillaume ordered.

The two soldiers started to beg piteously but were dragged away by their former comrades under the command of the young officer.

"My Lord, I praise your justice, but..." The townsman looked at him meaningfully.

Guillaume considered the unspoken request. He did not like the idea of parting with his money as a result of someone else's actions but on this one occasion at least he valued the support of the locals more.

"Your goods will be returned to you and due recompense for the harm done to your good name made." Guillaume conceded. His scribe made the appropriate note and the townsman was ushered away with little ceremony. "Come brothers."

Leading the way the duke recommenced what he had intended to be his regular tour of the camp. Behind him rode his two half brothers, Bishop Odo and Robert, Count of Mortain. In their wake came their servants and a mounted guard. In truth the duke had seen enough of the camp already, its condition had not changed any since yesterday but it seemed that the same could not be said for the men. As if in defiance to the violent weather he led the way down to the beach and into the teeth of the storm. For a moment he simply sat and watched the broiling waves pummel the shore, his mind lost in other thoughts. Eventually Robert moved his horse alongside the duke's and that prompted a response from his brother.

"The wind is my enemy," Guillaume muttered.

"It does not compare with the weather that Harold Godwinson enjoys in England," the Count of Mortain commented dryly. "It is as if the season mocks us. Here we have winds too strong to sail against; there they have a glorious late summer. Harold disbands his army so that the men can fetch in the harvest, a bumper crop they say."

"So contrary to our expedition are these winds that the English have retired their fleet. In truth nothing stands between us and their southern shore but this storm," Odo of Bayeux added as he came alongside Guillaume on the left.

"The wind is Harold's ally but all I need is one day of good weather," Guillaume asserted. He turned to look again at the fleet hugging the bay for protection. A spit of headland extended north along the river, like a protective arm, shielding the vessels from the worst of the weather that whipped up the waves in the dark sea beyond. The tents of the men where lashed by those same storm winds as they raced over the sands, raking the river and then tearing along the southern bank. There were thousands of soldiers here and they should be a marvellous sight to see. A terrible sight for the enemy to behold, but they were miserable. The wind was beating them down as were the months of inactivity. Desertion was not yet a problem but as winter loomed and they sat here exposed to the storms that would get colder as they raged through the channel between Normandy and England, the men would leave.

Mayhap the barons would leave sooner?

"We must do something and soon," Robert urged his older brother. "This idleness will defeat the men's resolve more certainly than any power that Harold could bring to bear. The crimes of those two this morning will be just the beginning. The barons too grow jaded with our plans. They long to return to the comfort of their estates and the warmth of their hearths. The promises that we've made concerning the wealth of the Saxon kingdom will grow empty and respect for your authority will be lost. All our enemies will laugh into their cups."

"And what, my brother, of Brittany?" Odo again reminded the duke. "If we do not act before the year is out Duke Conan will trumpet our failure throughout France. He will use it to stir up King Philip against us. Our enemies will grow strong on every border of Normandy."

"What would you have me do brothers? Everything is bent on this one enterprise and it has stalled due to the wind. I have the banner of God from the hand of the pope himself Odo but I lack His divine approval all the same. Is it not His breath that blows over these sands and keeps my fleet bottled in the river mouth? Can you not intercede in your capacity as a priest on our behalf Odo and can you not keep the adventurers in check with more tales of gold and land in Saxon England Robert?"

"There is no point in blaming the persistent weather. We Normans know what the winter seasons bring along this coast. The storm will blow out eventually," Robert replied. "More irksome is knowing that Harold basks in the sunshine of a late summer, seemingly untouched by these petulant storms. No doubt if they do breath upon his kingdom it is along the cliffs of England's rugged coastline, doing little harm to his army."

"His army! What army? A force of peasants and no more," Odo insisted. "The whole of the Saxon world is peasant in character. Even these eorls as you call them, their nobility, are but farmers with mud on their heels."

"They all live on the land but in many ways that is their strength, not their weakness. They defend that land with a bloody tenacity. Not even the Vikings have conquered them. Oh, they placed their Norse kings upon the English throne but that was more a result of Saxon in-fighting rather than by the keenness of Danish axes. For over five hundred years the Saxons have withstood the Norsemen, our ancestors I remind you. That alone makes them a dangerous enemy. These eorls and theigns that you dismiss so lightly are born to war. Their victories are measured by the gold that encircles their heads and pins their cloaks about their shoulders. Where is your circlet of gold Odo?" Guillaume retorted.

"One might think that you honoured your enemy," Robert noted.

"I do honour my enemy," Guillaume admitted, "because he is a worthy enemy."

"Harold Godwinson is a usurper," Odo insisted.

"Harold Godwinson has taken Edward's crown by expectation, not by right. His power as the greatest eorl of the kingdom gave him that expectation and, mayhap, the marriage of his sister to King Edward gave him a form of right, enough that the Witan recognised his claim over all others," Guillaume deliberated on the recent events in England.

"You were cousin to King Edward, a bond of blood existed between you, one recognised by King Edward himself when he acknowledged your claim upon his crown. Godwinson vowed to support that claim, over holy relics he made his oath; you cannot now admire his transgression when it is at your own expense," Odo insisted.

Guillaume only smiled.

"I announced to the world my revulsion at Harold Godwinson's breaking of a holy oath, an act that resulted in him being excommunicated by the pope, but I am minded that I would not have acted any differently if our roles were reversed."

"And Harold insists that the presence of the holy relics was not made known to him until after the oath was taken, and that under some duress as he was, as it might be said, a captive of our brother's court at the time." Robert added. The use of the relics had been Odo's idea of course, but Guillaume had been just as keen to keep Harold ignorant as to their presence. It occurred to Robert that mayhap now both of his brothers might wonder if their connivance was the cause of their bad luck with the weather.

"I do applaud his bravado but I regret the measures to which it now puts us to. An invasion of England is no small matter, it puts us in a vulnerable situation if we should fail, it strains my authority over the nobility of Normandy, and it empties our coffers," the duke said.

"Necessity demands it of us. Our Normandy is a duchy hemmed in by enemies and no matter how many battles we win eventually the weight of the King of France's arms will bear you down and Normandy will become but another vassal; a coronet to the French crown," Robert replied with a little heat.

"King Henry is dead and his son is still but a boy. This Philip may have taken the throne from his regent mother but the boy king poses no immediate threat," Odo insisted. "Under his father, King Henry, the French kingdom actually grew smaller and weaker."

"King Philip is surrounded by men looking to make their names and fortunes by extending the provinces of the French kingdom. They will do this by annexing lands to the crown that are either new or previously belonged to it. Normandy would make a choice addition," Robert countered with an argument that was already known to the three of them.

"I do not fear war with the French; did we not defeat them nine years ago at Varaville? Was that but a postponement of the inevitable? The French are jealous of our Norman independence and will always look for ways to curtail it." Guillaume looked at both his half-brothers in turn, enjoying their company and conversation despite the cold and inhospitable location. The same could not be said for the men who sat silently awaiting their lords. "In such circumstances what the Duke of Normandy needs is to become a king himself and organize the power of a kingdom against our enemies. No, the barons are wrong in their popular supposition that you espouse Odo; the Saxons are not weak, disorganised peasants, incapable of withstanding a Norman charge of heavy cavalry. They are stout of limb and strong of heart. They will make fine soldiers when properly trained in the modern method of warfare; our method of warfare."

The mood between the three brothers brightened considerably as they talked even as the clouds on the horizon grew darker and more threatening. They spoke then with more feeling about their plans. And of course there was the gold. England had more gold than anyone else it seemed. The gold alone, if he was to admit it, drew Guillaume's ambition more than anything else to this enterprise. That gold of England would make him powerful enough to resist the boy king of France and all his other enemies without fear, and with Saxon stock in his infantry his army would indeed be formidable; but first he had to get the crown.

How do you pull a crown from the head of a Saxon warrior-king?

"Have you made a decision?" The Count of Mortain asked. Guillaume looked at him.

"Yes." He replied simply.

"If we do not do something soon then winter will be upon us and all of this talk and planning may prove to be for nothing,"

Robert prompted him. "Too much money has been spent already. We must act, be it to England or to home."

Odo glanced from one to the other, knowing that the moment had come and eager to discover the resolution.

"We will move," Guillaume determined confidently.

"Where?" Robert demanded with a note of exasperation.

"Closer to England, give the order, the army is to board ship and the fleet is to head north-east to St Valéry-sur-Somme. That will give them something to occupy the men with." He looked a little pleased with his decision.

Robert looked out to sea where the waves continued to broil under the dark, oppressive sky.

"It's some 160 miles to St Valéry-sur-Somme from here," he pointed out, "the fleet will be at risk every day it spends away from the shore!"

"True, but not from the Saxons," Guillaume answered easily.

Robert knew him well enough to realise that the duke's mind was made up. There would be no going back and in truth he welcomed this decision.

"Then we move one step closer," Odo pointed out, not exactly dismayed either.

"When the fleet embarks know this, that there will be no turning back. From St Valéry-sur-Somme one clear day is all we'll need to land our power on English soil and that is all I pray for."

Sunday 17th September 1066

The City of York

The gloom pressed hard upon the weak light emanating from the lamps of burning mutton fat that were scattered throughout the long-hall. So sparsely were they placed that little could be seen of the dimensions of the building by the flare of the insipid flickering flames alone. The tapestries that decorated the walls remained in darkness. Trophies of war affixed to the beams high overhead were beyond the reach of the weak light. Their presence would be known only to one who had visited the Great Hall of York when it was put to its proper use; for feasting.

The hearth had burnt low, the embers still hot enough to emit an orange glow but in the shadow haunted gloom it looked more like a hellish pit than a source of warmth and comfort. There it sat, a glaring orange eye, in the centre of the hall, enclosed by stone shaped by the hands of craftsmen. Iron work hung over the hearth. A grill to stand pots upon, spits to impale large cuts of meat so that they could be roasted, and arms that could be swung over the centre of the fire and from which large cauldrons would be suspended. There was barely enough heat to warm a beaker of water right now but then the lord of this hall was not presently at home.

The scrape of a single, slow moving leather heel over the floorboards disrupted the suspended silence of the hall. Fresh straw balled behind that heel as it was dragged backwards exposing the wooden floorboards beneath.

Coenred sat hunched at the table with his back to the hearth, facing the main door at the far end even though it was lost to his sight in the dimness. His broad shoulders were arched somewhat, as if in weariness, and buried under a good quality woollen cloak that had, however, seen better days. The brooch that fastened the cloak around him was of cast iron inlaid with silver, formed into a stylised image of a horse. It was not the adornment of a peasant but neither was it the jewel of a great lord of men. On the table before him lay a gleaming sword, the naked blade reflecting the dull light.

It measured three spans long, tapered from the hilt to the point in a continuous line, with a fuller running down the centre of the blade to lessen its considerable weight. The core of the sword was iron with harder steel welded to the edges and merged into a seamless double-sided blade, sharpened to sever muscle and ligaments. It had an iron cross-guard that swept forward in an arc to protect the hand, the points directed away from the grip. The guard was inlaid with both silver and gold, woven into the intricate patterns that were typical of Saxon art. The tang was made of soft iron wrapped in wood to give it form and to help absorb the shock of impact. It was then bound in leather giving a secure grip. The pommel too was of iron, overlaid with bronze and adorned with chased silver and gold. It perfectly counterbalanced the sword and made it easy to swing in a trained hand. It was the required weapon of a huscarl, the badge of his rank and status as a member of an elite warrior brotherhood.

This was an old sword and he was the third generation of his family to bear it, but it was no relic. The sword's quality was beyond doubt and it was maintained with much care, but it was also a weapon that had seen use. The warrior's own father had carried it in the service of Leofric the

Long Lived, Eorl of Mercia. That great nobleman was said to have reached the grand age of 89 and still commanded his own wits until his last day.

Absently the warrior turned the sword in his hands, watching the dull light move slowly up and down the length of the blade, his mind lost in his remembrances. He recalled the imperfect forms of men, shadowlike in his mind's eye, gathered together on a dark field. They evoked once again the impact of the linden wood of their shields as the warriors came together in the frenzy of a pitched battle contained within the discipline of an interlocked shield-wall. The thrusting of the spears over the tall round shields, like the flicking of the poisonous tongues of the dragons painted onto many a shield. Balefire steel points glanced off steel helmets or pierced the cold links of mail and spilt warm blood. Danish axes splintering wood and brave men alike. His imagination conjured up a sky darkened by the flights of arrows and throwing spears, streaming like flocks of countless black ravens over the battlefield. The Vikings told tales of the dark angels, the Valkyries, coming to the battlefield to choose who would fall and who would stand as the missiles fell amongst the ranks. For a man who had seen the sky clouded by those volleys it was not difficult to imagine the forms of the Valkyries moving amongst the deadly missiles. Like shades of his past the images fluctuated as the light and shadows slipped over the cold naked blade in his hands. Lost in the mists of something that was both his past and his imagination he heard again the screams, the curses in many tongues, the unintelligible roars and howls of phantom men filling the darkened hall as with the voices of ghosts.

"My Lord?"

The words were spoken softly and yet they called out to the warrior through his dark reverie as if a beam of sunlight had penetrated the gloom of the building's interior, scattering the grim shadows of his recollections. Nevertheless, when he looked towards the source of the feminine voice his eyes remained dull and clouded.

He did not look threatening at all, thought the woman. Despite the size of the hall he was not diminished by the emptiness. His powerful frame contained a definite vitality, a masculine strength born from years of martial training and violent encounters, but there was no evil in his face, no malice in his eye. He was a weapons-man, a servant, not a wanton murderer nor a man to be feared by those who were not his enemies. The kitchen women were a feared of their own shadows and she would treat their opinion with the scorn it deserved in the future.

"I thought that you might be hungry, My Lord?" She proffered the board she carried. It contained a fine clay bowl holding hot pork stew and a roll of wheat bread. "Or mayhap you are thirsty?" An equally fine clay cup placed next to the bowl contained a fruit wine. Both of the vessels were the product of a slow wheel and not hand formed, the smoothness of their surfaces gave testimony to that. They were decorated with similar patterns painted on before they were fired in the kiln. Not quite the tableware to be put before honoured guests but also far from the cheapest crockery available in the kitchens of the great hall.

"My Lady, I asked no service of you," Coenred commented. Past memories still clung to his consciousness, lying like mists between his dream world of recollections and the real world before him. Nevertheless, he could not be anything but courteous.

"I am no serving maid," she replied with a soft smile. "Theign Aethelwine offered me sanctuary upon my widowhood."

"Noble friend. An apt name my lady for the High-Theign of York. If you be not a serving maid then would you not sit at my table and keep me company?" He said this mostly from his own innate sense of propriety rather than any real desire to surrender his solitude.

"Gladly, My Lord."

He had expected her to politely refuse his invitation and so was surprised by her readiness to join him. She placed the bowl and a spoon moulded from goat horn in front of him, followed by the bread, and then put the cup within reach of his right hand. As she seated herself opposite she kept her face down but glanced at him through her lashes. She admired his well trimmed beard, something else that was different with him from most men who shaved their beards, and followed the white scar that ran down across his left eyebrow and onto his cheek. Mayhap the beard was meant to mask that scar? Not that it disfigured him at all, it spoke to her of bravery and a spirit of adventure. He had a well formed face that she liked even more having at last come so close to see it. His eyes had brightened and his countenance softened as he reacted to her unexpected company.

"Where are my manners, my name is Coenred son of Aethelred, in service to the eorls Edwin and Morcar, sons of the late Aelfgar, once Eorl of Mercia."

He spoke with a strong timbre, heavy with the accent of Holderness; a northern man then. His tunic was blue linen, a little faded, but in good condition. The sleeve cuffs were rolled back revealing skin browned by exposure to the sun and thick with corded sinews. His dark hair was long, reaching to his shoulders, and tied at the temples with a simple braid woven in black and gold. She noted that his hair, like his beard, was clean and combed. To her eye he seemed to be some thirty five summers old. He wore no rings on his fingers and she could see no other jewellery on his person other than the brooch. It was said that he was not given to such displays of wealth. This encouraged her as it accorded with the character of the man as others better informed than the kitchen women had told it to her.

"I am Mildryth, wife of the late Aethelheard, son of Aldfrid. He was a theign, owing service to Gamal, son of Orm, killed along with our own son during the tyranny of Tostig Godwinson, when he was once the eorl of Northumbria. We lost our holdings and have no kinship to Eorl Aelfgar's house. I have scant expectation of being restored to the lands that were once ours, although I have lodged a complaint with the Hundred Court. It was passed up to the Shire Court but it has yet to be heard," she spoke quickly.

It was, mayhap, too much to tell someone on first meeting, but she did not know how much time there would be before someone else entered the hall and she had waited many days for just such an opportunity. Her heart beat quickly and beneath the table she wrung her hands nervously, but she hoped that her face did not betray her emotions. The intention was simple, to appeal to his sense of honour, but she was also aware of how easily her motive might be misconstrued if she said the wrong thing or acted in the wrong way.

He seemed thoughtful again, not as willing as her to rush into a conversation, least of all on the subject matter that she had just raised. Eorl Aelfgar had been no friend to Eorl Tostig, this she knew, but his sons, this huscarl's lords, had benefitted by Tostig's fall and that was a fact that might provoke the warrior to hear her appeal more sympathetically.

"Tostig Godwinson brought a dark stain upon his name with the murder of the lords Gamal, Ulf and Gospatric. Of Dane blood or not the law granted them and their retainers protection whilst they took counsel with the eorl at his own invitation. The great never worry about the pain they cause for such as thee. But Theign Ęthelwine gives you charity?" Coenred spoke after eating a spoonful of the stew that he was pleased to find to his liking. He wondered if she had cooked it herself?

"Not charity, My Lord. What he does for me he does out of duty as a friend to my dead husband, and also out of the greatness of his heart. He has indeed proven himself a noble friend. I accept duties to his household in return and carry them out as best as I can, in grateful repayment for the security and keep that he has given me."

"Then certainly he is well named," Coenred smiled and she saw a warmer character beneath the persona of the warrior.

"Are you not married too my lord?" She asked knowingly.

"Me? I am a huscarl to the eorls of Mercia. My trade is war and the training of the dead eorl's sons. A man should have the time to care for a wife and family, I cannot do that in these days of troubles and alarms."

"Would not the love of a wife give a desire to your sword arm to maintain your life a little longer? To bring you home safe again a little sooner?" She raised her chin and he saw the strength of character in her face. For a moment he forgot himself as he became aware of the power of her beauty.

She wore a remarkably plain dress. It was coloured a soft green, mayhap faded or effected, it complemented her combed hair well, like summer wheat against the green of the hedgerow. Her hair was tied back, fastened by a simple braid of yellow and green that ended in carved bone clips. That set her apart from the crowd; most women today were following the churches sermons on feminine modesty by wearing headdresses. Clearly she was of Nordic descent; as likely as not Danish as so many others in these parts were. Her jewellery was modest, bronze for the most part, or at least iron coated in bronze. Although beyond the reach of a peasant woman her adornments were tasteful rather than just expensive, showing a liking for animal forms. Many a woman, and many a man for that matter, wore jewellery merely as a means to display their personal wealth. This Mildryth was a widow-woman however, not looking to turn the eye of a young man but simply to pass in society according to her rank as theign-worthy. There was about her, however, a sense of self-possession that could only come from age and experience and that he found himself admiring. He began to wonder why she had come to him in this empty hall as he suspected that the reason was not contained within the obligation of hospitality alone.

"I have no doubt that your husband felt as such," he admitted, "but I know nothing of these things."

"Nothing?" She pressed.

"I have spent my life in the service of eoldermen. I have fought wars, stood firm in the shield-walls of great armies. I have known warriors take wives and seen the womenfolk in their despair when an enemy spear or Viking axe took the lives of those men. I have watched their tears and heard their wailing. Ask me what wood to make a throwing spear from or how to wield a sword against an armoured man. Ask me not about the kinder skills of a husband."

"I would rather ask you about the skills of a protector." Mildryth caught his eye purposefully.

"Protector?" He paused in eating, the spoon hanging between bowl and mouth; genuinely surprised.

"The word upon the lips of many is that the exiled Tostig Godwinson means to return," she looked at him intently but the warrior resumed his eating, breaking off some bread to dip into the stew. He kept his eyes on the bowl.

"I have heard it said that Tostig fled over the southern sea to Flanders when first exiled last year. His wife is the sister of Count Baldwin who rules there. They would be welcomed in Flanders I should think," Coenred replied in passing, keeping his voice level even as he pondered the import of her word, protector?

"There is a canker in the bosom of that man that will allow him to know no peace. Is it not true that he raised a fleet and landed in the Wight Isle where they gave him gold and provisions not so long ago and that he sailed north and raided the settlements of Mercia because he hates the sons of Aelfgar so?"

"You know much of the happenings of the kingdom, My Lady," Coenred conceded, "but know also that though Tostig raided the eastern coast of the northland he was defeated by My Lords, the eorls Edwin and Morcar; I fought under their banners. Tostig Godwinson's men deserted him before our spears and he fled first to Scotland, no doubt to claim sanctuary from King Malcolm, a good friend of his in the days when Tostig was second in the kingdom only to his brother; King Harold, then an eorl himself. Again I say, from Scotland I believe he went to Flanders where he can live out his days in peace. He is beyond doing harm to thee again I think."

"And yet my heart labours under a shadow," Mildryth persisted, "the King of Norway has laid claim to the throne of England, this he has made known through a common declaration, but My Lord King Harold sits in London awaiting Guillaume of Normandy to land his power in the south."

"With good reason, Hardrada has spent many a year fighting the Danes for their kingship and though he often defeated King Sweyn he never took the crown. Norway is spent, the king's money and army wasted on a fruitless war." Coenred once again returned to eating as if that were the end of the matter.

"So it may seem, and yet word comes to me from the Danes settled in Northumbria since the time of King Knut, that Tostig has sailed to Norway."

The huscarl fixed her with a serious eye, straightening on his wooden seat and placing the goat-horn spoon into the half empty bowl. His face became harder.

"Do you think me worthy of such news, My Lady? Is this not a matter for the Council of Eolderman?" His voice was stern now.

It was almost a rebuke and she wondered if mayhap she had indeed gone too far. However, he was a man of reputation, one of Eorl Aelfgar's fabled companions and it was said that in many a lord's eye his station was deserving of being equal to that of the two young eorls that he now served.

"It troubles me that you seem to know so much, My Lady."

"I have learnt to live by my wits, My Lord. I would rather be a vixen than a doe, for when they murdered my good husband there were those amongst Tostig's company that would have sported with me against my will before casting my body out to be used by their men, as such so often do with womenfolk!" Anger made her voice vibrate in the great emptiness of the hall. The moment had come and she would press on as she had designed. He would either concede to her appeal or he would not and the words he uttered next would reveal which way his intention lay.

"And what kept you safe that night?" Coenred asked, intrigued as much by her sudden passionate outburst as by the story that she clearly had to tell. "Not your wits alone I think."

"This helped."

From her belt she brought forth a scramseax and laid it on the table to accompany his naked sword. It was a little over two spans in length, but that included the handle that was made from carved antler. Coenred reached over and picked up the knife. The sheath was made from fine leather fastened down the seam with a strip of riveted copper. He took hold of the handle and grunted with satisfaction at the skill with which it had been formed to fit the hand so comfortably. A stylised hind had been carved into the handle, the animal in mid leap and surrounded by swirling patterns so typical of Saxon art. Power and grace in one image.

Gentle strength!

He recalled the literal meaning of her name. This knife was either made for her or given to her by her now dead husband, either way he who gave such a treasure thought very highly of the recipient indeed. He withdrew the knife and recognised the quality of the workmanship instantly. The main body of the blade was iron with the traditional rectangular body section. The top corner at one end tapered into a long thin spike that pierced the handle made from the carved antler, the lower opposite corner also tapered but less acutely from the thick top side of the knife down to the thin and razor sharp cutting edge at the bottom, forming a wicked stabbing point. There were larger versions called langseaxes that were used as tools for chopping wood or butchering animals, or even as swords by warriors who could not afford weapons carried by the likes of high-theigns, huscarls and eoldermen. These tools were effective implements indeed and what they lacked in decoration they more than made up for in utility. Most Saxons carried a scramseax of some description but the majority were nondescript tools meant for everyday work; the one he held now in his hand was something different.

The blade was patterned with, on one side, another hind, very similar to the one on the handle and on the reverse he recognised the name 'Mildryth'. He was not a proficient reader but he had mastered enough to be able to read simple inscriptions. So it had indeed been made for her. Steel had been welded onto the single edge of the iron blade and worked to a faultless seam making it an even more formidable blade. The scramseax would have taken a craftsman several weeks to make and was indeed a thing of value, not a tool for cooking or working but a weapon to protect someone, a person that another obviously held as precious to them.

"This is a very fine scramseax, My Lady," Coenred said with evident appreciation, "your husband loved you very much."

"And I him but now he is dead and I am cast upon the goodwill of others for protection and support." She kept her chin up and her eyes upon him, no sign of weakness showing, no plea for pity.

Mayhap he understood?

"I had hoped that with Harold of Wessex taking the crown with the Witan's approval a degree of peace might settle over the land. There are duties a huscarl should attend to by his lord's direction that do not call for the use of sword or spear. In that time there would be a place, I had thought, for the life of a family man. But dark clouds remain upon the horizon, the foreign duke threatens still, he does not respect the wish of the Saxons to choose their own king. I fear that my place in the shield-wall will be commanded again and that my blood will yet be spilt at my lord's bidding."

He replaced the fine scramseax back into its sheath and held it out to Mildryth to take back.

"Know this Coenred, huscarl to eorls; I am a widow with little property or wealth but I still have a station in this life and it makes me the object of many a man's unwanted attention. Of you, Coenred son of Aethelred, I have observed many times, even if you have not noticed me once since Theign Aethelwine gave me leave to reside in this great-hall of his that you frequent. It has been two years since the death of my husband and in that time I have heard your name spoken with honour and regard. In days of darkening clouds and gathering enemies a woman would be wise to choose a protector with the qualities necessary not only to survive such days but also to be able to shield those he counts as worthy of his protection."

There it was again; protection. He sat and thought for a moment, eyes on the blade of his own sword as it lay in front of him. He believed that he knew what she meant. Most women her age were indeed married and would look to their husbands for protection. Some, widowed as she was, would turn to surviving family members, fathers, brothers, uncles; friends as a last resort. And for those women who had no one, then mayhap not even the gods, pagan nor Christian, could foretell their fate. Of course, a woman might also seek out another husband.

Was it such a great step between being a protector of a woman to becoming her husband?

"Many a warrior will be cut down in the battles that may yet come. There is no promise that I, too, will not meet my bloody end on a field somewhere," he proffered her the scramseax again. "It is yours, take it. I would have you own some protection."

"It is mine to keep or to give as I see fit. Take this knife and wear it in your belt. Use it to keep the threat of our enemies at bay. Mayhap one day, in your last battle, when your shield is splintered, your spear broken, and your sword too heavy to wield, my knife will indeed come between you and death. It may preserve your life so that you may return it to me when the great lords' argument of the day is over and he who wears the crown of England cares little for such as we. I will await you."

She reached out and laid her hand over his and then gently pushed the scramseax back towards him. His heart missed a beat. The softness of her skin broke upon him like a revelation. He looked at her and knew that he had indeed seen her before, many times probably and within this very hall. He had noted her because she was a woman apart from the servants. That said he had always believed that there had been no place for a woman in his life, not when it had been dedicated to being the best weapons-man that he could be in the service of Eorl Aelfgar. Others depended upon him and he had won them much in the way of land and gold by virtue of being the finest huscarl in Mercia. His ambition had demanded sacrifice however, but of late his mind had considered a change in his path. This was too soon though, no decisions had yet been made. He was still the warrior, an eorl's man.

Although his most recent thoughts had been of war and killing they had arisen, it seemed to him now, in response to earlier thoughts of the farm that he owned and how he might prefer a life there, raising sheep, instead of hazarding his blood for lords who were little more than boys and who, in many a free man's estimation, were but pale shadows of their ancestors. If he took that path then maybe he might also take a wife and become a theign himself. He was aware that only a woman could fill this hollow space in his life, but not while he was a huscarl. Not while his sole purpose was to fight the enemies of his young lords. It was true that theigns fought as a duty to their lords too, but they did so as protectors of the families and ceorls for whom they were responsible, not solely to win treasure and fame as an eolderman's hearth companion.

"Without the protection of your knife the men who leer may well prowl all the closer when the likes of me are gone to war." His voice sounded slight even to his own ears. He actually believed that the threat of war was diminishing with each day. Since Tostig Godwinson had been driven from the land, no new threats had been realised, the Normans remained beyond the horizon, but he knew of nothing else to appeal to being a man of the sword.

"Take this knife and you will become my protection. None will dare to disrespect me knowing that Coenred, huscarl to the earl's of Northumbria and Mercia both, holds me in his favour," she smiled. "We are not young lovers Coenred, but man and woman, and in this world it takes such a partnership to make whatever happiness we might yet know. I ask you only for the protection that a man as mighty as you can give. Go to war, as you must, and fight for theigns or eorls or kings or crowns. Mayhap you might fight for me as I deem you as worthy a man as my dead husband, but do not join Aethelheard in death. Fight and live. Go when you must but come again to return my scramseax to me and then shall you and I sit once again, in peace and solitude, and talk about what future there might be for us."

Her eyes held his but did so without challenge. She was searching his face, his expressions, looking for something. Coenred returned her look without hesitation and realised that this had been her end purpose all along. His sense of honour would not allow him to deny her the protection that she reasonably asked of him. He was a huscarl; his duty was to protect the life of his lord and by extension the lives of all the people who owed fealty to that same lord. Whether granting her boon would take them towards a closer union was not clear, could not be clear yet. A part of him, a new voice within his head, wished that it might be so. The huscarl, so long the dominant character of his spirit, rejected that thought but he brought the scramseax back over the table all the same and looked at it once more. Wyrd decided many things in a man's life but mayhap it was not so absolute, mayhap men were left with many choices to make as well.

"As thee wish, My Lady."

The Village of Skaroaborg

Even the hardest of warriors, the most experienced of sailors, even a king of men, might stop and feel insignificant before the world when they witnessed such a change in the weather. The sky was rolling down upon them from the north, great tumbling boulders of dark granite for clouds that threatened to crush everything beneath them. The light faded quickly, as if it were being extinguished by an irestiable weight, remaining only as a thin ribbon as bright as silver but pushed to the far horizon. It was only a half-light, however, and it gave a weird aspect to everything that it touched. Beneath the keels of the ships the sea turned black and the waves began to roll in their turn as if a mirror image to the sky above.

The brave men within the great Viking long-ship crowded the sides of the vessel and looked with dismay at the changes that were being enacted all around them. The sky had been dark all day but the clouds were always moving, blown by a north-easterly wind that had aided them in their journey across the great northern whale-road that lay betwixt Norway and England. The voyage had not been a direct one, however, as they had lately come from Orkney. Their course had brought them down the eastern coast of Britain and that in turn had allowed them to stay within sight of land as the threat of a storm had been almost ever present since they had sailed.

"The old gods grow angry," Eystein Orre remarked as looked north past the stern of the great warship. "The superstitious read runes in the water and in the clouds."

King Harald Hardrada only grunted in response. He could read the signs as clearly as any man onboard but that was not sufficient, he had to weigh up his next choice of words carefully. Behind him there followed a huge fleet of ships in the wake of his vessel Long Serpent. They were not all warships, however, almost half were much smaller craft used to carry the supplies that a large army in a foreign land would need. The loss of any one of those ships would be regrettable.

"We must put into shore," Jarl Steinkel announced suddenly. He stood before the mast, his legs apart to allow him to ride the growing roll and pitch of the vessel. "Turn to shore!"

His voice called out over the growing wind that already made the cable sing. Those that heard it could not mistake the tone of command used, nor hidden their surprise at it.

"Run before the wind!" Hardrada cried out in an even more thunderous voice. "Run before the wind I say as there's naught to landward that will shield us from this blow!"

"Odin has turned against us!" someone commented from the rowing benches, his words were given quick support by many more mouths. Another even suggested that it was the end of the world.

"Ragnarok doesn't begin on this day," Hardrada asserted but his voice was lower in tone.

He still stood by the port side of the ship from where he had been watching the phenomenon of the threatened storm develop. The sea had become like jet, a shiny black flecked with silver from which they could watch the undulation of the waves as they grew in strength and size. Over their heads the clouds seemed to increase in magnitude so that the air around them began to feel oppressive. A few drops of rain began to fall, the precursor of what was to come; everyone expected it to turn into a downpour of terrible ferocity.

"We turn to shore or we die at sea," Jarl Steinkel countered the king.

He was joined now by two of his own men. Eystein Orre noticed that they had weapons at hand but that they were feigning a disinterest in everything about them despite the curious change in the weather, which alone had already attracted so much attention.

"It is not your place to give commands here!" Orre corrected the jarl and took a step towards him, laying his hand on top of the pommel of his sword as a warning.

Jarl Steinkel looked passed the faithful Orre and directly at the King of Norway himself. Hardrada seemed unperturbed as he stood with one hand on the timber rail at the side of the ship, but then that was to be expected. The giant Viking was not only tall but fully formed, not long and lank like some men of height. His arms and legs were thick with muscle made strong by many years spent sailing the known world and fighting countless battles against all kinds of peoples.

Despite his impressive stature and a formidable reputation Steinkel also saw a man who was somewhat down on his luck. Challenging the king in Norway had been unthinkable, the odds were too much in the old man's favour even if the people were much cooler towards him since the Danish war had led to naught but a miserable peace treaty. Within his own court Hardrada was surrounded by his loyal favourites, Jarl Siward, the captain of the king's companions, Jarl Orre, the steward of the royal keep, and of course the princes Magnus and Olaf. Here on the ship, even this royal ship, the odds were much better to his mind.

As the sky darkened further and the wind began to howl like a wolf the men at the oars gave fresh voice to their fears. They were all battle-hardened warriors but that did not mean that they were not ruled by the superstitions of the sea. They feared to drown.

"It is a Viking's right to voice his thoughts when the luck runs ill and we stand on the point of destruction," Jarl Steinkel answered Orre, all the time keeping his eyes on the king. "This expedition has been plagued from the first, that's what comes from making alliances with the enemy."

Eystein Orre was about to speak when he was silenced by a great hand that casually but firmly pushed him to one side. Instead the Norwegian looked to his right, craning his neck to see the face of his king as Hardrada stepped slowly past him and towards the rebellious jarl. It was a face of concentration and cold intent.

"Steinkel, I wonder why you journeyed on this voyage seeing as you have done nothing but bellyache since we left Norway?" Hardrada had to raise his voice to combat the growing wind but he seemed, unlike his men, unperturbed by the worsening conditions around them. "I wonder as well why you have lodged yourself on board my ship when you have one of your own?"

In truth Hardrada would have, if he had had the choice, postponed this encounter with one of his own jarls for when their feet were back on dry land but clearly Steinkel had decided to precipitate matters. He could appreciate the timing, however, what with the peculiar developments in the weather. Men were given to reading doom and disaster in such moments. It was always wise to seek an advantage over an enemy but it was not always wise to act upon the first opportunity without careful consideration.

He should, mayhap, have felt angry at the jarl's challenge but he found himself feeling surprisingly calm. Of course he knew very well that Jarl Steinkel opposed his rule, well not so much opposed him as sought to replace him as king. That was something that was never going to happen of course. Prince Olaf voyaged with the jarls of Orkney on their own ship, safe from a back-stabber's blade, and Prince Magnus sat as regent in the court of Norway.

Keep your friends close and your enemies closer!

In truth Hardrada had not imagined that Steinkel possessed the courage to launch a bid for power so soon. However, once the moment had arrived the king had already looked ahead and seen how this incident might benefit himself, and restore something of his reputation with the men as well. He was, after all, the War Wolf, a vicious, cunning and ruthless man and chieftan; the defeat of one of his enemies at court would not be a bad thing.

"You see where your leadership has brought us," Steinkel shouted back with no show of etiquette before his lord. It was clear that both men now knew that they had crossed a line but as to whether or not that would lead to violence no one could yet tell. "The black wind of the gods would dash our ships upon the rocks of England's rugged shoreline, drown our bodies in icy waters and wash us up for the plunder of the Saxons. What glory is there in this fate? What merit for a man of the sword and of the spear in this doom that you, great king, bring upon us?"

Jarl Steinkel had moved away from the mast and towards the bow of the ship but always facing Hardrada. He was a typical Viking, his body was strong and his hand practiced with the sword, but before the King of Norway he looked like a child. Those who watched the altercation wondered at his reasoning for picking such a seemingly unequal fight.

Hardrada now stood upon the deck between the rowers facing Steinkel with the mast to his back. His great hands closed and opened reflexively. A sudden peal of thunder erupted over them and many a man flinched at the sound that reverberated through the very timbers of the ship. Hardrada did not move a muscle. Despite this sudden reminder that the storm was at hand and their safety threatened no one could take their eyes from the confrontation.

The two men who had been with Steinkel when he first spoke were now behind the giant king and on either side of him. They exhibited an air of interest in the proceedings just like their fellow crewmen but their eyes often flitted to Steinkel as if they were awaiting a signal.

"Give me an oath of fealty," Hardrada spoke loud enough so that he could be sure the crew heard his command.

"Your day is done old king, die with some grace for the pity of all those you lead to hell!" Steinkel retorted drawing his sword and moving into a fighting stance. The jarl did not hurl himself into an immediate attack, however, that came suddenly and unannounced from the king's left.

A man holding a short-sword in his right hand launched himself at the great Viking chief. He voiced no challenge; his attack was both silent and swift, but not swift enough. Hardrada turned with amazing agility for such a large man. His right hand fastened around the throat of his attacker, his left closed like a vice on the other's right forearm. With a quick twisting motion he snapped the bones in the man's arm as if he were twisting straw between his fingers and then spun again to his left, lifting the man from his feet in the process.

Even though the ship pitched and yawed in the swell the great Viking never lost his footing. A second attacker had attempted to close with him from the starboard-side but he had been too slow. The position of the mast had protected Hardrada's back. Using the helpless would be assassin almost as a club the king crashed one body into another. They collapsed to the boards of the ship, the sailors scattering before them. In an instant Eystein Orre was upon them with his sword in his hand, which quickly emerged into the weird half-light stained with their blood.

Jarl Steinkel watched the seconds pass with disbelieving eyes from the moment the attack had begun to when Hardrada faced him once more, untouched by either blade and still without a weapon of his own in his hand. Steinkel felt the grip of his sword, the weight of the cold steel, judged the length of the weapon. He looked once more into the king's eyes and knew that it would not be enough.

"Your oath," was all that Hardrada said in response.

For a moment the two simply stared at each other and then the king started forward with a purpose to end the matter once and for all. Jarl Steinkel hesitated only to weigh up his chances and then he turned and ran to the bow of the ship. His pace did not slacken as he reached the rail but he jumped over it without breaking his stride.

"That will suffice," Hardrada commented.

Several seconds passed without a word from anyone else on board and then the silence was broken by another thunderbolt from the heavens.

King Harald Hardrada had stopped his advance just before the rail of the ship. He did not look down into the black sea that had closed above the head of his enemy but rather out further forwards and a little off to the west. The whale-road was becoming violent now, the waves tossing the great ship up into the air by many feet, the bow sending up a shower of black water as it crashed back down again. To replace the excitement of the violent encounter the fear of the storm seeped into men's hearts.

"To shoreward!" Hardrada suddenly boomed. He raised a great hand and pointed ahead of them. "Mark me, make for the headland."

"Where, My Lord?" Eystein Orre came to his side quickly and squinted into the almost darkness. The ribbon of silver light continued on the horizon and it gave them enough illumination to see a great formation of rock jutting out into the sea.

"You see it?" Hardrada demanded.

"Aye, My Lord, I see it," Orre grinned at his king.

Abiorn the Dane pulled his cloak around himself and scowled back at the black clouds quickly approaching from the north. It may prove a bad night tonight if the weather did not change. He fancied that the wind would shriek through the village and the rain would find a way in through the walls and roof, it always found a way in, but they would remain warm and mostly dry. He glanced eastwards out to sea and was rewarded by the sight of the last of the fishing boats coming back to shore. He bent down and picked up a woven bag from the grass at his feet, he was not sorry that this duty as watchman was almost finished. There was little to see now that the weather was closing in anyway. He desired nothing more than to return to his hearth and home and while away the evening with his family.

It was a decent walk back down to the village and he was eager to get under way, you did not have to be a man of the sea to know that the rain was coming. It was still a little early in the last hour of his watch, however, and so as if to make up for that fact he walked towards the edge of the headland and looked out to sea once more. The sky was grey to the south but there was nothing on the sea. To the east the last of the vessels making their way back home had slipped beyond his field of vision beneath the cliff upon which he stood and to the north....!

Below the roiling clouds and riding a pitch black sea Abiorn saw a vision from his nightmares. A great Viking warship was running before the storm and in its' wake came hundreds of other vessels. For several seconds he could not believe what he was seeing. Never in his life had he seen a fleet so large. It chilled his heart more than the threat of the great storm that drove those ships south to Skaroaberg ever could.

An echo of thunder rolled up to the headland and it gave the watchman a sudden impetus. He turned upon his foot and ran inland praying to the Lord Jesu Christ that he would be in time for his family's sake.

With a wave of his right hand Tostig Godwinson halted the party of armed men at his back. Obediently they stopped and let their lord continue his walk to the edge of the cliff. Only their captain, Oswyn, continued to follow in the nobleman's footsteps.

The grass-topped headland jutted out into the North Sea, rising some three hundred feet over the dark churning waters. Tostig turned and looked in land. The fresh kiss of the westerly wind was on his face, tugging at his clean and combed hair, held fast by a golden band. His blue cloak fluttered but the wind was much weaker now, having changed direction and losing its violence. Just a few hours ago it had threatened to wreck an unimaginable doom upon his expedition, to ruin all of his careful plans, but they had reached safety.

He moved closer to the edge of the cliff and looked down into the southern bay. He was, despite himself, impressed by the sight of so many ships moored there. The great headland protected the combined Viking and Saxon fleet from the worst of both the northerly and westerly winds. It was a natural harbour and the shallow beach made it an excellent site for craft to be both launched into and recovered from the sea. Many of the smaller vessels were indeed pulled up onto the shore and a small habitat of canvas shelters had sprung up around the beached vessels. Camp-fires littered the sands, each attracting a host of men intent on cooking or drinking or talking or singing ribald songs.

The bigger ships, such as the massive warship Long Serpent, the King of Norway's flagship, rolled majestically on the swell. They had been anchored in the bay and left to ride out the storm, their crews trusting to the strength of the ships' timbers and cables. Thanks to the protection that this superb harbour gave they had survived with little mishap.

The setting sun was painting the sky blood red in the west. Ribbons of wind torn clouds stretched out across the darkening horizon, vibrant with the hues of a wound, from bright crimson to the dark purples of a bruise. The blood light fell on the Viking long ships, their nodding dragon-heads rose and fell in the undulations of the surf, painted with light and shadows that constantly changed and made it appear as if they were taking on a life of their own.

All would be blood red soon.

Seagulls drifted like lost souls amongst the masts of the ships or rode the crimson coloured swell in between the vessels as if in anticipation of the killing to come. The sun was slipping behind the highland to the west beyond which an unsuspecting City of York lay.

Tostig pulled his fine woollen cloak closer around him but not out of a desire to feel warmer, if anything this September weather was milder than usual. He took no more notice of the fine weave of the cloth than he did of the ships below. Another Saxon may have envied him the good quality cloak so expertly made and so dearly priced but he had lived a life of privilege and such thoughts did not occupy him; his mind was elsewhere now.

"I have returned Oswyn!" he declared.

"Indeed, My Lord," his captain of weapons-men replied.

"When this land was mine, when I was the Eorl of Northumbria, I never thought to visit this place."

"Why would you, My Lord? It is just a stinking fishing village."

"I owned it though," Tostig glanced at his captain, "now they do!" He nodded down into the south bay where the Viking ships lay.

"I ruled over both Saxon and Viking alike then. I am no longer a prince of the kingdom, but a common adventurer now, at war with my own brother," he smiled ruefully.

A clamour from the cliff top further inland attracted their attention. In the faint light the shadowy figures of a number of Vikings could be discerned building a bonfire. They were drunk and being their usual boisterous selves.

"It amazes me that not a single one of them has yet managed to tip himself over the cliff edge," Oswyn commented derisively.

"Harold of Wessex, King of England, has everything now and I, our father's third son, have but the daughter of a foreign count for a wife and a band of mercenaries to command." Tostig paid no heed to either the Vikings or to Oswyn's observation about them. He was revisiting an old subject and a familiar anger was rising within him. "Brother. There is a word of treacherous portent. The most powerful nobleman in the kingdom is both my brother and my enemy."

"It's natural that brothers should rival each other," Oswyn commented, "that Harold shines now in the people's eyes is in no small part due to the poor light cast by Eorl Godwin's first born; your brother Sweyn."

"Sweyn! That man was an idiot who squandered every chance given to him. He actually believed himself to be the illegitimate son of King Knut," Tostig looked exasperated as he remembered with little love the brother who had been elder to both himself and Harold. "What fame he won the family by abducting and raping an abbess for which he was rightly exiled. Killing our own cousin Beorn and him the only member of the family willing to support his return from that exile and ready to plead his case before the king."

"He did indeed prove himself a nithing," Oswyn agreed.

Tostig smiled at the irony of his older brother's fate. He remembered how the news had come to them that Sweyn had repented his crimes and previous life of debauchery. He had gone on a barefoot pilgrimage to Jerusalem to atone. Only a few days after his return from the Holy Land God had, in Tostig's mind at least, so far absolved Sweyn for his many crimes that he bestowed a final blessing upon him; death at the hands of a murderer! That event had rid the family of an annoying fool but it had also left Harold as the heir to Eorl Godwin's title and fortune.

"Father always had a design upon the throne, I doubt not. He thought the now dead King Edward weak and undeserving and many shared that opinion even if they did not speak their own minds."

"Your father's breaking of the king's exile did little to strengthen Edward's hold on the crown," Oswyn agreed.

"He needed the strength of the House of Wessex to hold his kingdom together under the threat of the Welsh and other disgruntled nobles at home. Mayhap, like so many weak men, he hated those that his own infirmity made him lean upon? Mayhap that was why he chose not to consummate his marriage to my sister Edith?"

"But you were a friend to King Edward in other days, ever looking to broker a friendship, an alliance even, between him and King Malcolm of Scotland. Lady Edith supported you at court."

"To no avail Oswyn, to no avail, lesser men merely numbered me amongst the Norman advisors that the king had surrounded himself with. They understood me not. This land is so resistant to change and the eorls so jealous of their positions, they see a threat in every action, a challenge in every word. Like King Edward, who grew up in exile in Normandy, I have seen more of the world beyond our shores and it is indeed changing. It is growing bigger. Scotland, Ireland, Wales, France, Norway and Denmark, these are the powers against which England has to measure her strength."

"Your acceptance of Edward's Norman advisors made you unpopular with the eorls," Oswyn observed again, as he had done many times previously. This conversation was not new and it was often repeated. It probably would never be forgotten until Tostig had achieved his revenge on those he judged to have wronged him.

For Oswyn it was just one more burden that his position in Tostig's now much diminished household subjected him to. There were, however, advantages to being the right hand man of an eolderman, even one who was disgraced and banished. Tostig still had some wealth, the now King Harold had not denied him that, and should he prove successful in recovering all the power that he had previously lost then those who had stood by him would be justly rewarded too. The Godwins valued loyalty and they had always been generous in recognising it.

"They lacked the wit to see that my aim was to supplant those same foreigners with good Saxon advisors, but Saxons educated in the ways of the new world that is dawning around us. Craft must be employed at court. Clever words traded with powerful individuals to oust the Normans from their hold over Edward's court. So many men of title and estate have power over people and animals but little more brain than an ox driver. My mistake was in not recognising sooner that Harold had grown afraid of me."

"Mayhap there can yet be peace between you and Harold?"

"Peace?!" Tostig looked as if he had tasted something foul. "It was Harold who counselled the king to strip me of my eorldom when the people of Northumbria revolted against me. Murder and butchery were suffered by my own vassals while I hunted with King Edward at his pleasure; you know this Oswyn. Harold was commanded by the king to return me to my station but he saw a chance to be rid of an able competitor instead. I was the one man best placed to challenge him so he sided with the sons of Aelfgar and had me exiled."

"Weak King Edward could not choose any other path despite all the promises he had made to you, My Lord; Harold was too powerful." Oswyn agreed, still managing to affect an interest in what his lord had to say.

"Edward and his promises. There was a man who made promises that he never meant to keep and traded upon his reputation for piety to fool men into trusting him. It was King Edward's promises to brother Harold and to Guillaume of Normandy both that have brought these several claims to the crown. In such times as these might those who have been wronged not seek their revenge? In such times as these might not one brother strike down the other and suffer no sin for an act of war? Harald

Hardrada's claim to throne may be no more certain than either the Saxon's or the Norman's but it is the one venture that gives us a promise of retribution"

"Then there will be two more brothers who will not be happy to see the return of the rightful eorl," Oswyn grinned maliciously. "Edwin and Morcar."

"Cousins, but only by marriage not by blood," Tostig agreed. "They seek to emulate the achievements of the Godwins but with none of the Godwin craft. There is no sin to be feared in the spilling of their blood."

The sun had sunk lower now. The sky overhead was growing dark but the clouds on the horizon glowed like hot coals. With only a little use of their imagination they could see the undulating hills of the Wolds burning under the fire that was to come. Their ancient enemy's fire that they had willingly brought from across the cold sea to their own land.

The bonfire on the cliff top flared into life and was greeted by an outpouring of rowdy drunken cheers. As it blazed it silhouetted a group of men steadily following the path that Tostig had taken only recently.

The poor light could not disguise the approaching party. Tostig glanced at Oswyn, the captain signalled the bodyguard and they responded immediately. Moving in an unhurried fashion they surround their lord as he, in his turn, moved away from the cliff edge and towards the approaching king. The execution of their duty pleased Tostig. The warriors had not rushed so as to seem panicked, nor did they dawdle as if underestimating the threat that the Vikings could pose even to their allies.

Hands drifted unconsciously to sword pommels. Like two bears the lords of men approached each other with a respectful wariness. Both parties were capable of inflicting great hurt upon each other and although mindful of the need to maintain the status quo between them they were also keen to avoid any unnecessary bloodshed through either a misunderstanding or a lack of due etiquette. It had to be remembered that Saxon and Viking were in this instance actually allies and not the traditional enemies of yesterday.

"My Lord, you come to watch the sport?" The King of Norway's voice rumbled into the evening air.

Hardrada grinned in the torchlight but there was little humour and less warmth in his kingly greeting. He did not like his new ally being beyond his ability to watch and liked even less the inclination of Tostig's men to stand apart from the revelries of the Vikings.

"And to consider our next move, My Lord," Tostig replied without hesitation.

The king's train outnumbered the Saxon's own by several. Tostig recognised within it Siward, a friend so close to the king that they were almost brothers. Eystein Orre stood just behind him, another loyal companion accounted with the coolest of heads in the heat of battle, although the hair on that head was now turning grey. Norse huscarls accompanied them, without armour it was true but they carried swords, all except for one. He was a titan, bigger even than the great King of Norway. Blond hair flowed over his shoulders like a mane, braided into tails clipped at the ends with gold fastenings, and held in place at the temples by a gold circlet as thick as a man's finger; no doubt a prize given by the hand of Hardrada himself. This colossus carried only one weapon, a two handed Dane-axe that seemed to weigh nothing in his massive hands. His arms were thick with muscle and crossed with scars flashing white against a skin burnt by the sun of much warmer climes. In battle he had the honour of carrying the king's pennant.

Hardrada was older than this Viking Goliath and almost as big. The tales told of his exploits had seemed as exaggerated as the references to his size, with that personal detail verified, however, mayhap all but the most outrageous of deeds attributed to him were true. The King of Norway was indeed of heroic proportions, as were his tempers and his lust for power and wealth. He was indeed the War Wolf personified.

The king's son, Prince Olaf, was also in the party and that gave Tostig reason to relax somewhat. King Hardrada was a dangerous man but he had a habit of being more tractable when in the presence of his own kin. A pity then that he had left his womenfolk at the Isle of Orkney. No doubt the Viking Jarls of those islands felt the same way as it was said that they had their eyes set on King Hardrada's daughters. Those two young men also made up the king's train having become friendly with the prince. They believed that they could impress the great warrior-king with their own courage in battle. They had also brought much needed men and ships from Orkney to support this expedition to England.

"Ah, thinking. You should take time to enjoy the moment, My Lord; that's the Viking way. Today we own this worthless pit and use it to mark the return of the old days."

The king threw up a hand and a loud cheer went up from the Vikings at the cliff-side bonfire, which they then attacked with pitchforks. Burning bits of wood began to fall over the edge, tumbling down towards the abandoned village. Some struck the side of the cliff, bouncing off rocks and exploding into a shower of sparks in the growing gloom, beginning a literal rain of fire.

Harald Hardrada watched the Vikings as they laboured drunkenly but he also watched the Saxon lord too. These were not the old days; he would not fool himself about that. Thirty years ago a great war-chief like himself would have sailed to England with a mighty army of Vikings to crush the gold out of these Saxons, not make alliances with them. This Tostig was a clever man, however. He had climbed from being the third son of the Eorl of Wessex to a position of high prominence in the kingdom. The Saxons of the north might not welcome Tostig's return from exile but the lords of the south would be a different matter. Not every man was swayed to the banner of Harold of Wessex. Hardrada knew very well that today a man achieved as much, if not more, by the use of clever words than he did with the sword.

Slowly the bonfire started to topple over. It cascaded down onto the village sending up a huge shower of sparks as it landed amongst the wooden buildings. A great roar of approval went up and Hardrada added his own voice, smacking a warrior on his back with enough force to make the man stagger a step forward.

"Today we burn our enemies' homes, tomorrow we stick them with our spears and make them squeal like pigs!"

He laughed loudly and his men laughed with him. It was a good show of boisterous humour. Below them the fire spread quickly. It would not be long before every building in the settlement would be consumed.

Wooden hovels can be rebuilt, Tostig reminded himself.

"'Tis not the fisher-folk of Scarborough that we should be concerning ourselves with," Tostig said, showing no sign of enjoying the Vikings' sport. "York is defended with stout walls and a fyrd."

"This we know," Hardrada replied in a quieter voice. "If the storm had not threatened I would not have put into this place but the winds did rise and my men have an opportunity to enjoy themselves; that I would not deny them. Let the fishers of the sea become the fishes of the land, they will be caught in a much bigger net than this."

He waved to the settlement below. A column of dark smoke now poured upwards, lit from underneath by the voracious fires and speckled with bright sparks that both lived and died in the blink of an eye.

"They will head for York and alert them of their peril," Tostig pressed.

"Good! I find men hiding like sheep behind their walls are more given to fear than boldness. I will make them fear my name and know why my standard is called 'Land-Ravager'! Jorvik will fall to us and all of Northumbria with it."

He raised his voice towards the end of this speech and his men, hearing what they wanted to hear, responded with roars of delight.

"We should march on York before these flames die down," the Saxon lord suggested. "'Tis not that far over yonder hills to the Vale of York."

"As the raven flies no doubt, but that would still put some distance between us and our fleet. Though I fear no ill luck I would rather have my ships closer to hand than Skaroaborg." The king's tone was inflexible.

Clearly he had already made up his own mind on this subject and Tostig wondered fleetingly if the Norwegian had some misgivings over this adventure after all?

"And the fyrd of York alarmed," The Saxon mused.

He glanced down at the distant ships in the harbour below. They had taken on a weird aspect in the dancing light of the flames.

The army had to move, that was obvious. Whilst the local theigns may indeed choose to bar the gates and man the walls of York that did not mean that they would simply await their fate. The eorls Edwin and Morcar were probably in the north and Harold was definitely to the south in London. Messengers could be sent in both directions, however. If they did not act quickly this Viking army, as formidable as it was, might find itself trapped between two equal Saxon powers coming from different directions and the Norsemen would have no firm base from which to fight.

"I think, My Lord, that we might move both fleet and army within reach of York, though it would take us longer to reach the city walls," Tostig ventured at last.

"And how's that, My Lord?" The king demanded.

"We sail upon the wide Humber," Tostig suggested. The simplicity of the idea suddenly spurred him on. "We put the marshland of the Isle of Holderness to our northern flank and head west up the great river."

"And how would that bring us to York?"

"The River Ouse that flows by York flows also into the Humber. We sail to its mouth and then up the river, as far as your Long Serpent can still draw draft. From there we moor and make safe the fleet and come at York from the south."

"From the south? Ha! I like thy thinking, My Lord. By the time we reach a mooring point all of York may still believe us marching over the hills to the east. We might catch them with their heads turned with all the gods' luck."

"Should there be any need the men left to guard the fleet could be called to our aid also; they will be within distance of a messenger," Tostig further prompted.

The idea had genuine advantages and he chided himself for not thinking of it earlier. Mayhap he had suppressed the very notion at birth because sailing down the Humber would bring him close to the village of Grim's By again? He dismissed that notion immediately but it felt like he had touched upon an open sore all the same.

Hardrada looked down at the fiercely burning village, despite the distance between them and the flames they could feel the heat from the fire even where they stood on top of the headland.

"Let this be the end of our sport. Siward!"

The king's lieutenant stepped forward, the flames glinting on the gold that adorned him and reddening his blond hair.

"Once the flames have died down we'll ready the ships and head south to the Humber River."

"Aye, My Lord, the men have had enough of Skaroaborg; it offers no more in the way of distraction," Jarl Siward agreed readily enough.

"Then give my command. The sooner we are ready the sooner we'll be in Jorvik."

Siward turned and headed back down the cliff, making the long walk to the destroyed village with equally long strides and accompanied by a number of warriors to help get the revellers in line.

"It will take some time to get the fleet seaworthy again," Tostig commented.

"Hours!" Hardrada insisted. "They have only brought ashore what was needed and there was little found in this midden to fill their holds with. The fleet can be back at sea by first-light and if the wind is fair we will make the Humber well before evening."

It crossed Tostig's mind that he should voice his fears concerning the Saxon's being better prepared than they had so far allowed themselves to believe, but he also worried that he might appear weak before such a mighty warrior. And Harald Hardrada was a mighty warrior, there was no doubting that. It was said that he had not known defeat in battle since the very first time he had participated in one, and then he had been but a boy. No, Tostig decided, getting the Vikings moving again was all that was needed. Once this great army was landed and properly prepared, an accomplishment that Hardrada excelled in, then there would be little to fear indeed even if messengers did get to London in time.

The Vale of York

Shadows began to stretch over the Vale of York as the sun slowly slid behind the western horizon. A few clouds were strung across the sky, long and thin, catching the dying rays of the sun. A large flock of starlings danced along the tops of the trees that strode across the hills and into the next valley. They swirled across the darkening blue, twisting and turning, seeming more like a nebulous but singular being than a gathering of several hundred small birds.

The three horsemen sat upon their patient steeds and looked down into the low valley with predatory eyes. In the fading light they could make out the structure of a small farmhouse. It was roughly rectangular in shape with a thatched roof that came no closer than a rod to the ground leaving space in the walls for windows. Lights were lit within, illuminating the open shutters. It was still warm so no need to close them yet. A man and a boy of about ten were bringing a pair of oxen back to the paddock that was penned adjacent to the far end of the house. A hound ran before them, picked up a stick and returned to the boy, prancing from side to side, its tail lashing the evening air, as it waited impatiently for him to throw it again.

"How many others?" Wulfhere asked as he chewed on a stalk of grass in an absent manner.

"Three; a woman and two girls," one of his companions answered. "All ripe!" He added with a leer. The final horseman sniggered in response.

"You sure?" Wulfhere turned in his saddle to look the man directly in the face. "No brothers? No uncles? No slaves?"

"I've been past this place several times," the man answered with some surety. "I looked the place over like you said to. Never seen more than the man and his boy and the three women."

"And the hound." The other added this as if he felt he should contribute something to the conversation.

"Not much in the way of pickings though," Wulfhere complained.

He knew what interested the other two and whilst the presence of the women offered an infrequent opportunity that he was not likely to spurn himself it was money and valuables that motivated him most. Gold could buy the charms of any woman.

He glanced at his two companions and knew that his future did not lie with them. They were thugs and braggarts who lacked imagination, but they did do as he told them. In another life he had run with such as these down in the southern lands, there he had learnt the way of the outlaw. Up here, in the north, he had looked to live that life in a different fashion. Instead of living in the wild he gave service to a theign, one of some fortune and popularity with the Eorl Morcar. Under the guise of being the theign's man he traversed his lord's lands in Northumbria and when the opportunity presented itself to add some coin to his purse, as it did now, then he took it. Having willing muscle to add steel to his craft in the shape of these two helped him succeed even more, but still his takings were pitiful. A kind of peace throughout the land had not allowed him the harvest that he had hoped for. Nevertheless, winter was not too far away and the theign kept a warm hall with plenty of food and drink. Spring would be a better time to make any changes to his chosen occupation and the long, cold nights would give him time to think on how he might improve his situation. He did not intend to remain at this low station for the rest of his life.

The two thugs were happy with their lot, however. They were fed and billeted at the theign's expense and worked as hired swords to help defend his lands. Their time was for the most part spent as sentries or acting as messengers, which gave them opportunities to find places such as this farmstead, isolated and vulnerable.

"Ceorls!" Wulfhere sneered. He glanced again up at the evening sky. "Still, it'll be warmer and safer indoors rather than camped out on this hillside. Mayhap we'll find a hoard but my gut tells me we'll be lucky to get some weak beer and a loaf of bread."

"And a bed mate." The other two laughed together.

"A hard ride would see us in York before the night grows too late," their leader mused.

"But the eorls won't reach York until tomorrow afternoon. From here we could be in the city as the watch opens the gates in the morning and secure their lodging as ordered."

For a moment the two wondered if Wulhere had lost interest in the opportunity before them.

"Come then, if this be the height of your ambition today. Let me do the talking, you can do the killing."

They walked their horses down the hill and into the shallow valley. The man and boy had put the oxen into the fenced paddock for the night and were just entering the house, the door closing as the hound dashed inside. The shutters began to close also. Their timing was perfect. The horsemen had not been seen except by the oxen that stared at them with that dumb look so characteristic of their kind. The inhabitants would be caught totally unawares, less chance of resistance then.

They slipped from their horses and adjusted their cloaks and weapons. The other two both carried spears but Wulfhere preferred hefting a pointed langseax in his right hand. He intended to force his way into the house as quickly as possible and spears were less than useful in such cramped spaces to his mind. With a balled fist Wulfhere banged on the wooden door as hard a he could.

"Open up!" he shouted in his best tone of command. "Open up on the theign's orders!"

They had heard voices through the door coming from within but now the people on the other side fell silent. Wulfhere repeated his demand, this time using the pommel of his weapon for greater effect. The sound of iron on wood rang out into the evening air.

"Who be there?" A male voice called from behind the door.

"Huscarls of the Theign Ricbert. We are here on his business, open the door," Wulfhere answered, maintaining his role as a man of authority.

"What business has the theign with us?"

The man spoke with a nervous tone. The night was never a safe time but then a peasant never did well in earning the displeasure of his theign; especially not one as rich and as powerful as Ricbert.

"You owe him your obedience, you live on his lands. We are on his business to York and need to stopover. You will accommodate us and we will pay you for it."

"You will pay?"

Wulfhere smiled in the gloom. He had hoped that an offer of money would tempt the fool to do the one thing that he should not do.

"Aye, I'll pay. The theign don't allow us to take what belongs to him," Wulfhere assured him in a more placatory tone.

"Step back from the door sir," the farmer called.

They heard the bolt being drawn back. Light from several lamps burning tallow began to spill through as the door opened. As soon as Wulfhere could see the man himself he stepped aside and his rogue drove the head of his spear into the farmer's belly with terrible force.

The man cried out in alarm, the attack had been too fast for him to yet feel the pain from the spear head piercing his abdomen but it would come nonetheless. He was carried bodily back into the house, fixed on the point of the spear. His legs gave way and he fell to the floor where the thug seemed intent on sticking him permanently with his weapon. The other brute dashed in after his mate with Wulfhere bringing up the rear. The women began to scream as the man of the house lay moaning, his hands around the shaft of the spear that held him immobile.

Suddenly the boy attacked the intruders like a terrier. He launched himself bodily at Wulfhere who grabbed him by the hair, spun him around, glanced meaningfully into the face of his mother, and then he cut the boy's throat with the langseax, a sword that looked all the more deadly when held against such fair skin. The boy's legs gave way and Wulfhere allowed him to fall forward onto his face as blood spurted from his artery with each pump of his dying heart.

The snarling hound was dispatched with a single spear thrust, a yelp of pain being its last utterance.

The mother threw herself upon the body of her son, tears coursing down her face. The two older girls held each other and cowered in the corner, their screams having given way to whimpers of despair.

Wulfhere cleaned his langseax on someone's tunic that had been left out for mending and returned to the doorway. He closed and fastened the door securely. He then turned and looked on the wife and her two daughters, they were comely indeed. Their heads were covered in the popular modest fashion and each wore an iron crucifix on a length of leather. He looked over the house and was not surprised to see how poorly it was appointed. There was little chance of getting anything of value from this place but at least they would have somewhere comfortable to spend the night and warm food to eat.

"Women!" Wulfhere spoke loudly, "you have guests, bring us food and drink."

"Murderer!

The woman at his feet looked up with red eyes and a white face. She had dragged the now dead boy to her and held him in her lap.

"I am that and many other things," Wulfhere told her. "If you wish to bury your men-folk in the morning in a fitting Christian manner then attend us, or else we'll make this your last night in this middle-earth and it will be a hell the likes of which you've never dreamed."

Wulfhere's face was cold but his eyes burnt with malice. For a moment she glared back at him with a courage born from her immediate grief but she could not hold her own against such a baleful stare.

"I will hurt them," he promised her.

She cast her eyes down and spoke in a tremulous voice.

"Heresuid, Tatae, bring food and drink."

The girls hesitated and their mother had to tell them again in a more forceful manner. They moved towards the hearth staying close together and as far away from the men who had invaded their home as possible. They kept their eyes cast down.

Wulfhere smiled to himself. The moment when the mother's will had broken was to him as fine as anything else in life. He enjoyed exerting such power over others but was acutely aware that his brutes were incapable of that kind of appreciation. They looked at the women with eyes that were only hungry with lust. They would get their fill soon enough, but not until the women had ceased to be useful in other ways.

Outside the dark had fallen across the land and there was no one within hearing of the little homestead, no one who could come to aid of the women-folk this night. It would be their last night.

The Abbey at Waltham

It was late in the evening, well after vespers, and the church was empty. Dressed only in linen trousers and a linen shirt worn loose and not fastened with a belt, the man knelt at the crossing, facing the alter. His head hung forward and his unkempt hair fell over his face. He clutched both hands together and mumbled a prayer to himself. Candles were dotted around the nave, the transepts, the ambulatory, and of course on the alter itself, but they were not sufficient to light all of the building.

He wanted it that way.

So much of this year had sped at such a pace, the days becoming blurred to his mind's eye as he worked to consolidate everything that he had so far gained. It had seemed like a dream, the realisation of long held ambition, the desire of his father now dead these thirteen years. He had not expected success to weigh so heavy upon his shoulders.

Was he right to take the crown from the dead king's hand?

Did he act only for his own advantage?

Would God forgive him?

Had God cursed him in response to the pope's excommunication for breaking an oath made over holy relics?

Did Guillaume of Normandy have the just and sacred claim to the crown of King Edward?

Would God forgive him?

So many questions and as yet no answers, so he prayed here at Waltham Abbey as a pressed man under the weight of the world might do so. He prayed as he had done as a child when his father had brought him to visit the Holy Rood, the black stone cross of Theign Tovi the

Proud, kept here at Waltham. Then he had been an innocent, the second of six sons born to Eorl Godwin. What did it matter if he was prone to paralysis when so young, Eorl Godwin had a first born; Sweyn. Only Sweyn was not quite right, as people had said then.

Mayhap their father had foreseen the fate of his eldest son, my brother?

Mayhap that is why he had brought me, then so young, his second chance of success in the long game of intrigue that he played at court, to be blessed at Waltham by touching the Holy Rood?

He had touched the black crucifix and he had been blessed as a result. The sickly boy had grown into a strong and vibrant man, hale and hearty. Where Sweyn brought shame Harold brought honour. When Eorl Godwin looked to advance the fortunes of his house it was to Harold first that he entrusted his enterprises. It was always Harold that he expected to be the one to succeed and he had succeeded.

Before the alter of the church at Waltham King Harold of England wore no crown because there was only one king deserving of that honour to his mind and he wore a diadem of thorns. He knelt before Jesus Christ in willing and fervent supplication.

He surrendered himself to judgement.

If he had sinned so grievously then it must have been in the last nine months he believed. He began to trace his actions backwards, thinking hard about when and where he might have transgressed. Almost inevitably he thought of the early morning ride in January, some nine months ago.

The moon had been waxing crescent, barely half illuminated but still able to cast a delicate silver light onto the frosted earth below. The sky was clear and ablaze with stars. The horsemen appreciated that light as they wound their way through the narrow streets of London heading west to the gate by the river. They could not risk travelling at pace within the dark and shadowy confines of the city, too great a chance for mishap with so little light to ride by. Nevertheless they still possessed an air of urgency, an excitement picked up by their horses that strained at their rider's control as if already relishing the opportunity to stretch their legs on the journey to come.

The riders would have made an impressive sight at a more sociable hour of the day. Fine woollen cloaks with woven edges were draped over their shoulders, held in place with gold and silver broaches decorated with rubies and sapphires. Gold adorned swords held in finely crafted scabbards hung from leather belts fastened at their waists, tightened over expensive thick woollen tunics of the finest weave. Circlets of gold held their washed and combed shoulder length hair in place. Amongst their number there rode a man carrying a spear lodged into his stirrup onto which was fixed a pennant decorated with the Wyvern of Wessex. The animal reared up and held forth a foot armed with talons as if prepared to strike out at the world.

The watchmen by the western gate heard the approach of the horses long before they could see the riders, the fitful glare of their torches barely reached a few feet into the gloom. They came to attention more out of curiosity than alarm, their spears held casually in their hands as they peered into the darkness. The warmth of their brazier held them close to their post, however, for their breath misted in the cold night air and although their cloaks were woven with thick wool they still felt the touch of winter upon their shoulders.

"Open the gate," a voice commanded from the shadow with a tone used both to exercising authority and to being obeyed.

"It's the eorl! Quick, open the gate for the eorl."

The watchmen rushed to their task, removing the great wooden bar and swinging the thick gates outwards. With surprise they watched the nobleman and his party exit the city and disappear into the night, beyond the safety of the Roman walls. It was not normal for anyone to be abroad at this hour, least of all the most powerful man in the country after the king himself.

"The morn will break with a king's death and an eorl holding the crown I reckon," one of the watchmen pondered.

His fellows nodded their agreement. They would talk more upon it after they had swung the gates shut and returned to the comfort of their fire again.

The hard earth slipped beneath the horses with a blur, the animals' hooves thudding into the hard frozen dirt with the hot rhythm of the life that coursed through their powerful bodies. The party rode a beaten path westwards but could not allow their steeds to gallop at full speed due to the heavy frost and the poor light. Nevertheless, there was a spirit of exuberance to the group after leaving behind the confining walls of London and all the cares and demands that the city made upon the rich and powerful. To their left lay the great River Thames, glittering with a silver sheen under the naked moon, snaking eastwards out to the sea. It meandered to the great whale-road across which their ancestors had sailed so many generations ago. Before them and somewhat also to the left they could make out in the moonlight the dark bulk of the handcrafted stones of Westminster Abbey, begun in a religious fervour and now some twenty years old and still incomplete. It had become a familiar sight to them all as even in its unfinished state it dominated the landscape west of the city.

They closed upon the abbey with every heartbeat, the chill air abrading the skin on their faces and burning in their lungs. As they rode a barn owl appeared out of the night sky heading obliquely in the same direction as the riders. Its silent appearance unnerved more than one of the riders as it closed in slowly from their right. The starlight gave the bird's face and body a ghostly radiance made all the more unearthly by its total silence in flight. It did not reveal whether it noticed them or not, which only added to its eerie appearance. Free to ride the airway instead of being bound to the road the owl passed over the heads of the noblemen and their several retainers and flew on towards the king's palace at Westminster. More than one of the travellers tried to follow the line of its flight as it disappeared into the dark, wondering mayhap if it would come to rest on top of the palace roof. There were many who said that death visited the house upon which an owl chose to perch.

They had to travel a little over two miles and their horses were of a good stock. It was exhilarating to ride at speed with the cold night air breathing through their hair, their fine cloaks whipped back by the wind, the rhythmic pounding of the hooves on the hard packed earth, and the countryside laid out before them free and unbounded beneath the starry canopy. If anything the journey from London to Thorney Island was not long enough to allow them the full enjoyment of this unexpected moment in which each and every one of them felt alive. Too soon they reached the confines of the abbey and had to reign in their horses. Once more they were in the company of the watchmen and the purpose of their moonlit flight was brought home to them again.

A king will die.

A king did die, but not by the hand of Harold of Wessex.

His sister, Queen Edith, had been on hand to receive them at the Palace of Westminster, relieved that her messenger had been able to rouse three of her brothers at least at this dark hour. Also present had been Stigand, Archbishop of Canterbury, Ealdred, Archbishop of York, and Leofric, the Abbot of St. Peter's Burgh. The three clergymen had been keeping a bitter watch over many nights as the vitality of King Edward ebbed away and brought him nearer to the Kingdom of Heaven. There had been no time to formally acknowledge the holy men, however, it was allowed that the crisis facing the country excused their lack of etiquette.

"What news?" Harold Godwinson asked as he approached his sister, removing the gloves that had protected his hands from the chill night air during their ride.

She looked pale and concerned but strong nonetheless. His face was red in comparison. He closed the space between them almost penitently, aware of her pain, but his ambition burned in his eyes all the same.

"He grows ever weaker," she spoke sadly but without surrendering to any great emotion. "I fear the king will not last out this early hour."

They embraced with a genuine affection. Edith then nodded in acknowledgement to her other younger brothers, Gyrth and Leofwine, who had journeyed with Harold from London. Out of respect for their elder brother's rank, and mayhap the solemnity of the moment, they stood behind him a pace or two whilst he greeted the queen. Their retainers waited in the vestibule on the opposite side of the door through which they had entered. Three eorls travelling together would naturally be accompanied by a large party but the encounter with Queen Edith was in truth a family matter and not entirely subject to the ways of the court.

Of course Edith was all too aware of what most occupied Harold's mind, she was a Godwin too, but at least he had the strength of character to act with due consideration towards her. It somehow seemed important that Harold did not function solely upon his life's ambition and at this painful time she valued the brotherly love that was expressed in his thoughtfulness.

"He has ailed since December last. Even the consecration of the abbey here at Westminster could not rouse his spirits," Gyrth commented.

He spoke out of a genuine kindness towards his sister; they all knew how grave the king's health was. Of her five surviving brothers Gyrth was most alike to Harold in his treatment of others, softened also mayhap by a lack of the ambition that drove the senior Godwin.

"The Psalm Ninety tells us our allotted time on this Earth is three score years and ten, King Edward would not be the first man to fail to reach that total but he has come very close to it," Gyrth added.

"I wish that he had seen the consecration of his abbey," Queen Edith declared with some feeling now. Although the arrival of her brothers had brought her some moral support it had also awakened in her other conflicting emotions. "It is a work that will carve his name in history."

"You care for such a legacy from such a king?" Leofwine asked derisively.

"He is still my husband." A note of anger entered her voice as she shot her youngest brother present a challenging look.

Edith felt that her life was also slipping away, not the vibrancy that beat within her heart but the one she had known as Queen of England. She understood without consciously thinking about it that the death of Edward would change everything in respect of herself; not only would she lose a husband but also all the power that she had wielded through him. It seemed that even before the last breath had left his body there were already those keen to sully his legacy. She felt very defensive, determined to keep his reputation sacrosanct. Not for the first time Harold wished that Leofwine could learn to be more tactful.

"So much grace has fallen upon our house as a result of my union to King Edward, despite the character of several of my brothers!"

The last was added with some spite. She knew that many a man secretly mocked the piety of her husband, just as she was aware that two of their brethren, not present at least, were widely held as infamous for having far from pious characters of their own.

"This is neither the time nor the place to bring such matters before the light," Harold intervened. "What was done in the past will remain in the past. Have I not worked long and hard to reconcile the House of Godwin with King Edward?"

"And yet he still does not trust thee," Leofwine observed.

"King Edward has reigned long in difficult times; our own father did not always work to ease his government," Gyrth reminded them all but siding with his elder brother and sister against the younger sibling.

"Not when so doing favoured the prospects of our house," Leofwine countered.

"Must you always see the ill in every situation?" Harold demanded in an exasperated tone.

It seemed to him that Tostig had had too great an influence over Leofwine, certainly that kind of cynicism was a trademark of his brother's policy at court when he had enjoyed a position of power within the kingdom.

"King Edward was a weak monarch who disdained the Witan and favoured Norman advisors, giving them high positions and royal favours.

In truth I prefer your conciliation brother over father's confrontation, it has brought you that much nearer to success and I would see you successful," Leofwine inisted feelingly and with the energy that often prompted him to act hastily. "That Westminster Abbey will outlive us all in King Edward's name I do not doubt, and it will mark this city out from any other in any country we know of let alone England, but the king's obsession with religion also reveals his failure to minister his kingdom; we have no heir."

Queen Edith looked away from her brothers, feeling again some guilt in the matter that concerned the whole kingdom now as the king lay upon his deathbed. She had heard this speech so many times before and yet it still left her feeling frustrated because there was nothing that she could do about the situation. Many a mind was already made up on the subject and would not listen to the truth; that she and Edward had longed for a child and heir. Whilst Edward could accept their failing as God's will she was not so inclined, her desire to be a mother still ached deep within her even though the best years for motherhood had passed her by. It contested with her own religious feelings too, spurred on by the knowledge that most of her brothers enjoyed many children of their own. She did not resent them their families; she wished only to share in such happiness. It was, after all, a happiness that would relieve the kingdom of the fateful question of succession.

"The death of Edward Aetheling, the king's named heir, some nine years ago has brought us to this crisis," Archbishop Ealdred intervened as if recognising the queen's discomfort. He approached the children of Godwin respectfully as he spoke. "That the king and queen were not blessed with children is a blame that should be levelled at neither one nor the other; it is as God willed it."

Leofwine looked as if would counter the clergyman's predictable words but Harold chose to deny him the opportunity.

"There is still time to settle this matter in the best interest of the kingdom," he insisted.

"And yet even as we stand upon the precipice salvation is at hand," Edith told them, following her brother's lead. "During the days of his illness the king has spoken of you Harold, when the malaise allowed it of him. He does not, as some have put abroad, despise the safety of his kingdom in favour of the Kingdom of Heaven. Rather, he would see it left in secure hands, guided by a strong man of proven worth."

She gripped his forearm in her earnestness, looking directly into his face. It seemed important to her to return the support that he had shown her so often of late even though the misery of widowhood was about to break upon her.

"Does the king have yet the strength to state this before witnesses?" Stigand asked eagerly. All the clergymen had now joined the group.

"The hour grows late. If the king's final moment comes then witnesses of the best quality stand all around us and the Witan can be convened at a moment's notice," Edith replied. It was mayhap the last time that she could have a hand in the concerns of the court and she took a degree of solace from that fact. She could still play the queen before she became the widow. "I tell thee again, my husband, King Edward, would leave this life knowing that England and all that he values in it were left safe and secure. I know that this is what lies in his heart; that this is his will."

"My Lady!" A servant entered the room through the door the queen had used earlier. He was recognised as an attendant upon the king himself, a trusted man. "My Lord, the King, calls for thee."

The eoldermen and clergy all glanced at one another in silence. The moment that they had waited so many long days for had now apparently come upon them; their hesitation spoke of its weight. Without another word they all passed as a sombre procession down through the dark corridors and towards the royal bedchamber.

They entered a room that was lost to shadow. Around the head of the bed a number of candles were arranged casting their light onto the white bedclothes. It seemed on first viewing that the stately bed was an island of light in a pool of darkness, the fine hangings on the wooden walls, the expensive furniture, all the finer points of the room itself remaining untouched by the flickering candle light and, therefore, known only to those who had seen the chamber previously when it was better lit.

King Edward lay upon his bed looking old and weak. His eyes moved constantly around the room but never seemed to settle on any one point. His hair had always been fair but now it was white as if totally drained of life as much as of colour.

"My Lord, I come." Queen Edith spoke out to him with a voice edged with emotion.

She advanced quickly to his side, her footsteps silenced by the hides that covered the wooden floorboards around the king's bed. She took his hand up in hers to reassure him, noting how cold it was to the touch, and brought her face down to a level where he could see her more easily.

"So is my time I believe." Edward's voice was weak but he spoke clearly. His eyes fastened upon her face and he managed a sad smile. "The crown slips from my head I think and you will be my queen no more."

He glanced to where the crown rested on a stand beside his bed and then returned his tired eyes to Edith.

"I will live out the rest of my days as your queen My Lord, and only ever yours," she answered him passionately and squeezed his hand tenderly.

Tears welled at the corner of her eyes but she remained in control of her visible emotions and her vision was transfixed upon his wan face.

"Is the Eorl of Wessex here?" Edward asked with some determination.

"My Lord!"

Harold stepped forward and took up a position on the opposite side of the bed to Edith. He knelt down like his sister, a gesture of both respect and consideration that would allow Edward to look him in the eye also.

No one else in the room moved. Only two people had a right to be in the immediate presence of King Edward at this moment in time, the rest remained on the edge of the pool of light understanding that their moment to step forward would be upon them soon.

"My Lord of Wessex, I have loved your sister as my wife and queen," his tired eyes settled on Edith again, another quick smile before flitting back to Harold. "This woman and all the kingdom I commend to thy charge."

Harold glanced at his sister. A surge of excitement threatened to overwhelm him but his own sense of propriety battled against it. When he saw the tears now course down her cheek freely the inappropriate sense of celebration abated quickly. He looked back at the king.

Edward lay propped up on many pillows as he lacked the strength to sit up by himself. His head had been turned towards Harold Godwinson but now it had settled into a more central position, his eyes fixed upon a space between the queen and the eorl, sister and brother. Those eyes were now without life.

"And so passes the reign of King Edward," Stigand commented before all three clergymen began to mutter a prayer in Latin.

"King Edward began the work on his abbey by the sanction of the pope because he could not keep his vow to visit Rome. I will honour that work by being crowned within it," Harold spoke quietly but surely.

"Dependent upon the Witan," Gyrth reminded him.

"Dependent upon the Witan," Harold agreed, "although they have no other claim to consider."

But they did!

Guillaume of Normandy claimed the throne by right of being a cousin to King Edward, asserting also that the Saxon king had told him that he was the preferred choice following the death of his named heir Edward Aetheling in 1057.

But why should a foreigner rule over the English?

No one in England believed the words of the Norman duke. The witan had made its choice and voted for Harold of Wessex to make safe the throne and the country. He had undertaken that task with vigour and in this, the ninth month of his reign, he had so far succeeded.

Where was the sin that has brought down this judgement from God upon me?

Ealdgyth Swannesha?

Ealdgyth the gentle swan. My beautiful Ealdgyth.

A woman so virtuous, so beloved of the people of Wessex; how could a woman such as she house a sin great enough to curse a king? They had been handfasted for some twenty years and she had given him five healthy children. He loved her even though the church did not recognise her as his lawful wife and yet he loved the church as well.

The sin was not hers, it was his. He had put her aside after taking the crown. Archbishop Stigand had given him a reason, to marry in church and have the union blessed by God Almighty. Ealdgyth of Mercia had given him the opportunity, an accord that would join the fractious houses of Wessex and Mercia, making relatives of the young eorls Edwin and Morcar. Ealdgyth of Mercia was now Queen of England, not the Ealdgyth who was the gentle swan of Wessex. The motive was political; the marriage was blessed by both the clergy and by God, or so it seemed as his new wife was pregnant.

Was the betrayal of Ealdgyth Swannesha's love the sin that cursed this king?

In the gloom of the church Harold Godwinson, former husband to Ealdgyth of Wessex, raised his arms, each hand pointing down a transept; one north, one south. His head came up also and he looked towards the alter; looked eastwards towards the apse. He had paid for the church at Waltham to be rebuilt in stone, dedicated only six years ago. He had been generous in his endowments.

Could all the good works of a pious man be undone by one small sin compelled by circumstance, enacted in consideration of the welfare of others? Or had he always desired the throne too much? Had he sacrificed a good woman like Ealdgyth Swannesha to his ambition just as Tostig claimed he had sacrificed him, his own brother, to that same ambition? Was this the nature of his sin? Had Eorl Godwin cursed all of his kin through his hunger for power and his dream of seeing a Godwin sat upon the throne of England?

How could a son atone for a father when all he had done was honour and obey him?

The moment of judgement had come. In one scale he would deposit all that he had done to make the kingdom safe, in the other the sin as he understood it. He would let God decide now.

Several days ago he had fallen ill at Westminster. The healers were mystified but Harold had recognised the symptoms; his childhood illness had returned. The healers could do nothing for him, only God could cure him once again. God must lay hands upon him but he would not do that for a sinful man.

I repent all sins! I ask only for what I deserve!

He closed his eyes and prayed once more, his arms still outstretched. How long he prayed for he did not know nor care. His prayers seemed to come to a natural end and he found that his eyes opened of their own accord. His arms should have ached having been held aloft for so long but they did not. He clasped his hands together in front of him and said a silent 'amen!'

Slowly, as if testing the validity of his belief in the judgement received, Harold climbed to his feet. He took in a deep breath and felt the vitality of forty years of life course through his body. A joy rose within his breast that was difficult to contain but he mastered himself. He would not profane the church or the holy gift given to him here by acting without humility. He wept instead.

"We should not have come," Half-foot complained, "time is pressing and there is little that can be achieved here."

"You think only of the court," Father Egric accused him in his mild tone.

"I have employment there, here I am…well, I wait upon my lord's whim," the courtier retorted with a scowl.

"We could find you employment here if you wish, you are a man who can both read and write; a skill rare to find outside of the clergy." The priest smiled benignly.

"I am both grateful for my learning and for being outside of the clergy," Half-foot told him. "I have no wish to come any closer to your religion than my office brings me."

"Where does this ill-will come from my friend?" Father Egric kept his tone calm despite the other's hostility.

"I'm sorry Father. I wish you no ill in truth. I am just sore today," Half-foot apologised.

"Your foot pains you? We have skills in the healing arts, mayhap if you let me have a look at it?" He looked down at the other man's left leg as he spoke.

Half-foot was dressed like any other Saxon; except that his clothes were of very good quality and that his left leg and foot were somewhat different in shape. Beneath his linen trousers a piece of wood shaped to the contours of the back of his leg was strapped against the limb with leather fastenings. It was positioned beneath his knee and stretched down under the arch of the foot, which was quite pronounced. Although his trouser leg covered this support his fine leather shoes could not hide the twisted nature of the foot itself. His clawed toes pointed inwards to a marked degree and his normal stance reflected his tendency to use the outside edge of the foot almost exclusively.

To help with his balance he used a staff made from oak and decorated with carvings and inlaid with gold and silver. The craftsmanship was exquisite, taking pagan symbols for its theme. It had become something of a badge of Half-foot's office at the court of the King of England but then it had been given to him in lieu of a sword by Harold Godwinson himself when he had been the Eorl of Wessex.

"I thank you for your concern Father but I doubt that there is anything that your skill can achieve with my foot," Half-foot told him sincerely and took a precautionary step backwards.

"God gives us all our burdens to bear," the priest told him in an apologetic tone.

"Your god may." He noticed a flicker of resentment cross Father Egric's face and felt a moment of satisfaction. However he knew that he was only present at the church because his own master had commanded it. "Come Father, we have touched upon this before and it would make me an ill mannered guest to insult your hospitality by doing so again; you know my feelings on the subject."

"It pains me to see you so wilfully rejecting God's love," the priest smiled benignly. "There is much that the church can give you."

"Except an answer as to why I was born with this?" Half-foot pushed his left leg forward.

"God moves in mysterious ways," the priest told him with an odd tilt of his head that Half-foot found surprisingly patronising. "There is a purpose in everything that He does. Your lameness is a reminder to us of what his son, Our Lord Jesus Christ, did with the laying on of hands. Your pain teaches us to be accepting of the ills of this world in preparation of the joys awaiting us in God's Kingdom."

"Why am I put on this middle-earth to illustrate your god's lessons? Why doesn't your god choose one of his own believers?" Half-foot retorted with a degree of heat.

"We have the ability to choose for ourselves good sir, without it there would be no meaning to choosing God over the Devil. Although you may feel that he has taken something from you, you must remember also that he has given you other gifts with which to make your life somewhat easier," the priest adopted a placatory tone.

"He has given me other gifts?" The courtier sounded disbelieving.

"You have your mind, which so far exceeds others," Father Egric pointed out.

"I would rather hold a spear than a quill, but I am too lame on this side to make a warrior," Half-foot told him, indicating the left side of his body.

"A life of violence is no life at all. It brings only misery and destruction."

"Death is our final destruction and it will find us in any place where wyrd has thought fit to fix our final moment. For some, death upon a battlefield is a fine place, for others their beds will do."

Half-foot limped over to a trestle table and sat down at the accompanying bench, sighing as the soreness in his foot was relieved somewhat.

"I find you exasperating." Father Egric told him. "You are a learned man and yet you yearn to don armour and carry a spear like so many other loutish brutes. You dream of spilling blood and ending lives, putting homes to the torch and leaving only ruin behind you. With all that you know can you not think of greater things to turn your heart too?"

"I would be a man Father," Half-foot snapped. "In this world such as I do not thrive; are not meant to thrive. Of what use above a slave does a man who cannot wield a spear have?"

"Within the church no man wields a spear and your wyrd does not hold sway. And you do thrive, Half-foot, you do very well indeed."

"All by my own effort and not by the will of any god, that I know. At least my lord the king values my learning and is wise enough to know how to use me to his best advantage."

"The worldly trappings of the court hold you so tightly?" Father Egric asked with a disdainful look.

"At court the eoldermen mark me, they show me due respect. Even without a spear I am someone in the court of King Harold. I have made myself someone."

"Indeed you have but the court, like all things temporal, will pass."

"And I with it, I have no doubt, but in the meantime I am not the village cripple dependent upon alms. I am the king's secretary," Half-foot spoke this last with pride.

"I see that you are determined to live in your world and will not crossover to consider our spiritual life, for the moment then I will let you be. Your master has been good to this abbey and, as always, our hospitality extends to you without resentment," Father Egric spoke in his turn with sincerity.

"Then please understand that when I say that I wish King Harold a speedy recovery it is not without gratitude for all that you have done for him," Half-foot responded in a more conciliatory fashion. "I take it as a good sign that he wishes now to spend some time with his queen; that is, that he is indeed on the road to recovery and that his recent illness is now passing?"

"In that we all thank God for his merciful intervention," Father Egric was determined to achieve the last word on the subject.

"The king comes," Half-foot said.

Monday 18ᵗʰ September 1066

The City of York

"My but tha's a bold one!" Branda stated as she entered Midryth's small house through the only door.

Familiarity removed the need for ceremony, despite their difference in social class. Her presence filled the single room with an exuberant energy, she was a well built woman to begin with but her character dominated whatever area she found herself in making it seemingly impossible for Branda to pass anywhere without being noticed.

"Mistress Acha told me what tha did, approached Lord Coenred and made dove-eyes at him so tha did," she had a huge grin on her face and a knowing look in her eye.

"I look first for protection," Mildryth told her in reply, reddening a little at the accusation. "If Mistress Acha looked beyond the walls of the kitchen in the long hall then she might see the world outside is changing. My father was a Saxon but my mother was a Dane, I have kin amongst the Dane-folk, I still hear of things that happen abroad, beyond the borders of Northumbria even, and I tell you that the sky grows dark again. Tostig Godwinson's shadow may yet fall over us once more."

"Oh I ken the thinking behind tha's actions, but men are men and 'appen he'll grant one request to thee and that will lead to him making another of tha too," she gave her friend a salacious grin. "Not that those aint the kind of requests we women don't favour every now and then."

"He is a man of honour," Mildryth insisted, growing redder in the face.

"As is the theign who honours tha with his care and this…house of his." Branda glanced disdainfully around the small and dark interior of the building that Mildryth had made into her home.

It was not the grandest of constructions. The interior was dark and the roof low. There was scant furniture, some stools for sitting on and a low table for working at. The hearth was well built, however, but the door and shutter both faced north, which kept the place gloomy. It was a house more suited to a peasant but this thought did not prompt her to criticise it, Branda knew that to give her a dwelling more suited to her station the high-theign would have had to evict someone else. The ready compromise that freed the theign from a difficult position and saved another from the threat of eviction spoke much to Branda of her friend's character.

"I can't be resting on the kindness of Theign Aethelwine forever and the breed of men that have made their intentions obvious to me are far from my liking. This house is a blessing, such as it is, but I had one of my own, with my own man and a son to care for. 'Tis not the same. If I do not take steps to change matters for myself then I have no right to complain about the situation I find myself in."

"Aye lass, and why settle for less when thee can have more," Branda agreed in her expansive way. "Still, tha's set tongues a-wagging."

"If not me then someone else would."

"True enough; but tell me Mildryth, is this what thee want?" A more serious expression crossed the woman's face.

"A man of honour, courtesy and proven valour to act as my protector, what more would a woman want in these days?" Mildryth demanded.

"Well, something between the legs to match the sword at his side mayhap!" Branda laughed in return. "Aye, tha knows I've always had a liking for thee since tha came seeking sanctuary here lass, I mean nothing by my talk."

"You're a good woman Branda and a better friend," she smiled sincerely back, glad that the air had lightened between them again.

"That means something that does, coming from a lady such as tha self," Branda confessed.

"I am no better than you my friend," Mildryth insisted.

"But tha husband Aethelheard was a theign, a man of land and authority, we are nowt but ceorls, though my Hereward claims we be geneatas, though he's never carried a spear in anger, what with his back."

"People of my class turned their backs on me when it suited them," Mildryth reminded the other woman. "You and your good husband did not. His back is far straighter than some I once thought I knew."

"Ah but that's me, as Hereward would complain, always ready to take in another a stray or a waif."

"And I am a stray," Mildryth agreed, "but I like this man, this Coenred, in the first instance at least. He is a proven warrior and not one that just claims to be so. I have watched the men that come to the mead-hall on the business of their lords and he is unlike them all. His clothes are fine but he wears them to suit, not to impress. He has no gold upon him except in his sword. He speaks quietly but surely and the other men respect him. He shows respect to others too, with no mind to their station. He is not loud and vain like so many are today."

"In that tha's both right and wrong," Branda insisted. "True, he's not given to buying a new cloak just cos he 'as money in 'is purse but that's cos he's wise in such matters. His battle-harness is second to none, as becomes a companion of eoldermen, and, more to it than that, he's a great landowner too, almost a high-theign in his own right by property alone."

"He's a huscarl, a paid soldier of the eorls," Mildryth insisted, "what wealth he has goes to pay for his war-gear, his horses and his servant."

"That he is and more, as I said. He owns land in the Isle of Holderness, west of the River Hull and near the River Humber. Good sheep land my Hereward says. Wool's a good trade to be in he reckons. Lord Coenred's mother and younger brother are in place to run his land and mind the ceorls, more than nine hides they say, whilst he pays the eorls with his service so that they don't have to raise any fyrdmen."

"I know that huscarls must have the means to pay for their war-gear and such, but I thought only the sons of the rich held such lands. In truth I never thought Lord Coenred to be of such stock," Mildryth admitted.

"His grandda were a middling theign brave in battle, made a hearth companion during the dark days of the Danelaw. Tha knows his da also served as a hearth companion to Eorl Leofric, giver of rings, and Lord Coenred followed on with the same sword serving Eorl Aelfgar, son of Leofric. Each has added to the family holding, being one and all true weapons-men and not just given to saying so, as I said before."

"You never told me this lineage before," Mildryth accused her with a surprised look on her face.

"Ah my love, tha were so sad to see when first tha came here, me heart fair went out to thee. I seen tha eyes follow Lord Coenred of late and, though it were still close to your widowhood as some would judge, I knew tha needed a man in your life again and he's such a fine man when all's said and done."

"I look for a protector first," Mildryth insisted again.

"And what's a husband if not a protector of his family? My but I reckon tha couldn't of picked a better man in the whole of the Vale of York, what with my Hereward being taken already."

"But a landholder too?" She was still amazed by this revelation.

"Nine hides and maybe more, all his own. Lord Coenred added to his land with monies given to him by Eorl Aelfgar after they returned from exile in Ireland. That eorl much valued loyalty too and Lord Coenred stood by him despite the trials of banishment and the king's displeasure. My, what tales we told of those days around the hearth fire eh?"

"You know much of this man Coenred."

"Ah me lamb, what else's there for us to do in the deep midwinter but while away the time in idle talk and Lord Coenred is a more interesting man than most that are seen in these parts. Too good for the likes of the eorls he serves now, if tha'll forgive my boldness."

"I have not met the eorls so I cannot say."

"No doubt thee will. It's said that they'll come down to York and stay at Theign Aethelwine's expense for the winter. They miss their father's hand I say, though Lord Coenred does the best he can with 'em; God bless him."

"Yes, God bless him. They say a war is coming," Mildryth wore a more pensive expression.

"They've said that since tha old king died in January. I know tha's a feared of this Tostig, and it's no surprise thinking on what he did to thee and thine, but he seems to me to be farther away than ever," Branda sought to reassure her friend.

"He is the murderer of my family and I will feel safe only when my lord the king has strengthened his hold upon the throne," Mildryth spoke with a cold conviction and a sudden flash of fire in her eyes.

"Aye, the crown sits uneasy on Harold Godwinsons' head, though for me he's the better man to wear it. And that makes me wonder at tha timing my love?"

"Timing?"

"Tha made thy advance on Lord Coenred today but he's a warrior and must off to war sooner rather than later, so my Hereward says, and I got to thinking, forgive me but…what if he don't come back?" Branda looked at her friend with barely concealed concern.

"If he dies in battle then I will mourn him as a friend lost, like many others will do for their own I expect. If he does not come back because of some other matter, well then, all I've lost is my scramseax; but if he does come back…" she paused and lowered her eyes.

"Tha would make a fine mistress of that holding in Holderness," Branda assured her.

"That is not my thought."

"Nay, I doubt tha not. As tha said tha knew naught of Lord Coenred's land holdings betwixt the two rivers. Ah me." A look of sympathy now crossed over her face. "I don't know how tha do it lass?"

"Do what?" Mildryth was surprised by her friend's sudden change.

"My Hereward, he's no theign. He's good at selling though and we have more than most and he'd always use the last hour of daylight to sell another sack just so his family don't go without. That's why I love him. No great warrior or lord of the land but a good husband he is. Thy Aethelheard was dear to thee too. I can't imagine being widowed. I wouldn't survive it."

"Yes you would," Mildryth assured her in a quiet voice. "You have your children."

"Oh I did not look to upset thee," Branda saw the shadow pass over her friend's face.

"You haven't," Mildryth assured her. "What happened happened. It was our wyrd to be parted in such a manner; though I don't like to dwell upon it. Aethelheard was a good husband and Aelle a good son, but that was two years gone by now. It was another life taken from me by cruel men. The ones I loved live inside me still and I honour them by living because that is what my husband wanted of me; that is what he demanded of me. If I had surrendered when I learnt of their deaths then who would remember them? Where would all those good days that we had together be now? It would be like they had not happened at all. No, Branda, we women do have the strength to survive such things. In living I don't allow the likes of Tostig Godwinson to have a complete victory. In building a new life I defy him and his kind. It is better than revenge."

"We should talk no more upon this," Branda said nervously. "Talking ill breeds ill says I."

She looked uncomfortable now, glancing sideways at her friend, trying to read her thoughts.

"Then we will not talk of such anymore," Mildryth stated firmly but with no suggestion that she had been upset by her friend's words. "I doubt not that you have more idle talk from the kitchen though?"

Wulfhere bit into his apple and watched the two women through the open shutter. He was sure that it was her. He knew that it was her. He had spied the woman in the main street as she had made her way from the great hall only a short time past. Her dress was not that of a serving wench and she wore nothing on her head unlike many a woman these days. Those close to the church covered their hair in modesty but this one let it hang free in the old style, plaited and braided but hanging long down her back. Her manner was as haughty as he remembered, but then she is theign-worthy and that was one of the things that had attracted him to her.

He had arrived in the city with his two rogues early in the morning; none of them had wanted to stay any longer at the homestead where they had spilt blood last evening. They had found little of value, as he had expected, but the women had been a distraction. Their bodies remained with their men folk and the whole family lay now within the burnt out ruin of their hovel.

Wulfhere had acquired a lodge for his lord, which was their original purpose in coming to York, and had left the other two there to await the theign's arrival. The rest of the morning had been spent wandering the city in the hope of spotting some new opportunities for enrichment, as always, and it was the pursuit of this activity that had allowed him to spy out the woman and follow her back to this peasant house.

Why does she mix with ceorls so freely?

He knew her to be a theign's wife, widowed mayhap, but not belonging to the peasant class by any stretch. Yet here she was passing the time of day with a ceorl as if they were the best of friends when in truth their stations were far apart. He would not have allowed such a woman as that ceorl into the house never mind actually permitting her to talk to his wife. If she were his wife.

If?

That was a question to ponder.

But why not?

Her husband was dead and she had no family to fall back upon, that was clear from her current situation. He knew that her suit against the household of Tostig Godwinson had been passed up to the Shire Court, but that was just as expected. Going before the Hundred Court was only a formality but it had brought her to his notice. Everyone knew everyone else's business in this small world. The Shire Court would not sit again until Michaelmas and even then it might not make a decision at all, and if it did it might not be in her favour, considering how it would inevitably involve the King of England. Nevertheless it was worth a gamble. Although she might not receive a fortune in way of compensation from the Shire Court it would be enough to make life a little easier for a man like him. And she would make a goodly bed-mate for any man; that was for certain.

He bit into the apple again and again, devouring it noisily as he kept his eyes on the open shutter. He turned the fruit in his hand as he bit without pause. When he had taken all that could be had he tossed the core away and crunched on the fleshy pulp crammed into his mouth. Excess juice and saliva ran from the corner of his lips and he wiped it on his sleeve. He swallowed the pulp and marched up to the small house purposefully.

"My Lady, I thought it was you I saw in the street," he said, announcing his presence to the two women who seemed deep in conversation.

They glanced at him through the open window but there was no sign of recognition on either face.

"Do you know me sir?" Mildryth asked, looking a little bemused. Her lack of recognition irked him somewhat.

"Come now," he affected to be pleasant. "It was not so long ago when last we met."

Mildryth looked at the thin face and did not like what she saw there. He had a kind of knowing look in his furtive eyes. His dark hair was lank and not well kept. She could barely see his tunic through the open window but what she could see was far from impressive. He looked like a ceorl but he acted like something else, he seemed to believe that he was someone above the station that birth had placed him in. The immediate impression that she had of him said that he had so far failed to rise to the heights that he believed he should occupy.

"I think that you are mistaken," Mildryth told him, quite certain with herself.

"My name is Wulfhere. I am a weapons-man in the service of My Lord, Ricbert, High-Theign to the Eorl Morcar of Northumbria."

He spoke with some dramatic effect as if this pronouncement was supposed to impress them.

"I have naught to do with so high a man as an eorl," Mildryth told him firmly, "and I know nothing of a theign called Ricbert, though a good man I do not doubt he be."

"Your husband was a theign of Northumbria," Wulfhere responded. He saw the change of expression on her face and fancied that he had found a mark.

"There are many theigns in Northumbria, I know of some but not of all." Her manner was harder. "May I ask what you want with me?"

It was less of a question and more of a demand. Wulfhere was annoyed at the rebuff.

"We met at the Hundred Court in Ripon, I came merely to re-acquaint myself with you and ask after your health; you are well I hope?"

"I am thank you," her manner did not soften.

"You will be to the Shire Court soon I believe?" He prompted.

Again her expression changed. She appeared momentarily confused and then concerned. She looked more closely at him and he took this for a good sign.

"I believe that I will have to go before the court," She spoke carefully.

Branda could tell that her friend was in some discomfort and she did not like the look of the man presuming to peer in through the window. He was 'weasel-faced' as her Hereward would say of a customer he did not trust readily. She noted that he talked with a southern accent too and that was enough for her to dislike him.

"We have work to do, me and thee," She interrupted bluntly.

"Aye, we do," Mildryth agreed.

"No matter, my lord, High-Theign Ricbert, is a companion to the Eorl Morcar and they travel to York presently. I am here to secure a lodge for him, being a trusted servant, so I will see you again here and about I expect," Wulfhere told them.

He stepped back from the window, bowed in an almost mocking manner and then turned and sauntered up the street and out of view.

"Do tha know that man?" Branda asked.

"Not that I recall," Mildryth asserted vigorously. "Although I was at the Hundred Court in Ripon, as he says, but then so were many people. If he is in the employment of a northern theign then he might have had cause to be there himself but I cannot recollect ever speaking to him."

"Why would tha?" Branda agreed. "He fancies himself a fighting man does he? Well I say he's like a rat to a mastiff when tha compares him to your Lord Coenred."

"He's not my Lord Coenred!"

Mildryth turned away quickly, her face flushed. Branda stood and stared at the other woman, her own expression frozen. Then she broke out with a loud peal of laughter and slapped her thighs through her dress.

"My but you're a terrible woman Branda!" Mildryth berated her but with little anger.

Theigns!

Coenred had the world's most annoying itch in the one place that he could not reach and it was caused by theigns. First the High-Theign of York was away hunting and he had had to wait upon his return in order to carry out the duties given to him by the brother eordermen; Edwin and Morcar. Now the lesser theigns came to him early in the morning in his capacity as an eorl's man to make a decision that they should have been capable of making themselves even in the absence of their own lord.

Servants moved around the hall lighting lamps, trying to be as inconspicuous as possible. At least some life seemed to be returning to the building. Coenred stood before the raised dais where the high-theign and his guests of honour would sit on a more hospitable occasion. About twenty lesser theigns were gathered before him, townsmen all. Two dirty and tired looking individuals stood at the front of the assembly. His mood was not good considering that they had interrupted his breakfast.

"Speak again, what is this matter?" Coenred instructed them in his most authoritative tone.

He hoped that it would prove to be something more important than a petty crime or an incidence of disobedience. Although the two strangers looked unkempt, tired, and hungry, they showed no fear so he suspected that they had not been accused of some trivial offence.

"These men come to us from Scarborough with talk of a Viking fleet, My Lord," one of the theigns answered. "They claim a Norse army invades Northumbria."

The two men in question nodded their heads in agreement.

"You have seen this army?" Coenred asked them directly.

"Yes, My Lord, that is, we have seen the ships," one of them answered promptly.

"We saw them round the headland as they ran before the storm and made for the haven of the southern bay of Scarborough," the other added, each taking it in turn to nod their agreement to the other's account.

"You have seen the ships but not the warriors?" Coenred pressed.

"Not immediately. We knew our peril for what it was, My Lord."

"So you fled!" One of the theigns of York accused them. Several others voiced their disagreement with taking such a course of action; a luxury afforded them by the stout Roman stone walls of the city.

"We took our families and left for the safety of the hills, we are fishermen not fighters. None of us has seen a power so great before, even the eorls of the north may not be able to gather an equal force to challenge it."

"How can we know the truth of your words?" Coenred asked in a tone that suggested that he did not so much doubt their honesty as required further information before making a decision.

"I am Abiorn the Dane. My father settled in Skaroaborg some years ago and became a fisherman; he taught me his trade. We come together as Saxon and Dane so that you would know the truth of what we say."

"I am Sabert son of Cudberct, known as Saba throughout Scarborough. I was a lower theign myself before I fell foul of the opinion of Tostig Godwinson when he were Eorl of Northumbria. Though I be now brought down to the station of a ceorl my honour is as that of all the theigns gathered in this great hall. I swear upon that honour that we do not lie."

"Saxon and Dane united in delivering a warning," Coenred mused.

"They may still be lying!" One of the theigns of York suggested.

"To what end?" Another wanted to know.

"I don't doubt that they have seen something," Coenred interjected, "the question is what? How great was the number of the ships?"

"Our fishing boats number some thirty in the reckoning, the Viking longships numbered three times that," Saba asserted.

"With the same number again of smaller vessels carrying the stuff of war for them," Abiorn added.

"How would you know this with your backs to the sea and running for the safety of the hills?" A disbelieving theign demanded with a sneer.

"Saba and me returned to Skaroaborg from the south and spied out the enemy," Abiorn replied to the accusation but he directed his words to Coenred. "We tethered our horses and crept to the edge of the village. The storm out to sea was angry but the headland protected their ships in the southern bay. Many a fighter came ashore and helped drag the smaller boats onto the beach. Their bigger craft were anchored in the bay and left to ride out the worst of the storm."

"They put Scarborough to the torch!" Saba added.

Coenred could think of no reason why the fishermen would lie about this event. Norse raiders still plagued the eastern coast and would pillage such places as coastal villages, but these days it was rare for them to come in such numbers as the men claimed or land such a large force of fighters. If they spoke the truth then the objective of the Norsemen was clearly not some obscure fishing village.

"Know you anything of this army that might identify them?" He asked.

"I know one thing," Abiorn said with conviction, "King Harald Hardrada walked amongst them!"

This statement brought a loud torrent of scorn and disbelief from the assembled townsmen, tinged with a little fear as well. Coenred commanded them to be quiet and they fell to muttering amongst themselves.

"How do you know this?" He demanded of the Dane.

"The tales spoken oft around the hearth-fires of those of us with Danish blood tell of a warrior great in stature and he who walked amongst them was the greatest man that I have ever seen. He had grey in his hair and beard so that his years might total those of the King of Norway. He had a guard of mighty warriors dressed in the finest harness of war, helms and byrnies of steel decorated with gold and silver, and all who came before him showed due respect without fail. They say that Hardrada sails a ship greater than any other upon the sea and such a ship sat in the bay. It had a dragon head of wonderous size and the benches would seat eighty warriors at the oars with ease. I tell you, the War Wolf is amongst us!" Abiorn's confident reply was met with a fearful silence.

"There was another too," Saba said after a moment.

"Another?" Coenred prompted him.

"A Saxon lord with a circlet of gold upon his head, a strong following of weapons-men, and a rich cloak upon his back; it was Tostig Godwinson."

"Aye, we spied him also," Abiorn agreed.

Another outburst of disbelief followed this revelation. Mildryth's words concerning the king's brother Tostig sailing to Norway came back to Coenred's mind. It seemed that her news was indeed accurate after all. He raised his voice to silence the townsmen once again.

"I told thee that I was lowered in station by Tostig Godwinson," Saba snapped at the townsmen, "think any man here that such as I would not remember the face of the man who would do such a thing? My wealth and land taken from me and given to one of the devil's favourites, and me made a fisher for my living. I tell thee, if I had had my bow at hand I would have put an arrow in his hateful breast, even if the price of it be to die beneath a Viking axe!"

The hall was filled with more noise but it seemed that the men were now considering the news a little more seriously than before.

"I received word that Tostig Godwinson sailed to the court of the King of Norway," Coenred told the assembly, "if this power be a league of Tostig with Hardrada then they did not come to sack a fishing village, they came to take York."

The assembly met this pronouncement with the most energetic uproar yet. They did not question the huscarl's words but responded with panic at the thought of the War Wolf leading a force large enough to lay siege to the city and being within days of arriving.

"We must prepare," Coenred raised his voice to quell the noise within the hall.

"What must we do?"

"Send riders out, two to London to alert the king, he will send a force to aid us. Send another north towards Ripon to alert Eorl Edwin and Eorl Morcar, they come to York which is why I am already here but they will come all the swifter knowing that the city is in danger."

A general consensus was quickly reached on this proposal and finding that this action was well within their abilities the theigns fell to selecting and organising the messengers.

"I will go to London to tell the king," Sabba volunteered himself, "any payment in kind that I can do Tostig I will gladly undertake."

"You look tired already man, we can find messengers from within the city walls to ride to London," Coenred answered him.

"My anger maintains my strength, My Lord," Sabba said in a calm, cold voice. "Tostig took my title and lands first, now he takes my hovel of a home and burns my boat; he leaves me nothing. If I can wreck a ruin of my own upon his head by taking a horse to London and stirring up the king, his brother, then let it be so. Let the men of York defend what they have, their hearths, homes and families."

"Your family will stay with mine," Abiorn told him with sincerity. "I will protect them until you return with the king."

Wyrd, they say, decides all great events in a man's life. It seemed to Coenred that wyrd had worked its spell upon him also. He had volunteered to come to York on the eorls' business because it suited him, not because it was within his usual duties. Here, in this very hall, he had met Mildryth, a woman also well suited to him in terms of age and station, and she with words on the possible movement of the king's errant brother; words that looked to have been proven true. Those who believed in the power of wyrd would insist that that meeting was meant to happen. In one respect he found himself wishing that it were so, it suited the trend of his thoughts of late.

There was a shadow, however. It came, or so it seemed to him, with Mildryth too. If this new danger was indeed King Hardrada and Tostig Godwinson in league together then his sense of loyalty would not allow him to abandon the eorls in a moment of peril. The ties that bound him to his brother warriors held him tightly. He was the captain of the huscarls, a soldier of the Army of the North, his brother warriors would expect him to stand with them in the shield-wall. It went against the grain to consider leaving them when the old enemy raised their spears once again in the lands of the Saxon. He could not hang up his sword now, not until the danger was met and dealt with. Also, he could do no more for

Mildryth than extend his protection over her; at least as much as a fighting man could from the field of battle. Everything else would depend on whether wyrd had decided that he would survive this threat or not.

As his counsel was no longer called upon Coenred decided to leave the hall and attend to business of his own that awaited him outside. He paused in the doorway to Aethelwine's hall, tasted the fresher air, warm as it was, and took a moment to gaze out at the city. Just down the street of single storey, thatched roofed buildings his three tethered horses stood patiently. One was a fine steed well appointed with an expensive but much used saddle and bridle. The second was a similar animal but not so well appointed and the third was a pack horse. A man stood holding the reins of the lead animal exhibiting the same patience as his charges.

Looking from this vantage point Coenred was forced to admit what he had known for many weeks; Eanfrid was getting old before his time. As if to prove the point the man was wracked by a sudden and violent coughing fit. In truth he was barely ten years Coenred's senior but he looked much older. His clothes were of a good quality but hard worn and somehow seemed too big for him now, as if the years of service had thinned him and not them. His hair was lank, despite being washed, combed and tied back. Like him it looked as if it had no life left in it.

In his heart Coenred knew well what he had to do now that the moment had come but he found it no easy act to perform. Age caught every man eventually and Coenred did not delude himself that time would not lay him low too even though he could claim to be in the prime of his own life. Sucking in a deep breath of late summer air he stepped out into the daylight and walked over to where his servant and the horses waited patiently for their master.

"My Lord," Eanfrid acknowledged his approach with a ready smile, "are we to go to Holderness now?"

"Theign Aethelwine has still not returned and now his servants say that it may not be until tomorrow, the man loves hunting so much. So I must wait longer. I had hoped to have seen him yesterday and that would have allowed us the time for my business, but a high-theign, it seems, has much to distract him." Coenred had other errands that he had wanted to run but he could not see how his time would now be spent other than in waiting for the theign. "I must wait, as I say, but yet we must to Holderness - or at least you are to go."

"My Lord, I don't understand?" Eanfrid looked inquisitively at Coenred as if he had misheard.

"My old friend, time has caught up with you. The days will yet, I fear, be filled with alarms, fights and dashes that your body is not able to cope with," Coenred told him.

He decided not to tell Eanfrid about the news of the Viking invasion as that would make pensioning his retainer off almost impossible.

"I am as strong as ever," Eanfrid declared, straightening his back, squaring his shoulders and thrusting out his chest. A warrior's practised eye could see quite clearly that the man was fooling himself, he might have once had a fighter's physique but illness had robbed him of much of his strength. "Do not turn me out when war hangs like a shadow over us. You need me."

"Aye, I do, and you should know better than to think me the kind that would turn out so loyal a man as you. Nay, good Eanfrid, your time in harness is done; there'll be no more war-work for you," Coenred clapped him on the shoulder with affection. "However, I've not done with your service yet."

"What service could I do thee if not to be your shield bearer?" His face was a mask of disbelief and concern.

"Be the protector of my family," Coenred suggested.

"At Holderness?" A gleam of delight suddenly shone in Eanfrid's eye.

"Aye, at Holderness. Osred is a good farmer but he knows nothing of the wars. You know as well as I that when the fyrd is in the field the lawless take to the country and will plunder the weak and the defenceless. My brother tills my land and raises my animals but what knows he of war-work?"

"Nothing, My Lord."

"But you do Eanfrid. You have followed me these many years and know what it is to stand against the enemy. My heart will be lighter knowing that you are at Holderness to protect all that I hold dear whilst I am serving the eorls in the field. King Harold faces many enemies and we, as his subjects, face them also, whether in battle harness or behind a plough."

"Such have the Vikings ever taught us," Eanfrid agreed.

"I do service as a huscarl so that none from my holding have to go to the war as fyrdmen."

"And the Eorl of Mercia deducts it from thy pay," Coenred smiled ruefully at Eanfrid's comment. Such was the closeness between master and servant that he would allow him, in private at least, to speak in such a manner about the eoldermen.

"Then you will do this service for me?" Coenred asked.

"Of course, My Lord, if this truly be your will?"

"I know you like the life at Holderness Eanfrid; it is more suited to your summers. Tell Osred that I have pensioned you and that he is to have a house built for you-"

"A house?!"

"Where else will you sleep? I have no great hall like Aethelwine. A house is my gift in return for your many years of service, along with land for crops of your own. You have a woman by Tadcaster way I think?"

"My Lord?" Eanfrid looked flustered, almost embarrassed. Finally he added as if in justification: "She is a widow."

"Then take her to Holderness with you. You cannot spend your winters alone even in such a house as Osred will give you," Coenred laughed. He reached into his purse and pulled out a smaller cloth bag. "Here, old friend. I have put this aside for today. It is little enough for a man who has served me so faithfully and for so long but it will allow you to claim....?"

A long pause developed between them before Eanfrid realised that his master waited for his lover's name.

"Cynwise!" he finally blurted out, "She is called Cynwise!"

"To claim Cynwise for your wife as a man of means. Will you take her with you to Holderness and do me this great service?"

"If she come," Eanfrid replied earnestly.

"She'll be a poor judge of character if she does not."

Coenred gripped his shoulder and was struck at how thin the muscle underneath his hand felt. Here was a man who had carried on his back all that a warrior needed for battle, over many miles of rough country, either where horses could not go or when they had bolted before sudden attacks from enemies in greater numbers. He had done it without complaint; ever. He had even fought beside his master when the need was dire and the enemy too close.

In truth Coenred did not imagine that there were many years left in Eanfrid, he had never seemed to have fully recovered from the fever he caught during last winter. For a moment he chided himself for not having let his retainer leave his service sooner, but it was a fault of his not to let go too easily the people he loved.

He put the bag of money in his friend's hand.

"Take your horse and get thee to Tadcaster," Coenred told him, "then tomorrow onto Holderness."

"I will give the horse to Master Osred when I get there," Eanfrid insisted.

"Why? It is yours, as is the harness. You have ridden it so long that I doubt it would answer to another anyway."

Eanfrid looked up into Coenred's face. He had known this man since he was a boy on the farm at Holderness. He had grown to love him like the son he had never had himself. He was proud of the man that the boy had become. Of course he could not show the emotion that he felt, part joy at being released from the arduous toils of a huscarl's retainer, part delight at the thought of settling down in a house of his own at the family holding at Holderness, and part sorrow that he would not be there ever again when the call to arms came.

Their embrace was quick and awkward but said as much to either of them about shared experiences and a friendship that crossed the normal boundaries of master and servant.

"I will see you at Holderness before the year's out," Coenred told him.

"And I will see Holderness is still there for you when you come," Eanfrid returned.

He un-tethered his horse and swung up into the saddle with an accustomed ease despite his age and failing health. Without another word or a backward glance Eanfrid walked his horse to the south gate of York and onto the road to Tadcaster.

Coenred did not stand and watch Eanfrid leave; instead he turned and busied himself with the two remaining animals. It seemed that he would have to spend the night in York yet again so he would need to return his horses to the stables. Aethelwine's hall would be his bed chamber once more, as it had been on many other nights previously, but as he pondered that thought he found his mind being occupied by the subject of Mildryth. He had a sudden rush of emotion as a result, followed by a wave of confusion.

What did he have to do with the woman?

His hands no longer moved over his horse but simply rested on its side as he was lost once more to contemplation.

She was as fine a woman as any he had ever met and the fact that the largest part of her fortune had been lost did not concern him at all. He had money and land enough. Eorl Aelfgar had been a generous lord who took great satisfaction from acting the ring-giver to his companions. He and his father before him had respected the old ways, rewarding men according to their ability and not just their rank. Having followed in his own father's footsteps into military service Coenred had enjoyed both the eorl's patrimony and protection.

Protector.

The word brought Mildryth back to his mind yet again. She had asked for his protection and he had, without so much as saying it, granted her wish. Was that because he had been thinking of making Eanfrid's departure easier by suggesting that he be a protector for their people at Holderness? The idea of offering Eanfrid as protection was already in his mind, had Mildryth known that in advance through her feminine wiles? Of course he was honour bound to give protection to those who asked it of him, at least to those who owed their loyalty to his own masters; Eorl Edwin and Eorl Morcar. Protection was a necessary consideration when your enemies sailed out of the morning sea mist to attack without warning. Eanfrid had grown old but there would be none at Holderness to rival his experience of fighting with the sword and the spear, and so by a single stroke Coenred had extended his protection over his mother and brother and all the ceorls who lived and worked the land there.

And now Eanfrid, at his age, was to take the lover he had thought kept secret as a wife. This world was small and everyone knew everyone else's business. Eanfrid might have thought Cynwise was beyond Coenred's knowledge but the huscarl's shield-bearer and his widowed lover had been the subject of talk around the hearth of the companions on more than one occasion.

Had the remembrance of that hearth-talk opened this old ache in Coenred's own heart?

Were men so easy for women to read?

The truth was that he did not know because he was a huscarl, a professional soldier, and he had never given time to taking a wife or raising a family, only in being the best warrior that he could be to win the honours and rewards that he gave to his family. He was the source of their prosperity just as his father and grandfather had been before him. There was that new idea forming in his mind, however, one that had grown ever more attractive with each day that he spent in the company of Edwin and Morcar. He thought again about the quieter life spent on the farm raising sheep for the wool trade and crops to sell at market. For twenty years he had led the life of a warrior and hazarded his heart's blood against fierce enemies. It had been hard work but rewarding, through the gifts of his grateful lord he had added to the land that they owned; enough to qualify him as a rich theign in his own right.

Why should he not enjoy it?

Why should he not consider a future with a woman like Myldryth?

The only things that stood in his way were the oaths that he had sworn, first as a huscarl to defend the life of his lord with his own blood, and second, more personally, to the father of Edwin and Morcar in particular, promising Aelfgar that he would see them raised as fitting leaders of men. The truth was though that the youngsters he had begun working with were now adults. Edwin had turned twenty, five years into his majority, and Morcar was seventeen. Their relationship had changed. From respectful students they had become masters of men by the right of their birth and they were tired of being taught by one who was, to all intents and purposes, a servant also. They had outgrown his oath even if he had not.

As a huscarl Coenred had the right to end his service with his lord at any time he thought best.

Mayhap that time was now?

Mayhap he should hang up his spear and his gold inlaid sword and become a farmer instead?

Mayhap he should raise a family as well?

Dreams were one thing, honour was another matter. The eorls were due in York any day now and Coenred would let them settle in before speaking to them and withdrawing his service; that was the right thing to do. He knew now, however, that he may have to delay actually quitting their service if the rumours concerning Tostig Godwinson and the Viking Hardrada were indeed true. In his heart he knew also that he could not turn his back on the eorls and his own comrades, his brother warriors, in such a time of danger. He had enjoyed the benefits of his position, but he had always recognised the obligations that being the companion of a lord imposed. The gold decorated sword that hung at his side was not just a badge of rank, it was his tool employed in the defence of the said lord, his land and property and all the people for whom he was responsible. Many years of service had crafted his sense of honour to a degree where it dominated his thinking totally. He could no more make a choice that, from his perspective, benefitted himself only and left others in harm's way than he could refuse a woman, alone in the world, his protection when asked. He would remain a huscarl yet.

And now here he was without even a retainer, what kind of huscarl did that make him? Carrying his own shield to the battlefield!

"I'll be thy retainer, My Lord," a voice piped up behind him.

Coenred turned quickly, partly from instinct honed by years of training, partly because the voice had startled him.

The young man who owned the voice stepped backwards quickly. He raised his hands, both to ward off the danger threatened by the gleaming sword that had suddenly appeared in Coenred's hand and also to show that he had no weapon of his own and did not, therefore, pose a real danger.

"What say ye!" Coenred demanded with an angry tone. He quickly observed the young man's poor state of dress, the lack of a cloak, the unkempt hair, the dirt on his tunic, trousers and skin, the worn shoes and the hungry look. "Do you think to rob me?"

"No, My Lord." The other shrank back. "I offer my service."

"Service?" Coenred almost spat the word out but it was only for affect.

His instincts told him correctly that this youth indeed posed him no danger. Nevertheless he felt somewhat annoyed that he had been so careless of his surroundings that someone could have come upon him unknown so easily. He replaced his sword into its fine leather scabbard with its gold fastenings.

"What service can you offer me?"

"As a retainer, My Lord, a shield bearer," the youth prompted, relaxing and looking a little more hopeful when he saw the weapon being put away.

"And why would I want one?"

"Because you let the one you had go just now."

He stepped further back and straightened up, judging himself to be out of arms reach and so safe from a sudden attack. Huscarls were dangerous men even when in a good mood and it was clear to him now that he had upset this one by daring to intrude on his private thoughts. He hoped to make amends for his poor display of manners.

"Are you spying on me?" Coenred demanded.

"No, My Lord, I was hard by, over there."

He pointed a little way down the street to a small house that, like so many others, also opened up into a shop. It sold vegetables. The proprietor was busy dealing with two female customers. He said something that made them laugh and he joined in their merriment. Their disposition was in stark contrast to that of the youth who stood before him.

"I was going to ask for some spoils," he admitted, hanging his head in shame. Coenred knew that he referred to the damaged stock that the shopkeeper might decide to throw away or feed to his pig if he had one. "I heard you talking."

"And you thought that you could just take a loyal servant's place?" Coenred was now also more relaxed but maintained an aggressive attitude.

He was an eorl's man, a freeman of significance and social standing. It was both important and right that he acted according to his station, but mostly he thought to test this youth.

"Well, yes, My Lord."

Coenred turned to his horse and loosened his shield from the leather fastenings that held it to the saddle. It was three foot in diameter with a large steel boss in the centre. At his own expense Coenred had had a steel rim fitted to give the shield both greater strength and the edge a resistance to cutting weapons like axes or swords. The shield was made from linden wood; a light material that did not split when pierced and it had a habit of binding around cutting blades making them difficult to withdraw. It was painted in the black of Mercia with a stylised yellow dragon, glorious in the intricacies of Saxon art, rearing in the centre. For the moment this decoration was hidden beneath a cover of linen especially made to protect the shield's patterning when it was not on display.

"How strong are you?" Coenred asked as he turned to face the young man again, the shield held horizontally in his hands.

"As strong as an ox!" He declared with a grin.

The grin suddenly disappeared from his face as he saw the large shield hurtling his way like a skimming stone thrown across the surface of a pond. He started to catch it reflexively but it hit him on the shoulder as, in two minds, he suddenly ducked and turned away in fear of being hurt. The impact staggered him and he fell to one knee.

"And as slow," Coenred remarked with a small smile.

He walked over and picked up the shield. He also helped the young man to his feet.

"What know you of war?"

"Nothing," he admitted, "I was born on a farm and that is all I know."

"At least you're honest. What's your name?"

"Edwin son of Octa, My Lord."

Coenred smiled ruefully.

What would Eorl Edwin think to his servant taking a retainer with the same name?

"A huscarl's retainer is not just a servant; he's a fighting man himself. Eanfrid fought with me in many battles, he could use a spear and an axe as well as carry them for me, what can you do?"

"Learn; if you will teach me," Edwin's face brightened as he took in Coenred's words. It seemed that an offer of employment might be about to be made.

I doubt that there will be time for that!

Coenred thought to himself in response to Edwin's answer concerning learning weapons lore. He looked the young man over again and could guess his story from the dirty clothes and the hunger etched in his face.

A waif and a stray!

Nevertheless the boy had said that he was born on a farm, if Coenred did decide to hang up his sword and this lad proved his worth then one more hand at the plough might not go amiss. He was clearly not a stranger to hard work if the roughness of his hands was anything to go by and he certainly looked stocky and strong enough for the role.

"It's a hard life, Edwin son of Octa."

"So is being cast out with no kith nor kin to turn to," Edwin replied. "I never meant to come by this fortune but my father raised me to be an honest ceorl, a freeman always, and I will work for my keep; I'm not afraid of that."

"Nevertheless, a shield-bearer to a huscarl is not an occupation to be taken up lightly. There is danger in it as well as hard work," Coenred further pressed the youth's resolve.

"I have experienced danger," he replied but without any bravado, "'twas danger that reduced me to this; homeless and alone. It seems that you don't have to be a man of the sword to be met by danger; it finds you wherever you are. I will work hard, I will obey you in all things, I will take what training you choose to give me, and I will be a man to be relied upon."

"And I, as you pointed out, am in need of a retainer."

The young man's face lit up then but he kept his excitement under control, standing there with his arms tightly clasped against his sides but unconsciously shifting his weight from one foot to the other. It occurred to Coenred that the boy had acted with some initiative in offering himself in place of Eanfrid; it suggested a degree of character and that appealed to him.

"I will take you on sufferance only; if you do not prove yourself to me then I will turn you out."

"Yes, My Lord," Edwin agreed without hesitation, "but you will not come to that. I am to be depended upon in all things, I am strong of limb and sound of wind, I know horses and I –"

"You will buy some clean clothes," Coenred interrupted him. "Consider this your first test. Get a new tunic, shirt, a braid for your hair, some trousers, a belt, a cloak and some shoes. I am to meet with High-Theign Aethelwine and I can't have my retainer looking like he's spent the night in the hounds' kennel."

He fished in his purse and brought out some coins. As he counted them out he glanced at Edwin and noted that although he was watching it was not in a covetous manner.

"Here," he gave him the money, "this may seem like a treasure to you but know this Edwin son of Octa, if you think to steal from me the watch will know of it, I will raise a hue and cry and when you are caught I will have you flogged first and then tried."

"Yes, My Lord! I mean no, My Lord! I mean as you say, My Lord," the words gushed from him.

He cupped the coins in his hands and stared at them as if he'd never seen so many in one place before.

"Meet me inside High-Theign Aethelwine's hall after you are done," Coenred prompted as Edwin showed no sign of moving to find a clothes seller, "and wash your hands and face before you put on the new clothes."

"Yes, My Lord," he looked up, smiled with genuine elation and then turned and started running down the street clutching the coins tightly in his right hand. All of a sudden he stopped and turned round again. "My Lord," he shouted. "Where is Theign Aethelwine's hall?"

Coenred stabbed a finger across the street from where he stood. The mead-hall was the largest building in the area, some thirty rods long with a roof almost three times taller than the walls. Unlike the smaller houses that crowded around it, but came no closer than ten paces, the hall had a tiled roof that made it look all the more magnificent. It was the largest building in the vicinity and the hub of both the social and political life of the city.

"There," he answered in a gruff voice.

"Thank you, My Lord."

Edwin turned and disappeared down the street leaving Coenred to wonder if he had made the right decision. He looked at the horses and it occurred to him that he probably had, as long as the youth returned as he had promised and he did seem an honest lad; one that had fallen on hard times but who had so far resisted the way of the outlaw. That was something to recommend him by anyway.

"And it falls to me to stable you two then," he said to the horses, wishing that he had thought either to replace Eanfrid earlier or given Edwin the money for his new clothes after he had had him take care of the animals.

The River Humber

The Viking fleet struggled against the surging tide of the estuary after having turned into the Humber from the wild northern sea. Another time they may well have simply waited for the tide to turn to make their journey easier but they had no wish to remain away from shelter with the winds out to sea still strong and the threat of another storm just beyond the horizon behind them. The crews bent to their task of rowing the ships to aid what momentum they could get from the wind that had changed to a north-easterly.

King Harald Hardrada stood in the prow of his drekkar, the dragon ship known as The Long Serpent. He would have preferred to have been out in front at the head of the fleet, leading as always, but his vessel was indeed long, some ninety feet in total, and carried eighty Viking warriors at the benches. Although impressive in size it was not as manoeuvrable as the smaller vessels and as they sailed upon a river that none of his men knew well he did not want to run any unnecessary risks. Tidal estuaries were dangerous places for the unwary.

Before him sailed twenty or so snekke, in many ways similar to the Long Serpent but smaller, the biggest being a little over fifty feet in length. Over two hundred similar vessels followed in their wake, including many more drekkar. The snekke were not as impressive as the larger fighting ships but they were far more practical on an unknown river. Today they scouted the way ahead, looking for both an easy passage and possible obstacles to their progress; the Humber would have shifting sandbars that could trap their vessels. They excelled as watermen, however, riding their element with both confidence and joy.

Nevertheless, Hardrada would not be without his Long Serpent no matter how impractical it might be for close sailing on foreign rivers; what better way to impress upon both friend and foe alike the power at his disposal than this magnificent vessel?

They had turned round the curious 'Hook of Holderness' that formed the north bank of the River Humber at its mouth and were now heading west. The river was over a league wide at this point and the air carried the smell of salt. Rowing would do the men no harm, it would keep their muscles toned and fit for the fighting to come. Long arms burnt by the sun, hardened by use with both the oar and the axe. Standing in the prow of the Long Serpent the wily Viking judged their destination to be at least two leagues away, not so great a distance for a man on horseback but travel on the waterway was always slow in these conditions.

"We come at last to England," Jarl Siward commented as he approached the king, "this place be new to the both of us."

"It's too flat," Hardrada growled." We can be seen for miles. There's no advantage to be gained by this route."

The country was even and green on both sides of the wide estuary although there was some higher land in the distance both to the north and to the south. This made the river look even wider than it really was. Salt marshes lined the banks, home to wading birds that preyed on small fish, crabs and shrimps. Further up stream there were mud flats and where the river water ran fresh rather than salty the otter replaced the seals and dolphins as the main predator. Today, however, the men from Norway were the hunters to be feared most.

"Jorvik lies inland, this is the only way to reach it and keep the fleet at hand," Siward stated the facts as simply as he understood them.

"I know, I know," the king muttered. He rode the movement of the ship expertly, never losing his balance, not even being forced to change his footing or to reach out a steadying hand. He was like the captain of old once more, the man who had led them so far over the blue seas of the world in similar fleets to this one, not mayhap as large but always in search of treasure and adventure.

"It's good to be abroad again, bringing our swords to a worthy enemy and taking their gold," Siward laughed, the king forced a smile. "This is the way we should live."

"This is not the same kind of adventure," Hardrada stated, "back then we were happy to raid and plunder, to use the treasure to fund the war against Sweyn and his Danes when we returned home."

"That man has proved as elusive as an eel, still he sits upon his throne though now he lacks the spirit for war."

"Like us his force is spent."

Siward looked closely at the king, momentarily alarmed by this out of character utterance. He could not help but note the lines around the king's eyes, the furrows in his brow, the grey strands in his hair and beard. Involuntarily a proverb jumped into his head.

Silver hairs are the first blossoms of death!

"Nay, My Lord, we are as strong as ever!" he declared with a vigorous tone, wanting to rid himself of the images that the unlooked for adage had imposed into his mind.

"Are we?" Hardrada looked him straight in the eye. "Since when have we had to ally ourselves with foreigners to win a war?"

It was a good question and Siward had to think hard for an answer and it took him some moments to do it.

"We were mercenaries once ourselves, in Byzantium. You were the Captain of the Varangian Guard," he offered up hopefully.

"What we did then we did for the pay of others, it is not the same. Things have not gone the way I had planned. It seems to me that my enemies escape my sword now rather than die under it, and my own people curse my back. I have heard it whispered that they call me now the 'Old Hound' instead of the 'War Wolf'. You know that I have placed everything on this adventure Siward?"

"You are still the King of Norway," Siward insisted. He wanted to say more but his friend continued speaking.

"What is a king without a treasury? If we fail here then there will be a cold homecoming awaiting us in Norway. Sweyn of Denmark will be following our moves and he will be aware of what our success will mean for him. Fifteen years we spent fighting that man and not once achieved a decisive victory over him. Through his very stubbornness to fall before me Sweyn has forced me to make peace, to sign a pact that guarantees that peace for the rest of our joint lifetimes. Things may change, however. Things do change. England is the richest country this side of the Byzantine Empire and with all that money in my grasp Denmark will fall to me. We must be resolved to win this war Siward. I must lead you to foreign places again and you must do much killing. I will be the 'War Wolf' once more."

Hardrada spoke in a more expansive manner towards the end of his speech, as if finding some encouragement for himself within his own words.

"I have seen half the world following in your footsteps My Lord, seen things that were undreamt of. We sailed the Greek seas and put out the eyes of an emperor. I have put more treasure into the holds of our ships than I thought existed. We have lived as Vikings should, wild and free and feared. What matters this voyage to England now?" Siward spoke effusively in his turn but only demonstrated that he had missed the anxiety in the heart of his monarch and his friend. He had followed in the footsteps of his hero for so long that there were things about the man that time had hidden from his eyes.

Some men are born to follow.

Hardrada was glad that Siward's mind was at ease. He was not the most intelligent of men mayhap but he was a natural soldier, a good leader of warriors on the battlefield and a man to be trusted in himself. He had no vision, however, no understanding of the politics of court. For Siward there was no problem that a sharp spear and a brave heart could not find an answer for. Educated men knew that Hardrada's claim to the English throne was weaker than a spring frost. That King Harthacnut, the then Viking ruler of England, and King Magnus of Denmark had made a pledge that each would inherit the throne of whosoever died first was doubtful in itself. Probably no more than a folktale at best.

That the English Witan would respect such a claim was not even to be considered. No, it was circumstance that had lent Hardrada's claim any real substance, circumstance and the coming of Tostig Godwinson. He had promised to turn powerful Saxon lords who were not necessarily supporters of his brother Harold of Wessex to the cause of the Norwegian King. In truth, with Guillaume of Normandy looking to take the crown as well, Hardrada knew that he needed more than just a Viking army at his command, even one as large as this, he needed to win the popular support of those Saxon lords who could be swayed by Tostig, only then could he make the throne of England his own.

The king watched the surf ripple past the ship's hull and it reminded him of the days slipping by and his own hold on the throne of Norway growing weaker due in no small part to the Danish resistance. He needed to believe that this design would work.

"Aye, though Guillaume may have run to the pope in Rome for a blessing have we not made our own pilgrimage to the Holy Land?" Hardrada broke the comfortable silence.

"Aye, My Lord."

"Then let the Christian God smile on our venture if pilgrimages mean aught to him," Hardrada sounded lighter of heart. "Look!"

He pointed to the north bank. They had passed the mouth of a river, a tributary to the great Humber, that flowed down from the northern hills. They could just see the roofs of a Saxon settlement sitting in what seemed like lush grazing land. In between the Vikings and the Saxon houses there were dotted the white fleeces of a large flock of sheep, grazing lazily over a rich, green pasture.

"This country is richer than it has a right to be. No matter how many times our people have plundered it the Saxons continue to remain fat with mutton, warm in their woollen cloaks and bedecked in gold. Where does all this wealth come from?"

"I care not, My Lord," Siward admitted, "I care only where it goes; into our possession."

Hardrada laughed along with his trusted captain. He had always enjoyed Siwards uncomplicated nature.They had spent many nights under the canopy of stars that seemed to bedeck foreign skies, on some adventure and surrounded only by honest fighting men. Life was simple then. All knew what they wanted and all knew what was expected of them. Death, if it came, was glorious if you had a sword in your hand and a companion by your side. It was something to look for.

Now the trappings of the kingship that he had so long sought seemed to weave around him like a net. He had a kingdom at his command and yet he had failed to bring about the defeat of his enemies. He had achieved so much more with far less in the simpler days of his youth. He found himself yearning for those days now and it caused him some disquiet to realise that so many years had passed him by since he first set out to make a name for himself, to become the subject of his own saga. Fifty one years since he had come into this world and it found him now forcing himself to laugh along with a good friend.

"All the same, if we can see them then they can see us," he declared when Siward's mirth had passed. "I think that we should moor at the first suitable landing place we come upon and then prepare for battle immediately. The Saxons will know we are no longer in the east and will change their plans for defence. I do not want to be caught with half our men on the ships and the other half still unloading on the shore."

"They would never be so bold."

"These are strange times my friend," Hardrada replied. "The great moving star appeared in the skies during springtime, the one that comes every five and seventy years, or so the learned tell us. Who knows what things undreamt of might yet occur before winter closes its hoary grasp upon the land?"

"Edward was king at the beginning of the year, then Harold took the crown, you will be the third and final king, one who sits on the throne of both Norway and England."

"And maybe even Denmark?" He grunted to himself with satisfaction at that idea. "There are those who see a power in threes and three thrones would see me a powerful king eh?"

"One to rival the Emperor of Byzantium," Siward agreed, "the greatest Viking king of them all."

Hardrada did smile at that comment.To be remembered down the ages was always the desire of the Viking lords.

What point was there in pursuing these long voyages away from home if not to win glory for one's name?

How many men had walked this earth, lived their lives and died their deaths unknown and unremembered?

Only the weak of mind and body left such a legacy. They would sing sagas of Harald Hardrada, the third of that name to be King of Norway. All the gold and silver that he had amassed during his life time, from Norway to Africa and all the lands in between, had been spent in making his name one to be feared and one to be remembered.

He was the War Wolf!

He would not admit it openly to anyone else but doubt had plagued him over this expedition. Sweyn of Denmark posed no threat to Norway in the absence of its king; that was not the problem. His son Prince Magnus occupied the throne as regent in Hardrada's absence and the boy was more than able to deter any Danish transgressions. Rather he was aware that there was a touch of desperation in this action that they now undertook. He needed money and he needed allies; that was not a position of strength. Travelling to Orkney he had swelled the ranks of his depleted Norwegians with men not just from Orkney itself but also from other Viking settlements as diverse as the Isle of Mann, Icelanders, Greenlanders, Irish Norse, Scotland and Cumberland, and even men from the Faeroe Islands. There were Danes too, against whom he had fought for so long, still eager for battle and plunder no matter whom led them. It was a large number of swords at his command but they were of disparate origin. At least these men had the tie of Viking blood if not the same country of origin, unlike Lord Tostig's army of adventurers.

Nevertheless, Hardrada would have preferred an army of true Norwegians. He had seen during his time as a captain of the Varangian Guard in Byzantium both the strengths and weaknesses of a mercenary force. An army of one mind and one spirit was always more courageous than a collection of diverse warriors. At the heart of his army he had a large number of hardened veterans who were steeled in the fight and had a hunger for the spoils he promised them.

If the battle went not their way easily would they all stand by my banner?

What would be the outcome when their allegiance was truly tested?

"The sun begins to sink in the west," Siward commented, breaking the king's train of thought.

"We will row through the night," Hardrada commanded. "No doubt the Saxons of Holderness will be sending messengers to Jorvik; we cannot afford to stay long on the river."

It would be several hours in this late September before the light faded beyond use for navigation and they should have long since turned into the River Ouse before then. Making their way up that watercourse in the dark would be difficult but not beyond their skill as watermen. With luck they would come upon a good landing point not far from Jorvik in the early morning and then they could finally test their mettle against the northern Saxons and begin the task of taking the English crown.

The City of York

"At last I walk the streets of York again," Sigbert declared as they stepped out from the stables leaving their retainers to look after their horses and equipment. "Think on brothers, within a few strides I will be home and in the embrace of my beloved Hilda."

"Truly I do not envy you friend Sigbert, for I have known the embrace of many a fair woman and hope to know many more before I breathe my last breath," Thrydwulf responded with good humour.

"I am with Sigbert on this occasion," Hereric commented. "My lovely Eadgyd also resides within York's fair walls and tonight I will sleep a sleep not perfumed by the odours escaping from your foul bodies. I long to see my children again."

"And make another one I do not doubt," Thrydwulf grinned at him.

"We have ridden all day as bodyguard to the eorls, my limbs are stiff and my seat numb, let me walk in the sun and ease my aches," Sigbert said to no on in particular.

"We should make the most of it," Thrydwulf agreed, "the eorls are busy settling into their lodge, sooner than I want duty will call us back to the great hall and the ease of the eoldermen."

They walked leisurely into the sunshine and were seemingly unconscious of the deference shown to them by the people that they passed on the street. Their clothing was of the best quality and gold and silver adorned them, decorations for their weapons and belts, thick chains holding garnets, rubies and other precious jewels from the far east; the latter more so with the younger warriors. Around the head of each was a circlet of gold, a gift from their lord. No one could be in doubt as to their status as members of the warrior elite.

"You speak like old men," Aethelmaer declared with a smile. He was noticeably younger than the other three who had served together as huscarls for several years now. Like Aldfrid and Hengist who brought up the rear of the party he belonged to the next generation to take up the sword and swear the oath of the huscarl.

"The young know nothing," Sigbert declared.

"Except that they will grow old," Hereric added.

"I wonder at the miracle that the three of you were once young," Aethelmaer retorted.

"If you live as long as we in this occupation then you will have become wise indeed," Thrydwulf told him. "Your fair skin is yet to feel the cut of a blade or the sting of an arrow. I saw you bathe the other day and I mistook thee for a wench, so fair and flawless was thy skin."

The older warriors burst into noisy laughter whilst young Aethelmaer reddened. Hereric in his turn turned on the other two so far silent companions bringing up the rear; they were smirking at Aethelmaer behind his back.

"Getting your first scar is not like getting your first woman, as you'll know when both things happen to thee."

Again, there followed more raucous laughter from the older warriors and the reddening of young faces.

"We have stood our ground before the enemy," Aethelmaer insisted with some passion.

"Aye, we have seen the back of Tostig Godwinson when he turned and ran before the shield-wall that we stood firm in alongside thee at Grim's By," Hengist agreed.

"We do not doubt thy valour when you have us to stand behind," Thrydwulf told them, "we being a little taller than thee."

"More broader than taller says I." Aldfrid responded.

"My girth comes from good living got from living with a good woman," Sigbert replied with an easy humour.

"I know the wisdom of thy words brother," Hereric said in agreement.

"And we younger warriors will add to our slim girths by feasting in High-Theign Aethelwine's hall tonight," Aldfrid declared, smiling at the thought. "Though I doubt that he'll be glad to see the eorls and us, their companions, supping beneath his roof so soon again."

"In truth the eorls do test the man's sense of hospitality," Aethelmaer agreed.

"He is a high-theign, appointed by the king himself he has the obligation of duty just like the rest of us. Such is the fate of those who rub shoulders with eoldermen," Thrydwulf expressed little sympathy.

"My father would say different," Aethelmaer retorted.

"Your father would," Hereric told him, "your father is a royal-theign like Aethelwine. Picked by the hand of the sovereign himself to rule these lands in the king's name and apply the king's law."

"He bought that sword that hangs at your side." Aethelmaer glared at Thrydwulf's back in immediate response to that comment.

"We all come into our swords one way or another," Sigbert intervened, "mine is an heirloom, like many a man's, Aethelmaer's is a gift from his father, also like many another man's. What matters is that we are brother huscarls together."

They all voiced their agreement with this truth noisily. Thrydwulf was not a jealous man but he had earned his place as a huscarl the hard way, as a professional fighting man for lesser lords. He had invested the prizes he had received from their hands in the badge of his rank, the gold inlaid sword, as well as his necessary steel mail armour, the two horses, a shield-bearer and all the equipage dictated by law. His body carried many scars that were the testament of his achievements on the field of battle. The Saxon world respected talent and a man could win great wealth and great renown by proving himself to his lord in whatever field his skills excelled.

For his part Aethelmaer was the son of a rich man. He could have followed any occupation open to the theign-worthy, becoming a huscarl was as much his right as anyone else's who possessed the ability to thrive in such a calling. The law stated only that a man must own the required sword, not that he must earn it through the spilling of his own blood. Of course some wealth was necessary too, a huscarl was a full time warrior who was not distracted by the need to practice a trade or farm land; such was the fate of the fyrdmen.

The petty clash would quickly be forgotten, however. Aldfrid was quite correct; they would eat and drink well tonight in the companionship of the eorls and at Aethelwine's expense. Also, the bonds of brotherhood that they enjoyed had been proven more than once before the enemy. It was only peace and relative inactivity that gave them leisure enough to squabble like this.

"I am to my fair Eadgyd now; enjoy the city as best thee may," Hereric declared with a grin.

"I will walk a ways with thee seeing as our families both live on the west bank," Sigbert told him.

The two of them headed for the stone bridge that joined the eastern and western halves of the city. It had been built by the Romans and had remained strong and trustworthy to this day.

They entered streets full of buildings seemingly crammed into too little a space. Mostly they were single story houses of the traditional style, which in the city was of thatched roofs standing at least 6 natural feet from the ground. Windows with shutters were much more common here than in the poorer outlying settlements. There were also some buildings that were two storeys high as that was the only way to extend the property if the house on either side could not be bought by a man wealthy and determined enough to display his prosperity; a trait rich Saxons often indulged.

It was common for dwellings to also be places of work and more than one house had a front that could be opened up and turned into a shop. Through-out the city there were merchants who dealt in fish, grain, meat, poultry, fruit and vegetables, and drinks such as wine, beer and herbal teas. There were more practical wares to be had, implements such as needles, spoons and hair combs crafted from antler and bone work, practical and decorative woodwork, pottery turned on a wheel, and for those with less money to spend made by hand also.

As Sigbert and Hereric walked they browsed the shops they passed, stopping to look at the expensive glass and amber used for decoration or as windows to let in the light and keep out the cold. They examined knives and axes made from iron, in particular the more expensive steel. Hereric's eye was caught by items of jewellery made from precious and semi-precious stones, often set in bronze, silver and gold. He bought a delicate piece of amber suspended upon a silver chain.

"Eadgyd adores amber," he explained unnecessarily to Sigbert.

Clothes were abundant, caps, bonnets and mittens produced from sprang looms, woollen and linen cloaks, tunics and trousers, linen underwear or summer tunics and trousers, leather shoes, gloves and belts.

The city was a hive of commerce and full of busy people, although there always seemed to be plenty of men to sit in the small drinking houses enjoying cups of beer and discussing the great issues of the day.

"We part company here," Sigbert eventually said, "I wish all good things to you and yours."

"May you find hearth and home warm and welcoming," Hereric returned. "I will see thee anon at the great hall."

Hereric had only a short way to walk to his family's abode. His own father had been a theign of middle standing who had distinguished himself once in battle and had been rewarded by Siward the Sout, Eorl of Northumbria, with a generous grant of land north of York. That land and the settlement built upon it had passed to Hereric when his father had died some thirteen years ago. At that time he had been making the most of his status as the son of a distinguished warrior- theign, which led to Eorl Siward offering him a position as a companion and a huscarl. The life of a theign on a country estate did not appeal to the young Hereric who preferred the distractions of city life and when a neighbour had made a generous offer for the land, looking to build a bigger estate for himself, he had agreed willingly to the sale.

The death of Eorl Siward in 1055 saw the appointment by King Edward of Eorl Tostig Godwinson to Northumbria and he brought with him his own companions. Like many of Siward's former followers Hereric had drifted to Mercia where the energetic Eorl Aelfgar had always found a use for such men; even against their own king. Since 1065 Morcar, son of Aelfgar, had been the Eorl of Northumbria and it had been no trouble for Hereric to follow the young nobleman back to the place he loved best; not least because Eadgyd had remained in York and endured his long absences as a result.

They owned a large house that looked over the west bank of the River Ouse. It covered the area of four normal houses and had an upper floor. There were plans to have the thatched roof replaced with the more modern tiles, and the windows that looked onto the street were to have their shutters replaced with glass. Eadgyd had servants to help her look after the place, as was to be expected considering their station in life. In the immediate neighbourhood she was a woman of some note.

As Hereric approached the place where they lived he saw his children playing in front of their house. They were still very young, boys of six and four. Their mother chatted to several neighbours; ever did it seem that she had something to say to someone. She was so engrossed in her conversation that she did not notice him as he approached down the street. He watched her with an unconscious smile on his face, noting how her hair was tied with a braid, that she wore the soft yellow dress today, the one that reminded him of warm summer sunlight in the morning. Being only outside the house she had not put on a cloak. He noted that she was smiling, as were the women she was talking to and it broadened his smile too. He loved to see her face so bright as when she was happy.

"Da!" The eldest boy suddenly shouted.

He left his brother and ran excitedly to Hereric. The younger boy hesitated as if not sure that this large man coming towards them was indeed the person that he had last called 'Da'. Eadgyd turned then and saw him as he picked up his first born and swung him around in the air. He bent down and lifted the second child as if he weighed nothing, the sudden motion making the boy laugh, and then he grinned at her.

"Hereric!"

Her face became a picture of joy. Quickly she excused herself from the conversation that she had been enjoying. Her neighbours left with good grace, knowing that the man's duties parted the two of them more often than they were allowed to be together. She would have run to him too, and thrown her arms around him, but that would not be seemly so she walked demurely and put a soft hand on his muscled arm as he held their children who laughed and wriggled.

"The eorls return to York," he told her, "Morcar will be spending the winter here." He knew that she would rejoice at the news. They would be together throughout the hardest season and when he was called away to do his service he would still remain within the city walls, close to his family.

Eadgyd was barely twenty five summers old. Her Viking descent was obvious from her big blue eyes and golden hair, but then York was full of people who claimed a similar heritage. She had captured his heart almost at their first meeting all but seven summers ago and the birth of their first child had led to frequent talk of marriage but Hereric had just as often postponed the event. He loved her deeply but always felt a reluctance to tie her to himself whilst a violent death was the promise of his occupation. For her part Eadgyd did not seem to mind, there were many like them who had not even handfasted let alone taken a marriage vow in a church. They were happy together and wyrd had been kind to them.

People lived as best as people could, there was no condemnation to be faced from neighbours, though they might talk as they were always likely to do, it would not be with malice; just another subject for discussion around the hearth in the long cold night.

Hereric set the boys down. From a bag hanging by a strap from his shoulder he produced two hand carved wooden horses for them. There were many hours spent as a lord's companion that could be usefully employed in the carving of such toys and it was a popular pastime amongst many men, even those without children of their own to give them to; there were always younger brothers and sisters or nephews and nieces happy to receive such gifts. Needless to say the young Saxons were delighted with the surprise and lost any immediate interest in their father's return, falling to studying and comparing their new toys.

"This year has been one of the happiest I have known," Eadgyd told him, her face radiant with delight. "You are such a good man."

"And for you, the best of women, I have another trinket!" he produced the silver and amber necklace from the same bag that had carried the toy horses.

"For me?" Her eyes widened as she took the jewel from him, not noticing that he was watching every move on her face. "It is beautiful."

"So are you," he told her.

With an arm around her waist Hereric steered Eadgyd through the doorway of their house where, as soon as he was sure that they were beyond prying eyes, he lifted her from the floor and kissed her as he had been longing to do since arriving back in the city.

"The children should see you," Eadgyd suggested.

"Let the children play," he told her with a smile, "they have their game, we have ours!"

Sigbert was older and had served longer as a huscarl than Hereric, as a result his family was not surprisingly larger. He had four boys, the eldest aged thirteen, and two girls. His wife Hilda was a strong woman who was marked by both time and life but in his eyes there was none other to compare with her.

Their house was quite large as he had bought the property next to it and knocked an internal doorway through. In his travels he had seen such adjustments made by families who were prosperous, a quick and relatively cheap way to enlarge a home.

They did not depend entirely upon his pay and rewards from the eorls, however. Hilda was a woman of independent character and ran a modestly successful clothes selling business from one half of their house, catering to the theign-worthy rather than ceorls. She dealt in dresses, tunics, shirts and cloaks made from much finer wools and linens than the majority of the peasant classes could afford to buy. Richer theigns were less likely to wear their clothes for as long as a ceorl and, therefore, more inclined to buy frequently and at a greater price. If there was one truth of the Saxon world it was that those who were prosperous liked to show their good fortune to the world and quality clothing was always an excellent way to mark the higher social classes out from the lower.

The family home was well appointed with furniture, decorative hangings, pieces of intricate Saxon artwork, and the best tableware that they could afford. All of the family wore the finest clothes of course; they had easy access to them at a reasonable price. Like many families who enjoyed a higher social station they employed servants but Hilda would have nothing to do with the use of theow. She insisted that only free-folk had the spirit to work hard and work well, which they certainly did under her direction. Sigbert had also concluded that she deemed slavery as immoral, being something of a pious woman.

Their eldest son, Oswy, and daughter, Eabae, were working today with their mother in the shop. It was seen as a practical education and as Sigbert spent so much time away following the eorls he had little say in the matter. There was some discussion between Sigbert and Hilda concerning Oswy's future, however, whether he should follow in his father's footsteps and become a huscarl or not, but nothing was decided as yet. Hilda maintained that a successful owner of a business could make more than a huscarl without hazarding his life or having to spend long spells away from hearth and home at the whim of his lord.

As he grew older Sigbert found himself beginning to appreciate her point. The world turns, as the popular saying went. England was no longer a collection of petty kingdoms in which each king attracted stout warriors to his hall with the promise of ring-giving to those who acquitted themselves well against his enemies. One king ruled all and the eoldermen ruled their lands at his sufferance. It was true that Vikings and outlaws still raided settlements throughout the land, but it was noted that such incursions were caused by war-bands of smaller numbers these days. The opportunity for violent encounters appeared to be diminishing and with it went also the opportunity to earn the gold once given more often by the generous lord's hand. Eorls of the stature of Aelfgar of Mercia or Godwin of Wessex were hard to find these days and the time of adventure was surely slipping into the mists of the past along with the likes of those noble lords. The world was becoming more civilised.

"Husband!" Hilda smiled warmly at him as he came into her view. She confidently left the customers to be dealt with by her children. Together they embraced appropriately for being in the street, but warmly nonetheless.

"It always gladdens my heart to make this journey down our street and see thee busy," he told her with genuine affection.

"And it warms mine to see thee able to make the walk with no wounds upon you again," she returned. "How long do you stay this time?"

"For the season, according to Eorl Morcar, he likes York well enough to spend a winter before a warm fire within these embracing walls."

She smiled at his news just as he knew that she would.

"The children will be glad of it and I will be glad not to go to church without my man anymore. All are safe and sound then?"

"Aye, we have not spent much time in fighting. The eorls journeyed around Northumbria, doing what they must to govern the eorldom as the king commands, but there was little to employ the likes of us other than as the eoldermen's companions. That reminds me, I wonder where Coenred has hidden himself, he came to York before us and I had thought that he would be present to meet the eorls?"

"Leave off your talk of eorls and the likes of your companions man, I am here now and I will command the whole of your attention or you'll feel the heavy end of my ladle!"

Hilda threatened him with a frown that quickly gave way to a smile and a kiss.

"TO THE SOUTH!"

Edwin, Eorl of Mercia, spilt his ale as he slammed the bronze cup down hard onto the wooden table top. His voice tore through the hall like a thunderbolt leaving behind it only the echoes of his words.

"The Vikings were at Scarborough, to the east," his shoulder length hair, free of either a golden circlet or woven braid, flowed around his angry face, making him look even wilder.

How little like his father he is, Coenred thought.

They had met as arranged in Theign Aethelwine's great mead hall in York. It had of course been the reason for Coenred and Eanfrid coming to the city, to alert the high-theign to the impending arrival of the eoldermen, but now the meeting had taken on the aspect of a council of war. As expected Aethelwine had not been impressed by the news on his eventual return from hunting but he knew that there was little that he could do about it other than to mutter into his beer. Morcar was his lord just as Tostig Godwinson had been before him and he preferred neither one over the other. Although appointed by the king to rule York in his name his lofty station still fell beneath the authority of the Eorl of Northumbria.

Almost on the heels of the theign had come riders from Holderness alerting them to the presence of the Vikings on the River Humber and heading westwards. At that news Coenred had known immediately that his plan to withdraw his service could not yet be achieved. As he had suspected Scarborough had not been the Vikings initial target; they were indeed coming for York.

"So said the fisher-folk," confirmed Coenred.

His left-hand curled around the pommel of his sword. He had known that this would not be easy. The young eorls were given to flights of passion when messengers delivered news that would not be a joy to hear. Hardened by the real blows of combat Coenred had made it his duty to intercede on the messengers behalf because the boys, and they really were little more than boys despite their station, still needed educating in the ways of the court of a Saxon lord. He cared little for their railings and feared them as men not at all.

"But news now comes from Holderness to the southeast; they sail up the Humber and must be heading for the River Ouse. If they turn up that course it will bring them to Riccall, to the south."

The gloom within the building had been pushed back by the placement of many more lamps around the hall, revealing the boarded walls and the decorative hangings that adorned them. The hearth was better fuelled and this helped to change the atmosphere to that of a much more welcoming meeting place. Servants of the noble theign flitted about in the background, keen to go unnoticed but equally keen not to miss a service when one was required by any of the lords present. To be otherwise would certainly attract their lord's anger as it would reflect badly upon him in the company of the eoldermen.

Coenred had commanded his new retainer Edwin son of Octa to watch, learn and assist Aethelwine's people as part of his training. The young Saxon had returned as good as his word with new clothes, scrubbed hands and face, and even some coins that had gone unspent. Of course he was clever enough to know that Coenred's warning about the city watch had not been an afterthought, but the manner of his return and his apparent willingness to work in the hall made Coenred wonder if the crossing of their paths had indeed been a piece of good fortune for both of them.

Mayhap the work of wyrd again?

"We know where Riccall lies man," Morcar interjected with an arrogant tone and a dismissve hand gesture.

Coenred glared at the younger brother but bit his tongue. If it were not for the service he had begun with their father Eorl Aelfgar he might well have left these cubs for greater rewards with the likes of the Godwins. To talk in that manner to a seasoned huscarl in front of others, theigns, servants and slaves, was unacceptable behaviour, even from a young nobleman.

Aethelwine himself sat nearby, attentive but not presuming to intrude on the conversation. The muted light caught the thick circlet of gold that held his still rich mane of hair in check. A gold chain was suspended about his neck from which hung a large golden disc, exquisitely decorated with circles, each with a raised point of gold at the centre, and a large ruby fixed like the boss on a shield. Gold rings adorned his fingers too. He was a man of wealth and, in the absence of the eoldermen, the most powerful person in the city. He had no love for Eorl Morcar, however, who had a bad habit of over using the theigns' hospitality, but that was not a great bone of contention between them. Aethelwine was a man and a leader of men in his own right; he did not take kindly to being commanded by a boy of seventeen summers even if boys became men in the eyes of the world at fifteen.

"Let peace reign," Edwin interrupted quickly, a more thoughtful look upon his face. As the older of the two by three years he had more experience and knew all too well how close his brother had come to provoking a situation that no one but the enemy would profit by. "This news alarmed us, as I am sure you knew it would good Coenred, but let it not break us apart. Indeed, this turn of events may prove to our advantage."

"How so brother?" Morcar, as always, was quick to defer to his elder brother. Mayhap he also saw a chance to deflect the wrath of Coenred by not allowing him a moment to speak.

"They are heading for York and we are already here with our power. If this news is true then they can only achieve their ambition, the taking of York itself, by attacking from Fulford Gate," Edwin explained.

"Aye, that would be the lay of it," Coenred agreed, wondering what had possessed the young eorl's mind. He used the moment to breathe more deeply and assert his self-discipline. Certainly, he had little liking for young Morcar but Edwin could act more mature when the thought possessed him.

"King Hardrada would hardly have come with a raiding party either," Edwin continued.

"Nay, the fisher-folk numbered his fleet in the hundreds." Coenred agreed. "Although normally their estimate should not be relied upon too greatly, they are apt to exaggerate the number of the enemy so as not to lose face themselves. The other messengers, however, have given a similar number to the sails that they saw on the Humber. I expect further confirmation if and when they turn into the Ouse which will bring them to the city's southern gate."

"We have the power to match them," asserted Morcar.

"Mayhap brother, but do we have the wit?" Edwin rose and began to pace with a nervous energy. "Hardrada is a great war-chief. There are tales of him fighting many battles all over the world; how many are true Coenred?"

"Enough to trouble us, My Lord. I would not weigh this threat lightly." Unconsciously the warrior's hand drifted to Mildryth's scramseax that he had pushed into his belt. "There are those who call him the 'War Wolf', so many times and so cunningly has he fought; and so hungrily does he go to battle."

"Hunger draws the wolf from the woods, as they say," Edwin commented, his eyes gleaming with a nervous energy, "but what if we out-foxed him?"

"How so?"

Morcar and Coenred unexpectedly asked the same question simultaneously. Coenred kept his eyes on Edwin, the man he acknowledged as his lord and to whom he had renewed his oath as a huscarl when the boy's father had died. Morcar had glanced at the warrior unconsciously when he realised the coincidence but immediately wished that he had not. There was something in Coenred's refusal to look him in the eye that irked the young nobleman. Always it was Edwin to whom he deferred, even here in Morcar's own earldom where he was the principal lord. It seemed to Morcar that his brother also deferred more readily to the huscarl than he felt comfortable in doing so himself. Ever was Morcar conscious of the fact that he was an eolderman and this Coenred, although a hearth companion, was still a servant to them both.

Why does not Edwin demonstrate who are the masters here and who the servant? Morcar asked of himself.

"We invite him to battle on land of our choosing," Edwin revealed the thought that was uppermost in his mind.

"My Lord," Coenred interjected, surprised by Edwin's words, "Hardrada is not to be toyed with. He is a seasoned warrior and there's naught that thy can think upon with regard to battle that the Viking has not encountered upon the field before."

"You would have us cower behind the walls of York and await Harold's coming?" suggested Edwin with a note of scorn.

"If he comes at all," added Morcar. "The Ouse is not the only river to flow into the Humber; the Norseman's intent may take him away from York yet."

"Oh I don't doubt that he comes for York," Edwin told his younger brother. "If he wants to take Northumbria then he must come here and capture the city. Mercia is too far off for him to consider. No, this is the place where he will strike but he will not find us hiding behind Roman walls in fear of his presence."

"'Tis no cowardice to take shelter in a burh," Coenred replied. "King Alfred commanded such once before and the Vikings spilt their blood before the walls of Saxon strongholds over the whole of England. The walls of York are strong; the fyrd would be well protected. It is wise counsel to follow the practices of our forefathers against an enemy that was as much theirs then as he is ours today, especially as we do not have the number of warriors needed to fight a pitched battle."

"We have our power," Edwin insisted. "We have huscarls of our own as well as fyrdmen."

"Mayhap one thousand huscarls are at hand," Coenred conceded.

"And the fyrd," Morcar repeated as if to gain the attention of the other two, "some three thousand in the counting!"

"They may not be trustworthy," Coenred retorted. "Many are descended from Vikings come here under the rule of King Knut. They may have living cousins amongst Hardrada's horde. They may turn on us, especially if the battle does not go well."

"You are overcautious," Edwin insisted. "This is no whim Coenred, I have been thinking on this very event since we passed through York on our way to Ripon. I had hoped that an enemy would approach us from the south because I have walked the ground at Fulford Gate and there is a point there where even a poorer power than ours might hold a greater one than we face."

Coenred said nothing but he did not like the feeling in his gut. His instincts as a warrior told him to bar the gates, man the walls, and let the Vikings crash against them and break their heads. The handle of the scramseax felt reassuring in his right hand. He knew that Eorl Edwin could not bring himself to accept such a position, however, even if it were the best counsel, because of his own pride and his insatiable desire to match the Godwins. That family had a reputation in war second to none in the whole of England and these young eorls were over-keen to match it at the very least.

Edwin envied Harold, that much was plain to see, and this was both the source of his inspiration and his dislike for the Godwins. He appreciated the former Eorl of Wessex's achievements and needed to emulate them, but he lacked the Godwins' rich lands and the power that came with them. The recent marriage of Edwin and Morcar's sister Ealdgyth to King Harold had not built the bridges between the two families in the way that the latter might have hoped. The rivalry of the two families continued and the two young noblemen saw success in the field of war as a necessity to gaining the upper hand over the Godwins. Tostig had cheated them at Grim's By but now it seemed that Hardrada had given them an even greater opportunity to win glory.

What renown awaited the warrior eolderman who bested the greatest living Viking on the field of battle? He would be the man who tamed the War Wolf!

If Edwin could defeat Hardrada's army before the walls of York then he would indeed become a man of note, but vanity and aspiration were poor reasons, dangerous reasons even, for drawing a sword against a Viking.

"I think I know the place you refer to My Lord, but still I like it not." Coenred paced anxiously.

Every instinct cultivated by his warrior training was crying out to him right now. He was not a greatly religious man and barely acknowledged the church services and festivals that had become a part of modern life. He did this not out of disdain, nor out of an acknowledgement of the old pagan gods, he just did not feel the need to be a part of that aspect of the Saxon world. One thing he did admire about the clergy, however, was their education, their ability to both read and write, and that he lacked in any depth. He had often taken the time to talk to a priest when the occasion arose, not about spiritual matters, rather about what they knew of the old Roman knowledge, kept alive in the Latin of the popes. The Romans had known, like many fighters both before and after them, that the victorious general knew when to fight and, mayhap more importantly, when not to fight.

How can I teach Edwin the wisdom of this idea?

"Mayhap that is why, despite your strong sword arm, you are still a servant and I your master?" Edwin noted with a raised chin and a disdainful look. Morcar flashed a look of approval at his brother then turned a countenance of disdain upon their captain of huscarls.

Coenred showed no reaction, he was too well disciplined for that, but the words stung indeed. The boys' father had died when they were too young to learn the real lessons of leadership; they thought it came with their inherited titles as a privilege. Mayhap they would have learned otherwise if their father had lived to command it of them, but clearly they were loath to be taught by one they now saw as beneath them.

"Learn to obey before you command," Coenred said quietly. The knuckles of his right hand turned white as he gripped the carved handle of Mildryth's scramseax, it was the only visible signal of the rage that he held in check.

"What was that?" Morcar pounced as if he had been waiting for Coenred to say something objectionable.

"A saying given to me by a learned man, it comes from the ancient times, before Rome was strong I believe." Coenred turned and stared into the fire burning in the hearth but he did not see the flames dancing there, only a reflection of his own anger and frustration.

"Impudence!" Morcar spat.

"Hush brother," Edwin told him. ""Learn to obey before you command". I think I see the wisdom of those words Coenred. Come," he rose from his seat and approached the huscarl, "in the excitement of the council we have let our passions get the better of us. I am still minded to fight the War Wolf, but I will take your counsel as to when and where we stand. Will you not walk with me at Fulford Gate and study the lay of the land as my Captain of Huscarls?"

"Aye, My Lord," Coenred responded with a voice that was in ratio as loud as his misgivings were great.

"Good. We need you my trusty Saxon. We need your knowledge of war. In this matter I will be commanded by you and will obey your instructions, but we will meet Hardrada in the field," Edwin insisted. He clapped Coenred on the shoulder in a friendly fashion. "Early tomorrow we shall ride to Fulford Gate and I will show you the land of which I speak."

With that the young eorl turned away to find a flask of wine on one of the nearby tables. Coenred, knowing when he had been dismissed, ambled aimlessly lost in his own thoughts until he was halted by rough words spoken quietly.

"They will be the death of the likes of us."

He looked at the speaker and met the eye of High-Theign Aethelwine who sat comfortably with his back to a trestle table and his elbows resting on the wooden top, at ease within his own hall.

"My Lord, I thank you for your hospitality," Coenred responded in an uncommitted manner.

"Ah, Coenred, you are a man and all can see that, why do you waste your quality with boys such as these?" The theign spoke softly still, but nodded in the direction of the eorls so as not to be mistaken.

"Such words are ill-becoming," Coenred chided him, "besides, I respect their rank if not their character."

Aethelwine laughed loudly. The two eorls had occupied a table together with some of their retainers, of like age and manner, and spared the two older Saxons barely a glance.

"You are learning some wisdom then, it is true," Aethelwine asserted, "for such as I think in that manner and am I not a wealthy man? Gotten through my wiles I might tell you." He grinned knowingly but then adopted a more serious countenance. "So much greatness is gone from this middle-earth that whelps may wear a badge of high office and command the lives of real men."

"Careful, My Lord, I am in their service whether I like it or not, and I am an honourable man," Coenred warned him. In part he agreed with the theign but this left him feeling uncomfortable because his sense of loyalty also brought him to the defence of Eorl Aelfgar's sons.

"I said as much to Lady Mildryth," the theign smiled meaningfully, "and I see you carry her token." Coenred felt his face aflame in an instant but his tongue was too dry to retort. The theign laughed again. "Easy man, I jest not at your expense. Mildryth is ever welcome in my hall and I ask nothing of her, but she undertakes to do a service becoming of her station by her own mind and her own sense of duty. Such is the way of women, especially, mayhap, one of such quality."

"I am not the man for her," Coenred eventually blurted out.

"So think you but what does it matter? If Edwin stands at Fulford Gate you will stand with him and verily there's a good chance that neither of you will sup under my hall's roof again."

"Not if I have my way," Coenred asserted. "I have fought the Viking before, and won."

"But then you had an eorl who would listen to counsel and valued the lives of his men above any glory that might be won. Listen my friend, you are too good a warrior to be cast upon the spears of Old Hardrada, so I say to you, fight with your wit, not with your sword."

"Would you drink to that?"

"I'd drink to most things, but most of all I'd drink to the safe return of those I value. None of my retainers will be wasted in this stand at Fulford Gate," he insisted and saw the face of Coenred darken. "Oh, don't worry, I'll be there and I'll take my place in the shield-wall, but I won't throw mine or my men's lives away to feed the aspiring glory of your young eorls! I am not the seasoned warrior you are but I know when it is good to fight and good to withdraw. As long as there is a hope of victory me and mine will stand firm with every Saxon on the field, but if these two would-be heroes act out of turn don't blame me for returning to York before the day is done. There are many here who depend on me for their lives and their safety and I will not desert them."

He filled two beakers with beer as he talked and passed one to the huscarl.

"So, will ye drink with me?"

"Aye, I'll drink to thy strong arm and to living another day, what more can we warriors ask?" Coenred replied.

The Abbey at Waltham

"You should not have come," Harold Godwinson repeated himself again. "Better that you had stayed in London as I had wished."

He spoke kindly but in truth he felt exasperated. In part he had submitted to his own selfishness in coming to Waltham Abbey, in escaping to some degree the endless activity of the court.

Cannot a king indulge himself every once in awhile?

"You cannot ask that of me which you refuse to bestow upon yourself," Ealdgyth of Mercia replied, "you should not have come either, your illness were better treated in London." Unconsciously her hand stroked her distended abdomen. Harold followed the movement with his eyes.

Another son mayhap?

It did not particularly matter to him. He had spent some twenty years with Ealdgyth Swannesha and she had given him six children. At the age of forty-four another child was of no great matter but he would care for it all the same, very much aware that the child's birth cemented a marriage that had at first been prompted by purely political considerations. The baby would create a bond between him and Ealdgyth of Mercia too, and that was something that he had come to desire.

"I have good reason to be at Waltham," he told her.

"You forget yourself, we have been married only eight months and as renowned a man as you are for your part I do not know your whole family history." She refused to back down or allow him to use her condition as a reason for their separation. Ealdgyth was astute enough to know the prompting behind her marriage, but that did not stop her from determining to make their relationship work on a more personal level.

Her beauty was much admired and she had experience of the world that came with being the daughter of an eorl. This was also her second marriage to a king. She lacked neither the strength nor the craft to use her gifts and being the Queen consort of England was not such an intolerable position to hold.

She too had children from her previous relationship to Gruffydd ap Llywelyn, King of Wales, but they were catered for and it was in gaining the rightful recognition for the child she now carried that she devoted all her energy to. If it were indeed a boy, as the midwives claimed, then she would see him become a king and Harold's agreement on this, in preference over his other children, was necessary.

"Why is Waltham Abbey so important to you? Why would you prefer to convalesce here rather than in the palace at Westminster? Why would you, the king, wish to be without me, your queen?"

Harold sighed, but good naturedly.

"Ealdgyth, it is not you that I wish to be parted from, but for these many months I have dedicated myself to securing the kingdom, preparing to frustrate Guillaume of Normandy, doing all that is demanded of a king. When my illness fell upon me I saw a chance to retire for a few days from all the demands made upon me."

"And is not a wife's place at her husband's side, ever more so when he is ill?"

"At any other time I would say yes but you have your own condition to consider, the child is not long from being born," Harold insisted. It was not just a convenient excuse, he actually did care that she survived this pregnancy. The rooms that she now occupied at the abbey were sparse in comparison to those at Westminster Palace but they had been luxuriously appointed at his command. Her comfort was important to him and her chamber reflected his concern.

"And what better place to be than here, at this abbey that you love so much, with its father in attendance."

Again he sighed, trapped by her reasoning.

"Half-foot doesn't pester me as much."

"You should not call him by that name," Ealdgyth chided, "it is not Christian."

"It is his name," Harold protested, beginning to wonder if he could say anything right by her.

"It is not his given name."

"Mayhap, but he prefers it all the same. If a man as learned as he can go by such a name so lightly why should anyone else care?"

"He was born lame, a thing to be pitied and not made light of," she insisted. Involuntarily her mind conjured up the image of the child she now carried being born with a similar condition. It made her shudder.

"He would not thank thee for that," Harold assured her. "He cannot carry a spear like many of my companions but he is stronger with the word than any of them are with the sword. If he wishes me to call him Half-foot then I will know him by that name, and honour his ability rather than pity his lameness."

"I think that he holds a greater claim over your affection than I? You were ready to enjoy his company over mine here at the abbey."

Harold smiled, realising that Ealdgyth was unaware of how uncomfortable Half-foot found such places as Waltham Abbey. He was a curious man in that for all his education his sympathy, if not his actual beliefs, seemed to lay more with the pagan past than the Christian present.

"Half-foot is a loyal servant to me, and I judge him by his own worth to be a companion of my hearth. I find his ability to read, write and speak Latin and French invaluable to my court, and though I left the court behind me in London I think it wise to keep so useful a courtier close at hand. Without his skills my brothers can do little mischief in my absence."

"So you bring Half-foot and Osfrid, your gesipas, to Waltham because you have need of them in this place you love, but not so your queen?" Ealdgyth had identified some of those whom Harold depended upon so dearly and she was determined to get herself counted in their number.

"You would know why Waltham Abbey is dear to me?" A new direction for this conversation suddenly presented itself to Harold's mind and he decided to explore it.

"I would know why it is so dear to you as to drag you from the court in your infirmity. I would know why you would travel some twenty miles to pray here when King Edward's fine abbey stands but within a few steps of your home?"

He came and sat beside her on the bed, facing her so that he could look into her fair face as he spoke. He even took up her hand in his, a genuine gesture of affection on his part.

She was thirty two years old, a mother of several children, and twice a queen. When he looked into her eyes he saw not just her obvious beauty but a woman of experience and character. He valued these qualities because he knew that they would make her strong at court and a king needed a strong queen; the life of King Edward had proven that. Also, this strength of hers meant that their relationship could be more than just one of political expediency; they could be happy together if they were willing to accept each other as people as well aethelings.

"Have you heard the story of Theign Tovi the Proud?" His voice adopted a more conciliatory tone.

"He who dreamt of finding a black flint crucifix on top of the hill?" The queen responded likewise, knowing that she had made some progress in developing their marriage and that choosing now to indulge him would only further it.

"The same, it is said that he followed his dream and found the Holy Rood out in the wilderness. He loaded the crucifix into a cart and set off to take it home to the village of Montacute but that the oxen would pull the cart in no other direction than to Waltham, some many days travel. Here he came and here it has remained, a holy relic, much venerated by the clergy and often visited by pilgrims."

"Aye, the story of the Holy Rood is known well by one and all, but in Mercia that is all it is; a story."

"In Mercia mayhap, but not here in Essex. Here they tell how Tovi had the church rebuilt to house the stone cross. When I was a boy my father, Eorl Godwin, brought us to Waltham Abbey. I had an infirmity then that came upon me without warning; my limbs would seize and I could not move. During my father's visit, not long after such a seizure, I touched the Holy Rood and my infirmity was lifted from me. I talked of this with none outside of my family but a clergyman here at the abbey. He told me that God visited a healing gift upon the worthy who touched the holy stone. Since that day I have not been visited by the weakness, until a few days ago at least. If being in Waltham cured me once then mayhap it could do so again? If I was worthy of God's touch then, am I not just as worthy now?"

Harold did not mention that there was a longing within him to find such a validation to his most recent actions at least. He had enemies at home as well as abroad who spoke of his opportunism, his scheming, his breaking of holy oaths at the court of the Norman duke. Also, at the behest of Guillaume of Normandy, he had been excommunicated by the pope. If God blessed him now by removing the malady that had descended upon him so recently then that would put Harold's mind at rest.

If God did favours me, despite the pope's interference, then what enemy could stand against the King of England?

For her part she liked him better this way. In this private room without even a servant present he was himself, charming, caring, thoughtful, a husband. Previously she had only ever seen the famed eorl and the warrior, the man of politics who conversed with kings and the captain who led his own king's armies into foreign lands. He had never seemed an attractive man to her in those guises but then they were both the children of nobility and their sense of duty shaped their characters as much as their lives. Like him she had a visage that she presented to the world. In private she was Ealdgyth of Mercia, sister to Edwin and Morcar, wife to Harold of Wessex. The same situation was true of Harold of course, only he seemed to lack the time to indulge his private self with any of his family these days.

"And that is why you have bestowed so much upon this abbey in preference to all others?" She asked, wanting more to prolong the conversation than to discover an obvious answer.

"I find God in this place," he said simply. "It seemed right to rebuild the abbey in stone when I had the means to do so, to protect the existence of the Holy Rood and give thanks for my own deliverance."

"Then if God is here for you in Waltham why shouldn't your unborn child visit it too?" She wondered again if she should tell him that the midwives believed that she was carrying twins.

"For your sake, my queen, I would wait until the child was born and your pregnancy not hazarded by such a journey." Harold looked at her stomach once again. He never referred to the child's sex, he already had sons from his previous marriage and although the clergy did not consider them born in wedlock the eoldermen would not question their legitimacy. In this instance it did not concern him whether it was a boy or a girl; he would welcome it into his family all the same. The child was not intended to be an heir to the throne; it was an expression of the genuine affection that existed between him and Ealdgyth. Although political considerations had motivated their marriage it had proved to be not just for show after the formal church ceremony, they had grown to be fond of each other.

"I was an exile when my father betrothed me to Gruffydd ap Llwellyn, King of Wales; I hazarded many dangers then including your army," she smiled. Ealdgyth spoke as if the risk to herself before the advance of the English army led by her now husband against her late husband had been but a game.

"'Tis a curious wyrd that brings us together Ealdgyth, but I would have offered you my protection then as I would wish you take it now." He told her meaningfully. He reached out and took her hand in his again, enveloping the smaller fingers within his rougher grasp.

"You would not ask me to be less a Queen of England than I was a Queen of Wales," she teased him. "The Welsh might have something to say about their one time queen who stalked the mountains in younger days when Harold of Wessex marched through the valleys, wilfully sitting in Westminster whilst her husband seeks healing in Waltham merely because she is with child."

"And close to her time," he smiled at her. "You forget to mention that important point and the cause of all my concern; you are close to your time."

"I have some weeks left before the baby is due, My Lord, and I think that like you I welcome the quiet of the abbey over the bustle of the court."

"May that peace continue, Guillaume remains bottled up in Normandy with the winds blowing contrary to his design. By the time this little one sees the world mayhap the Norman duke will be forced back home to sulk through winter in his castle," Harold spoke with determination, revealing his hope for the immediate future.

"To return another day in the New Year," Ealdgyth pointed out the obvious flaw in his thinking.

"Guillaume does not act with nought but a free hand, his enemies prescribe his freedom. Duke Conan of Brittany loathes Guillaume and continues a ceaseless war against him. He will use any failure on the duke's part to weaken Norman power and things change in France, they have a new king and new kings always want to prove their strength." He slipped once again into his role as the king.

"Like you have proven yours?" She sensed that this brief moment of intimacy was coming to an end; she knew of course that this was inevitable.

"I have kept the wolf from the door so far, My Lady, within a few weeks I will have shut him out for the whole of the year and then we will have nothing to fear," he answered her confidently.

Tuesday 19th September 1066

Fulford Gate

The warm September sun gave a lie to the landscape as it hung in the west, late in the afternoon. The world looked beautiful in the soft, slow fading light. A heron majestically flapped over the wetland, hunting for a last catch. The approach of evening could be felt as much as seen. The smell of water was in the air, not just from the beck in front of them but to either side too; river water on the right, marshland on the left.

It might work, Coenred thought to himself.

They had ridden out from York, which lay only one and a half miles to the north, as Eorl Edwin had instructed. A little too late, mayhap, to get the clearest view of where it was proposed to hold the battle tomorrow, but light enough for Coenred to understand what it was that Edwin had in mind.

It seemed to the huscarl that he had passed the last three days in just waiting. First, he waited upon the return of High-Theign Aethelwine, then he had waited for the arrival of the eorls, and now he awaited the approach of the enemy.

The noblemen had feasted too well last night and slept most of the waking day so that now, with this most important of business at hand, they reviewed the proposed battlefield in the dying of the light. From the advantage point of being on horseback they looked south with Germany Beck immediately in front of them running west to east. On the left the ground was firm approached across the beck by a narrow ford running north to south. 'Foul Ford' the locals called it.

"What say you?" Eorl Edwin asked. "A good place in which to lay a trap for a wolf, eh?"

Further east stretched the marshland. Viewed from their position it looked like a natural extension of the grassland where Eorl Edwin hoped to offer battle to the Vikings, but an experienced eye could see the telltale signs of the change in the land.

Coenred dismounted and walked over towards the marsh. Due to the warm spell there were no obvious pools of standing water but just beneath the surface the ground was still sodden. He stopped when he head the water squelch beneath his leather shoe and looking down he saw it rise to the surface.

The marsh was punctuated with isolated mounds of trapped sediment that allowed plants better suited to drier areas to still flourish. Goat willow and alder were amongst the larger plants to grow there but there was also an abundance of soft rush grass growing in clusters and giving shelter to birds. Yellow Iris dotted the marsh like a scattering of golden coins. The air was laced with the scent of water mint too. The ground was too soft and wet, unsuited to men in armour or even on horseback. The Vikings could not outflank the Saxons there.

He turned and looked back to the west, to the River Ouse, from which the beck sprang. It was marked by the growth of willow, silver birch and alder trees. Another crossing point was located further towards the river but like the Foul Ford it was narrow and easily defended. The flanks appeared to be protected. The front was made difficult by the shallow beck, a natural but not impassable obstacle. It was a good place to hold against an invader, that Coenred could not dispute.

The problem was that the eorls had a little over one thousand trained warriors, huscarls like himself. The fyrd were not all disciplined warriors, they were trained whenever called to service but dependent on the settlements from whence they were raised for their equipment, which could vary alarmingly in quality. They owed an allegiance to their theigns and were conscripted to military duty as and when required. Some training would - should - have been given to them during their time giving service, but mostly they would only have experience of tilling their land or practising their trades. They could hold a shield-wall. They could fight with spears and when the battle turned their way they would prove as vicious as wolves when an enemy's back was presented to their spear points, but when the battle went against them?

That was the doubt.

Hardrada had a seasoned army, largely Viking warriors, some mercenaries and adventurers no doubt, but few if any of them would have the distractions of a farm or a business to consider running, or a family to protect. They were coming here to seize property, land and women; to build a kingdom for themselves. Their motivation for success was great and they carried little baggage to slow them down. The Saxons had everything to defend and that meant a loss of mobility. The fyrd was raised locally to defend locally and there would be many of Viking descent in their number.

Where would their loyalty lie?

"I say again, is this not a good place to meet the enemy?" Eorl Edwin had dismounted also now and marched over to Coenred in a manner that suggested that he was beginning to become frustrated with his retainers lack of enthusiasm.

"I am spying out the land," Coenred told him and continued walking towards the Rive Ouse

The village of Fulford Gate, or Gate Fulford as some termed it, lay close to the river but behind what would be the right flank of the army. A typical Saxon habitation, a collection of single storey and single roomed houses made from wooden frames with mud and wattle walls. Thatched roofs reached to the ground in many cases, although some of the better off families had adopted the newer style where the roof stopped higher to allow shuttered windows to be placed in the walls. Oxen, pigs, chickens, goats and sheep were farmed here but fish from the river and hunting in the marshland also supplied extra food to be either stored against winter or traded at the market in York. Across the beck, on the wrong side as it would happen tomorrow, stood the village of Water Fulford, almost identical to its larger neighbour of Fulford Gate, except that it sat closer to the river.

"We can hold them here." Eorl Edwin followed after the warrior but kept stopping as if unsure of whether or not he should be going after him. He wanted to speak his mind, however, and as Coenred showed no interest in standing still he was forced to walk quickly along the same trail. A part of Edwin needed to hear Coenrerd approve of his plan although he could not think why this should be so.

For his part the huscarl continued his musings. Their only chance of seizing the initiative was to force the location of the battle upon the enemy, as Eorl Edwin was looking to do now. It was a risky strategy, however, because it meant fighting outside of the protecting walls of York. The courage and support of the people could prove doubtful. Certainly the populations of the two villages here had something to fight for; their homes were not defended by stout walls. They could only expect the Norsemen to burn to the ground everything left unprotected but then these buildings were easy to erect again, they could be replaced, unlike the people themselves or their valuable farm animals.

The people of Northumbria had risen up against the tyranny of Tostig Godwinson previously, however, demonstrating that they had no love for him. They might fight all the harder knowing that he had returned and sided with their enemy of old. A victory for Tostig would inevitably result in retribution. The blood feud was a way of life here even though it profited no one.

"It is a place where an army such as ours might make a stand against an even greater force," Coenred conceded, "but I have misgivings."

"Tell me," Edwin demanded. "I want to understand."

The return of this manner of attentive pupil was refreshing. Coenred turned to face his lord at last.

"This is good ground for the defender, the river to the west and the Dam Lands to the east will protect the flanks. Across the front runs the Germany Beck, a yard deep and three yards wide with steep banks. The ground on this side is firm, to the south soft. There are the two fords but they are narrow and easily defended; the power that holds this ground here, where we stand now, may have the day."

"As I told you," Edwin exulted. "So what troubles you?"

"The front is some six hundred yards wide, from river to marsh, we have about a thousand huscarls; a thousand is not enough."

"This we know, but we do have the fyrdmen," Morcar offered. He had chosen to dismount also and had follwed them over to where they now stood near the beck. "They will be placed with the huscarls; they will form a strong shield-wall."

"We have sent out word to call in all the warriors that owe us allegiance. More huscarls and more theigns will come, yet still thee worry," Edwin observed. A shadow of impatience crossed his face.

"You will draw up in two groups, the largest on the left facing the main threat. The other on the right to resist the Vikings' should they push along the river." He snapped a branch from a nearby bush and then snapped it again, unevenly, so as to represent the supposed disposition of their forces. He held the pieces out before him in two hands, apparently joined. "If one flank moves forward without the other they will lose contact with each other." He moved the larger stick in his left hand as if it were pivoted to the one on the right and yet also moved them slightly apart. "They will risk being severed by an enemy attack at the point where they once joined. If this happens the Viking wins the day."

"Then it will not happen," Edwin insisted. His eyes were at least fixed on the graphic demonstration that Coenred presented to them. He could see the point of weakness that was being illustrated and for the first time a doubt entered his mind but he was determined to resist it.

"I have seen the enemy give way before a defending force when it is a feint. The defenders think the battle won and the foe preparing for flight. They leave the ground they held to fall on their enemy only to find him turning at bay; more fierce than at any other time in the battle. Then it is the defenders' turn to flee. Then is the battle lost."

"It will not happen thus," Edwin insisted again. His voice rose, mayhap more to quell the growing unease he felt inside.

How hard could it be for a shield-wall to stand its ground before the enemy?

"Do you know the art of the warrior before the enemy's shield-wall?" Coenred asked of both the young eorls.

"Do you take us for slaves?" Morcar demanded, his quick anger coming to the fore once again. He was too sensitive to his brother's moods. He had become aware of Edwin's unease and it made him defensive, consequently he failed to appreciate what was being asked of him.

"The warrior looks for a break in the shield-wall, a weak point," Coenred spoke on as if he had not even heard Morcar, "if he cannot see it he looks to make it with spear thrusts and axe hews, but when he does see it he must grasp it quickly, he must push his blade into the softer flesh of men and make the blood flow. This you know."

"As well you know we do," Edwin kept his voice calm whilst Morcar raged silently, "this has always been your teaching."

"When you hold the ground in a place like this, that is not the art of the warrior. The defender stands his ground no matter what. He lets the enemy break upon his wall like the sea upon rocks. When the enemy pulls back, like the surf, the defender does not surge forward but waits like the rock. Only when he sees the enemy's back, when he sees their power lying spent in blood and gore at his feet, only then does he move."

"I understand," Edwin said. His insistence came quickly.

"Do you? Hardrada is a warrior who has fought and won more battles than any other man I know of. Some call him the War Wolf because like that animal he is cunning, steeped in the craft of battle. If there is a weakness to this position that you mean to hold then you can trust him to find it. If he finds it, we are lost."

"Can you not see such a weakness then warrior?" Morcar asked with a hint of disdain.

"I've just shown it to you, if you do not see it for yourselves then we are lost," The huscarl said quietly. "There is one more thing; the land behind us is soft too. It will turn into a mire with the churning of so many feet. If we need to retreat to the city the going will be hard and many will be dragged down. There is a track, some yards wide, down which we just rode. If we must retire then that is the place to do it. The army will present as small a front as possible to the enemy as it moves up the road to York and disciplined soldiers will be able to protect the withdrawal of the men."

"Sound advice," Edwin conceded, "but it is not we who shall be withdrawing. We'll stain the ground red with Viking blood!"

"I would like this place better if our route to safety were more suited to an army," Coenred commented, "and that we had a thousand more huscarls."

He glanced up at the sky. The sun was turning red as the evening began. The cloud was light but enough to be stained by the dying rays. The shadows grew long over the ground.

"It is time to return to York," Edwin declared. He returned to his horse and vaulted back into the saddle with the vigour and agility of youth. "What time shall we muster the men?"

"At first light," Coenred responded. "We have no news of where the Vikings are or where they will land. If you mean to fight this battle here at Fulford Gate then we must have the men in place because Hardrada will not grant you the time to do it after he arrives."

"So be it. We'll feast tonight in York and be back here at first light on the morrow. Come; let's return to Aethelwine's fabled hall." He turned his horse for York and set off at the gallop with Morcar and their retainers following. Coenred watched them go but did not move. A murder of crows descended noisily into the trees along the riverbank, cawing and thrashing the branches with their wings. It was not difficult to imagine that they came so as to be close at hand for the feast that the battle would surely bring them.

Coenred's own retainer, Edwin, waited until the eorls were at least out of earshot before dismounting from the pack horse and approaching his master with both horses in tow.

"I have never been in a battle," he said simply, "I have no harness."

"You'll need none," Coenred told him. He looked at the young man and saw the anxiety in his face. For some reason it touched him. "There will be no time to fit you out with a battle harness and even less time for me to train you in the use of weapons. You will stay in York tomorrow after I have made ready, there's a service you can do for me there."

"I am not a coward!" Edwin insisted with some passion.

"There's no cowardice in avoiding a fight that you are not prepared for," Coenred told him, "neither does obeying his master's commands make the servant a coward. Tomorrow I will say to this or that man go to this place and do this thing for me and whether I stand him in the front line or at the rear of the army all will know that it does not signify the measure of his courage. He will do it as a thing that must be done and as a service to me."

"I do not want you to think me a coward," Edwin replied looking down at his new leather shoes.

"I think that you will have time to prove your courage to me yet Edwin. Besides, the service I will ask of you tomorrow will mean more to me than to have you stand here lacking arms and armour on this field. I have misgivings about this fight and there are things important to me that your presence in York might make safe."

"Then if it is understood between us I will happily do your bidding," Edwin insisted.

"Then if you understand that I value the lives of men, whatever their rank, and will not use them so that they may seem brave, I will command this duty of you." Coenred took his horse's reins from Edwin's hand and mounted quickly. "Come now, to York before we are missed. You will tend Theign Aethelwine a service again tonight and not get drunk in carrying out this duty, unlike many a lord is likely to do."

The River Ouse

The Viking fleet moved slowly up the River Ouse as the light faded in the west. Each ship carried a burning torch at the stern so that those behind could mark their place on the water. The several hundred vessels, warships and supply ships, were stretched out in a long line so that in the growing gloom it looked as if a giant snake of fire was making its way along the surface of the water. Seen in the dark it would not be too far a stretch of the imagination for one to believe that Midgard's Worm, the World Serpent, had released its tail from its mouth, rose from the ocean, and now looked to mark the end of the world as the well known prophecy said it would.

In truth it was only the ships of men, however. The dragon's head that led the way was carved from wood, as was the tail. The oars dipped and rose, dipped and rose, pushing the fleet further and further into the territory of the enemy, but they moved slowly because it was a tidal river marked by several pronounced bends that had to be worked with some skill. With the setting sun safe navigation became more and more difficult.

Tostig Godwinson stood in the stern of his ship and absently watched the slow progress of the fleet. Hardrada's Long Serpent was out near the front of course, closely following the smaller snekkes but staying to the mid-channel due to her large size. Some of the tighter bends had posed a problem to her but the skill of the Vikings had seen the ship rowed past any possible obstacles without mishap.

The weather was mild and the wind had dropped as it usually did on warm September evenings. The sails were furled and they depended entirely upon the strength of the oarsmen now. They operated in shifts so that no one became overtired; it was not forgotten that there would be a city to take on the morrow. There was a rhythm to their movement that was almost hypnotic, especially when accompanied by the gentle slap of the water against the ship's hull. Birds darted through the growing gloom chasing insects, one last meal before the night closed in.

Occasionally they saw lights off in the distance, indications of Saxon settlements. The people would be retiring indoors now, settling down to an evening meal accompanied with beer or fruit wine. Mayhap they would tell stories or sing songs to one another as they rested from the chores of the day. Larger villages might even enjoy a visit from a travelling scop bringing news of the outside world, songs no one had heard before and poems that everyone knew well. Of course the news of the Viking fleet might also be on the lips of the people already.

Did they know how close the Norsemen were right now?

Would they shutter their homes and cower in the dark praying for the terror to pass them by?

Would their sleep be haunted by the images of Vikings descending upon them in a bloodlust with fire and steel?

Tostig neither knew nor cared. His mind dwelled on York and what its capture would mean. If Harold was still in the south, which he did not doubt, then the fall of York would demand a response. He would have to push north but that would leave the southern coast undefended and open to Guillaume, almost tempting him to try a landing.

How long would it take Harold and his army to reach York?

A week would be a quick march. He would probably raise the local fyrd and have them watch for the Normans in his absence. That would take time to organise so it would have to be left in the hands of a trusted lieutenant, no doubt one of their younger brothers. Ten days then. If York fell tomorrow, a thing only to be dreamed of if the eorls of the north were not present to defend the walls, then Harold could be expected at the gates by the end of the month; that was plenty of time for them to consolidate their success in Northumbria. Hardrada would declare himself King and Tostig would become an eorl again, although he looked to take the family lands of Wessex when all was done and settled. They would raise fresh forces from amongst the peoples of the north, those of Viking descent who might be expected to sympathise with a king of their own blood and those Saxons looking to improve their lot at the expense of brother Harold's supporters. If they could raise enough extra men then it was possible that they could trap Harold between two armies, one commanded by Hardrada, one by himself. If only all of Tostig's enemies could witness the vengeance that he would wreck upon his brother. If only he was not alone on this adventure.

A sudden pang of loneliness interrupted his thoughts.

Judith.

He thought about his wife and their family residing at the court of Count Baldwin of Flanders; her half-brother. It was not such a hard life for them since fleeing Northumbria and enduring exile. The Count was a gracious man. He had even given Tostig ships and men to help mount his return to England. It was a pity that Judith's status as aunt to Matilda of Flanders, the wife of Guillaume of Normandy, had not resulted in any advantage when Tostig had visited the duke's court only a few months previously. All of Tostig's skills in diplomacy, learnt and practiced at the court of King Edward, and also that of King Malcolm of Scotland, had come to nothing before the duke. It mattered not; he had a king for an ally now.

Judith was a pious woman, however, and she had been very taken with King Edward; religion was an obsession that they shared. Her devotion rendered her submissive before authority, though. Judith had argued that they should accept the decree of exile from such a virtuous monarch as Edward and instead of making war on Harold that he, Tostig, should make the most of the honour and position as the governor of Saint-Omer that her half-brother had conferred upon him.

From an eorl to a governor!

How could he, a son of the fabled Eorl Godwin, be expected to accept such a fall from grace without lifting a sword in the defence of his own honour?

Taking Judith to wife had been a good move, or so it seemed, but she lacked the political insight of either her niece Matilda, who supported Guillaume fully, or even his own sister Edith who had been such an able queen to King Edward. Judith had given him two young children, although he had more by other women. The two legitimate children gave another impetus to Tostig's desire for revenge; he did not want them growing up dependent upon the favour of a foreign count for their success in this world. Tostig would bequeath them a worthy legacy by taking back that which was his own in England or die trying.

Whichever wyrd prescribed.

Stretching languidly Tostig sat down on the timbers of the deck. Like the crew he would sleep here tonight, rocked into slumber by the movement of the ship, at least those who were not required at the oars, and then tomorrow; tomorrow he would seize his destiny with both hands. If only brother Harold were there to see it!

King Harald Hardrada sat comfortably on a thick ox hide spread over the timbers of his ship. He was joined by his son Prince Olaf and the Jarls of Orkney; Paul and Erlend Thorfinnsson. Their youth reminded him of his own early vigour in the days when he was free to travel the world without any constraint other than which direction the wind blew.

The jarls had seen a little more than twenty summers each. Their father, Thorfinn Sigurdsson was known as Thorfinn the Mighty. That name was rightly earned too. He had ruled over Orkney for five and seventy years and had added nine Scottish earldoms to his control. In the west this made the young jarls men of note, a position reflected by their ability to bring a sizeable number of men and ships to add to the expedition. Of course the jarls had their own ambitions too; Hardrada had two eligible daughters to his first wife, Elsif of Kiev. Maria and Ingegerd would make fine alliances for the Jarls of Orkney but Hardrada had other plans for them, not that it hurt his most pressing concern to allow the young jarls to think otherwise, however.

At sixteen Prince Olaf Kyrre was very much the junior but he was already tall for his age and well proportioned. The fact that many at court commented on the prince's good looks, a fresh face framed by blond hair, secretly pleased Hardrada. He looked even fairer sat next to the jarls who had inherited their father's black hair and, unfortunately, a degree of his infamous harsh looks. He was not so satisfied with the boy's taciturn disposition, however. A leader of men who was reluctant to speak was not going to achieve great things in this life. The Jarls of Orkney were much more effusive, expressing more of the character that Hardrada liked to see in a Norseman. He hoped that by mixing the young men, along with some ale, he might influence the prince's disposition to be a little more like that which he considered proper for a future king.

"Your ships do you proud," Hardrada complimented the jarls, "the men who crew them are deserving of their Viking heritage."

"Thank you, My Lord," Paul replied with a smile, "amongst our islands a good ship is a necessity."

"Along with a good crew," Erlend added. "Our father would not have reached so far without the men who put the steel in his word."

"Thorfinn Sigurdsson was indeed a man worthy of remembrance." Hardrada nodded. "He fought long and hard with Rognvald Brusason for control of the islands and even though my nephew, Magnus Olafsson, once King of Norway and on whose throne I now sit, swore vengeance on your father I saw things differently. Thorfinn Sigurdsson was a man after my own heart and Orkney has ever been a friend at my court. He will be written into the sagas and so will you be when we have defeated the Saxons' power. For every warrior glory awaits upon the battlefield and I will bring you there, to the place where your forefathers can judge your merit before the spears of our enemy. They will sing songs in the mead halls across all the lands where I am known after what we will have done here in England."

"That will include a great many halls indeed," Paul flattered the king.

"What say you Olaf?" The King prompted his quiet son.

"That I will watch and learn as I follow where you lead," he replied with a little smile, hidden by the cup that he raised immediately to his lips. The drink was beginning to take its effect upon him and he felt himself relaxing more with the company. "Tell us how you mean to take Jorvik father?"

"How to take a city, eh?" Hardrada put on a show of contemplation, staring past their heads and stroking his beard. "There are many ways to take a city; it all depends upon the defences and the quality of the men manning the walls."

"You expect them to stay behind their walls then?" Erlend asked with genuine interest.

"Lord Tostig Godwinson says as much and he is the man to know such things. He was the Eorl of Northumbria almost a year ago, although the people liked his rule but little and cast him from his high station by a popular revolt. The Saxons know how to pursue a blood feud and they will not take kindly to his return. That matters little, however in regard to the subject that you have raised. How to take a walled city? Anyone of good sense would do what the Saxons have always done when we trod across their land; bar the gates and hurl javelins from the walls."

"You speak as if this is to our advantage," Olaf commented and the king smiled.

"It can well be. The truth is that people hidden behind walls are trapped. They hide there because they are a feared of the danger without. They are a feared of us. The trick is to make that fear grow and let it eat them from within. A terror imagined is often greater than the terror realised, and so we stoke their fear with the flames of our ferocity in war. I offer them with one hand survival through surrender, and the loss of whatever treasure they may own, and with the other death by fire and spear, and again the loss of whatever treasure they may own. If they spurn the first offer then they will know that I will give them no quarter."

"Must it be so ruthless?" Olaf asked. Hardrada looked at him as if he neither understood the question nor the speaker.

"Ruthless? It is war boy."

"Nevertheless, they are people; people that you hope to rule over," Olaf persisted.

"A people pressed too hard can prove most belligerent, as Tostig Godwinson found out," Paul agreed.

"And what if the people of Jorvik prove more resilient to the fear you would have us put in their hearts; they are Saxons after all and known for their stubbornness?" Erlend added.

"As I said, there are more ways to take a city than one." The king adjusted himself to a more comfortable position and Olaf knew instinctively that he was going to regale them with an often told tale of one his exploits. They waited patiently while the Viking chief ruminated on which story to tell them. "When I was in the service of the Emperor of Byzantium I was commanded to take a city with walls so great that no siege engine could hope to bring them down. The people within the city were supremely confident that they could resist us, and with good reason, so they feared us not at all when once their gates were shut. My mind recalled the tale of the Greeks before the great city of Troy, a tale often told to us when we were in those parts, and I schemed to have myself taken inside the city gates."

"You would not fool them with a great wooden horse, My Lord," Paul declared, mayhap knowing that indulging the king in retelling this tale guaranteed his good humour.

"Indeed, but with a dead body I stood a chance. The people were devout followers of Jesus Christ so I had myself laid out in an open coffin, dressed for death and burial in my finest armour. My good friend Eystein Orre went before the walls of the city with me in the coffin and appealed to the city-folk to allow me to be buried in hallowed Christian ground; then he would lead the soldiers away and return in peace to Byzantium."

"The people agreed?" Olaf prompted the story along from familiarity but with a good humour.

"That they did. They flung open their gates and the priests came out to conduct my funeral procession to the graveyard within their great walls. I lay with my sword upon my breast and my guard of honour carried only their spears, but it was enough. Before we had gone too far from the gates Eystein stopped and began a speech of thanks to the gentle townsfolk. When they became impatient with him I jumped from the coffin, sword in hand, and sealed their doom. My guard secured the gates and the rest of our men poured into the city and we took whatever we wanted. When strength of arms fails always turn to craft."

Hardrada took a great draught from his cup as if telling the famous story had given him an equally great thirst. The young men followed his example and a servant refilled their cups without waiting to be asked.

"But you let the townspeople live?" Olaf said.

"Yes. It is not good policy to kill all of those on whom you depend for robbing and pillaging, or, if in your own country, to tax and to rule," he paused a moment in thought. "In truth Prince Olaf has a point about being ruthless. I want to capture Jorvik, not raise it to the ground. Against their warriors I will be merciless because then they will fear me and know that I am stronger than they are. Against the townsfolk I will be less harsh."

"Less harsh than Tostig Godwinson?" Erlend inquired. The king shrugged.

"I know not to what extent he pressed those who owed him loyalty but I do know that a king must strike a balance. It is good that his subjects fear him to a degree, but it is also good that they know he is strong enough in mind and body to defend them against their enemies on the borders. The king has an obligation too, and tipping the balance too far one way will, as Tostig Godwinson found out even as an eorl, see the fall of any crown or circlet of gold."

The City of York

The evening before the battle was spent inevitably in the hall of High-Theign Aethelwine. The young eorls demanded a feast for the fighting Saxons who were to defend York from the threat of Hardrada and his horde. The beer and wine flowed and meat and bread were consumed in great quantities, most of it from the high-theign's own supply and it would probably go unpaid for. Serving girls wended their way through the ranks of men, some warriors, some dreaming of being such, many fooling themselves that they already were. The men letched and leered, as was their wont at such times, and many a couple would awaken tomorrow with only a dim memory of the drunken pleasure that had passed between them.

Music and song reverberated from the rafters and there was, for once, plenty of light. The hall was decked out far more gloriously than was usual, with plenty of lamps burning bright to reveal the wall hangings, the captured arms of dead enemies, hunting trophies, and the large number of benches that filled the great long hall. The eorls sat at the top table with Aethelwine, Coenred, and their usual favourites. Coenred's station entitled him to sit closer to the eorls but he found himself pushed down to the right by the placing of theigns who enjoyed the patronage of the eoldermen but it did not trouble him greatly. In truth his mind was not turned to the prospect of merrymaking being shadowed by thoughts of the coming battle.

He was not as superstitious as some here tonight but he felt an ominous weight settling on his heart. He ate and drank enough to be sociable but felt removed from the proceedings. Normally he would have happily indulged himself, eating too much and drinking somewhat more, knowing all too well that such moments of plenty, and of entertainment too, were to be relished in this precarious world. His very profession made him all the keener in this perception.

The boards before the top table were occupied by the companions of the eorls, huscarls such as Sigbert, Hereric and Thrydwulf, the richer theigns and the equally prosperous merchants of the City and Vale of York. Lesser ranking individuals occupied the remaining benches or stood behind them. The lowest ranking guests filled what space remained, many with their backs against the wooden walls. There was no complaint as everyone would be catered for eventually and it was good to be in the company of so many again, to see the hall being put to the use for which it was both skilfully made and artistically decorated.

So she was the guest of the high-theign and sat at the top table alongside the eorls?

Wulfhere's own lord had not been granted that particular honour; it made him wonder if mayhap he had indeed set his sights too high? Mildryth looked well suited to her position and it crossed his mind that she might not be quite alone and as vulnerable as he had first believed. He stood towards the back of the hall, amongst the lowest ranks of the guests and present only because his own lord was a favoured theign. Rubbing shoulders with the peasants vexed him but he soothed this complaint by enjoying the free food and drink that was being passed around quite liberally.

He had pushed as far forward as he dare. Although it was not customary in such a gathering he wore his byrnie so that he would be known as a weapons-man and would then be afforded some respect if not fear. Before him were the lowest tables, jealously occupied. To go any further into that social circle would be to invite a public rebuke; no one liked seeing someone else contravene the well understood social rules on such occasions as these. Besides, Wulfhere had no wish to attract any undue attention. He had long since learnt that the man of note was another's target. Better to stay in the background and move amongst the shadows, pouncing like a cat only when the moment was right to strike.

It had occurred to him that tomorrow's battle would create a moment of chaotic excitement in the city. Although he could not escape being in the ranks as a theign's fighting man there would still be time after the conclusion of the battle when people would behave a little wild. The talk was of victory of course, no one ever thought of defeat. To be fair the young eorls did have some experience in combat and they had driven Tostig Godwinson from England previously when he raided Lindsey with his war-band of adventurers. Wulfhere would hedge his bets all the same; even a defeat could prove profitable.

But what to do about this one?

He saw her glance down the table to the man who sat glowering at his board. It seemed that she was trying to catch his attention but he was distracted. Wulfhere did not like that. His eye was practiced enough to recognise a genuine warrior when he saw one and this man must be of an elevated rank to be sat with the eorls. It occurred to him then that Mildryth might have set her sights on the man with a trimmed beard and that did not sit well with Wulfhere's own plans for her. However, if the man was some celebrated warrior then it was to be sure that tomorrow he would be employed on the field of battle and not within the city walls. She may favour him but he would not be around when the battle was at its height. Wulfhere smiled to himself. If the glowering man was her protector then she would be no safer for having his service when all the weapons-men were fighting for their lives against the Vikings. He would just have to steal from the field a little earlier than everyone else but with a fitting reason so as not to anger his own lord.

"'Tis a grand table to be sitting at," Thrydwulf declared to his companions.

"The eorls make fine hosts," Hereric agreed, glancing at the eoldermen and their guests.

"I prefer this table myself," Sigbert told them.

"Would you not seek the honour of being counted one worthy of sitting with the eorls?" Aethelmaer asked; his young face already flushed from the drink.

"I have been sat before many such tables young Aethelmaer," Sigbert replied, "and few have noted how much I've eaten or drunk seeing as I was not raised to the sight of everyone else present."

"Nor have they seen how many times you've fallen from your bench all the worse for drink," Thrydwulf said with a laugh.

"I like a good drink," his friend agreed, "and that is another good reason not to sit so high; it's not so far to fall." Everyone laughed at his remark. "Oh they'll eat and drink their fill, you can be sure of that, but they are lords and ladies and must always seem so before our eyes. I tell thee, there is more merriment to be had down here in our company than to be had in such a vaulted band as the eorls and the high-theigns."

A round of hands banging on the boards of the table followed this statement as a hearty sign of agreement.

"At least they are allowed womenfolk as guests," Thrydwulf observed; he always had an eye for a pretty face.

"This is a battle feast," Hereric answered, "an occasion such as this is not meet for women. Brother warriors, we renew our death-oaths this night and promise to stand firm beside each other before the points of our enemies' spears. We will defend our lords with our lives, and if they die so do we. I would bring my fair Eadgyd to any other celebration but I say again, it is not proper for a woman to be here to remind her man of all that he stands to lose when his mind should be concerned with only one thing; killing our enemies."

Again the sound of fists banging the hard wood of the table broke out, but reverberating much more loudly than before and lasting longer.

The music died and the minstrels were applauded. One of the eorls' companions made them a gift of a gold ring and a horn of ale, an act that was warmly appreciated by the rest of the guests. As they departed an older man stepped forward before the lords' table. He wore a bright tunic of summer yellow and trousers of dark red. His face was lined with the passage of well over forty summers but his eyes sparkled with a vitality that a younger man might envy. His hair was greying at the sides, but clean and well kept. A simple braid was tied around his head to keep it out of his eyes. In his left hand he held a much used staff. He walked into the vacant space that the minstrels had recently occupied and stood a moment just looking around the great hall. Aware now that a new entertainer had taken the floor the crowd began to quieten. As he turned back to face the eorls he crouched dramatically and threw out his right hand, fingers splayed. The hall suddenly became silent and into the void a deep voice boomed from the scop's chest.

So often does the solitary one

find grace for himself
in the mercy of the Lord.
With a sorry heart he must
for a long time
row by hand
along the waterways,
along the ice cold sea,
and tread the paths of exile.
Events go as they always must!

He recited a well known poem that all had heard many times before but it was listened to with rapt attention. His voice had all the qualities necessary for the telling of the tale and he was clearly much practised in his art. Coenred appreciated the scop's talent too. 'The Wanderer' might seem to some a poor choice for such a feast as this but it echoed the misgivings in his own heart. He found himself quietly reciting particular verses as the scop spoke them.

Alone each morning
I spoke of my troubles
Before the dawn.
There is none now living
To whom I can clearly speak
Of my innermost thoughts.
I know it truly,
That it is in all men
A noble custom
That he should keep secret

His own mind,
Guard his thoughts,
Though he thinks as he wishes.
The weary spirit cannot
Withstand fate
Nor does a sorrowful mind
Prove helpful.
Thus do those eager for glory
Keep secure their dreary thoughts
Housed in their breasts.

Coenred felt as if the scop was at that point talking directly to him but when he looked up he found that the man had his back to the lords' table and was performing to the larger audience.

Those eager for glory!

He glanced down the table to where Eorl Edwin sat, watching with genuine appreciation the scop's recital.

What dreary thoughts does that young man have secured in his breast?

His constant competition with the House of Wessex mayhap?

A young man's need to prove himself to the world, felt all the more keenly due to his high station?

All to what cost?

He who has been given the trial
Knows how cruel
Is sorrow as a companion
To those who have few
Beloved friends.

The path of the exile
Holds him,
And it is not all twisted gold,
It is a frozen spirit,
Not the bounty of the earth.
He remembers well
The hall of warriors,
The giving of treasure.
How in his youth his lord
Accustomed him
to the feasting.
All that joy has died!

Mildryth glanced towards Coenred but saw that she still could not catch his eye. He was staring intently at the table before him. They were separated by several seats, she a guest of High-Theign Aethelwine, he the captain of the eorl's huscarls, and all other personages of note between them.

How cruel is sorrow as a companion.

She knew only too well the truth of that statement. For some reason, hearing it here tonight, on the eve of the battle, it made her think of him. Not her dead husband Aethelheard, although he had been dear to her, but rather of the living Coenred, who would hazard his very life on the morrow to protect them all. It crossed her mind that she had been foolish indeed in thinking to ally herself in anyway with a warrior, a fighting man, who could be so easily snatched out of this world.

Then the memory of the man called Wulfhere came back to haunt her. She knew what lay behind his eyes and feared the fate that might await her there if he had his way.

What was there in life that was worth having if it was not also worth hazarding?

Sorrow was indeed a cruel companion, but so was regret, especially the regret of not taking the opportunity when it presented itself.

Does Coenred felt nothing for me other than an obligation dictated by his sense of honour?

Could he not form an affection for me that might lead to something that would end my lonely state in this world?

Had her state fallen so low since being made a widow that she was beneath the consideration of such a man as he?

She knew only that the answers would not come to her if she sat passively and waited for wyrd to decide. Life was a gamble to begin with and she believed herself to be unafraid of a little more hurt if that was what wyrd had in store for her.

There was something about the man, however, that had attracted her attention even when the strands of her grief were still clinging to her soul. Her love of life was too strong to surrender all hope so soon. She wondered for a moment if seeking protection had been her only motive in approaching Coenred in such a manner and knew that it had not, she could not have asked such questions of herself if it had been so.

She wanted to live again.

Having manoeuvred into meeting him in the hall she had not been disappointed. He was handsome, proud but not arrogant, well thought of and lacking in vanity. She liked what she had discovered of him and knew, almost instinctively, that she could love this man if wyrd gave them the chance.

Must sorrow be my constant companion for the rest of my life?

I know not why
My spirit
does not darken
when I ponder upon
the whole life of men
throughout this world.
How suddenly they
Left the bright hall,
Those proud theigns.
So this middle-earth
Decays a bit more
Each day.
A man cannot call
Himself wise
Before he has his share
Of years in this world.
A wise man knows
He must be patient
He must never be too impulsive
Nor too hasty to speak
Nor too weak a warrior
Nor too reckless
Not too fearful
Nor too cheerful

Nor too greedy for treasure

Nor too boastful about his own deeds

Before he can see clearly.

A man must wait

When he speaks his oaths,

Until the proud-hearted

Can see clearly

Which way their heart will turn.

The wise hero will realise

How terrible it will be

When all the wealth of this world

Is lain waste.

Are you listening proud eorls to these words of wisdom? Surely this man was sent here tonight for a reason, to warn you off a vainglorious path?

Coenred glanced again at his young lords.

The bright halls fall into decay

Their lords lie low

Deprived of all their joy

All of their companions

Have fallen,

The proud ones,

The shield-wall,

Taken by war.

He speaks of the fate of the Vikings!

Edwin, Eorl of Mercia, gripped his gold cup tightly as the poem worked its magic on his mind. War would indeed take off some and that number would be great in the reckoning. His mind was alive with the images of battle, of great heroes clashing with spears, swords and shields, the fall of one and the victory of another. Fanciful imaginings drawn from the remembrance of poems and tales he had heard at the feet of his father in the great hall of Mercia.

Where is the horse?
Where the rider?
Where the giver of bright treasure?
Where the seats at the feast?
Where are the revels in the hall?
Alas for the golden cup!
Alas for the mailed warrior!
Alas for the splendour of princes!
All that time has passed away
Under the cover of the dark night
Now, as if it had never been!

So will it be in hall of the Norwegian King.

Edwin smiled grimly as he thought of what he might achieve tomorrow.

This fabled Viking king. This leader of a plundering mob. This reaver from over the great northern sea. This War Wolf! I will end this wanderer's journey tomorrow at Fulford Gate and it will be as if King Hardrada of Norway had never been. Then will my own glory rise and burn the eyes of the Wyvern of Wessex.

Those brave warriors
Were taken
By the glory of spears
Weapons greedy for slaughter
The famous turn of events
And do storms thrash
These rocky cliffs
And falling frost
Fetters the earth
The harbinger of winter.
Then does the dark come
The night shadows deepen
From the northern sky
There comes a rough hailstorm
In malice against all men

I will be that hailstorm from the north!

Edwin nodded his head absently in agreement with his own thoughts. This was indeed the sign that he had been secretly looking for, dispelling those dreary thoughts that the scop's perception revealed.

All is but trouble
In this kingdom of the earth
The turn of events
In the world under heaven.
Here gold is fleeting,
Here friend is fleeting

Here kinsman is fleeting
Here man is fleeting
Here the foundations of the earth
Turn to waste!

The audience sat enraptured, hanging on every word spoken by the scop. Lords and ladies at the top table, huscarls, theigns and merchants on the benches, frydmen and ceorls at the back of the hall, and servants standing wherever they could to hear the words of this most gifted of speakers.

So spake the wise man
In his mind alone,
Sat apart in his own counsel.
Good is he who keeps his faith
And a warrior must never speak
Of his grief too quickly
Unless he already knows the remedy,
A hero must act with courage.
It is better for the one who seeks mercy,
Consolation from our Father in Heaven,
Where for us,
All permanence rests!

As he spoke the final lines the scop turned and bowed to the eorls in a dramatic fashion. For a moment a silence hung suspended; in that instant no one dared to speak. The scop kept his head low, waiting.

"Yes!" Edwin sat back in his carved seat. "YES!"

He began to beat with his golden cup onto the boards of the table. Quickly his companions followed his example and then the rest of the people in the hall added their thunderous appreciation.

The scop rose and performed a series of similar bows to each part of his audience after which he was furnished with a horn of ale and Eorl Edwin heaped praise upon his head and a circlet of gold promising that, after the battle, he would also give so gifted a poet a grant of land to equal his talent. The assembled people were so moved as to give the young nobleman a resounding cheer of his own. They appreciated the generosity of the lord, the ring-giver of old, who rewarded the achievements of his people. There were many men who held the title of lord but so very few that seemed to acknowledge the old customs that went with the privilege of their station.

Coenred could see the delight in the eorl's young face. He had discovered the power of playing to the crowd. He grinned foolishly at people and became generous with his gifts to one and all. Although by no means a miser Coenred could not help but wonder if Edwin might not regret his generosity in the morning when his head ached and the stale taste of beer was in his mouth and his scribe read the list of endowments that he was recording this night?

If he survived the battle.

If they all survived the battle!

The heat and noise became oppressive, what with so many people crammed into the long hall. Drinking did not alleviate the din of so many talking disparately, nor was their conversation dulled by the musicians whose music had at first been listened to politely but was now largely ignored. After awhile Coenred took advantage of the distraction of a wrestling match to leave the table and make his way unnoticed into the quieter and cooler night outside.

The sky was clear and a myriad silver points shined down upon the city from above. Coenred stopped to marvel at the celestial display as he had often done as a boy on the farm in Holderness. He did not question what the stars were or how they shone or why they seemed to move in the night sky, he simply enjoyed their unrivalled beauty.

"'Tis a beautiful night," a voice out of the dark stirred him.

He turned to see a brother warrior lumbering from the shadows but it was a face he happily recognised.

"Sigbert," they nodded their greeting to each other, "do you tire of the feast?"

"I have attended and, like you Coenred, I think that I have both drank and eaten my fill," he returned. He showed no embarrassment as he passed wind noisily as if to prove his point.

"You go home to your wife then?"

"Aye, though some might think me upon a short leash eh?!"

They both laughed good-naturedly.

"Why did you marry?" Coenred asked suddenly. When he realised what he had said he found himself a little embarrassed.

"Why?" Sigbert looked at him as if not understanding what his friend had asked. "'Tis man's place to be with a woman of course."

"True, but you are a huscarl like myself. We fight for our lords, we fight for our pay. We die for our trade."

"Don't we all." Sigbert responded. "No man has to be a warrior to die on the point of a spear. The people of Fulford Gate and Water Fulford will be in as much danger as us when the Vikings come whether they take up arms or not."

"You do not fear for your wife if you should fall?"

"Aye, I do, and for that I make provision. I spend not all the money I have and I work my land holdings beyond the city walls well enough to provide a little extra. Hilda runs her shop too bringing in more coin. I have three sons and two daughters. Should I die tomorrow they will look after each other and use the money we have to buy their own protection if necessary. In time my eldest may even avenge my death. But even if I survive tomorrow death will come and find me someday, though in my sleep I prefer." He laughed to himself.

"It has always seemed strange to me that ones such as we, who live to kill and be killed, should seek wives," Coenred stated.

"Why?"

Coenred looked away, wondering if mayhap he had indeed drunk too much. Sigbert mused for a moment.

"Have you not known the magic of a woman? Ah, now when I lay me down and my sweet Hilda rests her head on my shoulder, her silky hair in my face, her arm across my chest and her leg across my thighs, I pull her close in my arms and thank the gods that I am a man." He laughed to himself again. "Coenred, you have an estate worked by your mother and your brother do you not?"

"Aye, in the Isle of Holderness."

"Then all you lack is a good wife, believe me," Sigbert asserted. "'Tis talked around the hearth-fire that a woman has her eye on you even now." He glanced sideways to judge the other's reaction.

"Much nonsense is talked around the hearth-fire," Coenred insisted. Despite the cooler night air he felt his face growing warm.

"You have not taken a wife because you fear your trade will leave her alone and widowed; 'tis the same for any man you know, be he a fisher, a hunter, or a king. I am no great thinker Coenred, that you know, but I say this to you, take her to wife if she will have you. Be handfasted, and enjoy your time together. Probably we'll all be dead by this time tomorrow anyway." He turned and started to walk away from the hall. "I'll see thee on the morrow Coenred my friend and if we die then I'll die the happier having come from the warm embrace of my Hilda instead of a cold and lonely bed like yourself."

He watched his fellow huscarl totter into the night, full of food and drink and good cheer. Sigbert had served the family of Edwin and Morcar for ten years and here he was alive, well, and to all appearances a happy man.

Mayhap there was some truth in his words after all?

Coenred turned and made his way back into the noisy hall. He was met by what seemed to be a wall of heat and sound, and he had to push his way past bodies as the men were now too far gone in their cups to recognise his rank or give him due respect. He did not mind, they would be fighting for their lives tomorrow and he was not one to demand the constant servility of others.

He made his way towards the main table where the lords and ladies were gathered and there he saw her. She was dressed in fine clothes but demurely. The jewellery that she had chosen to wear tonight was of good quality but sought only to enhance and not to shine. She sat as a guest of High-Theign Aethelwine, which indeed she was, but no one seemed to be taking much notice of her, mayhap because the followers of Edwin and Morcar were very much of a similar age and, therefore, younger than she.

Coenred took a deep breath and then made straight for where Mildryth sat. She saw him coming and smiled gently. He felt his knees go weak and hated himself for the sudden hesitation that came upon him but he continued to her side.

"My Lady, would you take some fresh air with me?" He shouted more than spoke because of the noise.

"Gladly," she replied, although she mouthed the words in reply. Rising she took the hand that he offered and he was once again amazed at the softness of her skin. "This way."

Mildryth had to lean into him to talk into his ear and despite the din, despite the press of other people, of the smell of hot food and warm beer, Coenred found his senses overwhelmed by her femininity. She led him towards the back wall and then along it to the side and through a doorway hidden behind a woven cloth.

They were in the kitchens of the great hall and suddenly it was surprisingly quieter. The servants and slaves were still busy working and they chatted happily enough to each other, but there were fewer people in here and a large shutter in the rear wall had been propped open so as to let the night air cool down the workers. Another door to the left took them outside and away from everyone.

Edwin, Coenred's retainer, sat on a stool eating some spare meat and drinking weak beer like many of the other servants in the kitchen area. They knew that their masters were too far into the feast now to be bothered about people of their low station. He watched Coenred leave by the unexpected route with the lady and wondered for a moment if he should follow, but he had been commanded to spend the night here in the hall. He decided that seeing as there was still plenty of food and a little more drink available that that would be the wiser course. He had spent yesternight out under the September sky with nothing in his belly and no coverlet to keep off the morning dew. Here he was now warm, fed, newly clothed and with companionship. Strange how a man's fortunes could change after a chance encounter.

"I had hoped to speak to you before the battle tomorrow," Mildryth said as the noise of the feast slowly faded behind them.

They continued to walk away from the hall, down a narrow path that curved gently as it went. He felt her grip loosen and her fingers began to slide from his grasp. He regretted it.

"And I meant to speak to you to, My Lady," he confirmed. "I am the captain of many men and there is much to be done to prepare for tomorrow, but I must have this time with you." He looked her in the face and she did not avert her eyes. "I have used women as men do, but I have never looked for a wife. I still do not understand why, when a single stroke can end a life on the battlefield, that men such as I should, and yet I find my thoughts ever turning that way."

"We are just two sides of the same coin, My Lord, only one a man and one a woman, but there is happiness in such unions also."

"The times, I think, are against us, My Lady. The Vikings return with blood and fire and the Normans cast their greedy eyes upon our lands from across the sea to the south; what chance have we of any happiness?"

"Only that which we choose to make for ourselves."

"I have made happiness for others; my mother and brother have a good life on the land I own. The tenants are happy too and work the land well. I have taken none of this for myself."

"I know."

"And you are widowed once already."

"But my heart is strong. I had a good life with my husband and my son but it was taken from us by cruel men who come again to take whatever else they can by force. Mayhap this time they will take everything? Mayhap it is wrong and foolish to try and build a little happiness in such times, or mayhap it's right to disdain the fates and take what we can while we can? Mayhap, knowing that they have something to fight for beyond the declarations of eoldermen, good men like yourself will fight a little harder and come back to us all the sooner?" She put her hand to his face and gently stroked the soft, neatly trimmed beard. "I do not think that you fear to lose your life but rather that you fear to fail those who would look to you for their protection. If you fall tomorrow your family will fare as best they might, as will I. If you last the fight then we all will have gained something."

"If I followed a better leader then I would have more hope." A shadow of doubt crossed his face, visible even in the starlight.

"Then be your own leader. You are the Captain of the Huscarls of the Eoldermen; lead them the way you know best."

"You are wise as well a beautiful." The words surprised him as they passed his lips but he meant the compliment.

"Those words come from another, my husband who taught me to love life and to be thyself. Tomorrow, be the leader the men need, whether in victory or defeat, and show the eorls what it is be a commander of men."

"I seek counsel from a woman!" He laughed at himself, not at her.

"A wise man takes counsel where he can find it."

"Then do you have any other wise words for me?"

"Only this." She leant close and kissed his lips. He remained rigid as if incapable of relaxing even though he realised that he had secretly longed for this moment. "I sought to commission you as my protector Lord Coenred, but I find in you a noble heart that I much admire."

He remained speechless, his mouth slightly open and a surprised look on his face. She laughed gently.

"Do not be afraid of me," she chided him playfully.

"I am not. I fear nothing. I…" his voice faltered and he felt stupid.

"Then prove it."

She looked him in the face and in the starlight it seemed to him that she was glowing. She had seen twenty eight summers and she had been a wife and a mother. He was aware that this lady was no girl but a woman who had lived a life before he had ever met her, and she seemed more beautiful than any girl that he had ever seen. He gave into his passion and pulled her to him and returned her kiss with longing.

When they separated it seemed to him that the world had grown immeasurably smaller, that it was encompassed by this very embrace. Certainly there was nothing of value to him beyond it right now.

"Lord Coenred, see me safely home and then go to do thy duty to those you will lead on the morrow."

When she spoke to him her voice was a like a caress.

"I will."

They released each other and she started to walk towards her small house. He moved to walk beside her and found her arm linked in his.

"Mayhap we are fools to make this happiness when the enemy threaten our walls but I would have you know that I do not regret it," She spoke softly to him.

"I once thought that men who pursued this happiness were indeed fools, but now I feel that it is I who've been foolish all along," he admitted.

"And here we are my brave protector," she announced.

He looked at the unassuming single-storey house with its thatched roof and lone shuttered window. They could still hear the noise of the feast from where they stood and he turned to look back at the hall as if he did not believe how short a distance they had travelled.

"I would that it were further," he declared.

She reached up and kissed him again.

"Now go as you promised."

She released him and went inside without looking back. Coenred stood there for a moment as if one lost. He looked up at the clear night sky again, turning his face to the silver starlight, and a huge grin broke out over his face.

Wednesday 20th September 1066

The Village of Riccall

Riccall was somewhat larger than Skaroaborg. There were many more buildings to begin with, some much bigger than any that they had seen in the fishing village. A street ran down through the village to the riverbank from the furthest limit of the settlement. It was surrounded by arable land of good quality, the fields in their turn bordered by forest. Closer to the river small fishing boats lay high on the bank. Trading vessels called in at Riccall, plying their wares the full length of the Ouse and down into the great estuary of the Humber. There were many shops, indeed it was a thriving town with a small wooden church and all the signs of prosperity.

From within the shadows of the treeline Siward and a hundred or so Vikng warriors stared out at the village as the occupants rose to greet the new day. They had left the fleet before dawn and headed north for two miles to reach Riccall. Lord Tostig had a man with them who claimed to know the area well and he had warned them that the River Ouse made a prodigious 'U' turn at the village and that this would make further progress difficult. The same man had led the party of Vikings overland to Riccall and his words had proven true.

"The Saxons awake," Siward commented.

"They look well to do for peasants," a warrior at his side observed.

"We are here to capture the village first," Siward told him, raising his voice so that his words carried to as many as possible without also alarming the villagers. "The king wants this place for a safe mooring for the fleet, why waste time pillaging a village when we are going to capture a city today?"

"A sail!" The alert came from behind Siward, brought by a man who had run from the river itself. It was both a warning that the advance ships of the fleet were approaching and the signal to begin the attack.

"Remember, secure the village. Let the people run if they have a mind to." Siward drew his sword.

"What if some stand and fight?"

"Then kill them."

The Vikings moved out from the trees and began to trot across the open fields. Riccall had no palisade so that the people who they could see moving around the village could also see them, but no one reacted. When the alarm was initially raised it was by a lone woman who pointed at the advancing warriors and called out to someone nearby. Suddenly the screaming started.

Almost across the fields now the Norsemen increased their pace and began to utter their war cries

Within moments the Vikings were inside the village itself and had met no organised defence whatsoever. The Saxons ran in panic and with no clear idea of where they wished to go, only away from their enemies. Some headed across the fields and to the presumed safety of the forest beyond. Others headed for the river and their boats. Many more attempted to shutter their homes but they found that their doors were no barricade whatsoever against the hard steel of Norwegian war-axes.

The first ships reached Riccall and quickly disembarked more warriors to make safe the village but by then Jarl Siward's men had effectively cleared it of all but the old and the infirm, Saxons too weak to do anything more than sit and watch the Viking army arrive and claim their village.

Siward stood in the centre of the road, his helmet removed to allow the sweat on his brow to be kissed by the morning air. Already the men were searching the village for anything that could be of use to the army, horses, food, drink, weapons even. He watched as more and more shipse arrived, the smaller snekke first and the larger drekkar following. Ships were tied alongside each other so that the warriors had to climb from one vessel to another to make it to dry land.

The crews were not sorry to give up rowing, however. It had taken them two days to reach this spot from the open sea and most of it had required the use of the ships' oars. Morale was high because they had finally reached their destination to undertake the task that they had set out to complete and the men were in good physical condition.

Tostig Godwinson took possession of a horse, mounted it and began to put his troops in order. Like the Vikings they were in good spirits and reasonably well equipped. It did not take them long to don their byrnies, shirts of mail that reached down to their thighs for some. The majority of adventurers, however, could not afford such armour. Their byrnies were the common alternative made from toughened leather and given additional protection by the sewing of metal rings or plates of iron to crucial areas. Some wore beneath this the woollen jackets if they owned them. Most had helmets, again usually light in metal with additional protection provided by toughened leather covering. All of the warriors carried large round wooden shields painted in a wide variety of designs from plain colours to intricate pieces of artwork with a large metal boss at the centre. They gripped several throwing spears along with the shield in their left hand; in their right they held a fighting spear. Some of the more seasoned mercenaries carried swords or axes as well, but few if any of these approached the quality possessed by the Viking nobility.

The Jarls of Orkney made a show of presenting to King Hardrada a large black stallion that their men had found. It was not in the best of condition but it still looked an impressive beast, even more so with the giant King of Norway sat on its back.

"Olaf!" The king shouted, his booming voice carrying over the noise of the war preparations.

"Father!" The young prince appeared on foot, already armed and armoured, with his retainers in tow, young men of his generation and of suitable rank. His face was flushed with excitement and for a moment it touched the old king that he would have to disappoint a son who did not need to be commanded to do that which was expected of a true Viking.

"Olaf my boy, you will guard the fleet," he spoke with his usual brusque voice but he hid a different emotion behind the words.

"Father no!" The Prince looked indignant. "I have not travelled to Orkney and Scotland at thy side to do a watchman's duty in England!"

"'Tis my command boy," the king's voice rose.

"You use my youth against me?" Olaf protested still.

His own anger was reinforced by the knowledge that his peers were standing behind him, not least the Jarls of Orkney who would be leading their own men into this battle, and that they were watching an altercation that might have been better carried out in private.

"No, my better judgement," the king indulged him like he would no other, certainly there were no men now living who had dared to raise their voices against Harald Hardrada in such a fashion.

"And you were much younger than I when you first fought on a battlefield!"

"Aye, fought and lost and then hunted like an animal. I'll not risk that for my son."

"You fear to lose?"

"No warrior goes into battle believing that he cannot be defeated. Though there is much in our favour the Saxon is not a weakling and their ways are cunning. You would make a good prize for them and if I should fall Norway would have no king."

"There is Magnus who sits now guarding your thrown in Norway. You will not rob me of this glory!"

"Siward! Siward!"

"My lord." The Norse jarl walked over to where the royal family argued. His manner was neither hurried nor concerned as if he had witnessed scenes like this played out before and already knew what the outcome would be.

"Tell the Prince why I could not take him into battle; you have his ear more than I," the king commanded.

"But I would say take him," his friend responded. He looked at the king directly.

"WHAT?!"

"My Lord, the Saxons are caught unprepared. Harold has his army in the south fearing a threat from Guillaume the Bastard and our men are as keen as their spear points. I see no danger in Prince Olaf witnessing the fight."

"Damn you to hell Siward, would you ever take the prince's side against me?" Inside Hardrada rejoiced in the opportunity to change his mind without a loss of face. Siward was a good friend, a close friend;

closer than a brother. He was also right of course, they had the upper-hand and it behoved the royal blood of Norway to learn the ways of war. He cursed the inner voice that had counselled caution on this day; that was not his normal disposition. "Very well Olaf, you come with us, but I make you Siward's ward and my wrath will fall heavy with you if he comes to any harm."

"That will not be," Siward assured the king. He turned to the prince and flashed a quick grin. "Get yourself a horse My Prince, for such as we do not suffer the dirt of England on our heels when we go to war against her own."

"Thank you Siward, for a moment there I thought the old hound would have you keep me here after all."

"Son or no son, don't let him hear you using that name," Siward warned. "Now get thee prepared and let's spill some Saxon blood."

Fulford Gate

It would be another warm day in this long, glorious English summer. The sun was climbing into a clear blue sky over Fulford Gate against which the green of the trees looked so vibrant and so full of life. Birds flew across the heavens with no care for the worries of men. They fought their own battles for survival, whether predator or prey. The ravens and crows, however, would be spared the need to travel far for food; a feast awaited them after the bloody business of the day was completed.

Coenred stood leaning on his fighting spear in an attitude of relaxed waiting. The leaf shaped blade of the spear was highly polished and glinted in the morning light. It had a central ridge running from the socket to the very sharp point to give the spearhead strength. The shaft felt smooth under his hand. Made from the wood of the ash tree it was both strong and supple, allowing the spear to absorb the impact of thrusts against linden shields, impacts that would shatter more brittle woods. Fighting spears did not come in any one size. Coenred's was cut to a length of eight natural feet, a length that he found easily manageable. Others might be shorter depending upon the skill and strength of the man who was to wield it.

His great round shield, now free of its protective linen covering, was swung onto his back where he could carry it comfortably. The yellow dragon of Mercia scowled out at the world from a black background. A leather strap fixed to the inside of the shield held in place his three angons or throwing spears. Each measured up to seven natural feet in length, with barbed tempered iron heads on long iron shanks attached to a wooden shaft barely half that length. Some warriors placed iron rings in the shaft to mark the exact point of balance in the weapon so that they would know where to hold it when throwing the spear. Coenred had no need for such devices; he knew instinctively how to launch this necessary and deadly weapon.

His armour consisted of a byrnie made from steel mail links, an expensive long coat that provided protection against cutting weapons such as sword blades or axe edges. This was a thing of great value as most warriors could not afford such a large amount of metal in a single protective garment. The pattern of the byrnie was basically a 'T' shape with a hole for the head to pass through. The sleeves reached down to his forearms, whereas the body of the mail shirt reached to the bottom of his thighs. It was gathered at the waist by a leather belt that helped to distribute the two stones of weight more comfortably. Suspended from this belt, which was decorated with gold fastenings, were his double-edged sword housed in its leather scabbard also suitably decorated, Mildryth's scramseax, a double handed Dane-axe, and a bottle filled with weak beer.

Underneath the byrnie he wore a padded jacket made up of several cross-ply layers of wool encased in linen. This garment helped absorb impact blows and could stop the progress of piercing weapons that penetrated the steel mail.

Coenred wore a pointed helmet of a simple conical design made from polished steel sections riveted together with strengthening crossbars welded over the riveted seams. A strong nose guard extended down to offer some protection to his face, accompanied by solid plate cheek guards fixed to the helmet by leather straps. The cheek guards had bronze plates attached to them, each of these decorated with a stylised image of a horse chased in silver. At the back, riveted to the helmet, fell a curtain of mail to protect his neck. Linen trousers and strong leather shoes completed his battle dress.

He had left his horse and his retainer Edwin back in the safety of York. This soft wet ground would cut up badly under the hooves of horses so he had issued a general order for the fyrd, from eorl to ceorl, to assemble here on foot. Eorl Edwin had given nominal command to him as Captain of the Huscarls, the elite of the fyrd, but Coenred had no misunderstanding about the appointment; Edwin and Morcar would not surrender real command because that would mean surrendering the glory too. His was the job of organisation, not leadership upon the field when the battle was about to be joined.

"How's your head?" Sigbert asked jovially. He was a stocky man to begin with so the addition of his battle harness, of an equal quality to that worn by Coenred, seemed to make him even more rotund, as if he were almost as wide as he was tall.

"Fine," Coenred responded truthfully with a grin, "how was Hilda?"

The other huscarl laughed roughly before answering.

"Like silk beneath my hands and as warm as a fire. Rare are the times when I've lain with my wife before a battle but every time I have we've won and I've escaped wounding, or we've lost and I've just escaped."

They laughed together.

"May wyrd grant you the same fortune again today," Coenred smiled.

Even as experienced warriors they were both anxious to a degree though neither wished to show it. Mirth might not seem appropriate before a battle but it let them vent the nervous energy that they felt building in an acceptable fashion and it gave no reason to others to doubt their courage. They knew what was coming better than most men that morning and there was nothing like the threat of enemy spear-points to make the mind appreciate the immediate moment of living all the more readily.

They stood on a swath of grass that looked to be ideal grazing for oxen and sheep. The late summer sky was a limitless blue, the kind of hue that seemed to turn a man's mind to the sea and the cooling breezes that could be found there. The rhythm of life could be felt everywhere, in the season that was beginning to close, in the trees that were just beginning to show their autumn colours, in the flowing of the beck that rippled over stones and over which countless insects darted. Flowering plants marked the marshland, painting the landscape with bright colours. They could feel it coursing through their veins as the beating of their hearts drove blood through powerful limbs. They could taste it with every breath taken. This precious life that seemed so fragile but to which they clung with dogged tenacity, normally without conscious thought. Today they did think about that life, about all that it had given them and all that they shared with the other people who mattered to them.

The threat of war brought with it an awareness of how good it was to be alive at that very moment. For those who had hazarded their lives on the spears of the enemy before now this was a time to place a value upon their lives and all that they had enjoyed and loved. There would be no other moment like it once the battle was begun.

Together Coenred and Sigbert watched the army assemble slowly. Lesser eoldermen and theigns walked down the road from York with their men, mostly ceorls, some could call on lesser theigns to bolster their numbers, and some of the richer lords could even afford the services of mercenary butescarles, warriors better equipped and more experienced than fyrdmen but whose loyalty was counted in coin and not in terms of obligation.

The men wore a variety of armour ranging from mail coats to leather byrnies. Some wore only padded jackets and there was a large number who did not even have that slight protection, they came to the battle in their everyday tunics. There were many bare heads too, a few with light helmets made from iron hoops riveted together and covered in leather. Some could afford helmets with steel structures also covered in leather; very few could afford the best quality of head protection. The only piece of defensive equipment that they all had in common was the great round shields that every weapons man carried. Again, the quality of decoration presented on each shield reflected the means of the man who held it.

Their weapons were just as varied ranging from bejewelled swords to mean langseaxes formerly used for the butchering of farm animals. Experienced warriors carried battle axes whereas their poorer comrades brought wood axes. The commonest weapon was without doubt the tall fighting spears that every soldier was trained to use and the majority of the army also used throwing spears although not all were of the pattern of the angons with their heavy metal heads and sockets. Simpler versions were merely shorter fighting spears that were not as effective as the angon because they were lighter and their shafts could easily be broken at the head to lessen the encumbrance that they caused when fixed into a shield or even a man's body.

Some of the lords made a great show of their arrival, bedecked in their gold and jewels and pointlessly ordering their battle horns to be blown as they strode in the morning sunlight trying to impress everyone. Wiser men like Aethelwine came more discreetly, paying heed to the younger and more inexperienced of their people who even now would be clutched by fear at the thought of what the day might bring.

The High-Theign of York spent time talking to his men, encouraging them to be brave, to seem so before the eyes of the men of distant Mercia who served Eorl Edwin. He had no need to put on a show to the other theigns. His armour was richly adorned as became his high station; his weapons were second to none in quality. He was already a man of note and a warrior of some experience. However, in his own eye he was a father to his people. He understood that many of them had misgivings for this day and concern for the loved ones that they had left at home. The Vikings were not feared without reason. Nevertheless there always seemed to be some self-important fool who had to strut in their battle harness and act the bold warrior before all the men. Such are the ways of those who have not experienced the reality of violent conflict. True heroes were cut from a different cloth.

"Here they come." Sigbert nodded over to a group of heavily armed and armoured men who approached both him and Coenred. They were all huscarls, attired much the same as their captain, although some favoured the large, two handed Dane-axe over the fighting spear. These were the elite force of Edwin and Morcar's army. In particular these men were the most experienced and best trained warriors. They would also be the men most to fear as far as the enemy was concerned. The Vikings had the violent fury of the berserker; the Saxons had the determined loyalty of the huscarl.

Coenred moved to meet them half way with Sigbert at his side. Verdant grass blades bent beneath the sole of his leather shoes as he walked, each recovering slowly as his weight was removed with the following step. He counted the warriors quickly and was surprised at their number. He estimated there to be some one hundred and fifty of them, each a captain of one hundred huscarls. This was good news.

"Good morrow brothers," he called.

They returned the salutation willingly and in loud voices. It would not be lost on the fyrdmen that the huscarls were in such good spirits.

"Where are the eorls?" Thrydwulf asked the question that was on many minds.

"They'll come soon, though travelling by foot might take them a little longer than they are used to," Sigbert said and raised a hearty round of laughter. They all felt the nervous energy that seemed to be generated by the growing number of men and mayhap they laughed a little too quickly in their attempt to dissipate it.

"I call you here as your captain," Coenred said when the mirth had subsided. "Tis known around the hearth-fire that we hold this ground against my counsel but the eorls command it and so we must do battle against the old foe as best we can."

"Seems we must draw our line along the beck as deep as we can though the front is long," Hereric observed.

"The order of battle is clear enough to see even without the September sun," Sigbert answered, "that's not what concerns us."

"No." Coenred agreed. "The ground looks good for a defence but I doubt the eorls can resist the call to glory. I fear that they will not be able to defy moving to the attack."

"Mayhap we should if the opportunity presents?" Hereric suggested.

"Mayhap, if this were not Harald Hardrada that we fight. He's won honours in the Varangian Guard of Byzantium, the Emperor himself is said to have rewarded him for his service. He is the King of Norway and the canniest, most experienced warrior to take the field today," Sigbert responded. "He is the War Wolf and against him we have two youths-"

"And us!" Thrydwulf interjected and raised another roar of approval.

Coenred smiled grimly, he liked the spirit that they were displaying at least, they not only looked like warriors, they acted like warriors.

"Aye, and us. I don't doubt that we stand a chance of turning the Viking back today if we hold the ground but I am wary that if the line is breached or turned we will be trapped with the wetlands to our backs. That would mean the capture of the eorls and Harold, our king, would find himself caught between two hard enemies."

"The eorls may fall or be captured as any warrior on this field today."

"True enough, but Tostig Godwinson rides with Hardrada," Sigbert told them.

"Then the rumours are true?"

"Aye, Tostig Godwinson returns to exact his revenge with Hardrada as his ally. If they take the eorls alive then they take York and all of Northumbria too. Even Mercia may be counted as having fallen. Tostig is a friend of the King of Scotland, Hardrada's back would be protected in the north; Malcolm will not interfere. Mayhap those of Dane blood will join his banner if he wins this day and holds or kills the eorls?"

"Then you want us to bodyguard the eorls?" Hereric asked.

"Aye," Coenred nodded, "'tis no easy task in the midst of a battle to watch a man's back but that is what we must do. We must fight the enemy and make sure that neither eorl falls to either capture or death."

"More than one eolderman has fallen in battle before and the enemy has not profited greatly," Thrydwulf commented. Several warriors nodded their heads in agreement at this truth.

"How many of us fought in a time when three different men would wear the crown and two of them foreigners?" Coenred looked round at the faces of the warriors. "The Witan chose Harold for King and that sits well with me. Hardrada is another Viking adventurer looking to add

England to his crown since Denmark escaped his clutch. Guillaume is a Norman and we know what his kind did at the court of King Edward. No, if we hold Hardrada today then we save King Harold an unnecessary battle, leaving him all the stronger to face the Normans should they come. If we lose but save the eorls then Northumbria escapes Tostig's control. As long as the eorls live Hardrada will enjoy no real victory in the north."

"They may have the city but they won't have the people. Tostig will find that he has not so soon been forgotten," Sigbert added.

"If the eorls fall beneath Viking spears then our death-oaths demand the same fate for us, or the crushing of our enemy," Thrydwulf said this with notable pride and vehemenance.

"Then that is another reason why they must not fall," Coenred answered him. "If we lose the day but keep the eorls alive then the heart of the Army of the North remains to fight another day. If Edwin and Morcar die and us along with them then who will remain to protect the people of Northumbria? Who will be here to protect your families?"

"Then we either win this fight or spirit the eorls to safety if it goes against us," Hereric observed.

"So let it be," Thrydwulf said in a grim tone.

He threw back his head and growled a roar into the summer sky. The group of huscarls followed his lead and sent up a war-cry that rolled across the field. The rough sound of their voices drew many an appreciative glance from the assembling army, eoldermen, theigns and ceorls alike. If the elite troops of the eorls' of Mercia and Northumbria were in such good spirits then it seemed they all had a firm reason to expect to survive this day.

"Hereric, I give you Morcar," Coenred told him.

The big Saxon puffed out his chest with pride. He was not the tallest man there but his limbs were thick with sinew and muscle and he could swing his two handed Dane-axe with the same dexterity that the best of them used with their fighting spears.

"You give me command of the largest number of huscarls," he declared acknowledging both the responsibility and the honour that his captain was bestowing upon him. He would tell Eadgyd of this tonight, when the enemy were scattered and he sat before the warmth of her hearth with his children around him. It would become an oft told tale in the long nights of winter; it would make her so proud of her man.

"That I do. Morcar will hold the left flank along the beck to the dam-lands; Edwin will hold the river bank. Thrydwulf, you'll stand with Edwin." Coenred looked each man in the face. They were brother warriors, men of the same mind and ability; they commanded his respect. He knew that he could rely upon them one and all and that in the coming fight none of them would let him down or stain their own honour. "I will stand at the centre where Mercia and Northumbria meet. I expect the Vikings will try to push the two flanks apart; we will hold them together."

"There will not be enough of us," Hereric recognised. "We are some fifteen hundred strong but the length of the battle line is beyond us."

"Of huscarls there will never be enough," Coenred agreed. "The theigns and the fyrdmen will take their stand too. We will be the rocks onto which they will build their shield-wall. Behind us such ceorls as have skill with a bow will darken the sky with their arrows and behind them the village men will stand. They may be no good for fighting in a shield-wall but they will swell our numbers and give the enemy good reason to fear our strength."

Many of the villagers from Fulford Gate and Water Fulford were even now heading up the same track down which the Saxon army was still coming; they were heading towards the safety of the city walls. Children drove the family animals before them, pigs, sheep and oxen. One or two had horses which they used to carry the belongings that they believed they could not afford to leave behind. As Coenred had observed many of the village men of fighting age had taken up positions at the rear of the army, close to the Ings Marsh which was to the north of the battleground and stood between them and York. Those with bows would be the most useful if they could be made to loose their arrows together, although the common practice was for bowmen to act individually and find their own mark. Many were saying farewell to wives and children and hurrying them off to safety. Their villages would be close to the battle site and few were expecting to find their homes intact if the day was lost.

It was surprising, however, that despite the common consensus that the Vikings would put both villages to the torch no matter what happened in the battle itself many villagers had decided to stay with their properties. These were mostly men who intended shuttering their doors and windows and staying put, but a few were joined by their women who seemed to be of an equally pugnacious spirit.

"Go now to your places and form the lines. Remember your oaths as huscarls; brothers of the sword, we know no defeat when our lord has fallen, only death or victory. May your shields be strong and your spears longer than the enemies."

"DEATH OR VICTORY!"

The shout went up at Coenred's words and afterwards they departed with a mind to make war.

"Aethelmaer," he called to his own huscarls.

"My Lord." Aethelmaer responded eagerly advancing towards Coenred. Although a young man he was tall and strong and had the makings of a captain. With the other huscarls, Alfrid and Hengist included, his troop numbered only twenty, but they were proven men.

"We will form in the centre the same as the others but stand back from the main line. I want us to be able to respond should we see a weakness in either our shield-wall or the Vikings'. Muster another eighty huscarls from the line if you can. See if you can get a reserve of fyrdmen behind us too."

"Yes, My Lord," Aethelmaer responded, eargerly. His young face showed none of the concern that dominated so many others. He seemed to be revelling in the prospect of a violent encounter with the Vikings, proud of his station as a huscarl, proud of his immaculate armour, proud of his brother warriors.

"I like that lad. He has a comely head on his shoulders supported by youthful strength. Hopefully they won't be parted from each other by some Viking Dane-axe today," Sigbert said. "Where do you want me then?"

"At my side of course where I can keep an eye on you," Coenred told him. "I fear your wife's wrath more than any Viking's spear point!"

The City of York

The City of York was alive with excitement. People from the surrounding areas were flocking to the gates seeking sanctuary behind the stout walls and the palisade. Many had also climbed the same walls hoping to gain a view of the coming battle.

Mildryth could not.

She felt a sickening knot in her stomach. At first she went outside to get some fresh air but the throng of people and their excitement only made her feel worse. She returned to her small house but had to open the shutter. Despite her house standing at the end of the street, far from the main road, she seemed to hear and feel all the noise and emotion generated by the city-folk.

Do any of these people have anyone they care about risking their lives today?

Coenred came back to her mind and she tried to recall last night when all this had seemed so far away. She struggled to remember how he had looked in his fine tunic and trousers, his hair banded by a silver circlet, not as showy as the young lords but far from being a mean man of war too. The image of her remembrance seemed to change all too quickly, however, and unwillingly she saw him as he might look dressed in his armour and battle harness. The thought chilled her and she felt the sick feeling take hold of her stomach again. She needed some distraction, something to take her mind off the terrible events that were about to unfold barely two miles to the south of them.

"My Lady!"

She heard an unfamiliar voice calling from outside and on going to the open window she saw a well dressed servant stood in the street looking towards her house.

"Do you call me?" She asked through the open window.

"If you be the Lady Mildryth, yes," he replied. "I am a retainer to Lord Coenred. He has sent me to be of service to you."

"Of what service can you be to me?"

Thoughts of the other man who had presumed to speak to her through the window cast a shadow over her mind.

"Protection." He moved aside his new cloak and she saw the langseax hanging from his belt. "However the battle goes I am to stay with you until Lord Coenred returns or we must flee. I can do him no other service on this day but I will not fail him in this charge."

Even now my protector thinks of me.

"Then come in," she told him and went to open the door. Edwin entered with a small, nervous bow. "Please, be seated."

Edwin took a small stool from beside the wall and sat down near the open hearth. Mildryth went to pour him some wine.

"I should do that, My Lady!" He rose quickly when he realised that she was about to serve him.

"You are Lord Coenred's servant, not mine," She replied handing him the cup. "Under my roof you are my guest."

He smiled his gratitude but his unease was obvious. After seeing Coenred leave the great hall with this lady Edwin had asked in the kitchens after her and quickly discovered her story. The fact that she was theign-worthy had made a great impression upon him and he now found it difficult to sit in her presence as a guest when in his mind he should be a servant to her.

"You were working in the great hall last night," she chose to ease his discomfort with some polite conversation.

"Yes, My Lady. Lord Coenred thinks that it would help me to learn how to serve. I wasn't born a retainer."

"Where are you from?"

"A small holding near Inderawuda, just to the southeast actually. Near the river that runs into the Humber. It was attacked by raiders in the night some weeks ago. My parents were killed, my brother also."

"These have become lawless times," Mildryth observed. "I am sorry for you. Excuse me, you know my name but I do not know yours?"

"Edwin son of Octa, My Lady. Like the eorl only not so great." He took a sip of the fruit wine.

"Greatness is earned through deeds Edwin, not by birth alone," she told him. "Do you know anything of battles?"

"No, I am no warrior," he replied meekly.

"Good, then you will not feel the need to tell me what might be occurring out there in the field."

She sat down on another stool placed near the hearth but found her hands clutching each other nervously. For a moment there was a strained silence when neither could think of anything else to say and yet both felt that someone should.

"I think that it is as at least as bad to be on the fringe of a battle and capable of doing nothing as it is to be in a battle, My Lady," Edwin finally suggested.

"Mayhap you are right, therefore we will do something," she asserted rising to her feet again.

"What would you have me do, My Lady?"

"We'll cook an evening meal," she said quickly. "Yes, for when they return. It will keep both our hands and our minds busy."

Fulford Gate

The sound of horns announced the arrival of the eorls Edwin and Morcar at Fulford Gate. Against Coenred's advice they came down the track from York on horseback but at least only their individual banner carriers shared that honour, the rest of their men walked as they all should have done.

"Coenred, isn't it a fine morning for a battle?" Edwin shouted as the huscarl made his way over to the two young noblemen.

"My lords, the army assembles as you ordered," was all that he could bring himself to say in return.

"Then let's to it men." Edwin swung down from his horse and a servant disappeared with it. Saxons did not fight on horseback; a horse was just a means of getting to the battle. "Morcar, my brother, I give you the left flank, the greater number of men and the greater glory," Edwin declared effusively.

The two brothers embraced fondly and the men cheered at the sight of their leaders in such good spirits.

"Brother, the glory will belong to every man who fights under our joint banners this day," Morcar returned.

Coenred was grudgingly impressed by this uncharacteristic generosity of spirit on the younger brother's side.

Is the gravity of their situation giving the young men older heads?

The two young eoldermen were dressed in the best quality battle harness. Their metal byrnies gleamed in the morning sun, polished by servants so that they looked resplendent. Edwin wore a simple conical helmet with a nose-guard inlaid with gold. A curtain of mail hung down the back to protect his neck. Morcar's helmet was more lavishly embellished with long cheek pieces and an exaggerated nose-guard. It reminded Coenred that the Eorl of Northumbria was indeed young. Each wore an expensive sword decorated with gold, silver, and jewels but their shields and spears were carried by servants dressed as soldiers.

The retainers followed their lords and began to spread out along the line of the Germany Beck. Theign Ricbert was a companion of Eorl Morcar's and so positioned himself and his men on the right of the eorl's banner and near the centre of the line. He was in good humour with his warriors, encouraging them to form their lines without the need to employ threats or the flat of his sword. He saw a figure seemingly lurking in the back row.

"You man! What do you do there?" He called out, suspicious of the man's loitering.

"My Lord," Wulfhere replied with a loud voice and marched up to the theign in a proper manner.

"Wulfhere! 'tis you."

"Aye My Lord."

"What do you in the back row?"

"I was forming the lines, My Lord. Seems some of these fyrdmen know not how to position themselves," he spoke disdainfully and attracted one or two scowls from men close enough to hear what was being said. "In my experience 'tis worth having a man who has been in the wars stand in the back row to keep fyrdmen in check. They're as like to run after touching shields to the spears of the enemy thee know, My Lord!"

Ricbert studied Wulfhere's face. He could not say that he liked the butescarle particularly but the man seemed able and trustworthy.

Certainly no one else in his household had spoken ill of him in particular. Of course there were duties that necessitated the employment of such a man, although in truth the theign wished that he might afford the service of a proper huscarl rather than this poor replacement. Mayhap if the battle went well today a boon from Eorl Morcar might allow him to retain the services of a real huscarl? Wulfhere seemed genuine enough, however, always eager to serve when tasked, and in one thing he was right, the fyrd could sometimes take flight at the first provocation so it might be wise to have an experienced man like him in the back row to steady them.

"So be it. Keep them steady but when I call you to the front I want to see you there promptly." The theign turned and pushed his way through the ranks of his men to take his rightful position in the front row. As soon as he was out of earshot Wulfhere turned and looked at the fyrdmen around him. He chose one who looked less formidable than his fellows and cuffed his ear with the back of his hand.

"You heard the theign," he roared, "get into line and don't let me catch a man of you casting longing looks back to York. Eyes forward only."

It was a job half done to acquire a position at the rear of the shield-wall. If the battle went against them he would not have to fight through other fleeing men to reach the safety of York from this position. If the battle went their way then he would have leisure following the advancing line to pilfer the bodies of fallen heroes for their gold and jewels. Yes, he was set for a good day no matter how the world turned. He wondered if he should call his two rogues to him, they were so eager for the fight that they had positioned themselves in the second road convinced that they were mighty warriors destined for greatness. He remembered how small had been their ambition when they had stopped at the farm on the way to York; he knew that he could do better than them. Let them stay in the ranks of heroes then, if they survived he would drink a cup of beer in celebration with them, if not, well it was no great loss. First, as always, he would look after himself.

Coenred continued to watch as the men formed up. The huscarls, resting their heavy shields for the moment with the rim on the ground, were interspersed with well-equipped eoldermen and theigns and their companions as he had ordered. Nevertheless the Saxon shield-wall would barely cover the full front with properly armoured men.

Behind them would stand the second row made up almost entirely of lesser theigns and better equipped fyrdmen. Their job was to thrust the long fighting spears over the shoulders of the more heavily armoured front row. The poorer equipped fyrdmen and all of the villagers who had volunteered to fight today would make up the third and fourth rows where their weight could be used to hold the line against the push of the Vikings. Inevitably men in the front row would fall and their place would have to be taken by those behind them, then would the lack of armour and quality weapons tell; then would the true resolve of the Saxons be tested.

The army began to become a thing of discernable proportions and evident control, not just a multitude of excited, chaotic individuals. There was much shouting, much cursing, and more than one man regretted having drunk so much at the feast many had enjoyed last night. Banners were raised to mark the presence of important individuals, lesser eorls and royal theigns alike. Battle horns were readied against the onset of glory.

Young boys walked through the throng carrying pitchers of weak beer for the soldiers to quench their thirst. The sun had climbed above the tree line and burnt down upon them from a clear sky. It was unseasonably warm still. Men would be getting hot even without the weight of their armour. The huscarls and theigns wearing both padded jackets and mail would sweat most uncomfortably today.

Coenred turned and looked at his men. They were either standing and talking quietly or sat upon the ground. There were some one hundred huscarls; all that he believed could be spared from the front line to make a reserve force. They were supported by another three hundred fyrdmen, carefully chosen by Aethelmaer for their training and experience; men that could be relied upon to follow orders and stand their ground. Others, who seemed lost or confused, not knowing where to stand or whom they should follow, had congregated nearby, mayhap fooling themselves into thinking that as this collection of warriors were not already in the front line of the army then they would be safer associating with them. Mayhap a little later they might have reason to regret their ignorance.

Coenred mused on their dispositions. He had some one thousand five hundred huscarls, mayhap another one thousand theigns and a hundred or so eoldermen of quality. In addition there were two thousand fyrdmen and poorer theigns and another one thousand villagers and townsmen who would be of little use unless the real fighting men forced the enemy to turn and run. He would count on four thousand five hundred warriors, not a small force by today's standards.

How many would the Vikings number?

He thought over the number of ships reported by several different messengers, the totals being worryingly consistent. Based on experience he estimated Hardrada's army to be at least seven thousand that could be put straight into the field with possibly another three thousand to act as a reserve and a guard for the fleet. If pushed the Vikings could send forth into the field an army twice the size of the combined power of Mercia and Northumbria.

Eorl Edwin would hold the riverbank with three hundred and fifty huscarls supported by seven hundred fyrdmen. Eorl Morcar would hold the longer stretch of the line with one thousand one hundred huscarls and two thousand two hundred fyrdmen. It would be left to Coenred with his reserve to try and stop any breaches of the line, especially where he knew it to be the weakest.

"This is not a good day for a battle," Sigbert declared, breaking Coenred's contemplation.

"You have read some portent? Some sign in the sky that keeps your eye attracted?" Coenred glanced upwards mockingly.

"That I have," Sigbert admitted, "the bloody sun climbs high and burns hot with no sign of a cloud to offer us shade!"

"As it burns us so it burns the Viking, although they've had further to walk than either of us this fine morning."

"True enough friend, but I hate this waiting. 'Tis true, there's nothing worse than a battle begun if not a battle waited upon."

"I think you will not have long to wait then friend, for your misery to abate. There comes your enemy!" Coenred used the point of his fighting spear to aim southwards across the beck. Sigbert looked and squinted into the morning sunlight. Dark shapes were forming themselves into the recognisable body of a large number of men in armour.

The Vikings were coming.

Fulford Gate

"They are braver than what I took them for," Hardrada grunted. He turned to Tostig. "Only boys you said."

"That they are," the Saxon nobleman replied with some scorn. "No doubt they look to impress brother Harold with their valour."

"Whoever chose this ground did well; I do not like it," The Norwegian King declared. He looked along the Saxon shield-wall, noting the river bank to the west. "And a river before them too."

"'Tis shallow," Tostig asserted, "it will be no obstacle."

"To a man in armour charging a shield-wall under a rain of throwing spears it may well prove to be an obstacle," the Viking asserted. He knew that Tostig had experience of battle but he wondered if the man's lust for revenge was clouding his judgement. In battle even a row of bushes could become an obstacle. He had seen men trip and fall and break their own shield-wall for losing their footing on a root or a stone. It was usually men like Tostig who failed to consider such things and men such as that who lost battles. "Lord Tostig, form your men on my right."

"Aye, My Lord." Tostig moved his horse away and called his captains to him, pointing out where he wanted his men to form up.

"He has some fine men," Prince Olaf commented as he pushed his horse up alongside his father's in the space made by Tostig's absence.

"Think you so?" Hardrada shot a hard glance at his son. "What say you Siward?"

"Some Scotsmen. Some Franks. Some Northumbrians too, mostly mercenaries. Experienced but not Viking; not to be relied upon." Jarl

Siward spoke in a matter of fact tone, not even bothering to look at the men under discussion.

"My thoughts too," Hardrada agreed. "They will do for the task in hand though. My Jarls of Orkney take your valiant men to the centre and let Jarl Siward here give you positions of glory!"

Paul Thorfinnsson raised his battle-axe in salute and followed the king's friend towards what would be, if Hardrada's quickly forming plan succeeded, the hub of their battle line.

They had a reputation for ferocious wildness in battle but when it came to forming as a body in preparation for the fight the Vikings displayed a surprising amount of discipline. They began to line themselves up along the south bank of the beck but not within a spear's throw of their enemy. The jeering started quickly, punctuated with the odd thrown stone. Most fell short or clattered harmlessly off the large round shields that both sides carried, but occasionally one would hit a helmet and reverberate with a clang, an event that would be greeted by a louder jeer from whichever side had thrown the stone.

"Why do you send Tostig to the right?" Prince Olaf asked. "Is it not a position of honour, to fight on the king's right hand?"

Hardrada grunted in reply and then dismounted.

"Follow me," he commanded.

Just behind the forming Viking line there was a patch of higher ground that allowed them to look over the heads of the warriors and even beyond the Saxon lines to the north.

"The ground here where I make our line is firmer," Hardrada told his son. "My eye tells me that on the right flank it is soft and wet, disguised mayhap by trees like the alder, but I can smell the marshes from here; not good for attacking troops. I can only rely on Tostig's men to hold a short while if the Saxon's attack but that would be enough."

"Why would the Saxon's attack, they have an excellent defensive position?"

"You can see that eh?" Hardrada allowed himself a brief smile at his son's perceptiveness. "Do you also see that the Saxon army is commanded by at least two eoldermen?"

He pointed across the beck. Amongst the Saxon ranks many banners flew, mostly one coloured and simple, but there were some standards that were larger and more intricate. One was a large black square with a yellow dragon rearing on its hind legs, not far from it there was also a blue rectangle with yellow diagonal lines that crossed in the centre.

"The Pagan and Christian flags of Mercia," Hardrada explained, "and there!" The king's arm swung further to the right and pointed out a banner of eight alternate stripes of red and gold. "The flag of Northumbria." He grinned as if this were some just discovered advantage. "Lord Tostig told me to look for those banners to know the positions of the eorls; allies have some uses you see."

"I mark their place of stand but to what advantage is it to us?"

"Edwin and Morcar are kin now to Godwinson but not necessarily friends of his. If this were not so they would have remained behind the walls of Jorvik and awaited relief from the king's army. No, they come to the field to meet us and win glory. The Saxons will attack, and that meets well with my plan."

"To overwhelm them?"

"To destroy them. If we break these in front of us that guard the riverbank while the Saxons to our right push Tostig back the line of the battle will change-"

"They will have their backs to the Dam Lands!" Prince Olaf realised excitedly.

"And, if my plan works, our warriors will face them on three sides," The Viking king smiled grimly.

"And if they stand firm?"

"If they stand then we will lose more warriors than is my want. The outcome of a battle is only ever certain where one chieftain is a fool and the other possessed of craft. Someone has chosen this land and chosen well, we will see if it is the eorls and if they have the strength to match their ambition." Hardrada glanced back over his shoulder. The Viking army was still making its way up to the front, captains directing the men to each flank according to their lord. It would be at least an hour before the bulk of their forces had arrived and deployed.

The King of Norway had brought seven thousand men with him, a strong force by anyone's reckoning. A further three thousand under the command of the reliable Eystein Orre had been left at Riccall to both guard the fleet and their line of retreat if it were needed. Looking back north over the Germany Beck he calculated that the Saxons could not match that number. The front line looked impressive, armour and helmets glinting in the sun. Huscarls, warriors that should not be underestimated when it came to battle. His keen eye told him that a significant number of the men behind the front line were poor quality soldiers, however.

"If I were the Saxon commander I would attack now whilst we're still forming our line," Hardrada muttered.

The City of London

The northern gate of London rose before the thundering horsemen at last. Waltham was only some twenty miles behind them but in the heat of the king's urgency it seemed an age since they had set out in advance of the main royal party, leaving the queen to travel with the baggage train and the few attendants that had travelled with Harold and Ealdgyth only a few days ago for the peace of the abbey. In himself Harold felt well again, as if being in the presence of the Holy Rood had indeed worked God's healing power into his body and soul once more. God had blessed him; he knew it to be true.

Half-foot had interrupted the king at his ninth hour prayers, judging quite rightly that the news brought by the messenger from London was deserving of his immediate attention. He had also judged correctly that their leaving Waltham quickly was inevitable and had given orders to that effect even before the king had heard the news. The queen would follow at a more leisurely pace and retire to Westminster where she would probably complete her pregnancy. What King Harold chose to do next was beyond even Half-foot's ability to judge, however.

Osfrid had ridden out at the first receipt of the news to inform the king's brothers that Harold would return to London that very day. Half-foot rode with the king, a small band of loyal companions and the inevitable bodyguard of huscarls. Unlike them he did not carry a sword at his side but he was counted as one of their number all the same.

Harold, for his part, rejoiced in the moment, not least because it signalled the end of his withdrawal from the court and a return to the trappings of kingship. The touch of the mid-morning air on his face and the pounding of the horses' hooves on the road brought back memories of another flight, not so many months back at the start of the New Year. Then he had been leaving London as an eorl and riding under a night sky full of stars, this time the sun was still warming a September day and he was now a king.

It had taken them almost two hours to reach London from Waltham, the Saxon horse was not bred for speed but they did have stamina and if they could not gallop the full twenty or so miles then they did at least canter most of it. Inevitably the green woodland and golden fields gave way to the closer confines of the city that forced the royal party to slow down as they passed through the gate. It seemed as if the streets were thronged with a countless number of people, not there to see the passage of the king particularly but merely to go about their daily lives, trading, working, and of course talking; always talking.

London was a vibrant place these days but sometimes Harold felt as if it were too enclosed with too many people pressing in on every side. The old Roman walls offered protection still and yet they also seemed to serve as a stone fetter binding the people as well, restricting their movement and freedom to breathe clean country air. He could foresee a time when the city would have to escape those all encompassing walls.

In the king's absence the Royal Court at Westminster had been closed and the nominal running of the kingdom continued by his brothers, Gyrth, Eorl of East Anglia, and Leofwine, Eorl of Kent, at the Godwins' lodge within the city walls. The house had been built by their father and was fit to entertain royalty. It stood two storeys high with a tiled roof and it covered land that could accommodate at least eight normal dwellings. The windows facing out onto the street even had glass worked into them, a very public display of the wealth of the Godwin family.

Servants, alerted by the earlier arrival of the Royal Companion Osfrid, waited outside the grand house and took charge of the tired horses as soon as the party dismounted, leading the animals around to the rear of the building where they would be stabled.

King Harold marched through doors held open for him by more household servants, down a corridor, past storerooms and quarters and into the grand opening of the main hall. Trestle tables were strewn about and occupied by busy men; the atmosphere within the hall mirrored the king's own energetic disposition.

"Gyrth!" He called out to announce his arrival.

Immediately Harold's younger brother detached himself from a group of courtiers and answered the call.

"You come so quickly," he observed.

"As needs must," Harold removed his fine linen cloak, a servant whisking it away unasked. "What news?"

"As I sent to you at Waltham. A large Norse fleet landed men at Scarborough and they put the town to the torch."

Harold drank a cup of weak beer in one draft, the servant took the empty vessel away quickly.

"The people fled into the moors of the Vale of York," Gyrth continued, "but they had the sense to send riders to the city itself and they in their turn sent messengers south to alert us of the danger."

"And you think that I have travelled quickly?" Harold grinned at his younger brother. "Then this is no raiding party?"

"Nay, the King of Norway himself leads them," Gyrth confirmed emphatically.

Osfrid, the captain of the royal companions, joined the king and nodded his support of the younger eorl's declaration.

"This is not to be trusted," Leofwine finally spoke. He had stood almost on the outskirts of his two elder brothers' meeting with barely controlled frustration. He resented the fact that they judged him, wrongly in his opinion, to be too young to participate in such councils. "They fled the village without a fight, now they seek to save some honour by exaggerating the threat that they faced."

"Mayhap," Harold conceded knowing full well that they would not be the first Saxons to do so before a Viking invasion. "What makes you so sure that this is the army of Hardrada of Norway?"

"Tostig marches with him," Gyrth replied.

For a moment Harold said nothing but a surprising range of emotions flashed quickly over his face; surprise, disappointment, anger. He still held onto the hope that Tostig would return to the family and this news was a bitter draught to swallow.

"Are you sure?"

"One of the riders is a lower theign who served and suffered under Tostig's rule of Northumbria, brought down to become a fisher of the sea when he fell foul of our brother's opinion. He tarried long enough when the Vikings put ashore to witness Tostig stride up the beach in the company of Hardrada."

"His testimony is beyond doubt?"

"He described Tostig well," Osfrid agreed with Gyrth. "Also, his description of Hardrada matches that which we know so well. Mayhap the wolf is in the fold?"

"The messenger is here himself if you wish to speak with him?" Gyrth made a hand gesture to two huscarls, men dressed in normal clothes but possessed with an evident martial bearing. Between them stood Sabert son of Cudberct, known as Saba to many. His clothes were stained by his long journey from York but he had been told to wash his hands and face, and to comb his hair, before he was presented to the king. He looked both tired and in awe at the same time.

"He has made an heroic effort to join us here so mayhap I should also make an effort to hear his story from his own lips," Harold conceded.

The warriors approached with their charge who glanced around him as if he was indeed a stranger in a strange land, and not a little afraid of the company that he now found himself in.

"Repeat for the king your account of what happened at Scarborough," Gyrth instructed the fisherman. Saba did as he was told, relating almost word for word the same report that he had given the Eorl of East Anglia. This fact only confirmed the veracity of the messenger's story in the mind of Gyrth. "I see no reason for the riders from Scarborough to embellish their tale with these personages merely to save face," Gyrth added when Saba had finished his report. "This is why I thought it best that you should know, even whilst in retreat at Waltham Abbey."

"You were right to do so," admitted Harold. He turned his attention again to Saba. "You have had a hard journey my friend, to bring us this news from the north. Your family will be missing you I expect?"

"Aye, My Lord, but a good friend has taken them into his care until I can return to them again at York," Saba answered, after a moment's pause he added; "He is of Danish blood but his heart is English, My Lord."

"There are many of Danish blood in Northumbria," Osfrid observed.

"Aye, My Lord," Saba agreed, "many are like my friend Abiorn, settled here with kith and kin and very little to tie them to their Norse homeland."

"Of what need is there to talk of this?" Leofwine demanded.

"There are many people in Northumbria with blood ties to the Norse; Norwegians as well as Danes," Gyrth answered him.

"If King Hardrada has indeed sailed to England with an army I doubt that it will be wholly Norwegian, his war with the Danes is reported to have thinned out his forces somewhat. He may look to recruit new swords to his banner from amongst the Norse settled in the north of our kingdom." Harold pointed out the danger perceived by himself and Gyrth to their younger brother.

"Hardrada will make no friends amongst the Danes of Northumbria," Saba spoke up for his friends, "they have chosen their lot, made their lives and raised their families in England. The Norwegians burnt Danish homes as well as Saxon at Scarborough."

"They will do the same at York," Osfrid added.

"Enough." Harold interjected in a calm voice. "There's no cause to give you greater worry," he told Saba, "you will remain here and rest; food and a bed will be found for you."

"My Lord, I would return to my family at York," Saba replied.

"You will my good man, when it is safe to do so, when I have made York safe from this threat. Besides, your horse, I dare say, will be all but broken after such a hard pressed ride. Half-foot!"

"Yes, My Lord." As usual he appeared promptly when summoned.

"This man is to receive a boon for his loyalty and courage," Harold instructed him. The command was noted and as the huscarls recognised that he had been dismissed Saba was escorted out of the hall.

"I had weighed Hardrada's claim to my crown as little more than Norse bluster from across the whale-road," Harold admitted, "I did not expect him to make it good with an army of conquest."

The three brothers fell into a moment of silent reverie with both Osfrid and Half-foot as the bustle of the court flowed around them.

"Do we know where they are now?" The king asked eventually.

"No, but all thoughts go to York; it is the capital of Northumbria. It would make sense for Hardrada to attack it and take it if he can," Gyrth answered.

"Where are Edwin and Morcar?

"Edwin was with Morcar in Northumbria, up at Ripon the last we heard," Half-foot answered. It was one of his habits to keep an up to date account of the movements of all the important eoldermen wherever they might be in the kingdom.

"Surely you will not rely upon them?" Leofwine asked.

"They are eoldermen and family," Harold told him, "they will do their duty."

"Their power may not be sufficient if the numbers of ships suggested in this report be true?" Leofwine insisted.

"All they have to do is bar the gates of York and hold the walls against Hardrada; I expect nothing more of them," Harold replied with confidence.

"That might indeed frustrate the immediate plans of Hardrada," Gyrth agreed, "but it will not stop him, he could lay waste to the whole of the Vale of York and the Isle of Holderness in the meantime. What will you do?"

"What of the storms in the southern channel?"

"They blow as strong as ever. My eyes and ears in Normandy tell me that Guillaume has moved his troops further up the coast but that the wind defeats his purpose still. Winter approaches and he does not have long left to make his move," Half-foot once more answered.

"I would feel easier about that if the fleet were not called back to port," Leofwine added.

"The fleet could no more survive the storms on the whale-road than the Normans could," Harold countered. "The ships needed refitting and the lithsmen resting, the winds gave us this respite and the fleet will be all the stronger for it when the storms eventually blow out. I think that the Norse in the north present a greater danger to us than the Norman's to the south. We will march north."

"To York?" Gyrth asked in surprise.

"Aye, to York. Leofwine, you will stay in London and manage the kingdom from here. Gyrth and I will summon what power we can and march north to rescue Edwin and Morcar from the threat of the Viking." Harold spoke firmly, his mind was set. "Half-foot, you like to ride?"

"Well it is better than walking, My Lord!"

"Then you ride with us to York. Mayhap we will be able to make our presence felt in the north and do some good there after we have dealt with this presumptuous King of Norway."

"This thing you propose has never been achieved before," Gyrth pointed out.

"Then mayhap even the great Hardrada will not think of it," Harold replied with a grim smile. "Both he and Tostig will know that should York fall I must head north to recover Northumbria so the journey must be made at any cost; sooner rather than later say I."

"Our own power is not so great since the fyrd was disbanded to bring in the harvest," Gyrth commented.

"True, but the eorls of Mercia and Northumbria do have their own power, such as it is, and if we come upon Hardrada camped outside the walls of York he will find himself between two Saxon forces."

"But what if Edwin and Morcar give battle before the walls of York?" Leofwine asked.

"Against the War Wolf? They are not so stupid as to contemplate such an action," Harold assured his brothers. "No, they will do the right thing and stay behind the walls of York; they have no reason to act in any other way."

Fulford Gate

Strike now!

The thought kept coming back into his mind.

Morcar looked the length of the Viking line before him and swore that he could see holes in the shield-wall created by groups of men who had not yet formed up properly. The road north from Riccall was narrow; the Viking army was stretched out in a long column to the south. Most of it had not yet taken up its place in the line of battle even though they were being encouraged to advance at a trot by their captains.

How long has it been since the first of them had arrived?

One hour? Two hours?

Who decided when a battle was to be begun?

Who threw the first spear?

Who claimed first blood?

Now was the time to strike.

He glanced up at the morning sun and judged it to be ten of the clock. If that was right then they had been waiting well over an hour since the first Vikings had arrived.

The church bells in York rang out the hour only minutes ago surely?

September had been warm this year. It would soon become uncomfortably so, exhausting weather in which to fight a battle. He felt sweat trickle down the back of his neck, under his byrnie and moistening the padded jacket that he wore beneath it. His shoulder length hair, bound by a woven plait to keep it out of his eyes, itched from the warmth of the helmet. The day would only get warmer; that was for certain.

Strike now!

Edwin's plan was to hold this position along the beck, to resist the Viking onslaught by the strength of their shield-wall, but what if another opportunity offered itself?

What if he saw an advantage that was denied to his elder brother? How many weapons-men had Hardrada and Tostig brought with them?

If their force was greater than that which he and Edwin had been able to muster then did it not make sense to strike before the full strength of the Vikings was assembled before them

How many Saxon lives might be saved by taking the advantage and pushing the Vikings back before they had time to exert their full power against an outnumbered Saxon fyrd?

He glanced around at his own men. He had eleven hundred huscarls, all heavily armed and armoured. He also had the pick of the fyrd; the richer theigns and the better equipped fyrdmen, over three thousand in all. Behind them was a motley collection of peasant villagers who would fall on the wounded enemy like hounds on a deer.

Hereric glanced at the young lord. The expensive helmet was a little too large for the boy; it almost hid the whole of his face from this angle making it difficult for the huscarl to read his emotions. As he stood beside his lord, however, he was loath to move so as to make it obvious that he was concerned. It had impressed him greatly that Morcar had taken up a position in the front of the shield-wall, a duty demanded by his noble birth but not always honoured by a man of title. This would make protecting him somewhat easier as Morcar would use his shield to ward off the weapons of the enemy and Hereric could assist him if necessary. If the battle should turn against them then Hereric was ideally placed to rescue the eorl.

He looked at the enemy troops forming across the beck and was not impressed. They looked like adventurers only, nithing, men without honour. That did not sit well with his expectations; this was supposed to be the army of the fabled King of Norway! Hardrada had fought everywhere from his own land to the steppes of the Rus and from there to even the Holy Land. His Companions were warriors of great repute, heroes who haunted the hearth-talk of the Saxons in the long dark nights, not this ragged collection of mercenaries! The War Wolf had turned into a mangy hound. The Saxon warrior grunted his disappointment into the morning air.

Tostig Godwinson turned in his saddle and looked back down the road that led to Riccall and up which the army was even now still marching. Siward had taken the Jarls of Orkeny and their retinue to the centre of the line. Hardrada was over on the left and his men were beginning to bunch up behind him. Tostig had barely two thousand men, only half of whom had so far arrived. It crossed his mind that Hardrada might offer him up as bait in a trap and that thought might have taken hold if it had not been for a Viking captain leading several hundred Danes over to Tostig's line to help bolster his men.

A small flock of starlings flew overhead, possibly early arrivals coming to spend winter in England. He wondered if the Vikings might stay as long as those raucous birds.

Where should I stand?

There was a number of Danes immediately to his left and he knew that they probably would not take commands from a Saxon even if he was the ally of the King of Norway. His right wing was weak but important, it would benefit from a leader, but should it be a captain or an eolderman?

"I will take the flank, My Lord," Oswyn announced as if reading Tostig's mind, "will you give me that honour?"

"It will require a steadfast heart to hold," Tostig commented. He looked at Oswyn with genuine appreciation. His father had always taught his sons to value true loyalty and Oswyn had proven a very loyal vassal. "I doubt not that you possess the quality to do this thing though. My only command is that you survive this fight Oswyn," Tostig spoke with genuine sincerity.

The captain smiled at his lord's words and started directing men to form the far flank as best as they could.

Tostig turned now to assess the enemy from the advantage of his horse. The Saxon line looked strong and he prayed that they would not have the foresight to attack just yet!

Strike now!

Eorl Morcar gave the signal, raising his sword in the air and slowly bringing it down and pointing at the enemy. A strident peal erupted from the battle horns behind them, raucous enough to set teeth on edge. From the rear of the Saxon army archers began to loose their shafts towards the Vikings. Most of the arrows would fail to find flesh, but many would strike the great round shields and, if they held, they would add weight to tire the warriors further.

"No, My Lord!" Hereric shouted in alarm but his voice was drowned out in the initial din.

Morcar gave out his war-cry and, hefting his own shield higher, started forward. He felt a rush of blood as the excitement took him. For a moment he was totally unafraid. Above his head the flag of Northumbria flew, spread out more by its movement through the clear September air than by any wind or breeze. He was young, rich, powerful, and he commanded an army. He had never felt so alive.

A great cry went up from his troops as they followed the young eorl's example. They marched to the bank of the beck and then down into the cool water through which they splashed without concern for their leather shoes or linen trousers. Like a machine they came on shields locked and spears gleaming. Those behind the first rank struck their own shields with their fighting spears and set up a thudding rhythm as if marking the time of their enemy's doom. The ground shook with the impact of their leather heels marching in the thousands. The chests of men felt the reverberation of wood on wood. The air bore the rhythmic, almost guttural chant of the warriors as they sought to bolster their own courage and incite fear into their enemies. Battle horns gave out long peals of strident notes that threatened to rend ears by their volume alone.

Hereric could not break the shield-wall once the march had begun; he was borne along with it. He knew in his mind that this was what Coenred had feared but still another part of him, the warrior steeped in the blood of his enemies, rejoiced. He found some pride in the bravado of his young lord who stepped so boldly to carry the fight to the hated enemy. His mail chinked as he walked, the leather fastenings of his harness creaking. The point of his spear glinted menacingly in the morning light and his vibrant blood coursed through his body. Hereric sucked air into his lungs and bellowed a war cry like an angry bull.

What had promised to be a fine late summer morning now became something far more threatening and, despite the clear sunlight, much darker.

Tostig, still on horseback, looked over the heads of his warriors. He glanced at the wet ground, already turned into a muddy hole by the passage of so many feet. Despite the sun the ground was damp from lying so close to the marshes. They were stuck here and he saw that Hardrada had indeed used him. His men could not retreat because the mud would hold them, they would be hacked down with their backs to their enemies if they tried to turn and flee. The Northumbrian throwing spears would scythe them down without mercy. No one expected any quarter when Saxon and Viking met on the field of battle and they were right not to do so.

He also saw the Saxons marching forward and felt, for the first time, a moment of misgiving. His own men were not properly in position yet. His archers were still approaching the field and more spear-men were still making their way north. There was seven miles between Riccall and Fulford Gate and it remained lined almost its entire length by Viking warriors hurrying to the fight. It may yet prove to be a moment of good judgement to have launched the attack so early.

The Saxon's were coming on in good order, their shield-wall looking firm, and their spears held high, ready to strike down into their enemy. Tostig's men began to murmur their misgivings too loudly; too freely. The mud clung to their feet, their calves, sucking at their shoes. It made movement difficult. It robbed them of their mobility, their strength; their hope.

We are stuck here in the mud like wildboar at bay, well, let's show the hounds of Morcar our tusks!

Tostig swung down from his horse and grabbed his shield from his servant. It was not a traditional round shield, such as both the Saxons and the Vikings used, but after the Norman fashion with a long tapering point that covered almost the whole of the side of his body that he would present to the enemy. Quickly he donned his helmet and swung the distinctive great shield onto his left arm. He drew his sword to mark himself out as a lord and a leader of men and ran forward into the Viking shield-wall commanding them to stand with a voice that expressed authority. The men around him were wavering but the arrival of Lord Tostig seemed to do something to bolster their nerves. Whatever else men might say he was they could not deny that Tostig Godwinson was a brave Saxon warrior in the mould of his father, Eorl Godwin had raised no cowards amongst his many sons.

At thirty paces distance from the enemy the Saxons stopped. The chanting and shield striking ended just as suddenly and in its absence the silence was even more unnerving. Instinctively the seasoned warriors in Tostig's line lowered their heads as a volley of throwing spears shuddered into their shields. Those who had not followed their example suffered, some fatally. Although the volley had been purposefully aimed at the shields of the Vikings some spears sailed higher than intended and if they did not strike an unguarded man in the front row then they might draw blood in the second line. The barbs on the spear heads made the weapons difficult to remove from either wood or flesh without doing further damage. The iron shanks of the angons made them impossible to sever with either sword or axe. Whatever they penetrated they made useless.

Immediately the Saxons began their march again at another peal from their battle horns. Hereric felt a surge of pride in the men, that they marched and executed their battle drill with such frightening discipline. Even the less experienced seemed to be in step with the huscarls around them. He knew that there would be a response from the enemy and hoped that the men, his men, would now have the courage to face it when it came. Some Vikings hurled their own throwing spears but they lacked the co-ordination and impact of the Saxon flood. Where a shield was hit the man simply stopped to rid himself of the spear and his comrade behind him would take his place, filling the opening in the wall.

Amongst the Vikings there was little movement to enter the front rank. Men attempted to free their shields of the encumbrance of fixed spears alone leaving themselves exposed to the approaching army. One Norse warrior wrestled with his shield and stepped from the line in his attempts to free the angon. Unconsciously he turned his back on the approaching enemy in his efforts to be rid of the annoying weapon.

Another Saxon volley followed. At the closer range the javelins bit deep into the linden wood of the shields. Some were thrown with such fury by practiced arms so as to pierce flesh as well as wood; joining the two together. The warrior who had strayed from the safety of the shield-wall presented too good a target. The warnings from his brother warriors came too late, before he could react to them a large spearpoint thrust through his back and exited red and gory below his breastbone. His face expressed his shock and agony as he fell to his knees before his countrymen.

The Saxons continued their march. Inevitably the two sides came together.

Morcar felt the impact of the shield-walls as wood and metal met, he felt the vibration run through his body, jarring his teeth and shaking his bones, and then he felt exultation as the enemy gave way. They did not collapse but they took more than a step backwards.

"Push!" He yelled, keeping his head behind his shield.

"Push!" Hereric echoed.

The Saxons pushed. Tostig's men attempted to hold them, warriors throwing themselves bodily against the pressing shield-wall. Their feet slipped in the mud. The weight of four thousand Saxons bore down upon them and it was fuelled with hate and violence. The Viking line was pushed back, pressed by numbers greater than their own, and by a ferocity seemingly greater than their own as well.

As if in answer to his prayers more men arrived behind Tostig and they lent their shoulders to the task. Even though they were badly outnumbered still the Vikings fought back against the advancing Saxon war machine. Eventually they succeeded in slowing the push of the Saxons. Where it was joined to the centre of Hardrada's army, where the Jarls of Orkney fought, Tostig's line was strongest and that part had held firm, but the further to the right of the flank it extended it proved weaker so that the most extreme reach of his men had been pushed the furthest back. They were almost in danger of being on top of the Viking centre and the reinforcements still hurrying up the Riccall road.

Oswyn cursed the mud. He cursed the men around him and he cursed the Saxons, his own countrymen, in front of him. Their feet slipped in the mud and the greater weight of the Saxon shield-wall pressed them further back. He knew that they needed more men urgently but he did not waste time on that thought. He was a warrior-theign, a man trained to war. For better or worse he had committed himself to be Tostig Godwinson's man and he had enjoyed the benefit of the good times; he believed that his lord's alliance with the Vikings would bring those good times back again. He would stand his ground knowing that Tostig would prove a true giver of rings when this day was done.

From behind the Saxons a sudden flurry of spears were launched again. They sailed over the front rank of the Vikings and fell into the bodies of the men behind them. Screams and the scent of warm blood filled the morning air, assailing the nostrils of Saxons and Vikings alike.

As the Saxon warriors in the front pushed again with their huge shields the men immediately behind them started to stab over the shoulders of their comrades with long fighting spears aimed at the heads of their enemies. Some of these weapons were equipped with backwards pointing barbs as well as the sharp spear head. They did little damage in the forward thrust but as a strong Saxon arm pulled the spear back the barbs bit into metal, removing a helmet, flesh, ripping a face or neck, shield, pulling it down. One Norseman found his shield pulled forward by such a spear, the barb caught on the steel rim. As he stepped involuntary forward an axe chopped into his body, splintering his fine chain mail and crushing his ribcage. In the space created by the fall of the warrior spears thrust in to stab into the flesh of the warriors positioned behind him.

Morcar hacked over the top of his shield at the men in front of him. He did not colour his sword with their blood, they were too canny for that, but he kept their heads down and a warrior behind him would jab a long spear into the space vacated by the Viking helmet hoping to reach the man behind.

Hereric stabbed with his fighting spear and screamed obscenities at the hated enemy, goading them into being careless, daring them to respond, knowing that any poor judgement or weakness on their part would be instantly pounced upon by the Saxons around him and a savage toll exacted.

Blood began to stain the mired mud beneath the combatants' feet. Bodies fell to be trampled under the advancing Saxons. Tostig's line was beginning to give. He could see that by the marshlands his men were desperately trying to move back without turning but the mud was hampering them. Their shield-wall was disintegrating and fighting spears, swords and axes were beginning to cut into bodies. Arrows flew like angry birds over his head to fall into the men who were still advancing to join the battle, and still the Saxons pushed on with a relentless fury.

Coenred cursed passionately. Morcar had done exactly what Edwin had promised he would not do, and what he had known in his heart that he would. The Saxon line was now changing into an 'L' shape as Eorl Edwin remained where he was and Eorl Morcar pursued Tostig's bending line. The Vikings at the centre were holding, however, as those nearer the dam lands gave way and the enemy on the right had yet to move.

He ordered his men to spread a little more thinly in an attempt to keep the two flanks connected, but he knew that this was also a dangerous move. Their strength lay in a close, disciplined formation; the shield-wall. It would lose effectiveness if the warriors were placed too loosely. However, he hoped to spot a break between the two flanks and plug it with his own body and those of the men he commanded and to do that he would have to move quickly, something that the a close formation could not do.

"A bad beginning makes a bad ending says I," Sigbert muttered.

"Mayhap a stumble might save a fall," Coenred countered.

"There'll be some running to do this day I tell thee," Sigbert complained further.

"Towards the enemy or away from them?"

"From one end of this battlefield to another methinks. I hate running,"

"In this heat it'll more likely be the death of us than any sharp spear or Danish axe," Coenred mused.

"Mayhap, but it seems to me that this fight is about to reach a point of decision my friend. I hope to see thee on t' other side of it!"

At the centre of the Viking battle line the Jarls of Orkney stood and fought in a manner that would have made their famous father, Thorfinnsson the Mighty, proud. Each were joined by their own companions, men well appointed with arms and armour, and together they made firm the shield-wall so that at this point the line remained unmoving even as Tostig Godwinson's men were forced to give ground step by step to their right.

They stood beneath the mythical raven banner of Orkney, an imitation of the ill-fated flag used by Jarl Sigurd the Stout. The folktales spoke that he had been granted victory whenever that banner flew before him but it was also said that the man who carried the banner himself was doomed to die. Legend maintained that eventually the jarl was compelled to carry his own banner because of the reluctance of his men to do so following too many of their comrades dying. Inevitably the jarl was killed by the spears of his enemies.

Today the banner man stood firm, brave and strong before the Saxons. The Raven of Orkney, a carefully embroidered stylisation of the bird of black on a sky blue background, stretched out its wings in the September sun without falling once. The men of Orkney retained their stand around their young lords, giving not so much as an inch before the pressing Northumbrians. In so doing they brought the battle to a critical moment.

Hardrada grunted absently as he stood on the small patch of high ground behind the Viking lines. He was not so vainglorious that he could not see when a battle stood to be won or lost. He had no love for Tostig but he still had a use for him. From his vantage point he could see the change in the two opposing lines on his right and he knew instinctively that the time to act was now.

"Siward, take men to the centre and send others to the right flank to offer Lord Tostig some relief," He commanded. "Olaf, come here boy and learn what it is to be a man."

The prince dismounted and joined his father, followed by his own retainers.

"Unfurl my banner Styrkar; it is time to win this battle."

His giant bannerman stepped forward with a pole that he lavished great care upon. He removed a canvas bag from the end and shook free King Hardrada's infamous banner, Land Ravager! It was a triangle of red cloth with a rounded outer edge from which hung a series of tassels. A rod extended from the pole when inserted to uphold the top edge of the flag so that the symbol could always be seen even if there was no wind to catch it. On the cloth was painted a stylised Nordic representation of a black raven in flight, its head pointing up into the top of the triangle. This was Odin's bird and with it Hardrada would invoke the power of that particular god to strike terror into the hearts of his enemies.

"Now Styrkar," Hardrada clapped the warrior on one massive arm, "show my bird to the enemy and run with me into their shield-wall so that we may see the fear in their eyes."

The Vikings gathered around the king grunted with satisfaction. They had listened to the sound of conflict to the east for long enough, now they were ready for their own moment of glory.

Jarl Siward hefted his shield into a more battle ready position on his left arm and gave the call to the Viking horns to announce the charge. With several hundred experienced warriors he ran in a loose formation into the left of the Viking's centre. Their arrival sent a ripple of encouragement through the battered line. Siward led them on into the right flank of the Northumbrians where they collided with savage violence. The influx of these new reserves gave the Norse army new belief and they began to fight back against the Saxon push.

Vikings painted blue, scorning armour, and carrying single handed axes and long knives did not pause to use throwing spears but launched themselves bodily into the Saxon shield-wall. A young Saxon theign stared disbelievingly as one of these berserkers leapt high in the air and came down bodily onto his shield. The theign staggered at the unexpected blow and his knees gave way. He fell to the ground with the wild Norseman on top of his shield. Over the bodies of both Viking spears shot into the opening that had been created and drew blood from the warriors who had been standing behind their theign.

The young Saxon tried to rise and felt the weight suddenly lift from his shield. He thought that he had a chance to rejoin the fight but instead the blue contorted face of his enemy appeared snarling over the top of his shield. The theign never saw the knife that flashed across his throat.

Coenred saw the Vikings making the push through the centre; it was exactly what he had feared would happen. He called his men to him and readied his weapons. He spoke a single word and the huscarls formed themselves into a wedge with their captain at the point. Sigbert fell in on his left-hand side. Coenred composed himself, watching the Saxons before him beginning to give ground. He opened and closed his grip on his great fighting spear, feeling the smooth grain of the wooden shaft beneath his fingers. With a great cry, he led the counter charge. Just as the Viking attack had staggered the Saxon line with its violence so did this unexpected surge of huscarls, supported by their fyrdmen at their centre, do the same to the Norsemen.

The first that Jarl Siward knew of the enemy's response was when a sliver of steel flashed into the neck of the man who stood next to him and release a crimson fountain from his neck.

"Thorald!" Siward shouted in alarm as his cousin staggered, the man's life blood pumping through the open wound. Thorald's eyes bulged and his mouth was open but no words ushered forth. The press of bodies was at this point so close that Thorald was kept upright even as his life ebbed away and his legs could no longer support him. He died whilst still upright.

A blood red anger descended upon Jarl Siward and he launched himself at the nearest Saxon, beating down his shield with the butt of his spear and then doing the same to the man, ramming the wooden shaft mercilessly into his chest and rejoicing in seeing him collapse before the onslaught, coughing blood.

Sigbert the Huscarl felt the impact of his spear as it collided with a shield. He pushed knowing what the warrior should do, try to deflect the blow away and behind him bringing the Saxon closer. The Viking did not disappoint and Sigbert lurched forward with all the power in his squat, muscular legs. He rammed his shield bodily into the Norseman and lifted him from the ground. The force of this prodigious display of strength carried them both into the ranks immediately behind the Viking warrior.

The Saxons behind Sigbert dashed forward in support and struck with spears and axes and swords and langseaxes into any opening that they could find. Sigbert roared his challenge and engaged the men immediately in front of him again, his darting spear point glancing off one helmeted head and leaving the wearer with a thunderous headache in its wake.

Hardrada moved to the front of his men as was the Viking way, his bodyguard forming around him. He urged them on with words designed to fire their blood lust. His plan was simple. As Jarl Siward led the feint into the centre he would take the best of his own men along the river bank against the Saxon right flank. Part of the force would engage the Saxon's directly; his section would push hard against the edge of their shield-wall nearest the river and break through.

With a howl the giant Norwegian King raised his sword, swung it in a great arc and then charged towards the enemy. Olaf fell in behind him and marvelled that his father, despite his age, still had the strength and vitality of a wolf, if not also the awesome threat of violence that animal possessed too.

They ran down the narrow ford across Germany Beck but their numbers were so great that many had to wade through the waters themselves. It slowed them down and lessened the impact of their onslaught, but what an impact they made.

Eorl Edwin looked towards the sudden sound of the Viking advance and felt a cold chill run down his back despite the warming September sun. He had allowed himself to think that his brother's successful advance was turning the battle in their favour but now he saw before him what he feared the most; the real Viking strength.

"HOLD!"

Thrydwulf commanded his men in his deep, booming, voice. They hefted their shields and stood their ground. Throwing spears hammered into their defence, adding to the weight of the shields so that the weaker warriors began to let them droop. Then came the berserkers again. One individual ran towards the front line, a Viking spearman fell to one knee before him and the wild warrior used his back to launch himself over the heads of the Norsemen. He came down with one foot on the chest of a Saxon eolderman and the other on his shield.

The Saxon had been unable to anticipate the attack but he was as strong as an ox and instead of falling he stumbled backwards, remaining on his feet. The berserker landed on his side on the trampled grass before him but sprang back to his feet like a cat.

The eorl recovered his own balance and attacked with his shield held forward and his sword ready to fall. The Viking showed contempt for the eorl and came at him with a flurry of blows delivered by the two short-swords that he wielded. The eorl retreated before the furious attack but not without purpose. As the berserker tried to close the ground between them fyrdmen loyal to the eolderman and armed with spears rushed around him and surrounded the Viking. As one they closed on him and then raised their spears upwards. Impaled upon the bright steel the Nosreman was lifted into the air screaming as his blood coursed down the wooden shafts.

Eorl Edwin could feel the resolve of his men melt like butter in this un-seasonal heat. The noise was suddenly terrific. The beating of axe, sword and spear on wood and metal sent vibrations through their bodies. The screaming of war-cries and death cries together intermingled like an insane cacophony. Battle horns blasted the air as if seeking to do violence to one another. The world had gone mad around him. His teeth jarred as a great axe bit into his shield. He held his ground against the impact but was almost pulled off his feet as the Viking warrior corded his muscle and sinew to drag the axe blade free. The shield would not relinquish the blade but the impetus pulled Edwin forward. If it had not been for the equally strong arm of a warrior behind him that twisted itself around his waist Edwin would have been dragged bodily out of the Saxon shield-wall.

"Stay with us a little longer, My Lord," Thrydwulf grunted as he righted Edwin.

The young nobleman looked backwards over his shoulder at the huscarl but showed no signs of recognition. His senses had been shocked by the violence of the impact.

The Viking battle horns rent the morning air again and again, announcing that the battle was now joined near the river.

Now Eorl Edwin knew fear.

Now Eorl Edwin stared death in the face.

This was not Edwin's first battle but it was the first time that he had ever encountered the ferocity of the Vikings. He had heard the tales told around the fires of the long halls when he sat, just a boy, at the feet of his father and his father's companions. He had listened to the poems of the Battles of Brunanburh, and of Maldon, but the words had not captured the terror of the violence. They had spoken of courage, of glory, of noble deeds and of brave warriors. They had not talked of the blood that soaked the ground, the stench of butchered men and the wild viciousness of an enemy that sought not a noble combat but simply the destruction of all those that stood before them; clothed in blood and gore and touched by madness.

It was all that Edwin could do to keep his head down behind his shield as it was battered by spears and swords and axes. He dropped his own spears but had the presence of mind to draw his sword. The rain of blows against him did not cease but just the feel of the weapon in his hand gave him some renewed courage.

Men shouted all around him, in Norse, in English, with accents as varied as the lands from which they came but it did not matter; in the chaos of the battle little of it made any sense. Their bodies were pinned together and Edwin could only move if the men on either side of him moved too. He felt ineffectual. His rank did not matter. His status was little higher than that of the dead man at his feet and only then because he still drew breath. He felt death closing in on him like some hungry animal. He did not see his banner fall but fall it did. The dragon of Mercia surrendered the English sky to the raven of Odin.

Tostig Godwinson paused to recover his breath. His helmet was dented; his sword scratched and dipped in blood. An armoured Saxon, once a high-theign of Northumbria, stepped into his place in the front of the shield-wall so as not to allow the enemy any advantage following his lord's withdrawal. The warriors carried so much weight in arms and armour that even the strongest of them had to rest after twenty minutes of violent activity. As a rule the well armoured men in the front row concentrated on keeping the cohesion of the interlocking shields that protected everyone, relying upon their comrades standing behind them to deliver telling strokes with spears, axes and swords. As a leader of men Tostig had taken a place in the front rank and used his sword whenever possible to inspire those around him by his example and like many a warrior he could not resist the urge to attack the enemy when faced by them.

As he drew in long breaths of hot summer air, interspersed with sips from his flask, he took the time to try and assess their position. He could see that the far right flank, which was the weakest point in the line, had been pushed back a long way from its original position adjacent to the eastern marsh despite Oswyn's best efforts. The left had remained anchored to the centre, however, meaning that they had now pivoted at that point so that the wetlands were almost in front of them.

In his heart he knew that Hardrada had offered him up as bait to tempt Morcar into leaving his position of strength. It had worked. As a tactician he could not fault the king's thinking, but as a man facing those determined Saxons he could rue the loss of so many of his own men all for another's advantage, not to mention the threat to his own life that Hardrada's plan had engendered.

A fox is not taken twice in the same snare!

At that moment Tostig Godwinson, once judged to be a man of craft, swore an oath not be used again in such a fashion.

Now, however, the Norwegians were committing their reserves and Tostig could see that his position was improving as fresh warriors came to bolster his tired adventurers. The only flaw he could see in Hardrada's plan was that it still left the far right flank dangerously weak. If a resolute group of Saxons pushed hard on the edge of the flank then they might break through yet and reverse the Norse army's gains.

With this dire thought in mind Tostig began directing the men new to the fight to support the line where he saw it was the weakest, hoping that his own actions would be in time to avert a possible disaster.

For his part Oswyn had no time to appreciate the extra men directed by his lord to help his position. He was exhausted, overheated, his throat ached from thirst, but he refused to give way. Only the press of bodies before him and the fact that his shield was locked in the formation forced him to take steps backwards, but every step was marked with a swing of his sword. He rejoiced whenever he saw it stained with blood.

Coenred swore under his breath again. He felt no better for having warned against this. The Vikings were fighting like demons and his own counter-charge seemed to have done little to halt the push against Eorl Morcar's right flank. It was getting pressed away from Eorl Edwin now, there was a real danger that the two Saxon forces would be separated creating a gap into which Hardrada's forces would pour, splitting one brother from the other.

In desperation Coenred pushed on into the Viking ranks once more. His spear darting in and out of flesh, using his shield and even his helmet as a weapon but no matter how many warriors he cut down there seemed to be two or three more to take the place of the fallen. His men followed him but their wedge formation had now lost its cohesiveness and they were no longer as effective. Indeed it seemed that they were merely diverting the greater part of the enemy's reserves into Eorl Morcar's right flank and it was being driven further and further away from the Mercians. The tide of the battle was truly turning.

"Things go ill for us," Sigbert declared as he took a breather just behind Coenred. His fighting spear was broken and cast aside, his double-edged sword was in his hand now and it was already stained with the blood of the enemy. "There are more of them than I feared, I admit to that."

"Then we can do no more than what we are meant to do," Coenred replied tersely.

"Aye, kill more of the bastards," Sigbert agreed.

Thrydwulf could see it even if Eorl Edwin could not, but then the huscarl did not stand in the shield-wall with his head buried, too terrified to look at the enemy in their onslaught. The Mercians had not recovered from the initial attack and a large knot of Vikings pushed now with real intent along the riverbank. By weight of numbers alone they were rolling up the Saxon's right flank. He could see the large triangular red banner that led the Viking charge and he instinctively knew that he would find the famous King of Norway there. If he had been a younger man he might have sought out that banner man and come upon the legendary Norse warrior-king to try his own mettle with the War Wolf, but not today. He was a huscarl with a sworn duty to protect his lord or die trying.

"Step back," Thrydwulf ordered.

His voice was deep and booming, a voice trained to command in this chaos called battle. The huscarls, ever the professional soldiers, responded with cold determination, taking a measured step back and then anticipating the sudden rush of the Norsemen as they found an unexpected space between themselves and their enemy. The Saxon spears shot forward and pierced the unwary or foolhardy Viking but it was not enough.

Thrydwulf knew that he could not reverse their fortune by such tactics alone. He was looking to withdraw the best of the Mercian army in good order, not win the battle. As he knew they would the villagers took this sudden and repeated manoeuvre to mean defeat was imminent. They threw down their weapons and ran for safety, wherever it might lie.

He did not blame them, they were little more than eager amateurs caught up in the excitement but not knowing what madness they had let themselves in for. The reality terrified them. No, it was the reaction of the fyrdmen that concerned him.

Again and again he gave the order and the huscarls responded with discipline. Those fyrdmen who stood close to a huscarl seemed to copy their example but those in the rear, seeing the villagers bolt in panic, became nervous. They looked behind them rather than to where the danger lay and Thrydwulf could see the disaster about to take shape. He had no choice, however. There was no other way to extricate these brave men and the eorl who led them than to sacrifice the weaker fyrdmen to their own fear.

Jarl Siward took in great breaths of warm September air and quickly reviewed the situation. The battle was almost won, he could sense it. The

Northumbrians had lost touch with the Mercians and the Norse were beginning to push in between the two. Only a small band of huscarls fought to retain the integrity of the line. Siward resolved to shatter that resistance knowing that doing so would spell the end of the Saxon army.

He chose a large huscarl in splendid armour and came onto him like a charging bull. The Viking rammed into the Saxon shield to shield taking him by surprise and forcing him back several steps until they collided with the warrior behind him. Only then could he regain his footing and stop the Viking's charge. The two separated and glared at each other with a wary hatred.

"Saxon, I am Jarl Siward, Royal Companion to the King of Norway. Know that you have killed my kinsmen and I will have vengeance upon you," Siward declared. He did not know if this was indeed the warrior who had killed his cousin Thorald but it did not matter; any Saxon would do right now. He hoped that his words would instil a little fear into the Saxon's heart and make this fight all the easier to end.

They seemed to find some space in the madness of combat that surged around them as if the lesser warriors knew that two champions had come upon each other on the field of battle and chose now to try their arms in a fight to the death; no other dared to intrude.

"Fight if you wish but save me your words, they are as unwelcome as you in this land." The Saxon huscarl lunged with his spear almost catching Jarl Siward on the left thigh. They parted again and assessed each other cautiously as the battle surged around them, lost in their own individual confrontation. It was just one more violent engagement upon a field turned a dirty red by the outcome of countless other such contests.

Siward judged his enemy with experienced eyes, noting the quality of the other's armour, with its lack of any unnecessary decoration, the kind that appeals only to the vainglorious. He observed the ease with which the Saxon held himself in full battle-gear. This was no fyrdman but an experienced warrior, a huscarl like himself. He rejoiced inwardly at the prospect of crossing spears with a weapons-man of quality at last.

Two, three, four times they swapped strokes, their spear points flashing forwards and backwards, but neither drew blood. Jarl Siward pressed the Saxon, testing his skill, and found him well versed in the art of combat. Once more he attacked; a fearsome flurry of blows from both his spear and shield. When they parted again Siward noted that the Saxon let his shield dip a little, the point of his spear came closer to the ground, and he took shorter, faster breaths.

Siward read the signs and smiled darkly.

This Saxon is tiring!

He launched another quick series of strikes against him, barged into him with his shield, the two metal centre bosses clanging together. The Saxon gave ground. Siward increased the pressure, raining blows down upon him, stabbing incessantly with his spear. He became ever fiercer in his desire to kill his enemy.

The Saxon huscarl counter-attacked but Jarl Siward defended himself easily with his shield and went back on the offensive, putting everything into a forward lunge so as to put even more power behind his spear. The huscarl moved with a particular intent. As the spear came in looking for his stomach he stepped both forwards and to his right, swinging his own shield away from his body. He brought his left arm back down swiftly and momentarily trapped the spear point against his mailed body with the weight of his heavy shield, his flesh protected by his byrnie.

Jarl Siward was momentarily surprised by the manoeuvre, then he was thrown off balance as the Saxon lunged forward, throwing the

Viking onto his back foot. The huscarl's spear stabbed out like lightening. Its point went beneath the other's shield, below the protective mail byrnie, and dipped into Siward's left thigh.

With a quick twist the warrior extracted the spear before it went too deep and became stuck in the thick muscle where it had struck. Jarl Siward tried to free his own weapon but the Saxon still held onto it with his shield arm and sent his own spear out again, this time into the Viking's right side, bursting the fine links of his bright mail coat.

Jarl Siward collapsed to his knees, his fingers losing their grip on the shaft of his fighting spear. The world seemed to become remote to him. He could hear the sounds of battle still but it was as if he were underwater, swimming. It was darkening around him also. He was swimming too deep.

What will the king do without me now?

I must remind Olaf to sharpen the axes.

It is so hot here and yet I feel so cold.

These and many other thoughts drifted through his mind with no apparent association. He was seemingly aware and unconcerned about his fate at the same time. There was no fear and surprisingly little pain. A shadow was growing around him and he noticed that the tiredness that came from his exertions in battle that day was leaving his bones.

I die a worthy death and this grim Saxon grants it to me.

Coenred felt no elation as he sent his spear into the Viking's flesh once more, this time aiming for the throat. He spilt his enemy's lifeblood without celebration, but also without a second glance as he turned away and looked for Eorl Edwin. At his command the men closed around their captain.

"That were some grim fellow thee killed there," Sigbert commented.

"To Edwin," Coenred commanded, he gave the death of the Viking no further consideration. "There's naught more that we can do than save the eorls now."

With harsh determination Coenred plunged into the Saxon wall in search of Eorl Edwin. To his credit the youth had maintained his proper station in the front ranks of his Mercians, but this now isolated him from escape and safety. Fear began to run through the hearts of the men. The Viking reinforcements had pushed through the centre too, coming between the forces of Edwin and Morcar. The Mercians were in danger of being surrounded.

"Give way!" Coenred commanded to the men about him. "Give way and fall back to York!"

They needed little encouragement but they ran instead of walked. The Saxon warrior cursed them, even hitting one or two with the shaft of his fighting spear. The fyrdmen were the first to crumble, many throwing away their weapons as they turned and ran. The huscarls held their nerve, holding the shield wall even as it shrank around them, always falling back in good order.

"Coenred!"

"Thrydwulf!"

The two warriors pushed towards each other against the tide of bodies.

"I have Edwin," The warrior declared.

Coenred saw the eorl at the warrior's side, looking somewhat small, lost and afraid. The Saxon shield-wall continued to attempt to move backwards without disintegrating. Behind them they had the fleeing fyrdmen, in front of them the bloodthirsty enemy. Once more Thrydwulf gave the command to step back. He was glad to have a seasoned warrior like Coenred at his side but he knew that even with Coenred's men there would not be enough of them to hold back the wave of Vikings.

"Stand and fight if ye be men," Cried Sigbert in disgust.

There was hope, however. Not all the fyrdmen were running. Many of them recognised that there was a greater chance of safety in staying with the more disciplined huscarls and that was what they chose to do. Within a sea of confusion and despair Thrydwulf's men became a rock of cold determination. They retreated one step at a time, their shields still closely woven and their spears protruding. From behind this protection some even threw javelins at the Norse ranks, a further reminder that not all of the Saxon resistance had crumbled. Coenred and Sigbert momentarily joined the huscarls and their men followed their example, adding to the core of warriors that refused to be routed.

For their part many of the Vikings were out breath due to the ferocity of their assault and although they still thirsted for more blood they were cautious about pressing too close to such a resolute band of warriors. The gap between the two forces began to widen.

Wulfhere saw the men running for the path over the Ings Marsh, and heading for York. They were Mercians and that could mean only one thing; defeat. For a moment he had believed that the young eorl might succeed. His attack had been well timed with the enemy still lacking its full strength. He had marched forward, prompting the rear ranks with the butt of his spear, but always he had kept an eye on the proceedings around him.

He glanced forward. The Saxon wall had stopped its advance and showed no signs of continuing. The Mercians were running, his path was clear. Wulfhere the butescarle, the sword for hire, turned and started to run. He did not panic because he could not see the enemy to his left. He jogged in an easy manner but kept looking to the west as he headed north. He would not drop his battle gear unless absolutely necessary because of the expense of replacing it.

Mayhap it might be time to try a different profession other than that of a mercenary weapons man?

He thought of the haughty woman in York, alone now, and decided that his warrior days may indeed be well and truly over.

Hardrada laughed madly. The battle was all but won. He had always known that the riverbank was the key. The ground was firmer here and he could launch a force forward to take the remaining Saxon army on its right flank now that he had dislodged the smaller but still significant band of Mercians. Styrkar planted his feet and waved his King's banner so that the whole of the battlefield could see to where it had advanced. The Vikings would take heart knowing that their king had pushed back the enemy on this side of the battlefield. The Saxons would lose heart knowing that the War Wolf had won the ground and probably the day.

He let the Saxon huscarls withdraw before a light harrying force, they were too few in number to be of trouble to him but there was no reason to let them think that they could return to the battle while his own back was turned to them. Although victory was at hand it was not yet assured, the next important objective was to destroy the Northumbrians of Eorl Morcar.

"Come now, the Saxons by the dam lands await your blades my sons," Hardrada encouraged his men.

They trotted forward towards where the Jarls of Orkney and Tostig Godwinson were still fighting the Northumbrians. The sudden violence of battle had winded them, but they had the stamina of seasoned warriors. They followed their king and pushed to the east where Morcar seemed yet able to get the better of Tostig Godwinson.

Coenred grabbed Edwin unceremoniously by the shoulder and spun him around. The warrior's face was grim, the youth's frightened.

"Leave with your men. Go in good order showing only your shields to the enemy," the huscarl commanded. The eorl looked at him but said nothing. "Edwin, do you hear me?"

"All is lost!" Edwin moaned at last. "Morcar is lost!"

"I will retrieve Morcar but you must to York. These Vikings will not let you return but I doubt that they will follow you far whilst there is still a battle to win. Get you gone and I will see you as soon as we can quit this fight."

"Coenred, we are lost."

"Mayhap. Thrydwulf get thee to York and then beyond to the safety of the vale."

"We can fight for you," the mighty warrior insisted, his visage grim and his eyes blazing.

"No. Your duty is to protect the eorl; it has not changed. Get him to a safe haven; now go. Sigbert."

"No need to shout, I'm at your shoulder as always," the huscarl complained.

"Then get thee with Thrydwulf and back to York," his captain commanded him.

"There's war work yet to be done if Morcar is to join his brother," Sigbert pointed out.

"Aye, that there is but it will mean a hard run from here to Morcar's position and unless you lied to me you're not a running man?"

"Running eh? I'm not built for it. Hacking and hewing is my strength."

"Then get thee to York and I hope many will see thee walk rather than run and take some courage from your resolve."

Sigbert put his sword in his left hand and clapped Coenred on the arm.

"I cannot thank thee for this but Hilda would," he said.

"Follow Edwin and I hope to see thee after this matter is settled," Coenred told him. He watched as Sigbert joined Thrydwulf's party and then turned his attention back to his own men. "Come Aethelmaer!" He barked at his retinue.

The hundred loyal huscarls with whom he had hoped to stop the eorls from losing touch with each other would now be the only force at his command with which to rescue Eorl Morcar from capture or death. The fyrdmen that he had also selected, and whom had proved both brave and steadfast, he now ordered to follow their fellows back to the presumed safety of York. At least they would retire with their pride intact and the safety of the Eorl of Mercia as their duty.

Coenred pushed west whilst Thrydwulf took Edwin and his men north to safety over the track between the Ings Marsh and the Dam Lands. Most of the Vikings sent to harry the Mercians followed the larger body of men but some began to track the smaller determined group of Saxon warriors. They exchanged throwing spears but did little harm to one another. As the Saxons turned south-east towards what remained of the larger battle the following Vikings seemed to lose interest, no doubt expecting their comrades would deal with them whilst they began to search the bodies of the Saxon dead that littered the field around them for gold and silver.

The City of York

"What do they shout?" Mildryth demanded of Edwin who stood at the opened window.

"They say that men come from the battlefield," He replied. His face darkened.

"What more?" She pressed but somehow she knew in her heart that it was not good news. She continued to stir the pot of simmering pork stew although her mind was no longer on the task.

"The battle is lost," he said simply.

Her heart sank like a stone dropped into cold water.

"Come with me," she commanded.

Dropping her cooking utensils she flung a cloak around herself. She closed the door to her house and it crossed her mind that if she returned to open it then her world might not be the same again, it would be irrevocably changed from that to which she had awoken to this morning. Her new protector might be dead and Tostig Godwinson returned to complete his destruction of her life.

Together she and Edwin made their way to the southern gate were the largest part of the throng was gathered. The earlier mood of excitement had given way to something much more fearful. They saw men with muddy faces and clothes, some had blood upon them; they were streaming into the city. It was not long before they were walking amongst the wails of women crying over the bloodied bodies of their men-folk laid out on the dusty floor.

"These are just the wounded," Mildryth asserted.

They had been brought from the field when the Saxon army had held the advantage. Her eyes ranged hungrily over the many faces, looking for his and yet praying not to see him.

"They have run from the field," a man suddenly cried in alarm, "the Vikings have the day. Flee!"

He turned and followed his own advice still hollering. Panic began to set in. The number of fyrdmen coming through the gate was not that great and this seemed to work in the minds of some people who suddenly decided that through that very gate lay safety even though that was where the enemy were fighting and killing and winning.

"Mayhp we should go, My Lady?" Edwin suggested nervously.

"We cannot leave," She replied desperately.

"Not York. Not unless we must. This place will turn ugly."

Edwin could feel the palpable change in the air about them. Fear would quickly induce violence in the mob. None would be safe. Within the walls of the city lurked a criminal class that was only too ready to exploit any situation where the normal rule of law broke down; such a situation was quickly coming into existence. Thievery, rape and murder would be the new order of the day.

Mildryth thought of Coenred and of Aethelwine.

Were they dead out there already?

Were they fighting still?

Should they just abandon all hope and flee like cowards only thinking of their own lives?

"I will not leave until I know that they are dead," She said emphatically.

"Or safe," Edwin suggested.

"Or safe," she agreed.

"But we must get away from the gate," he told her.

Gently he took her arm and began to lead her away. She moved slowly but did not resist. A fight broke out not far away, although it was difficult for her to imagine what Saxon men might find to fight over amongst themselves at a time like this. Edwin, however, saw that one of the men had stolen a silver crucifix from a wounded man and that that someone else now sought to make it his own.Panic erupted like fire and people started screaming.

The Vikings are coming! The Vikings are here!

Wulfhere pushed through the southern gate and loudly cursed the idiots who were fleeing the city through it. He knew better. The Vikings would indeed be coming and they would not stop their slaughter on seeing unarmed citizens. Their blood lust was up and it would not be sated for some time yet.

Should I pay her ladyship a visit?

His primary concern, however, was to go northwards, away from the enemy, and save his own skin. There might be a chance of some easy pickings in the chaos as well.

He saw some men fighting each other as he made his way into York. He knew not what they had to fight over and cared even less. Panic was in the air and people were running around like headless chickens. His quick eye did not miss the bodies of the wounded fyrdmen lain out in the road, however, some were being tended by their families, many were not.

This was an opportunity the likes of which he knew would come his way with the loss of the battle. He moved to the first body that was not minded by anyone and crouched down as if looking to identify the man. Using his shield to cover his wandering right hand he searched the stained tunic for valuables. He found a large silver cross and quickly snatched it away.

The man's eyes snapped open and a hand stained with both blood and dirt grabbed the front of Wulfhere's byrnie. Without a second thought the butescarle drew his scramseax from his belt and pushed the sharply honed point into the other mans ribs. He watched as the wounded warrior's face registered the initial pain. A gasp escaped his dry and chapped lips. With a cold expression Wulfhere gazed into his victim's eyes as the life left them. He glanced quickly around to see if anyone had spied his actions but everyone else seemed busy with their own fear.

It is better to murder during time of plague!

Wulfhere thought grimly to himself, a cold smile being the only evidence of this cruel deduction crossing his mind.

Moving quickly but with one eye ever on his surroundings Wulfhere worked his way through the casualties, careful to pick someone who was either unconscious or delirious with pain and always unattended. He soon amassed a small treasure-trove of rings, coins, crosses, and bracelets, mostly silver but some gold too. It was as he moved to another potential victim that he glanced up and saw her.

She stood with a cloak pulled tightly around her neck with one fair hand. In place of the haughty look that she had bestowed upon him the last time that they had met there was now an expression of fear. A young man stood beside her, seemingly trying to lead her away by the elbow. He looked like a servant.

This was the work of wyrd!

He took little convincing to believe that wyrd was leading him to his ultimate goal. Quickly he stashed the stolen goods inside his leather byrnie and rose to approach her. He cursed loudly as it seemed that she had been swallowed in the chaotic crowd of frightened people but then he caught a glimpse of her dark blue cloak, the quality of the material setting it apart from the ceorls that surrounded her. He set off in pursuit using both his spear and his shield to shove people out of his path. A townsman reacted violently to being heaved out of the way by the butescarle. He held a spear in two hands but seemed the most unlikely of warriors, although in that regard he was far from alone.

"Be steady man," Hereward shouted at Wulfhere, "this be a time to help another body not hurt them."

"Out of the way peasant, I have no business with you," Wulfhere snarled back. The man did not look particularly formidable and so he felt confident about playing the warrior before him.

"I am a tithes man, you will obey me," Hereward insisted with a note of self-righteousness.

Wulfhere's temper was already up and all it took to push him over the edge was a rebuke from a mere peasant. He hit Hereward with the butt of his spear in the chest. The grain seller stumbled backward, lost his footing and fell heavily onto his back. The butescarle stabbed him with the spear point in the stomach as he lay helpless on the ground and then Wulfhere continued his interrupted pursuit, the unfortunate Saxon's pitiful cries left in his wake.

A few yards into the city the crowd thinned appreciably and Wulfhere was able to see the pair not far ahead of him. He could close the gap easily but it suddenly occurred to him that the other man might not be a servant at all but a rival for the lady's affections. Remembering where she lived, and hoping that she might be heading back to the small house, he hung back. After a short while he congratulated himself as they went past the mead-hall without approaching it, continued on for a several yards and then turned down the small street immediately to the north of the hall. It seemed that she had nowhere else to go.

Wulfhere quickened his pace. The earth was sun dried, as hard as stone, and his leather shoes made no noise as he rushed after them. He turned the corner and began to increase his pace. At the last moment Edwin turned, mayhap warned by some sense or instinct. Wulfhere hit him full on with the shield and with such force that the young man was lifted from his feet and thrown some distance through the air. The youth landed heavily with a cry.

Mildryth cried out too, shocked by the sudden outbreak of violence. She stared uncomprehendingly at the mercenary and then at the fallen young man.

"Edwin!" She called out to him.

"Come." Wulfhere commanded. He placed his spear in his left hand and took hold of her arm. "The city is no longer safe; we must fly before the Vikings come."

"No!"

She tried to pull away from him but his fingers closed like talons on her arm. His grip was both strong and painful.

"I come to save you," Wulfhere insisted as he dragged her back up the street. "If ceorls will attack you in the open street think what several Norsemen will do to your body." He used lies and fear to try and subdue her resistance but it did not work as he hoped.

"Let me go. He's my servant," Mildryth insisted, but Wulfhere kept a tight hold and continued dragging her up the street.

Fulford Gate

The mood of the men changed like the wind and like the wind it could be felt. For a brief moment they had dreamt of victory like their lord; then they had been stopped and held, unable to push on any further. Now they knew that defeat was upon them. Morcar was very aware of the change and tried to rouse his brave warriors but his voice was lost, like his banner, in the clamour of the battle.

Aethelwine still stood with a group of fellow theigns and their retainers with whom he had formed the line, fighting as hard as anyone else. They were positioned on the far left of Morcar's position and here they had enjoyed the greatest success, cutting down Tostig's men like wheat for the harvest. The world had turned, however, and it was now brave Saxon men that were being cut down where they stood. As the Vikings pressed hardest against the Mercians and the centre of the battle-line Aethelwine saw their chance to escape. It would be achieved only by more fighting, more swinging of swords and axes, thrusting of long spears, by tired arms carried on equally tired legs. They must continue their push west, however, because here the enemy were still weak.

"By all the gods I'll not stand to be slaughtered like swine for this man's vanity," Aethelwine declared. "Push west lads. Push west."

His cry was taken up by his brother theigns. They called their men to them and pressed hard, cutting a bloody swathe through their enemies who simply were not strong enough at this point in their lines to resist this last desperate Saxon charge.

Oswyn felt a presentiment of doom wash over him. His warriors were exhausted; they could barely hold their shields aloft as the Saxons' weapons rained down upon them. He found himself facing a large theign, well appointed with arms and armour. He seemed like a most formidable warrior, the very kind a tired man would hope to avoid when his breath came too quickly and he had already been too long in the fight. From deep inside Oswyn called up his last reserves of strength and prepared to stand in one more epic battle between well matched individual warriors.

With his spear shattered and his strength waning Oswyn opted for his sword and struck at the theign. Aethelwine parried the blow easily with the blade of his Dane-axe and shoved the mercenary backwards with his shield. Stepping forward he swung once, twice, thrice, his keen blade biting into the linden wood of his foe's shield. Each time he twisted the ax after it impacted to stop the wood from holding his weapon fast.

Oswyn relied on timing, knowing that he could not match the other for strength now. Aethelwine looked to keep the gap between them to an arm's length. He was ever mindful of the larger battle going on to their right and that it had gone against his people. It would not be long before the advantage that lay with the enemy elsewhere on the field began to tell here too.

He feinted another push with his shield and stepped forward looking to over-reach the mercenary's defence with his axe. Oswyn was not deceived and stepped forward rather than backwards, bringing his sword over the edge of the theign's shield and into his face.

Aethelwine's vision was suddenly lost in an explosion of pain. The edge of the blade of the sword cut into his left eye socket. Instictively he reacted by lashing up with his heavy Dane-axe held in one hand. Neither of them saw the blade flash upwards, slipping under Oswyn's shield. It bit into the man's steel byrnie, bursting the mail links. The cold steel cut effortlessly through muscle and organs, stopping only when it met his sternum on its upward swing through his stomach.

The impact of the blow staggered Oswyn and sent him backwards on failing legs. He collapsed into the churned mud as his life's blood seeped from the terrible wound in his abdomen. He was dead before he rolled onto his side and the damp mud stained his face.

Someone grabbed Aethelwine's weapons-arm and pulled him along as the rest of his men continued forward. The blood flowed freely from his wound on the side of his face. Pain wracked that face and rendered him blind. The noise of the battle seemed far away from the foreign place that his consciousness now occupied. He followed the prompting of his fellow warrior, not questioning them nor minding the fate of his foe.

The Saxons pressed on and did not stop even after they had passed through the main body of the host, but kept on, turning south down the same road to Riccall that the Vikings had used to reach the battle ground. That way stood fewer of the enemy and, therefore, safety.

They abandoned their fellows on the field of doom to whatever fate wyrd through the Vikings would bestow on them. Not that it sat well with Aethelwine but he thought of his wife and children, he thought of his retainers and their families too; for all of those for whom he was responsible, a charge given to him by the king. He thought of those people and it inspired him to keep encouraging his men to fight as they made their way south. His vision slowly returned in one eye. They came upon contingents of Norse warriors still making their way to the battlefield and they slaughtered them without mercy as if in penance for saving their own lives.

Chaos now reigned as the once solid formation of the shield-wall was torn apart. Warriors were reduced into fighting in small knots of determined resistance and desperate combat. Eorl Morcar felt fear taking him. This was not his first taste of mortal combat but it was the first time in his young life that he found himself staring death in the face. A cold and sickening feeling filled his stomach. He felt certain that the moment of his doom was upon him as he stood in the front rank of the crumbling shield-wall, then he felt a force dragging him backwards. He turned to see a fierce huscarl, his armour spoilt by blood, glaring back into his face. Even as his mind began to run wild with fear a semblance of familiarity came to the young nobleman.

"Hereric."

"My Lord, this battle's done, we must get thee away."

"They're on all sides, only the marshland is safe."

"We'd flounder in there like hunted deer with hounds at their heels; their arrows will pierce our backs," the huscarl declared, "come with me."

Still gripping the eorl by the arm the warrior steered him towards a patch of much trampled grass that was a few paces from the front line. They seemed to be surrounded by hectic activity where nothing was clearly discernable. Still gripping Eorl Morcar by the arm Hereric gave a shout. With impressive discipline a number of warriors obeyed his command and approached them. An armoured man appeared next to Hereric holding a battle-horn in one hand and a sword in the other. The huscarl repeated the captain's command with a series of blasts on the horn.

Within a few moments both Hereric and Morcar were surrounded by a group of some five hundred Saxon huscarls. The men had successfully detached themselves from the front rank earlier as the shield-wall disintegrated around them. They had remained in the back rows to offer what help they could but it was for this moment that they had been waiting and preserving their strength.

The huscarls were grim and bloodied, their once bright armour smeared and stained but their valour was still intact. At the command of their captain they formed a protective ring around Morcar, pulling in tight so that their shields overlapped forming an apparently invulnerable barrier. Long spears jutted forth with those in the ranks behind holding their spears upright, partly to deflect the arrows that were expected to come their way, partly to make the formation look larger and more formidable than it really was. Hereric's voice called out again and as one man they began to edge north towards the hoped for safety of York but they moved slowly, painfully slowly.

Morcar's army of Northumbrians was being destroyed. Men, wild with fear, began to run into the marshland, throwing away their weapons and armour in order to flee more quickly. Vikings followed them to the edge of the marsh from where they hurled throwing spears or used bows to cut down the slow moving Saxons in their hundreds. It was no longer fighting, it was a sport; it was a massacre. The Vikings rejoiced at every death blow or mortal wound inflicted and the Saxons knew no mercy.

Braver, or more desperate men, stood back to back fighting with a waning strength as the Vikings ringed them all about. No quarter was expected and none was given. Saxons were pierced several times with spears, their blood running freely down their trousers or the sleeves of their shirts, each drop taking their strength with it. There was no haste to end the game, no respect for the Saxon warriors' bravery in the face of their enemy. When a leg gave way or a man stumbled, Viking steel would cut into any exposed body part. They were literally hacked to pieces before they reached the ground. When one fell, the others would pull tighter together but they only delayed the inevitable and failed to exact any cost from their tormentors. It was slow, bloody work but the Norsemen went at it with an obscene will.

The City of York

Where she came from Wulfhere could only guess but he cared little after losing his helmet to the upwards swinging stroke that he took from her broom-shaft.

"You let her go!" Branda demanded. Her eyes were wild and her face flushed.

Mildryth pulled free at last and stepped out of the mercenary's immediate reach as Branda attempted to land several more blows on his exposed head. Wulfhere raised his shield and took a step forward towards the large angry woman. Branda stepped back but the butescarle followed his military training and quickened his pace, giving her a shove with his shield that sent her sprawling. With his hand now free he took hold of his spear once more and moved it to a higher position, the clenched fist close to his head.

"NO!" Mildryth screamed at him.

Genuine fear crossed Branda's face as the mercenary's right arm drew back, the point of the fighting spear aimed directly at her heart. As the arm started forward the butescarle was suddenly catapulted away from the helpless women as Edwin careened into his side. The young Saxon let out a short cry of pain but unlike Wulfhere he kept his feet. For a moment he staggered but it was only in response to his already bruised side. Mildryth saw that the langseax was out of its scabbard and in his hand. It seemed that blood was sure to be spilt.

Wulfhere managed to turn as he fell and landed on his hands and knees with his back to them. It was an undignified position to find himself in and one that offered no protection against his attacker whatsoever. He tried to push himself off the ground by bringing his right knee up to his chest but the shield on his left arm gave him no proper purchase and the fingers of his right hand were trapped beneath the spear that he still clung to. He rolled to his right in a cumbersome manner instead, hindered by both his armour and weapons. Lying on his back he found himself looking up at Edwin and realised that his position had not improved any. Without hesitating Edwin kicked the spear out of the butescarl's hand and pointed the tip of his langseax at his chest.

"You wouldn't dare," Wulfhere insisted, not without a little fear, "I am a fighting man of the eorls."

"You fight women and attack men from behind," Edwin accused him angrily.

"And you are quick to leave the field without any hurt." Mildryth observed.

"A hog never smells its own stink!" Edwin spat at the cowering man.

Branda got to her feet and gripped her broom menacingly again. Several people noticed the commotion and despite the distraction of the battle beyond the city walls they were curious enough to come and see what was happening. One of them called out to Branda by name. Wulfhere was quick-witted enough to realise that the odds were going against him now, the townsfolk would be sure to defend one their own against a stranger. He scuttled backwards, releasing his shield so as to be able to use his left hand more easily. His spear lay where it had been forced from his grasp. Edwin followed him with grim determination, his knuckles turned white from the force he exerted in holding the long knife.

"Go," Mildryth snarled at the butescarle with contempt, "be gone wretch!"

Wulfhere required no further prompting. He jumped to his feet and ran north, pushing his way through the people. Edwin glared after him but made no attempt to pursue the fleeing coward. Instead he returned his langseax to its scabbard and retrieved the fallen shield, helmet and spear.

"Tha's trophies of war young warrior," Branda congratulated him, a wave of relief sweeping over her as the encounter concluded more peacefully than that it had promised to do.

"Are you hurt much?" Mildryth enquired coming to his side.

"I feel like I was kicked by a horse," Edwin admitted, "but I think I will live."

He held the spear upright and looked up at the steel point. This war gear cost more than he had ever earned in his young life. They were indeed trophies won in combat; although they were not quite the fabled weapons and it had not been the epic encounter that the scops sang of in their sagas and heroic poems.

"I ne'er liked the look of that man," Branda asserted.

"Thank you for your assistance Branda," Mildryth said, "he attacked Edwin from behind and gave him no chance."

"I doubt it not," Branda told her, "but I came not looking for a fight. I'm at home with the bairns; Hereward has carried a spear to Fulford. I thought we might pass the time together until the men come home again?"

Mildryth glanced quickly at Edwin and hoped that he would understand the meaning in her look. He stayed quiet, which persuaded her that he did. Clearly Branda did not know the way the battle seemed to be going.

"Why would Hereward go to the battle?" She asked, genuinely amazed that a man of such mild manners would take up a spear.

"He said it was expected of him as a tithe man," a look of concern crossed her face. "Will thee not come sit with us?"

"Of course, but I have also a duty at the mead-hall. I will sit with you until they have need of me, however. Come Edwin, you will join us."

They headed back to Branda's house and Mildryth marvelled that the woman seemed incapable of sensing the panic that was beginning to grip the people around her. She hoped that her attempt at suggesting the need to see to normal duties might delay the terrible news that she knew was coming their way, the loss of the battle, at least a little longer; long enough for two men at least to return home.

Fulford Gate

King Harald Hardrada looked around the battlefield and saw what he sought most. He levelled his sword and pointed at a group of armoured Saxons who were making a disciplined withdrawal using a tight defensive formation.

"There," he said with certainty.

"We have won," Prince Olaf declared. His face was flushed with excitement and exertion. "The Saxons flee before us. It was just as you said it would be father. We have victory."

"But the eorls escape us," Hardrada growled.

The King of Norway wanted to make examples of the Saxon noblemen so as to suppress any further resistance from the people of Northumbria and he knew what they meant to Tostig Godwinson as well. He had seen the Saxon banner of the lord who commanded the force by the riverbank disappear, but so had the lord himself; to safety he feared. He remembered now the disciplined group of Saxon warriors who had headed north from the riverbank in an orderly fashion and how he had let them go in his haste to win the battle. It occurred to him that one of the eorls must have been in their midst and that he had allowed him to slip through his fingers. The presence of the huscarls should have told him as much. In the frenzy of the battle he had lost sight of his greater strategic objectives. It was a slip of his judgement that might endanger the entire expedition, not that he would admit such a fact openly to anyone; not even to his son.

Observing this other group of huscarls moving slowly in good order suggested that the second lord was amongst their number, certainly it was one who was highly valued; the Eorl Morcar the king hoped. There had been at least two senior eorls upon the field this morning, the capture of just one of them could yet make this battle decisive.

"Come!" Hardrada barked.

With his loyal Viking warriors Hardrada advanced on the Saxon formation. The Norse weapons were bloodstained and their resolve tempered by a victor's disdain for the conquered. They trampled the once green grass beneath their heels, weighing it down with the blood of their enemy so that it did not spring back upright in the wake of their passing so readily.

Coenred saw the situation and realised the intent of the Vikings immediately. His band of men moved quickly over the battle ground in loose order like wolves closing in on a hunted deer, only this was not a hunt; it was a chase for survival. The huscarls to the south moved slower because of their protective formation. They were heading for the northwards track that led safely over the marsh of Fulford Ings to York. It was a narrow point where the Saxon warriors could fend off a Viking attack, but Hereric's men were losing the race. Norse warriors were closing in on them from three sides now, drawing close like a pack of hounds on a wounded bear. It would not be long before the Vikings furthest to the north were able to prevent the Saxons from reaching York and denying them any safety that the city might offer.

"Come."

Coenred set off at a fast trot, ignoring the weight of his harness and weapons. He pushed through his own tiredness. The pain from the several violent encounters that had left bruises and cuts on his body was suppressed by the force of his will. That was the difference between the huscarl and the frydman; they had the discipline to overcome their own fear of pain and death. They had the strength of will to do that which was necessary no matter what the cost was to themselves. Their death-oath was no grand gesture, it was more than words; it was the foundation upon which their honour was built.

His men followed him and they were all of a like mind. They ran along the northern edge of the grassland towards the point where the huscarls under Hereric's command were heading. The Vikings following the raven banner of the Norwegian King were just to the south of them, slightly behind but ahead of Hereric's men. They were spreading out as they came on, determined to halt the northwards movement of the Saxon formation.

What had been the centre of the Viking line, now commanded by the Jarls of Orkney since Siward had fallen, formed the main pressing force advancing from the west of the field. They were being joined by Tostig's warriors from the south who had now slaughtered the Saxons in and around the marshlands. Morcar's fate was truly hanging in the balance.

Coenred reached the beginning of the track where the ground was firm and turned to face both the approaching Saxons and the Vikings. His men formed around him, maintaining their loose order, awaiting his orders. They all took deep breaths of the warm September air and it gave them a little respite. Those who had not yet drained their flasks of warm weak beer took the opportunity to do so now.

Hereric and his huscarls were so close to Coenred's group that the latter could see the individual designs upon their comrades' shields. Their brother warriors were painfully near to safety and yet a bloody doom was breathing down their necks. The Norse army pressed hardest from the West, separated by barely three spear lengths so that they could see the blood smeared clothes of the enemy. Yet these Vikings hung back. Although vastly outnumbered this troop of determined Saxons still posed a dangerous threat. Their spears protruded from behind their shields and their faces were dark and glowering. The men in the second and third rows hefted swords and large double-handed axes. There was no weakness in this formation that could be exploited by taunts or threats alone. When the final encounter came it would be paid for in blood. So it seemed that the Viking host were waiting for their fellows under Tostig's command to catch them up whilst Hardrada's men advanced quickly to close off the escape route to the north.

It pained Coenred to know that he had too few warriors at his command to influence the outcome. They could advance and engage some of the Vikings but it would be a short, sharp fight that would not aid Hereric and Morcar. If the worst were to happen all that Coenred's men could hope for was to recover the eorl's body or die trying. They knew that the latter would be the most likely outcome unless something unexpected occurred.

"You must go now," Hereric commanded. He had one hand on the eorl's arm as if the young nobleman was incapable of being left to his own mind.

"Go. Go where?" Morcar asked in a plaintive voice.

They stood at the very centre of the formation, shuffling in step with the other tightly compacted bodies. For his part Morcar was not quite tall enough to see over the shoulders of the men who ringed him.

"Go north My Lord, go to the city," Hereric explained. "Coenred awaits you."

"We are too far," Morcar observed. He stood up on tiptoes and could see the small group of Saxons waiting to receive them but they seemed so distant and the enemy too close. "We cannot cover the distance. This armour is too heavy, the sun too hot. I am too tired. We cannot run that far with the enemy so close."

"You must run," Hereric returned. "Drop your shield and run to Coenred."

"…too far." Complained the nobleman again.

"If you do not go now everything will have been in vain. Good Saxon men will have died for nothing. What we are about to do will be for nothing and no one will remember it." Hereric gripped him by the shoulders and started to push him towards the safety of Coenred's huscarls. The men moved to open a passage through their formation for him. Hereric flexed his muscles. "Go now."

Morcar staggered forward under the impetus of Hereric's fierce shove. He stumbled two, three, four paces and then stopped as if the effort had been too great for him. Like a confused child he looked around him, seemingly unaware of the danger that he was in. An arrow suddenly hit his shield with a solid thud and it seemed to sting him awake. He dropped the large circular piece of wood as if it had been a poisonous serpent rather than a missile. The shield fell face down, snapping the arrow that was imbedded in it and miring the painted abstract design that he had once liked so much. He let fall his fighting spear and began to move as fast as his weary legs could take him towards the only route to safety left open to him now.

Coenred swore under his breath once more. He could see what the eorl could not and instantly understood the nature of the action that was about to be undertaken. Hereric and his warriors had stopped retreating before their enemy and having shot Morcar from them like a stone from a sling they now advanced on the prowling Vikings. Their demeanour had changed. They spread a little further apart to give themselves room to use their weapons. A battle chant broke out into the midday air, a simple rhythmic mantra to focus their minds on their enemies and away from their fate. Spears shafts and axe handles beat against metal rimmed shields in time to their growing song; a sorrow song through which they prepared themselves for leaving this world; this middle-earth.

"Easy lads. Ready lads," Hereric spoke to them in a calm but firm voice, "there's a lot of scum blood there for us to spill yet my lads."

The sun had reached its zenith and the day was at its hottest for the warriors. Hereric was tempted to loosen his helmet and feel the kiss of the air on his head but he knew that that would only invite death all the sooner. Death was coming anyway. He thought about sweet Eadgyd and his heart ached for her.

I should have taken her to wife, stupid man!

She had given him two strong, healthy boys and he had been afraid to handfast with a woman as fine as she was. Well he would make her proud of him this day if nothing else. He would stand unafraid before the enemy with his sword in his hand and he would die a hero on the battlefield. If Morcar was not quite the man of quality to honour such an action then he at least knew that Coenred was. He would not let the eorls forget this moment.

"Aldfrid! Hengist!"

Coenred spoke only their names but the two youngest of his retinue pounced at once like hunting dogs. Comrades took their heavy shields and long fighting spears so that they could move all the faster. As they sprinted forward several Vikings from the group furthest north who had seen Morcar separate from the huscarl formation realised that he must be the lord that their king wanted so badly and began to trot after him also.

They were wary of coming between the two enemy formations, however, and not as fast as the two young Saxons who reached the stumbling and terrified eorl before the Vikings could come within yards of him. Aldfrid and Hengist stopped only to hurl the last of their throwing spears at the nearest of their enemies, then they unceremoniously grabbed the nobleman by his arms and ran back to where Coenred waited, literally dragging Morcar with them.

Hereric turned away from Coenred and Eorl Morcar and looked back at his hated enemy. His fingers opened and closed on the hilt of his sword. His senses now seemed so finely tuned that he was experiencing everything in the minutest detail. He could feel the sweat that soaked his hair and the quilted jacket beneath his mail byrnie. The leather that bound his sword's grip was smooth to the touch. His muscles were sore and tired and yet still full of vitality so that the weight of his arms and armour seemed as if nothing to him. His sword was so light within his grasp that he might doubt its ability to deliver a killing stroke. There was the distinct chink of metal against metal, the rasp of ash spear shafts over the iron rim of painted shields, the heavy breathing of the men; his men. As their final moment came it was if they all lived that very instance to the full.

It would be sweet and short.

"Now!" Hereric ordered.

From within the five hundred Saxons a warrior blew a battle-horn as if with his final breath. It cracked the air with a voice of doom. More horns within the formation joined it. The huscarls howled their derision upon their enemies, clashing spear and sword against shields with abandon now. They turned at bay with a terrible fury.

Hereric pushed his way to the front rank and screamed his hatred at the waiting Vikings. Without fear and as one body the Saxons lurched forward and slammed their spears into the Norsemen. Battle was joined once again as the Vikings responded in kind and fell on their greatly outnumbered foe.

Coenred watched from their place of safety. His eyes were dark and brooding underneath his helmet and his hand gripped the shaft of his spear tightly. Hereric had led his men into the heart of the advancing Vikings and in doing so sealed his own and his men's fate whilst probably securing Morcar's safety. The Vikings fell on the huscarls' formation. They came from all sides so that they quickly enveloped it, their spears stabbing, their axes chopping, their swords hacking.

"Coenred."

Morcar gasped for breath, bent over with his hands placed just above his knees, facing away from the field of battle.

"Look."

The warrior pointed with his spear at the mass of bodies before them. Like the men around him he could, if he so wished, make sense of the chaos that they were witnessing and visualize the demise, stroke by stroke, of their brother warriors. They would kill as many of their hated enemy as they could before the last of them fell, he knew this in his heart, but the enemy were too many. The strong links of the huscarl's mail would be sundered. The linden wood of their shields would be split. Hammer falls would dent the once bright steel of their helmets. The spear shafts would be broken. Blood would soak their quilted jackets and the life would go out of their once bright and eager eyes. One by one the five hundred would fall beneath blows too numerous to counter. And brave Hereric would be the last of them, but all of them, huscarls to the end. They died a warrior's death.

He glanced at Morcar and saw that the eorl was still facing north, still looking towards the city.

"Turn and pay witness."

In a cold voice the servant commanded his lord. There was no deference in his tone whatsoever, anger mayhap, one held tight in a steel hard grip forged in a warrior's training. It gave metal to his words. Morcar responded hesitantly, as if turning to gaze upon a vision that he already knew would haunt him for the rest of his days.

In truth little could be seen but for the blurred figures of the Norsemen swarming around the five hundred. The Saxons were totally obscured by their enemy now.

"Why?" Morcar asked.

"For your life. They are huscarls. They swore an oath to protect your life with theirs. We are huscarls. We do not break our oaths. But you will not leave this place without acknowledging those men who die for you. HAIL HERERIC!"

Coenred raised his spear into the air, holding it horizontally over his head.

"HAIL HERERIC!"

One hundred voices cried out in unison, a salute to the fallen. Morcar may or may not have joined with his own.

"Now we go so that their deaths may mean something."

Coenred signalled the withdrawal. The two young warriors renewed their grip on their charge and hastened him down the track towards the walls of York showing little respect for his rank. Coenred and the others brought up the rear in a loose formation so that they could move more quickly but with alert eyes on the scene behind them. For now it seemed that the Vikings had forgotten their original purpose. Nevertheless the Saxons withdrew in good order, prepared to meet any foe who came after them. None followed.

The Vale of York

Thrydwulf and Sigbert had passed quickly through the city with Eorl Edwin safely within their charge. They had not paid heed to the frightened citizens knowing that there was precious little that they could do now to help the people of York. Wyrd would decide their fortune at the hands of Hardrada of Norway. This did not sit easily with Sigbert who looked longingly to the west of the city, he even considered deserting Eorl Edwin and looking to the safety of his own family instead.

The inclination passed quickly, however. Honour dictated Sigbert's every action. Whilst his children might rejoice at his safe return from the battlefield Hilda would not accept being married to a nithing. When the children had slept on the first night of his return home he had discussed this very eventuality with Hilda. Defeat had always been a possibility, and it was agreed that she would keep the family together and do whatever it took to survive. There was a cache of gold and silver hidden not far beyond the city walls and she would use it to buy their protection if necessary. He would rely upon her good sense and do everything he could to stay alive and return to them at a later time, but to do that he had to keep Eorl Edwin safe.

They were but an hour's march from York which now lay to the south of them. Members of the eorls' household had had the presence of mind to empty the stables and take the horses out through the northern gate where they waited not knowing if they would see their masters again. Meeting up with the servants had made the flight all the swifter as the horses had been made use of.

Eorl Edwin himself now sat disconsolate upon the warm ground, his head in his hands. All bravado had left him. Even though he still wore his armour he looked less of a leader of men and more like a frightened youth, a boy who needed his father.

"The watch is set," Sigbert told Thrydwulf, "if more come upon us then we will know of it and they will receive a friendly welcome."

"And if the enemy come upon us?" His brother huscarl growled.

"Then we will know of it as well and have time to spirit the eorl away. It worries me that we have seen no sign of the Norse though?"

They watched silently as in ones and twos more Saxons came upon them, only a few carrying light wounds. All those that could not run had been abandoned.

"If Eorl Edwin hopes to regroup his power here then he is going to be sorely disappointed," Sigbert commented.

"Where there were thousands this morning there are now only hundreds," his brother warrior observed disconsolately.

"Morcar is dead," Edwin moaned. "We are ended."

Sigbert glanced at Thrydwulf and from the expression on his face he gathered that they were both thinking the same thing; they wished that Coenred was there with them to deal with the young nobleman. He had known them since birth and although the young noblemen, since entering their maturity, had strained their relationship with him Coenred was still able to exert some influence over the brothers.

As the hours passed their small group grew but not into anything formidable. They were a collection of huscarls, eoldermen, theigns and fyrdmen but they all had one thing in common, irrespective of their station they were beaten men.

"We should think of moving," Thrydwulf suggested, "there are but stragglers coming this way now, our brothers have fallen."

"Except for those," Sigbert pointed south.

They were in the late afternoon now but the light was still good. In the distance they could see the largest body of men yet to come from the city appear over the brow of a small hill.

"The enemy?" Thrydwulf pondered.

A part of him almost wished that it was, a black despondency had settled upon him since they had escaped immediate danger and it was one that made the prospect of death on a battlefield seem glorious to his mind.

"I think not," Sigbert answered, "they move too slow for a chasing pack of hounds and too disciplined for fyrdmen alone, also they have horses."

"I could have stayed with the Lady Mildryth," Edwin insisted.

He walked the pack horse, one hand on its bridle. A silent Eorl Morcar rode Coenred's horse with the huscarl walking just behind it. His men marched in a loose column so as to be able to respond to any threat of danger but since leaving the battlefield they had not seen anything of the Vikings. Coenred had expected them to send a determined party after the eorls but so far they had not detected any sign of a pursuit.

"Your duty was to protect Lady Mildryth and yet I found you out on the main street awaiting the enemy," Coenred replied with a hard tone to his voice. He glanced back over his shoulder, the sight of Edwin with his new war-gear had surprised him initially and he still had not yet come to terms with it.

"She was safe in the house of her friend Branda," Edwin insisted, "I only went to see if I could find her husband, a man by the name of Hereward. He went to the battle with a spear like many other townsmen."

"Then likely he went to his death," Coenred said bitterly.

He found the thought that Mildryth was at least not alone comforting and it had already occurred to him that the Vikings would not treat a Saxon man carrying weapons kindly regardless of his peasant rank.

The sight of the gathering ahead of them was in no way encouraging, other than to suggest that Eorl Edwin was also safe. He passed this thought onto Morcar but the young nobleman remained silent, his head hanging low as he brooded in a world of his own.

It occurred to Coenred that Morcar might be outraged by his treatment since leaving the battlefield; they had been less than respectful towards him. Not that this concerned the experienced warrior greatly, but he knew how easily the younger brother could give in to his passions and it would not be beyond him to seek to punish the very men who had saved his life simply because of a matter of etiquette. However, when they drew within shouting distance they saw the Eorl of Mercia rise from where he had been sat and heard him call out to his brother. Morcar raised his head and life returned to his eyes. He slipped from the saddle and ran on tired legs to embrace Edwin. Even for men who knew the pride and occasional arrogance of the two eorls there was something touching in their joy at being safely reunited.

Coenred told Aethelmaer to rest the men, his brave and loyal men, while he went to talk to the eorls. As he walked towards them Sigbert and Thrydwulf intercepted him.

"What news?" Sigbert demanded.

"Hereric is dead along with all the huscarls he commanded at the last," Coenred replied bleakly.

"All of them?" Thrydwulf said disbelievingly.

"All of our brothers, with the last five hundred huscarls of Northumbria Hereric held back the Viking advance long enough for us to spirit Morcar from the field. They honoured their death-oaths."

"They honour those of us who yet live," Sigbert commented sadly.

"How does Lord Edwin?"

"Not so well until thee came with his brother safe," Sigbert glanced at the two noblemen. "Whatever else they may be they are loyal brothers to each other."

Coenred left his friends and approached Edwin and Morcar.

"My Lords," he announced his presence.

"Coenred, you honour your oath, you brought Morcar back to me," Edwin actually managed a smile. He had his arm around his brother's shoulder and it seemed as if he would not release him again.

"We must take counsel."

"For what purpose?" Edwin asked.

"To decide what plan of action to take next," Coenred explained.

"Plan of action. What action could we possibly take? Look around you man, this is the extent of our power that survived this day." With his other arm Edwin indicated the tired men that were gathered around them. "There is nothing more that we can do."

"We will not gamble our lives again," Morcar added.

"You are still responsible for the people of York," Coenred told them, "we must do what we can for them, even if it is only to know their fate."

"Their fate is sealed. The Vikings will do as they always have done in the past. They will murder, rape, pillage and put the town to the torch. We will rebuild after they have gone," Edwin retorted with pessimism.

"I do not think that they plan to leave."

"What makes you think so?" Edwin demanded.

Coenred pointed south to the city.

"There is no smoke," he said simply, "they have not put the city to the torch. Tostig Godwinson did not return with the King of Norway as an ally, a man who has made a public claim to the Crown of England, simply to raid the City of York. The city does not burn because he means to own it."

"You cannot be sure of that," Morcar insisted.

"No, but it would explain why the Vikings have not pursued us, they have taken the city instead and look to make it secure."

"So what would you suggest?" Edwin asked with a derisive note.

"That we discover their plans whilst retiring to Tadcaster to rebuild your power."

"Tadcaster! That place is to the south, why should we go there and not north where we will be safer?" Demanded Morcar. "Durham would make for a place of safety."

"Before you arrived in York I sent riders south to London to warn the king of the Norse invasion. King Harold will send a force northward to meet this danger and it will pass close to Tadcaster as it moves up Ermine Street."

"You sent riders to Harold Godwinson?" Edwin looked momentarily angry.

"In the absence of High-Theign Aethelwine and yourselves I was asked to make a decision as an eorl's man. It was the correct one," Coenred insisted.

"And now you expect the Godwins to ride north and save us?" Edwin could not keep the emotion from his voice.

"I expect the king to defend his kingdom."

"Do what you will, I am finished with this!" Edwin said abruptly.

"My Lord?" Coenred looked at him in amazement.

"Go to York and discover why Hardrada doesn't put it to the torch. Go to Tadcaster and see if the Godwins do send help beyond the borders of their beloved Wessex. Do what you will just don't expect me to take a care over it. We are beaten and can take no further part in this. Wyrd has decided so."

"No, you have decided so," Coenred glared at him.

Edwin only turned away and stalked back to the place where he had been sat before his brother's safe arrival. Morcar, as always, followed. For his part Coenred wasted no more time on the pair, he could read their defeated spirits easily enough. They contrasted starkly with their father who had never surrendered hope, even when in exile at the king's command. Always he had sought a way around his problems, sometimes directly but also occasionally with guile and craft. These were not the gifts that he had seemingly given to his sons. Coenred left them where they moped.

"What do we?" Sigbert asked when Coenred returned to them.

"I am minded to return to York, we must know what the enemy will do next," he replied, his tone suggesting that this was no great undertaking.

"That is a dangerous task to brave," Thrydwulf commented.

"And better done alone."

Coenred began to remove his armour. Edwin his retainer came to assist him.

"If you do this thing there is a favour I would ask of you?" Sigbert said.

"I know, speak no more of it. If I can I will do it." Coenred grasped his friend's forearm to indicate that he would indeed tell Hilda that her husband was safe. "I also intend to let Hereric's woman know of what befell him today. He has children I believe?"

"Two," Sigbert confirmed, "boys."

"Where are you going?" Edwin son of Octa wanted to know.

"Where you cannot come this once," Coenred replied. Edwin's face darkened.

"I am your shield bearer; I should go where you go," he insisted.

"You will stay here and help the men rest. They will need what food and water you can gather. When I return I am making for Tadcaster to await the king's power. The eorls have given me leave to do what I think best, they are for heading north, for Ripon and then for Durham most likely. Each man is to make the decision that best suits them, they can come with us or go with the eorls and carry a clear conscience; the war-work has been done this day for many a man. I would like them to have chosen before I return though."

"That is not a difficult choice when your family resides within the power of your enemy," Sigbert said with feeling.

"Nor when revenge for fallen brothers burns in your heart," Thrydwulf agreed.

"The men are to choose for themselves," Coenred reminded them. "Those who go to Tadcaster with us must do so with a will to fight again."

"So be it," Sigbert agreed.

As there was nothing left to discuss the huscarls left Coenred to finish his preparations.

"Have I failed you?" Edwin asked. He carefully placed Coenred's belt with the heavy sword, the Dane-axe, and Mildryth's scramseax upon the ground.

"You mean by not staying with the Lady Mildryth?"

"Yes, and mayhap in other ways?"

"No." Coenred answered with conviction. "You said that she was safe with her friend Branda and safe is where I wanted her. You have done your duty. As to other ways, I know not of what you speak. Time has not been given to us to get to know each other better Edwin. From what I have seen of you I believe you to be a loyal, reliable and hard working man. These are qualities I value, but you must be obedient too. You do not realise that when passing hidden amongst the enemy one can move much faster, and more safely, than two. I tell you to remain here not out of any failing on your part but because there is no service that you can do for me in this matter. Stay here, look after my war-gear and the horses, we will need them. Help the others if you have a mind to. Tomorrow we will go to Tadcaster and there I hope to have time to train you so that you can use that war-gear of your own and not just carry it about."

Edwin looked upward as if he could see the helmet that was upon his own head. He wondered for a moment if he should explain how he came by these things but then remembered Mildryth's insistence that it remain a secret between them two alone. He was heartened by what his master had said and decided that there was no dishonour in obeying the wishes of either him or the lady to whom he had extended his protection.

"Help me now," Coenred instructed.

He bent over and stretched his arms out before him. Edwin understood what was required and gripped the mail byrnie with both hands. He pulled the heavy armour over Coenred's head and gathered it to himself. It weighed a surprising amount and the young man wondered how the warrior had been able to spend most of the day fighting and running in such a garment.

Next Coenred removed his quilted jacket and gave that to Edwin too. The cooler air on his skin was a relief. There were several noticeable scars on the warrior's body and Edwin found himself staring at them unintentionally.

"A sword is not the only badge of rank a huscarl carries," Coenred told him.

He dressed quickly, putting on his linen tunic and woollen cloak. He removed Mildryth's scramseax from his leather belt and placed it securely in a woven belt that he fastened around his waist over his tunic.

"I hope to see you soon."

Edwin stood and watched as his master turned and retraced his steps back towards York. He knew himself not to be a coward but as the warrior strode away Edwin the ceorl wondered if he, an untrained peasant, could truly summon such courage to face the victorious enemy so soon again. After all that Coenred had witnessed that day, all the death and the destruction of the fine men who had been his comrades, to go now back into danger for the sake of others. Edwin felt that he had had a glimpse into what really made a warrior and it was not the war-gear that he now stood there wearing, nor the dreams of glory painted so bright in the poems. It was the spirit within the man.

"God go with you," was all that he could say.

The City of York

"Know that my temper is hardly soothed by your open gates," growled King Harald Hardrada of Norway.

He sat in High-Theign Aethelwine's hall and faced the Saxon men who were all that was left in the way of authority to govern the City of York. The high-theign's own chair had been placed on a trestle table to raise him above everyone else and with his own substantial height this made the Norse king seem an even greater conqueror. He was surrounded by the best of his own men who all still carried the stains of battle upon them. Styrkar, the giant who carried the king's banner in battle, was now chief amongst them since the death of Jarl Siward.

"I have lost many good men today, particularly one good friend, because your young eorls were so ill-advised as to make a stand at Fulford."

Tostig was suitably impressed by the king's behaviour. The force of his character was both terrific and terrible. He had taken control of the army even as they had hewed the fallen five hundred huscarls who had made such a futile sacrifice in the closing stages of the battle. He had stopped the Vikings from rampaging through the city's open gates in search of more blood. The news of Siward's death had been greeted by a fine royal fury, a display of anger that had even brought the hairs on the Saxon's own neck to stand up. Just for a moment, he had thought that everything would be lost in a callous instance of personal revenge, but Hardrada had mastered himself just as he had mastered the army.

Mounted once more on his black stallion he had parleyed with the remaining villagers of Fulford Gate, promising them no harm would befall them if they stayed indoors and respected his authority. Both sides had kept that bargain, which let the Vikings advance on the City of York without distraction.

The city-men had seen that further resistance was useless after the destruction of the northern army and allowed the king and his warriors within the walls without a struggle. Now they stood, bowed and beaten men, before this artful monarch. Despite the fact that there were barely a hundred of the king's warriors present they exuded a threat that was domineering. There was no fight left in these Saxons, only fear, and Hardrada knew it.

"My Lord," one of the city-men stepped forward, raising his hands in supplication, "it was not by our counsel that the eorls met with you so violently. They are young and headstrong and desired of glory."

"It is because I know this that I choose to spare you all your lives," Hardrada replied. That at least brought some relief to their faces. "In times past I would have razed your city to the ground for the loss of a man like Siward; one I held to be as close as a brother. I do not come for plunder though; I come for the crown that was promised to the Norwegian kings in days gone by. I will make a pact with thee but know this; none have broken faith with me and still live."

The threat was implicit and clearly understood.

"We accept your authority, My Lord," the Saxon affirmed.

"Then these are my terms: I will take hostages now, men of import whose lives you value, and what supplies you can muster. In four days time you will send to me at Stamford Bridge more hostages and supplies as a sign of your goodwill. I will reside there with my army but a garrison will be put in command here and you will not dare to touch them. For every man of mine that you harm I will kill ten of yours."

"As you wish, My Lord," the Saxons acquiesced.

"Further, all men of the city are to stay within their own homes at night-time and this rule to be obeyed until I say otherwise. My garrison will be given authority to kill any they find out of doors after eventide. They will not, however, harm any who abides by this curfew. Nor will they take anything that is not theirs. Northumbria is now part of the Kingdom of Norway and I give leave to spoil what is mine to no man. Now go, leave us."

The Saxons were quick and undignified in following their new lord's commands. Tostig Godwinson glanced at the king with barely disguised surprise.

"I thought the plan was to stay within the city?"

"And now I think differently Lord Tostig." Hardrada rose from his seat and with an easy agility descended from the table. He took the offered cup of ale from the hand of one of his men. "In truth I do not trust these city walls until I have stamped my full authority upon this land."

"My lord-"

"Oh, I know, you thought that you might remain here with the garrison eh?" He drank noisily. "Indeed, why would you not?"

"It makes sense," Tostig protested, "I know this city-"

"That came to my mind also Lord Tostig, you may have friends here eh?"

"You doubt my loyalty?" Tostig looked offended.

"Come man, you're not stupid and neither am I," Hardrada declared, "and that I am still alive is testament to at least half of that truth."

He laughed good-naturedly but Tostig was now on his guard. Of his own men here within the hall he had but a handful, certainly no match for the king's warriors. He wondered if Hardrada had decided that he had no further use for their alliance.

"We are allies for it suits us to be. You want your brother's head and I want his crown; neither act has been achieved yet. There may be those who call themselves your friends who might counsel that you could yet succeed without my help?"

"My lord, I have fought for you, counselled you true-"

"I am not saying that you haven't," the king interrupted, "but just suggesting that you might be tempted by those who do not know the full extent of our plans or abilities." He smiled, almost benignly, but Tostig understood the hidden meaning.

The truth was that if he could secure his own return to England without the Vikings' aid then no doubt he would do so, but Harold, his own brother, would not allow that to happen. No, he needed Hardrada for he doubted his own strength to keep a hold of the crown when Harold died, and that event must happen if he was to succeed in his plans. Hardrada was more the man to take and keep the crown, Tostig already knew that, just as he knew the King of Norway was as generous in his gifts to those who stood by him through loyalty as he was vindictive in punishing those who broke faith with him.

"I will not break my word," Tostig asserted.

"And I am glad to hear it. Now, my Saxon friend, let's drink to our victory before we mount up once again and return to Riccall. I will spend this night in the shadow of my Long Serpent."

"As you wish, My Lord." Tostig picked up a cup of ale and joined in the toast to the victory that they had enjoyed.

"My men tell me that there were so many Saxons slain that they could fill the beck with their bodies and walk end to end without getting their feet wet!" Hardrada announced to the hall. A general roar of approval went up at this macabre statement. Despite declaring his intent to leave the city Hardrada showed no haste in quitting the hall, at least not whilst the ale was still abundant. He left the ordering of the garrison to one of his captains and instead drank with his favoured warriors, bestowing his praise upon them in lieu of the prizes that they had yet to win.

Mildryth watched the events unfold from behind a group of Saxon ceorls. She had left Branda when it had become clear that the battle was over. The declarations of the people running past the house where they were all shuttered in made the result obvious. Edwin had gone to find Branda's husband Hereward if he could, but he had not returned. She feared the worst for him as he had insisted in wearing Wulfhere's war gear. It had been her intention to go to the great hall knowing that that would be the place where she would find Coenred; if they had won the battle. She had not thought about what to do if the Saxons were defeated. Here, however, seemed to be the best place to gather any news of their friends following the catastrophe and she believed herself best suited to the task. Besides, Branda had her children to keep her at home.

For her part Branda had implored her not to leave but Mildryth could not resist the urge to see what fate might now befall them all. In her mind it seemed safest that she go alone, whether that was true or not was a different matter. She was somewhat reassured when the Vikings had entered the city in good order, marching in a column behind their giant of a king mounted on a black stallion. It had not been difficult to enter the great hall through the kitchen and find a place to observe the proceedings. She watched now as Tostig Godwinson broke away from the Vikings and began to wander in a distracted manner through the hall. Her hand went unconsciously to her belt and found the vacant space where her scramseax would normally be. She glanced down as her hand failed to find the familiar handle and the truth dawned upon her.

She swore under her breath.

It came to her mind that the kitchen was but a few steps away and she knew that in there she could find a replacement, something long and sharp. She felt the desire for revenge burning inside her at the sight of the man who had murdered her husband and son, and possibly caused the death of her new protector.

Moving through the throng she headed towards the kitchen, trying not to attract attention. She walked to the nearest wall and followed it as if hugging the shadows there that resulted from the flickering light of the lamps and the numerous people in the hall. A rough hand suddenly grabbed her arm and spun her around. Mildryth found herself staring into the face of a Viking. He was all beard, stale breath and drunken eyes.

"Ale woman!" he bellowed but he did not release her. "My but you're a fair one for a serving wench!"

"I'll bring you more beer," Mildryth said quickly. She had seen that look in men's eyes before and knew what it might mean for her.

"Mayhap you'll do just fine instead?" He turned to his comrades with whom he shared the table. They voiced their encouragement for his obvious lust. Mildryth pulled hard as soon as he was distracted and broke away from his grip. "Stay thee!"

"More ale! Straight away!" She tried to calm him.

The Viking turned back to her with an oath and reached out to grasp her again. She spun on her foot and made to dash away, heading away from the wall and back towards the centre of the hall. Having gone only a few steps, her eyes on the table behind her expecting to see the warrior chase after her, she collided with another man. She looked up into his face and her blood froze.

"You should be careful," Tostig Godwinson advised her, "Saxon women can expect little courtesy around victorious Norsemen."

"My Lord…" she floundered. Mildryth cast her eyes down almost believing that he could read her intent through them. With the Vikings immediately behind her and the murderer right in front she was effectively trapped.

"You do not look like a servant," Tostig commented. He looked her up and down and noted that her dress, although plain, was better than what most ceorls could afford.

"I am a friend of High-Theign Aethelwine. This is his hall," she replied.

"Was," Tostig corrected her, "now it belongs to King Hardrada of Norway and soon of England."

"Mayhap…"

"Fear not. King Hardrada comes for a kingdom and has commanded his men to behave accordingly. He does not want his new subjects punished for the poor decisions of their former lords," he continued to look at her and Mildryth began to feel a cold dread seeping into her bones. "Nevertheless, you should be careful. A woman of your rank had best keep to her own."

"My rank?" She raised her head and looked back at him, almost as a challenge. "I have no rank."

"No rank? You look to deceive me. Even if your husband is dead you still hold a station above the common people."

He knows me!

Fear flooded her being.

"There will be many such as you," he told her, "battles leave many widows behind but even if your husband lies dead at Fulford Gate you still have his property, wealth and name. You are obviously theign-worthy."

He knows me not!

"I would counsel you to look for another husband, My Lady, but from amongst the victors if you wish to keep all that wyrd has left you with." He smiled and then turned away.

Even as she realised that Tostig had presumed her to be the wife of one of the fallen theigns who had fought for the eorls, Edwin and Morcar, her fear gave way to anger. She understood then that not only did he not know her but also that he did not even remember the crime that he had committed against her family. Her resolve returned with a burning edge and she started once more for the kitchens.

Inside the close room she dodged between terrified servants and slaves, looking for a scramseax, one with a long thin blade that she could hide in the sleeve of her dress. She saw what she was looking for but as her hand closed on the handle a larger, ruddier hand enclosed hers.

"No, My Lady," Branda said quite firmly.

Mildryth looked at her but the desire to do violence misted her eyes.

"Release me," she demanded.

"No, My Lady," Branda repeated. "If tha even attempt this thing tha'll bring about tha's death."

"What matters that to me? The man who murdered my husband and my son stands within the hall; within my reach."

"I know, but even if tha struck him down tha would bring death upon us all." Branda argued. Her grip tightened on her friend's slim hand.

"I alone will suffer and gladly too."

"No, tha won't. We all heard the Viking's decree. Many will die for the death of any one of their own. They know it in the kitchens so they know it in the hall. Besides, did tha not set Lord Coenred to be thy protector?"

"Likely he is dead," Mildryth declared angrily.

"No, he awaits thee at my house."

The words came easily, almost carelessly, and yet they robbed Mildryth of her breath.

"Your house?!" Her voice was barely a whisper.

"Aye, my friend. He survived the battle and more. He asks for thee. Come."

"Tostig-"

"Can wait," Branda said quietly. She still had hold of her friend's hand but her grip had relaxed. "He's in danger every moment that he waits for thee and truth be told having a huscarl in my house after this day is a great danger to me and mine too; but I do it for thee."

Mildryth could not deny the truth of Branda's statement. If the Vikings found Coenred they would know him for what he was if not for who he was. His life would be taken, violently, and the people who sheltered him would fare no better. She felt her anger wane before this new conflict. Her fingers released the scramseax.

"Take me to him," she implored Branda.

"Then put tha arm through mine and cast tha eyes down. We be but two serving maids going outside for more of anything the Viking scum might want," Branda told her.

As they pushed through the frightened kitchen staff Mildryth felt waves of competing emotions rage through her. She berated herself for not returning to the hall with a suitable weapon and taking her revenge on the smirking Tostig.

Had Coenred been hurt?

What he had done this day to not only survive the battle but to find his way into the captured city?

She chided herself for discovering so late that the living now meant more to her than those who were dead.

Within a heartbeat they rushed through Branda's door which was firmly closed and barred behind them. The house stood on the main street that ran north to south through York. The front was wide, one half being a store for the grain that Hereward sold. That part of the building was fronted by two large doors that opened out onto the street so that customers could enter directly. There was a more normal door giving access to what was properly the living area. The house was unusual in that the residential part was spread over two floors with bedrooms situated above over what for most Saxon families would be the main living and sleeping area. Downstairs another room had been added onto the rear and an open doorway knocked through the daub and wattle wall. This was where Branda cooked although a hearth was maintained in the other room as well. Tradition placed great domestic value on there being a lit hearth at the centre of every home but few peasants knew the luxury of owning a home with more than one room.

Branda's children were laid on the floor wrapped in blankets in the room at the front of the house. They looked up with fearful eyes that did not diminish even upon the recognition of a well known face. They knew that all was not well. Mayhap that was why they chose to be downstairs and not in the privacy of the children's bedroom upstairs.

The larger Saxon woman led her friend into the back room. It was dark with only one lamp burning fitfully. Someone lay on the floor, covered in a woollen blanket. Instinctively Mildryth went to the bed and crouched down. In the low light she recognised Branda's husband, Hereward; the pallor of his face shocked her.

"Hereward?" She could not help but voice some confusion.

"He's been wounded," a familiar voice told her.

She turned and saw him for the first time, cloaked in shadows in the corner of the small room. Coenred stepped forward. He no longer wore his battle-gear, just a normal woollen cloak, a linen tunic and trousers. There was no sword at his side but Mildryth's scramseax was tucked into his belt.

"I found him amongst the throng at the southern gate."

"And I thank God that it was such a great man as thee who did," Branda declared.

"It is no great thing to help a wounded friend," Coenred told her, "I only wish that I were skilled in the arts of healing."

Mildryth looked at Hereward and saw that his eyes were distant. He moaned lightly and moved his head as if in response to a memory but no words passed his lips. She rose and looked at Branda who was making a brave attempt to hide her fear.

"I owe you an apology," Mildryth said.

"Oh hush now," Branda looked embarrassed.

Mildryth crossed to her and took her hands.

"No. You housed Lord Coenred despite the danger to you and yours and you left your husband to come and fetch me when he needed you most. That is twice today that you have looked to help me when I needed assistance. You are a greater friend than any I have ever known."

She hugged Branda and felt the other woman's sobs erupt. There was a long moment when nothing was said.

"I must get some water," Branda gently broke away from the embrace.

She looked longingly into Mildryth's face and then turned and left the room without another word.

At last Mildryth turned to Coenred.

"You survived."

"Too many did not."

He saw her eyes cross to Hereward and then back to him and knew what the look meant. He shook his head. Hereward had suffered a spear wound to the stomach. A warrior's experience told him that there was little chance of the man surviving the night.

"What was he doing there?" She asked almost angrily. "A battle was no place for a kind man like you Hereward."

"The fever of the moment caught him like so many others," Coenred explained. "They thought that they would be part of a great victory, not victims of a slaughter. Edwin told me that he had gone to look for Hereward on Branda's behalf so when I returned to the city I carried out his duty for him. I called out his name and he was then strong enough to answer, that's how I found him amongst the throng."

She looked back at Coenred and found herself assailed by conflicting emotions. A part of her wanted to rail against him for encouraging the belief in these people that they could fight and defeat the Vikings, but she knew that this was untrue. It was not Coenred who was to blame but rather the people he represented; the eorls. They had hungered for glory. They had excited the people into believing a weak truth. As if to assuage her feelings she placed a hand on his right arm. The touch was reassuring.

"I am glad that you survived," she told him, "if not for you Hereward might have died out there, on the field, alone and unknown."

"Then you do not blame me?"

It was as if he had read the emotions in her heart through the expressions on her face. She could not hide her feelings from him any longer.

"You are a warrior, battle is your trade. You were where your lords told you to be, but you did not ask for the likes of Hereward to be there with you."

"If I had been in command none but warriors would have fought, but then if I had been in command the Vikings would still be banging their heads on our closed gates and high walls, and all the people of York safe within."

She looked up into his shadowed face and saw the weariness in his eyes and with it also a sadness that she had not expected to see. Instinctively she put a hand to the side of his face. She felt a sudden wave of relief and would have wrapped her arms around him then and there but for the return of Branda.

"I have sent for a healer, mayhap they will bring my brave Hereward some relief eh?" She blustered about making a fine pretence that the situation was not as grave as they all truly knew it to be.

"I cannot impose upon you any longer," Coenred told her, "the fewer people who know that I am here the safer it will be for you and yours."

"But where will you go?" Mildryth asked. "How did you even get into the city?"

"I came from the battlefield with Morcar and what few of my men I had left to command. We passed through the southern gate on our way north to meet up with his brother Edwin. That's when I met with Edwin son of Octa, my retainer, and some curious war-gear that he had come by. I was not happy with him as I had thought that he had deserted you but he told me that you were safe here with Branda. The eorls decided to head for Ripon, against my advice. Why Hardrada had not pursued us I did not know, he has won a battle but not the war. I thought that we should find out what his plans were so I returned."

"With the danger so great?"

"The danger seemed no greater to me than it was to anyone else left within the city," he told her, gazing down into her lovely face hoping that she would understand what he could not bring himself to say in front of Branda, "I left Edwin with my horses and harness just a few miles to the north; he was not happy. Mayhap he will tell me how he came by his new shield, helmet and spear? It was no difficulty to re-enter the city amongst the confusion and I wandered to the southern gate where I came across Hereward amongst the wounded."

"And I thank God for that!" Branda declared again as she gently wiped her husband's face.

"And what now?" Mildryth pressed.

"I will go south." He said firmly.

"South?"

"Aye, messengers were sent to London at my command before the battle today. King Harold will either come north or send a force to meet the peril. The raid on Scarborough may not have worried him overly but he cannot afford to ignore the fall of York. The whole of Northumbria may now be lost and King Harold will find himself between two hard enemies. He must act if he wishes to keep his crown and I mean to meet with the army he sends before it reaches York and tell them how things stand here."

"'Tis a pity that there are not more of you," Mildryth commented.

"I think that there are," Coenred told her. "I have talked with many survivors and I have learnt that a large group of theigns and their retainers broke from Eorl Morcar's left flank when their fate was made clear to them. They cut their way through the Norse lines and pushed south. I believe Aethelwine was amongst them. The safest place for them now would be Tadcaster, there they could re-group, distant from the immediate attentions of Hardrada but still close enough to York so as to know what befalls the city. I will make for Tadcaster and then decide where to go from there."

There was a knock at the door. Branda glanced up at them with a worried expression.

"I have stayed too long," Coenred admitted.

"It maybe the healer," Mildryth told them both, "I will go and see."

She left Coenred and Branda to exchange worried glances in the low lit room. The children had remained where they had been when Mildryth had first entered the house. They watched her silently as she opened the door. To her relief there was not a party of the Viking garrison but only a woman in a hooded cloak.

"Branda sent for me," She said in a tired but sharp voice.

"Yes, this way. Through to the back."

The healer did not stand on ceremony but walked straight through the house with Mildryth following.

"I need more light," She insisted curtly, "and space."

"We were just leaving," Mildryth said, "come husband."

She looked at Coenred, slightly embarrassed at using that word again and yet feeling it necessary to explain his presence. She did not know the healer and so did not completely trust her.

"Branda, I wish you good fortune," Coenred said.

He walked to Mildryth's side. They moved through into the other room with Branda following.

"Send for me if you need anything," Mildryth told her before they opened the door, "I will come by in the morning."

They embraced quickly in farewell. Coenred opened the door carefully and looked about outside but could see no one in the dark street.

"God be with thee both," Branda said.

"You need Him more than we," Mildryth replied.

They stepped into the quiet night and the door shut behind them. She started to slip her arm through his but Coenred moved quickly so that she was on his left-hand side. He had only her scramseax as a weapon but still he preferred to keep his sword arm free should he need to react quickly to danger.

"What now?" She asked quietly.

"I must leave the city before dawn," he answered.

His eyes roved the shadows ahead of them and his ears strained to discern the approach of danger in the scant sounds of the late evening. Branda's house was close to the hall, but not as close as Mildryth's. It also stood on the main street that led from the great hall to the church of St. Peter's where resided the Archbishop of York when present in the city. At Mildryth's house they would be uncomfortably close to the Vikings and they would have to walk down the widest street to get there.

He did not fear the enemy but he did worry about what his discovery might mean for Mildryth.

The closer I am to danger, the further I am away from harm!

Mayhap there would be some truth proven in that saying?

"Have you eaten? I prepared a stew earlier. I can warm it up quickly. You must have something to eat before you leave. There is drink also." She spoke rapidly, trying to disguise the fear that ached in her stomach.

It occurred to Coenred that he had not eaten since the early morning when they had prepared for the battle. He did not feel particularly hungry; the sight of so much death and violence had suppressed his appetite. However, he found himself in no hurry to leave Mildryth now that he was back in her company.

"You can rest too. There is time yet and the dark of the night will help hide you from the watch when you must leave York." She continued nervously.

"'Tis too soon to go yet," he agreed with her, although in truth this was just an excuse, "Edwin is not alone and can wait a little longer for me."

They reached her small house without incident and passed quickly over the threshold, barring the door behind them. Mildryth lit a candle with a taper from the low burning hearth and then set to with warming up the meal.

"You are not hurt?" She asked him as she worked.

He shook his head in reply. He had some cuts and bruises but they were nothing to complain about.

"Edwin was very good; I must thank you for sending him to me. It was a comfort not to be alone during that time, although if I had known that Hereward had been so foolish as to pick up a spear I would have gone to reassure Branda sooner."

She decided not to mention anything about the fool Wulfhere. Nothing had come of it and Coenred, she believed, did not need thoughts of the cowardly mercenary to occupy his mind when he would be leaving the city again so very soon. She was glad that Edwin had clearly not said a word about the incident either.

"It was the least that I could do," he told her, knowing that she was talking because she was nervous and not just being polite. "Many good men died today to no avail. I have visited others in the city to bring them the grim news."

The breaking of their hearts reminded him of why he had chosen to remain unmarried but he found that he could not admit to such a thing in front of Mildryth. She had made the first move in asking for his protection and he had followed her lead almost blindly.

Mayhap it was the thoughts of retiring from this life as a warrior and going to the farm in Holderness that had allowed his feelings for her to grow so quickly?

Even the violence of the day had not dispelled them; rather it had seemed to make his heart beat more strongly. Eadgyd's tears at the news of the death of Hereric had touched him but her sorrow could not make him regret his own situation now. The truth was that here in Mildryth's company he had quickly realised that he was glad of what had happened between them; as little as it was so far.

"I am sorry for Hereward's injury. He is a good man but no fighter. His death will go hard with Branda I fear."

"Mayhap he will not die," she said this more in hope than expectation, "if the healer is skilled mayhap she will mend his wound."

Coenred did not look to correct her even though he knew for certain that the man's injury would prove fatal. He moved to sit down beside the hearth and rest his wearied limbs.

"What were you doing in the hall?" He asked her.

She glanced at him and then returned her attention to stirring the stew that she had placed on the hearth to warm up. She left the hearth to pick up two clay bowls and a couple of spoons.

"I think that we should not talk of such things in the time that is left to us." She eventually answered him with some degree of conviction. "I had not thought to feel this way about anyone again after my Aethelheard was slain, but today I found myself fearing for you. It was not a good feeling and yet it made each minute of the day drag out into an hour seemingly, and I knew that I was alive. I prayed for you. I prayed that you would return alive to me. You have captured my heart Coenred."

She looked up and at him from across the hearth, the warm light from the glowing coals bathing her face with a soft radiance. She smiled at him, almost shyly as if she had admitted a great secret and did not know yet how he would respond.

"In times past I have entered battle with no one on my mind except the enemy and then my thoughts were ugly," he told her. "Today I thought of you, often. You said to me, when we first met not so long ago, that love for another might give a desire to my sword arm to maintain my life; you were not wrong. I thought that concern for another might be a distraction, that my guard might slip if my mind were not upon the danger at hand, but it did not. Instead I fought harder and better than I had ever done so before and I escaped injury."

"They say that a mighty Viking warrior, a Royal Companion who fought at the side of the Norwegian King for many years, was killed today by a Saxon huscarl upon the field of battle. The Norse King told the city men of the death of Siward and how it vexed him so that he thought to burn the city and kill all its inhabitants."

"I killed a Viking who called himself Siward," Coenred admitted.

"Then you are indeed a mighty warrior, mightier even than the greatest of the Vikings," she declared.

"And you have made me this great fighter of men," He smiled grimly.

"No, My Lord, you have always been this great, but only now have you found the need to prove it. If I have given you reason to discover this then I am glad because you have given me reason to discover that life is still worth living, even for a widow." Her smile was tinged with sadness but heartfelt all the same.

"I should not leave you."

"And betray who and what you are? No, you are now what we need. The eorls have abandoned us and the king is still, as far as we know, in the south whilst the enemy is within the walls and proclaims himself our conqueror. The people need someone to give them hope."

"I am but one man."

"So is King Harold but we look to him all the same," she replied quickly. "I know that you would say that you are no king, but consider what you have already told me, that you already plan to go south and meet the king's army and bring them against the Vikings. This is the action of a real leader of men. This is what the eorls should do. This is what you would do. I said before that I had found in you a noble heart that I much admired, you will not maintain that admiration by using me as an excuse to act in a way other than what your honour tells you to do."

He felt a weight lift from his shoulders as he listened to her words. In truth a conflict had been growing inside him between the soldier that already knew what must be done and the would-be lover that was still uncertain as to what was the right thing to be done in favour of her. He did not want to leave her in danger but he knew that as long as the city men obeyed the commands of Hardrada then there would be peace in York. Her danger would be no greater than at any other time. Of course that might change if he did indeed meet with the king's army and they pushed north to re-take the city.

"You are making it easier for me to go."

"I could be selfish and keep you here, that is true, but then Tostig Godwinson would bask in his victory and I would have no revenge upon him. Also you might be discovered and that might result in both our deaths with nothing to show for it. Now is not the time for selfish actions," She recalled her recent intent to kill Tostig within the great hall and it seemed to her that that had been a totally different woman. "You must go to the men who fought and survived this day and I must go to Branda and offer what comfort I can to her. These are our callings."

"You are indeed a wise woman Mildryth."

"And a good cook too I hope," she passed him an earthenware bowl full of pork stew and a spoon. "Or at least I hope you find me so." He thanked her and made himself comfortable. "Now rest and eat, we have some hours to enjoy each other's company yet."

They ate for awhile in a comfortable silence.

"Another time and some would make sport of your name to know that you had invited me in after dark," he said at last, breaking the peace between them.

"We are man and woman Coenred, what we choose to do behind a shuttered door is no one else's business but ours. I care not for the gossip of others, and there is no sin where our hearts truly agree with one another."

"There is no sin where the intent is honest," he agreed with her, putting down his now empty bowl.

She rose and came to sit beside him. Again she surprised him with her quiet confidence as she raised his arm and wrapped it around her shoulders and nestled her head on his chest. He could not resist the urge to stroke her soft hair with his other hand. With her free arm she embraced his body and pulled herself more tightly into him.

"For now there is no one but us," she said quietly.

He kissed her head and squeezed her gently but firmly.

The Castle of St. Valery sur Somme

The wind could rage against the castle walls but it could not topple the stones carved by human hands. Like a bastion of the duke's hopes the fortress resisted the elemental weather that had plagued his designs for many weeks. It neither bowed to the powerful gusts that destroyed the wooden hulls of ships unfortunate to be caught out at sea, nor leaked beneath the constant torrent of rain. As Guillaume moved down the passage to the great hall the only sign of the continuation of the autumnal storms was the occasionally more excited flickering of the torches that lit his way.

Within the confines of the castle the barons were quartered with some degree of comfort whilst their men huddled inside tents close to the fleet with only the thickness of the canvas sheet between them and the elements.

All eyes turned to the door as a guard flung it open and the duke entered at pace and with a purposeful expression. He glanced over their faces quickly and noted the scowls on more than one. Delay plagued them again only this time it was not the offence of two idle soldiers that threatened the future of the expedition. This was more serious; the barons themselves were talking of returning home.

"My Lords, you look well." Guillaume spoke in a jovial manner although he knew full well that he could not expect the same from those already seated as he joined them at the large table. As he sat down he looked first at his brother Robert, seated strategically half way down the table on the left, and then at his other brother Odo, sat further down and on the right. It had been tempting to place them closer at hand but that risked creating factions over the length of the table, this way he hoped to break the dissenters up by placing his most loyal men amongst them.

"We have waited too long," Protested Ranulf, Vicomte of the Bessin. Several others voiced their agreement. "If we cannot move forward then we should disperse for the winter and return in the spring."

"To what advantage?" Guillaume asked reasonably. "Our power is gathered here at St Valéry, the fleet stands ready. For all this to be dispersed and then collected again next spring, so much time would be lost, so much money would have to be spent again."

"And Harold Godwinson will grow more secure upon his usurped throne," Robert added in support.

"We have our own estates to tend to, My Lord, we have been absent too long to little effect. Autumn passes us by and winter marches closely upon its heels. I would know that all is well with my property," Ranulf countered.

"You should appoint men of trust and merit to the administration of your estate," Guillaume said simply. "This is not the first time that you have been abroad from your lands at my command; were they ruined by neglect the last time that you took to the campaign?"

Ranulf paused a moment before answering. The tension in the room was palpably growing.

"My lord knows that I have supported him in this endeavour as with many previous endeavours, but the weather intercedes. We sit here in St Valéry as we sat in Dives Sur Mer, merely waiting. The men laze and consume the rations that are paid for out of our purses and return us nothing in service."

"What service can a soldier sat on his arse all day render?" Another interjected to popular agreement.

"It is not that we wish to avoid our duty to you My Lord," Ranulf continued, "but rather that the elements set themselves against your design. We can make no further headway. There are no ports further along the coast that are friendly to this expedition. We are stalled." A general assent rose from the other lords sat around the table.

The dissent was beginning and Guillaume knew that a key moment had arrived. His authority as the Duke of Normandy was stronger than it had ever been, his ducal court the envy of princes, the lands over which he ruled at their greatest extent, but all of his achievements were now threatened. He could dismiss the army and suffer a little loss of respect and reputation for an act of commonsense amongst these nobles, but his enemies would present the facts differently. He was walking a fateful path as thin as a blade-edge. He could exert his ducal authority and keep these barons here all winter if he wished but their loyalty to him would only be eaten away by resentment and their support ultimately lost.

To what purpose should I act with an iron fist? To only satisfy my own pride?

There were the lesser-noblemen too; those here under duress that had been forced to present hostages to the duke's court to guarantee their compliance. They would surely look to turn any failings on Guillaume's part to their own advantage. Dissent could quickly turn into rebellion and the enemies beyond the borders of Normandy would exploit that situation to his destruction. He felt the weight of the moment pressing down on his shoulders. His future would rest on how successful he was in keeping the Norman nobility in line with his own desires. Any weakness now would spell disaster but at the same time he had to respect the power of his allies. Individually none of them posed a real threat but collectively they could overthrow him. The danger was very real.

"My Lords, I hear your words and you should know that they have been considered already," Guillaume told them, affecting a conciliatory disposition. "In truth none here thought that this expedition would fall foul of such un-seasonal weather. Our spies in England tell us that there the storms are restricted to the coasts only, that the sun shines to ripen fields of gold, a bumper harvest to be brought in by the people on the land. The Saxons bask whilst we shiver."

"Then does God favour the English?"

"God favours the just and we carry his banner, given to us by the hand of Pope Alexander the Second himself," Odo predictably answered.

"Then mayhap you should unfurl the banner and let God see it," someone suggested. "Mayhap Harold has one of his own, flying over England's golden fields, and God mistakes it for ours?"

Nervous laughter followed the comment. Guillaume sat with his chin resting on his hand but allowed a weak smile to crease his face. He glanced at Odo and wondered if his brother the bishop might assail the speaker with religious indignation.

"If God declines to send us a favourable wind by the Feast of Saint Michael the Archangel then I might concede that very point." Odo eventually replied. "However, I think that there is some merit in reminding everyone that we do have the pope's blessing in this enterprise and Harold Godwinson has been excommunicated for his unholy crimes. It might do many a soul good to see the banner unfurled and paraded around the camp."

"Would you be willing to undertake this duty?" Guillaume asked.

"Of course, My Lord," Odo smiled in return. "I have many priests who seem as indolent as your soldiers. I will stir them to it."

"As welcome as this event may prove in lifting our spirits it is only a momentary diversion from what concerns us here. After the parade of the banner the men will return to days of inactivity again." Ranulf observed.

"I have a concern of a more military nature," Fitzosbern spoke up. "Even if the weather does improve we are left with a considerable obstacle at this time of the year. Should we land successfully in England we will find ourselves in a foreign and undoubtedly hostile land facing the onset of winter. The longer we are delayed the closer we come to finding ourselves in a situation where only the food that we can carry across the sea in our ships will keep body and soul together. The Saxons for their part will have their bumper harvest to see them through to spring and will, I do not doubt, come at us all the stronger for it."

"Our wooden castles will prove of little comfort in a hostile land when winter tightens its grip and the food runs low." Another agreed.

"Our strategy is to provoke a response from Harold Godwinson as soon as we land," the duke told them. "You are right Fitzosbern; the time we have lost here in waiting will count against us once we have landed on the enemy's shore."

"Then it seems that we should have a day by which we either leave for England or leave for home?" Ranulf pressed.

"His Grace the Bishop has suggested Michaelmas!"

Odo glanced up the table to his half-brother hoping to express that he had done no such thing by looks alone.

"The twenty-ninth of September? That is but days away," Robert, Count of Mortain, protested.

"We spent how many days from July to September sat in Dives Sur Mer, and then again here?" Ranulf countered.

"Enough." Guillaume raised his voice at last.

The room fell instantly silent, only the logs on the fire made a noise as they burnt in the grate. He let the silence remain for a long time as he stared hard into all of the faces gathered around the table. It was indeed time to exert his ducal authority.

"There are many valid concerns that beset us here and I have spent time considering all of them. Michaelmas is too close to bring about an end to these preparations when the winds may yet blow themselves out in a day or two or last a few days longer. I will wait until the end of October for a chance to cross the water, beyond that I dare say that even if we did find a day for safe sailing the Saxons would put out to sea also and threaten our supply line so as to let an English winter thin our numbers." He looked around the room and noted the suggestions of dismay on several faces. "To keep the men busy I suggest that we practice boarding the ships whenever the winds lessen to make it a task that can be achieved without great risk of loss or damage."

"And should we land successfully in England what provision will we have to cope with the coldest season?" Ranulf asked in a respectful tone.

"I am not ignorant of the land," Guillaume replied. "I have been to England previously and I know where I want to be when we do set down our power. There is a town close to the sea and within marching distance of London. London is where King Edward sat his court and where Harold the usurper maintains his. If we are penned in to endure the winter then the town will give us shelter and an opportunity to gain supplies by sea. We will not sit out in the freezing countryside digging for roots waiting for the Saxons to come."

"I and my priests will pray daily for a change in the weather before Michaelmas," Odo told them firmly.

"I know that you would have me bend my mind more to your own immediate wishes. I understand the lure of hearth and home at this time of the year, but know also that by bringing this enterprise to a successful conclusion every man in this room stands to see his wealth and reputation increase in proportion to the energy he exercises in our design. If you can find nothing else to occupy your minds while we wait upon the weather then think of how rich your lands will be in both Normandy and England, and how much poorer will be those who spurned our invitation to press my just claim to a crown stolen by a thief."

The nobles banged the table but it was not with spontaneous enthusiasm. The duke signalled the servants who brought wine, the council was unofficially ended, the duke deciding to leave matters whilst the barons' spirits were seemingly high. Robert left his seat and joined Guillaume and Odo near the great stone hearth.

"Well spoken," he told his brother.

"It was nothing that they have not heard previously." Guillaume did not smile. He looked into the fire with eyes full of concern. "They are being drawn taught like the cables on a ship's mast, like a master-mariner I must judge the right moment to come about before they snap."

"They will hold," Odo insisted.

"The desertions will begin soon," Guillaume told them, "amongst the mercenaries first I believe but once it starts it will travel through the ranks like the pox. Desertion will injure us more surely than any Saxon arms."

"If any of the barons dares to break ranks..." Robert let the rest of his thought go unspoken, they already knew the consequences.

"There is little more that can be done other than to trust to divine providence," Odo observed.

Guillaume glanced at his brother with barely hidden disdain. He never trusted to providence.

"I trust only to the strength of our arms in this matter," he asserted.

"Whether arms or providence one thing is clear, we remain dependent on that over which we have no influence." Robert commented. "We must while away another evening listening to the storm winds outside whilst the Saxons repose themselves in comfort and have little need to go out of doors."

Thursday 21st September 1066

The City of York

Coenred slipped through the shadows of York, finding his way down the dark, narrow streets as he headed towards the River Ouse. The moon was in its first quarter so there was very little natural light to guide his movements by. Not a single light shone from any of the houses he passed by, all the doors were barred and windows shuttered; the city now lived in fear.

He had expected the Vikings to put the city under a tight curfew but they appeared to have shown little interest in securing it properly. King Hardrada had forbidden them to pillage the city, clearly he already saw it as his own; his capital in the north of England. The garrison had set about a half-hearted patrol but those pressed to walk the streets of the city were only too aware that their comrades sat in the Saxon mead-hall drinking, eating and finding pleasure with the easier serving wenches. Their minds were not on their duties.

At least the earth underfoot was hard, baked by the late summer sun. Coenred's leather shoes made no noise as he stalked the shadows. He had to be careful, however, for sudden dips where occasional rain and frequent use had scoured out potholes in the ground, hazards that he could not see in the dark and threatened to make him lose his balance or make a noise.

He made his way silently up the dark, narrow street where Mildryth's house stood and turned left when he came to the main street. Here there were bigger houses and the street was broader but just as cloaked in shadow. He became like a wraith, flitting from one dark place to another but stopping frequently to listen to the sounds of the city at night. Before him, on the right, he could see the tower of St. Mary's Church rising higher than any other building. Its dark mass stood out against the cloudless and slightly lighter sky and helped to guide him on his way.

He slipped past the Church, its grey stonework blending into the shadows created by its mass. The size of the structure set it apart from the mostly single storey timber and thatch buildings that crowded around it. The area immediately surrounding the church was fenced off allowing for an oasis of space. Grave markers dotted the dark ground but none were particularly large. There were several new mounds in the cemetery and work on a new grave had begun but then left off for the morrow for completion. He kept the church to his right as he headed west and soon came upon the bank of the River Ouse. Here he turned north and followed the slowly moving river against its current, keeping low and treading quietly.

Alder and willow trees were dotted along the riverbank and they offered protection through the deep shadows cast by their branches, still thick with foliage. There was grass underfoot now, guaranteed to keep his footsteps quiet. Coenred flitted from tree to tree, but he continued to take the time to stop and listen to the night sounds around him.

As with the rest of York there were no lights showing in any of the buildings he passed that faced the river. People were keeping their homes tightly secured, afraid as to what the loss of the battle and the presence of their old enemy might mean for their immediate futures. A few stray hounds roamed the area but they were wary of the skulking Saxon, more concerned with scavenging for food than in seeking a confrontation. A more superstitious man than Coenred might have hesitated at the sight of the hounds not far from the church and its cemetery. The black hound, a particularly feared omen, was renowned for appearing in graveyards after a funeral and there would be many of those services occurring soon.

Up ahead the old Roman walls that protected the northern limit of the city rose out of the night. They continued down to the riverbank but they did not bridge the Ouse. The original walls had enclosed a fort on the eastern bank of the river whilst a town for civilians had been founded on the west-bank, and that also enclosed by stone walls. This was the nucleus of York, the settlement that both the Saxons and the Vikings had developed after the Romans had left the governance of Britain some five hundred years ago.

He passed the stone bridge built by the Romans to connect the two halves of their town. The military fort had been swallowed by the houses of the new settlers, Saxon and Viking alike. This part of the city was dominated by the Church of St. Peter, first built to baptise Edwin, King of Northumbria, and rebuilt in stone by his successor King Oswald some four hundred years ago.

Coenred moved to the very edge of the riverbank and stalked forward in the darkness, progressing slowly and carefully. The last of the trees were situated some distance from the wall and he was forced to move in the open, depending on his stealth and the weak moonlight to remain unseen and unnoticed.

A Viking coughed then spat from on top of the wall, giving away his position. He was supposed to be a sentry, looking out to the north for enemies but everyone knew that there was no fight left in the local population, and no army out there to threaten them. The Vikings saw no danger and treated their guard duty with a lax attitude accordingly.

The huscarl treated them with more respect. He dropped to a crouch and proceeded forward almost doubled over, his outstretched hands skimming the grass before him trying to detect any obstacle in his path before it tripped him up. He came to the foot of the wall and was swallowed in shadow. With his back to the stones he moved to his right, following the stone work with his hands. The wall jutted a couple of feet into the river and that made this point somewhat more treacherous to pass. The ground began to give way sharply underfoot as he descended the riverbank. He used the wall for support. The soft lap of the river against the stone told him that he was almost at the water's edge. He gathered up his cloak so that it would not get wet, being woollen it would soak up the water quickly and become uncomfortably heavy. With a searching hand he found the lip of the wall and then stepped carefully down, moving slowly, tense and with his ears attuned for any sounds of alarm from up on top of the wall.

The water was cold as his right foot disappeared into the river. He waded further in but kept his right hand on the wall. His linen trousers became soaked and his feet felt uncomfortable in their sodden leather shoes. The current was strong but slow and he was able to swing around the edge of the wall without mishap. The water made little noise as he moved carefully through it. He used the Roman stonework again to help himself climb up the riverbank on the opposite side of the defences. Being at the foot of the wall also gave him some protection from being seen from above as the sentries would have to look straight down to spot him. He would only attract their attention now by giving himself away with some careless noise.

Pausing for a moment in the immediate shelter of the wall Coenred let the water drain from his clothes and lowered his cloak. The September air was still warm even with dawn only an hour away. It would not be long before he was dry again.

Of far more importance would be getting away from the city before the light betrayed him even to the eyes of such disinterested sentries as the Vikings seemed to be. Again he set off, moving close to the top of the riverbank and following the curve of the river as it swung north-west. There were no trees within a hundred yards of the wall; this was the most dangerous part of his escape from York. He moved as cautiously as ever, even though running in a crouch made his muscles ache, and he was rewarded by the sounds of a quiet night unbroken by cries of alarm from the watchmen.

He rose from his crouch when he slipped under the branches of the first alder tree that he came to and stopped to turn and look once more on the City of York. A few days ago it had just been one of the many places that his duties as a huscarl to the House of Aelfgar demanded that he visit. He liked it enough, certainly he had not found the high-theign's hospitality wanting, but now he had another reason to be fond of York. He thought of her lying on the floor of her small house where he had left her; so close to the enemy. He had risen quietly and found enough light from the hearth to be able to gather his clothes without disturbing her. As his eyes had become accustomed to the warm half-light he had looked at her often and his heart had ached. It hurt worse than any wound that he could remember.

"You leave me now without a word," she chastised him softly from the bed.

"I would not leave you at all," he responded.

"I know, but you must go. They wait upon you to return."

"You must bar the door behind me," he told her as he pulled on his shoes. "If they ask you have never seen me other than at the great hall."

"They will not ask," she told him. "They think me nothing more than a widow-woman, a pitiable creature at best. What would the likes of me have to do with huscarls who fought them yesterday?"

"I ask myself what a woman of quality like you would have to do with a man as mean as myself?" He retorted.

She smiled at the compliment, still wrapped in the warmth of the blanket, Mildryth felt a world away from the horror that had visited them that day.

"If the world was as full of men as mean as you huscarl, it would be a better place for it," she declared.

He fastened his cloak about himself with the brooch in the fashion of the stylised horse that he wore everyday. It was made of iron and inlaid with silver, an item beyond the purse of a peasant but far from an expensive jewel. It had been a gift from, of all people, his younger brother Osred, given in recognition of the sacrifice the warrior did for them all. It was the only expensive decorative item that he regularly wore.

Again he simply stood and looked down at her, following the outline of her body as it was betrayed by the folds of the blanket. He was swept up with a surge of emotion for her, not desire but a longing to wrap his arms around her and just hold her tightly. He wanted to hold her so tightly that she could never leave, as if he could, through the power of these muscles that were hardened for war, squeeze the two of them into one being and know peace.

"Mildryth-"

She rose quickly and stopped his speech with her lips pressed tightly against his, her hands cupping his face.

"Say nothing," she implored him. "No speeches of farewell, no words of comfort. I need neither. We know a truth that nothing in this world can take from us Coenred. We can be happy together but first there are things that must be done, things that it is not a woman's place to have a hand in. All I can do is stay here and look after the others, friends like Branda, and watch the tide of events crash over us like the waves of the sea. But I will be strong, strong for Branda, strong for you. The best that I can do is to survive these days without you and I will. Go now without fear for me, I will be here when you return with the king's army. Go now!"

They kissed again and this time Coenred did crush her in his arms, but gently, ever so gently. When she pulled her face away it was to rest her head against his chest, warm and strong beneath the soft linen tunic, and hide her tears. She felt him rest the side of his face on the top of her head and she squeezed him just a little bit more tightly.

That her heart could love again!

"You must go!" she implored.

It would be so easy to be selfish, to give into this moment and keep him here but she knew that in trying to win that one moment, in the hope of making this embrace last that much longer, she ran the real risk of losing him altogether.

"You must go!"

"Then I go," he agreed. "Bar the door."

Without another word or glance he crossed the threshold and stepped out into a night full of danger.

The moment of leaving now seemed so long ago. It was a dream, a moment from a life now gone and one that he may never recapture. He shook his head, as if trying to dispel those memories. He had to be strong now, stronger than he had ever been before. He had to put her to the back of his mind because there was nothing more that he could do for her. Whatever wyrd given fate she faced it would come without him there to protect her and all he could do was trust in her abilities and strength of character. He had to believe in her because he did not believe in anything else other than his own martial strength. He had to surrender her to the world and it was the most difficult task that he had ever faced.

He turned his back on York and in doing so became once more the warrior. A coldness set upon him. A coldness of intent for vengeance not born from the chill of the river he had waded through to escape the enemy. As he walked into the night he thought of Hereric and his brave five hundred huscarls who had given their lives to protect Morcar from the Vikings and in so doing kept their oaths to defend their lord with their lives. He thought of the Viking warrior who called himself Siward and how his death had angered King Hardrada. That brought a grim smile to his face. He thought of the traitor Tostig Godwinson and the hurt he had done to Mildryth in a life now past and he resolved to put an end to the source of that particular pain. It even occurred to him that he had had just such an opportunity at the village of Grim's By; he vowed not to fail a second time if he should ever come within a spear's length of Tostig. He thought of the young eorls and how they had succumbed to their defeat so readily, showing none of the character of either their father or their grandfather. He thought of his own grandfather's sword and how good it would feel in his hand once more. He thought of the vengeance that he would deliver with that bright, shining weapon. He thought no more of the woman he had come to love but only of blood and death and the horror of battle that he would visit on his enemies.

When the night closed in around him he was more deadly than any danger that he might meet in its shadows.

The End

of

The War Wolf

The Sorrow-Song Trilogy

Part One

By

Peter C. Whitaker

Author's Notes

The Battle of Fulford Gate marks the opening of the campaign of 1066 and yet it remains the 'forgotten battle'. Most people can name the Battle of Hastings, some can recall the Battle of Stamford Bridge, but for reasons unkown Fulford Gate has never entered into the popular history of this apocalyptic year.

For King Hardrada Fulford Gate was an important opening engagement that vindicated his gamble to invade Northumbria with the largest Viking army ever to set foot in England. His total defeat of Edwin and Morcar plunged the kingdom into crisis and forced King Harold to make a fateful decision that was to have serious ramifications for both him and Duke Guillaume of Normandy.

The events depicted in 'The War Wolf' are as true as I could make them based upon the historical resources available. This period of history used to be referred to as the 'Dark Ages', an inaccurate label if ever there was one. The recent discovery of the Saxon gold hoard in Staffordshire validates the portrayal of the Saxon period as a vibrant, culturally rich epoch; a culture that I have tried to reflect in my novel.

The battle depicted herein progressed as described by posterity with the Vikings turning the Saxon line and forcing the Mercians to retire. Somehow both Eorl Edwin and Eorl Morcar did escape with their lives but the fate of the five hundred did not change.

York passes once more back into the hands of the Vikings and Coenred is forced to abandon his new love Mildryth to the mercy of his ancient enemy, but he will return to fight again at the Battle of Stamford

Bridge under the fighting man banner of King Harold of England, in part two of The Sorrow Song Trilogy; 'For Rapture of Ravens'.

Peter C. Whitaker

If you enjoyed this book, which I hope that you did, I would be grateful if you would leave a brief review and a rating of it at the vendor's website. New authors need such things to attract new readers. Thank you in anticipation!

For more information about The Sorrow Song Trilogy, and a little bit about me as well, please visit my website:

http://www.petercwhitaker.co.uk

Historical Personages

King Edward the Confessor.

Born 1003 and died in January 1066. He spent his early years in exile in Normandy before returning to England as the recognised heir of King Harthacnut and ascended to the throne in 1042. He married Edith of Wessex, daughter of the powerful Eorl Godwin, in 1045. This union failed to produce an heir, which in turn plunged Anglo-Saxon England into crisis upon the death of Edward.

Harold Godwinson.

Born the second son of Eorl Godwin of Wessex in 1022, Harold succeeded his father as Eorl of Wessex following the latter's death in 1053. Prior to this he had handfasted to Ealdgyth Swannesha who gave him at least 6 children. Harold met Guillaume of Normandy in 1064 after being shipwrecked. The two seem to have formed a deep respect for each other. On the death of King Edward in 1066 Harold Godwinson claimed the throne. In the same year he divorced his common-law wife and married Ealdgyth of Mercia, possibly a political move to try and unite the kingdom. Harold was killed in battle at Senlatche Ridge near Hastings in 1066.

Tostig Godwinson.

Born in 1026 as the third son of Eorl Godwin Tostig was promoted to the Eorldom Northumbria in 1055. His rule there was considered harsh.

He was implicated in the murder of several theigns who were nominally under his protection when visiting the eorl at his request in 1064. In the following year Northumbria revolted while Tostig was away hunting with King Edward and elected Morcar of Mercia as his replacement. His brother, Eorl Harold, chose to support the rebellion and King Edward exiled Tostig as a result, an act that created a fatal schism in the Godwin family. Tostig made several attempts to return to England but they all failed until he allied himself with King Hardrada of Norway. He died at Stamford Bridge in 1066.

Eorl Edwin of Mercia and Eorl Morcar of Northumbria.

Edwin was born around 1046 and Morcar around 1049. Their father was Eorl Aelfgar of Mercia, a powerful and active rival of the Godwins of Wessex. Edwin was promoted to the Eorldom of Mercia following his father's death in 1062 and 3 years later Morcar became the Eorl of Northumbria, succeeding the banished Tostig Godwinson. The brothers continued their father's rivalry with Wessex, an ambition that was not altered by the marriage of their elder sister, Ealdgyth of Mercia, to King Harold Godwinson. Edwin survived the Norman Conquest but died as a traitor in 1071 after attempting a rebellion against King Guillaume. Morcar survived this rebellion as an exile but was imprisoned for several years during which time he appears to have died.

King Harald Hardrada of Norway.

Born in 1015 King Harald lived to become the greatest Viking of his day. He was exiled early in his life and lived successfully as a mercenary abroad, even attaining the captaincy of the Emperor of Byzantium's

Varangian Guard. He returned to Norway and in 1047 forcibly took the throne. It is said that he dealt with opposition violently and so earned the name Hardrada or hard rule. He began his long and fruitless war against Denmark almost immediately and it was this that led him to form an alliance with Tostig Godwinson when he looked to restore his wealth and reputation by making good a weak claim to King Edward of England's crown. By all accounts Harald was a very tall man, easily exceeding 6 foot. Throughout his long military career he went undefeated until he encountered King Harold of England at Stamford Bridge in 1066 where he died.

Duke Guillaume of Normandy.

Guillaume would become more popularly known as William as the English found his French name too difficult to pronounce. He was born in 1028 as the illegitimate son of Robert, Duke of Normandy. In 1035 Guillaume became the Duke of Normandy following the death of his father. His transition was not easy and it was not until 1047 before Guillaume was able to consolidate power within his duchy. Even then it was not until 1060 before Normandy itself was free from external threats as represented by the King of France who frequently changed his allegiances. Guillaume's claim to the English throne is founded mostly upon a promise made in 1051 by King Edward of England to choose Guillaume of Normandy as his heir as he was the grandson of Edward's maternal uncle, Richard II of Normandy. When Harold Godwinson declared himself King of England the Duke of Normandy set about his plans to make good his own claim. In 1066 he succeeded Harold. King William reigned until 1087.

Anglo-Saxon and Viking Lexicon

Aethelings   highest branch of the aristocracy including the immediate royal family

Angon   throwing spear

Bairn/s   child, children

Bondsman   a freeman who has surrendered his freedom due to debt or poverty for a fixed period

Burh   a stronghold, later known as a 'borough'

Butescarl   mercenary soldier

Byrnie   coat of steel mail or toughened leather

Ceorl   the peasant class of freemen who owed fealty to their appointed theigns

Dane-axe   large two handed war axe popular with both Vikings and Saxon warriors

Danelaw   that part of England ruled by Vikings between 884 to 954, including large parts of Northumbria

Drekkar   Norse longship, typical Viking warship

Eoldermen	the highest rank of the aristocracy beneath the aethelings.
Eorl	an eolderman, the modern day equivalent is an earl
Fyrd	the Saxon army
Fyrdman	a freeman who fulfils his settlements obligation to provide warriors for military service
Gambeson	a padded jacket worn under a byrnie
Gebur	the third and lowest class of free peasant
Geneatas	the first and highest class of free peasant
Gesipas	king's companion in a military capacity
Grim's By	Viking name for the town of Grimsby, Lincolnshire
Hadseax	small knife, usually a domestic utensil
Handfast	traditional marriage system predating the Christian church
Hide	unit of measurement, 1 hide considered sufficient land to feed 1 family

Hloth	troop, band, gang, often applied to thieves and robbers
Huscarl	professional elite warriors recruited by the king and later by those lords who could afford them
Inderawuda	the market town of Beverley, East Yorkshire
Jarl	Nordic equivalent of the Saxon eorl
Jorvik	Viking name for York
Kotsetla	second and middle class of freeman peasant
Langseax	larger variant of the scramseax knife used for heavy work and also as a sword by fyrdmen
League	unit of measurement, 1 league = 3 miles
Lithsman	sailor
Mercia	Former Anglo-Saxon kingdom bordering Wales and extending over what is now the midlands of modern day England
Michaelmas	church festival held on 29th September
Midden	dunghill, refuse tip

Natural foot	unit of measurement, 1 natural foot = 9.8 inches
Nithing	man without honour
Northumbria	former Anglo-Saxon kingdom extending from the River Humber up to Scotland's southern border
Rod	unit of measurement, 1 rod = 5.5 metres
Rus	Russia
Sandwic	the town of Sandwich, Kent
Scop	poet, story-teller
Scramseax	knife ranging in size from 3 to 30 inches
Skaroaborg	Viking name for the town of Scarborough, North Yorkshire
Snekke	Viking ship similar to the larger longship but commonly used to carry supplies as well as smaller numbers of warriors
Span	unit of measurement, 1 span = 9 inches
St. Peter's Burgh	Saxon name for Peterborough

Theign	members of the warrior class granted a minimum of 5 hides of land by the king or an eolderman, divided into lower, middling and higher classes, responsible for imposing the king's law on the peasant classes
Theow	slave, usually captured in war, or a bondsman
Tithe man	the head man of a group of ten, a common unit of Saxon society
Wergel	Anglo-Saxon system of compensation for the death or injury of a free person
Wessex	former Anglo-Saxon kingdom bordering Cornwall in the west and Kent in the east
Witan	council of leaders constituted from the athelings, eoldermen and bishops

Printed in Great Britain
by Amazon